Grayton Winds

First Edition
Copyright © 2011 by Michael Lindley

A *Sage River Press* Book

All rights reserved.

This book is a work of fiction. Names, characters and events are the product of the author's imagination. Any resemblance to real persons, living or dead, places, or real incidents, is purely coincidental.

ISBN 978-0-9794670-2-8

Grayton Winds

In the tumultuous days of Prohibition along the glorious white sand shores of Grayton Beach, Florida, the story of a young man's journey through the heartbreak of lost loves, bitter memories of family betrayal and the ultimate salvation of a gifted young blind girl and her wayward mother.

Michael Lindley

A *Sage River Press* Book
2011

Grayton Winds

ACKNOWLEDGEMENTS

What a marvelous journey this has been these past years, sharing stories of life and love and families. I am deeply indebted to the many people who have helped me through this maze of the writing and publishing life; fellow writers, my screenplay writer's group, editors, publishers, distributors, retailers, librarians, reviewers and ultimately the readers who provide so much kind and honest feedback and inspiration. And , of course, my own family who continue to offer their support and patience with my time away, lost in these stories.

By no means is this book intended to be a concise historical review of the time and places depicted, nor did I intend to represent any real people, places or events, other than the hurricane of 1926, that did indeed cause considerable damage in the area. From the beginning, I hoped only to capture a sense of what it may have been like to walk the shores and paths of this beautiful part of our country nearly 100 years ago, seen through the eyes of truly fictional characters that are purely the product of the author's imagination.

I would like to thank the early readers of this book who helped me to see the story and characters in a more objective light. I would also like to thank the organizers and guest authors of the 2010 Rosemary Beach Writer's Conference for their inspiration and enthusiasm for the writing life.

M. Lindley

Novels by Michael Lindley

The Seasons of the EmmaLee

On Past Horton Creek

Grayton Winds

There is a wisdom of the head, and a wisdom of the heart.
- Charles Dickens

This book is dedicated to all of you who continue to encourage this tireless pursuit.

GRAYTON WINDS

MICHAEL LINDLEY

Prologue

Grayton Beach, Florida *1985*

In my life there were choices that often cause me to lie awake at night and think back on how different things might have been. I try to remember that there were always other people to consider, other consequences.

As I sit on the deck of our house along the beach, the curve of cloudless sky stretches to the far horizon with nothing to stop the push of the outgoing tides and winds for a thousand miles. The brilliant white sand and storm-swept live oak nestled through the dunes, give a sense of wild timelessness. Between lapses where I've dozed off for a time, I've found the memories of this place coming back to me in rushing swells of joy and regret. I first came to these quiet shores nearly sixty years ago as a young man searching for something new in my life. Behind me were the scars of war and lost love, and bitter memories of a family mired in deceit and corruption. I close my eyes against the glare of the late morning sun and think back again on all that came to pass in those early years after the first war in France, and the people and events that led me to this little town of Grayton Beach along the northern Gulf Coast of Florida.

Later today we will gather with family and friends to celebrate another collection of birthdays, including my own eighty-fifth. It will be a joy to have so many of us around the big table again this year. My daughter will play the piano and lead us all in song. I always read a few passages from one of my books or short stories when we're together.

My last book was published shortly after my wife's death ten years ago. I rarely put words to paper anymore. Arthritis in my hands keeps me away from my old typewriter, and I haven't the patience to work with anyone to have them transcribe any more stories. I felt it only fair that the book not be released until some of the people in my life had passed on. I knew that the threads of truth in the story may have been painful to some, but in the end it seemed important, at least to me, that this version of the story be told. I offer no apology at this late age for an act of clear selfishness.

One of my granddaughters is calling me now to come downstairs. There is someone at the door to see me. With only one leg that works and old age doing its best to render that one useless, I make my way down the steps slowly and with great care. My granddaughter, Meredith, is standing at the open door and a woman is there on the front porch. She has a scarf on and with the bright sunlight behind her from the outside it's difficult to see. Her face is only a shadow.

"Is that you, Mathew?" she says softly, her voice barely a whisper. A gust of wind blows in from across the white dunes of Grayton Beach. When I hear her voice, I feel the burdens of the past lift from my heart.

Chapter One

Paris, France 1918

    Through the gauzy haze of the morphine, I heard the American doctors agree that my leg was beyond saving. I tried to sit up and yell out, but my body wouldn't respond and the words caught in my throat in a thick, garbled moan. A nurse was instructed to administer more painkiller. I barely felt the pinprick of the needle. I tried with all my will to stay conscious, to fight back against their planned mutilation. I felt myself slipping away, powerless to stop them, until there was only darkness and echoes of the battle in the French countryside.

    Her name was Celeste. The badge on her nurse's uniform was the first thing that came into focus. I watched the young woman move around my bed as she adjusted the blankets. Random strands of auburn hair fell out from her cap. She placed her hand on my forehead and I felt the warm softness of her skin.

    Then it all came back to me in a rush; the doctors and my shredded leg. I felt no pain anywhere, only a heavy sluggishness pushing my body down into the bed. I tried to lift my head and reach down, but was unable to move more than a few inches before

I fell back. The nurse saw that I was awake. She helped to lift me and prop pillows behind me. Then I was able to see down to the foot of the bed.

I drew in a deep breath and let it out slowly, my chest barely moving. I saw the form of two legs and two feet beneath the blanket.

"They saved your leg, Private Coulter," the young nurse said in a heavy French accent.

I looked at her face and was unable to speak. Tears began to well up and my arms felt too heavy to lift. She took the corner of the sheet and dabbed at my eyes.

"It was your brother," she said.

"My brother?" I was finally able to say.

"Your brother, the captain. He came in as they were preparing to take you to the surgery."

"Jess?" I asked. "What did he do?"

"Oh, he raised a terrible fuss," she said. "He demanded that they wait, and then a general came with a new doctor."

"A general?"

"Your brother said that he was a friend of your father's back in America."

The next day there was a medal on my chest. It was the first thing I saw when I woke up. The medal was lying there on the white hospital gown. It wasn't pinned, merely lying there. It was a ribbon of many colors with a dull gray metal heart attached. Memories of the night along the scarred battle line outside Verdun came back to me; the flash of flares in the dark night sky, the deafening sound and concussion of the shells exploding all around us. I winced as I remembered the relentless fire from the German machine guns cutting into our line and the sickening wail of men hit and dying. I covered my face as the smell of gunpowder and death swept over me again.

"Private Coulter?"

I heard the soft voice of the nurse, Celeste. She had come up quietly beside me, checking on all of the men in my ward lined up in beds along both walls of the long room.

"How are you feeling this morning, Private?" she asked and placed the medal on the stand beside me.

"It's Mathew," I said as I pulled my arms away from my eyes. "My name is Mathew."

"Yes, I know," she said with a smile.

There was a glow on her face from the soft morning light coming in through the window. Tiny brown freckles spread beneath her eyes and across the bridge of her nose. Her eyes were a pale green and stood out against the drab grays and whites of the hospital ward. The sound of her voice and her accent were like a soothing melody.

"Your brother tells me that you're from Atlanta."

"Atlanta, Georgia. That's right," I said.

"Is that near New York?" she asked.

I laughed, unable to remember the last time I had reason to feel happy.

"My father visited New York once before the War," she said.

"No, it's quite far from New York, in the South," I said. "Does your father have business in America?"

She looked down for a moment to gather herself. "No, he had no business. He was visiting his brother's family."

"Will he go back?" I asked.

She paused again. "No, he was lost in the first weeks of the fighting."

"I'm sorry. Do you have other family?"

"Yes," she said, brightening some, "my mother and two little sisters. We live north of the city in a village called Les Mureaux."

"Was there fighting there?" I asked.

"No, no, it was further to the north and the east. We have been fortunate."

"You speak English quite well," I said.

"My father taught us to read English when we were very small," she said. "He wanted me to go to school there some day… in New York."

"Then you'll have to go when this is all over," I said.

"No, I think not." She pulled the bedding back to check the bandages on my left leg. I saw they ran from my ankle to the top of my thigh. There was an ugly blue color in the skin that was exposed at the edges. Blood had seeped through the white dressing overnight in dark red splotches.

"We will have to change this again," she said.

"Why does it look so bad?" I asked. "Is it infected?"

"No, this is only normal. Your leg was very badly hurt."

Her words gave me some comfort, and then I thought again about what she had said earlier. "Why won't you go to America?"

"I must wait for someone," she said. "Is there any pain?"

"You all keep shooting me full of medicine. I can't feel anything." I managed to reach over and placed my hand on her arm.

"I must get the doctor to look at this," she said and began to turn and walk away.

I held her arm a moment longer. "Can you tell me who you're waiting for?"

She paused, considering the request, then quietly she said, "His name is Jules. He is away with the Army."

"He hasn't returned since the Armistice?" I asked.

"No, he has been lost since the early days," she said. "There has been no word."

***

There were too many times when the truth would find its way back. There had been no glorious act of heroism that night on the attack outside Verdun. It's one thing to know in your heart that you carry a weakness of spirit, that when you were really tested you had failed to measure up. It is another to have others believe just the opposite of you.

The surge of our attack had been pressed back. Our men were falling all around us under the murderous onslaught of the German guns. Some had started to run back to the cover of the fence behind the small farm. Through the chaos and dim light from the flares overhead I saw our sergeant yelling and waving us on. A shell exploded at his feet and I fell to the ground as his body was hurled lifeless across the field. When I looked up I saw another man from our unit fall to his knees, holding his face and screaming out into the night before he fell over into the mud.

As the images and sounds passed again before me, I felt someone touch my arm and I opened my eyes to see my older brother, Jess, standing there. He was dressed in a clean U.S. Army uniform and several medals and ribbons adorned his chest. He took off his hat and smiled down at me.

"You look a little better today, brother," he said, and then looked down at my legs. "Looks like you've still got all your parts, too."

"Jess," I started, "how did you ever find me here?"

"I got word from your unit that you had taken a shell," he said.

"I don't remember."

"Your commander told me that you were carrying a man back during the retreat," he said, and then sat softly down on the bed beside me. "You're quite the hero, little brother."

I shook my head. "They tore us up, Jess."

"I know," he said. "But the next night your unit broke through."

"I heard the bastards finally surrendered."

"Yes, two weeks after you were hit the Armistice was signed."

"So you're all in one piece?" I asked.

"Got a little shrapnel in my back," he said. "You can feel it if you want."

"No, that's okay," I said, and then smiled as I reached out to see one of his medals. "Looks like you did real well."

He just shook his head and I saw the surge of memories that were taking him back. "They kept you in the field hospital shot up with morphine for a couple of weeks," he finally said. "Couldn't get your damn leg to heal, so some asshole sends you up to this meat locker. Damn good thing I got here when I did."

"Yeah, thanks, brother," I said, and felt the tears beginning to well up again. "They're telling me that it won't bend real well, but they'll be leaving it on."

"Damn right," he said. "Brought in General Morris. The old man knows him from back in Georgia. He got the best doctor in the damn city to work on you. You're gonna be okay."

Jess turned his head. Celeste was coming into the ward for her shift. Several men along the way called to her and one always whistled at her when she came into the room. She walked over to my bedside and stood beside Jess.

"Hello, Captain," she said.

"I forgot you'd met," I said.

She reached down and held my wrist, counting out the beat of my pulse as she looked at the second hand on the clock on the wall.

"You two seem to be getting along just fine," Jess said, and then he went on in French, talking to Celeste.

I was surprised that he knew the language so well, but we had been apart for most of two years. When he finished, she laughed and her face blushed a bright red.

"What did you say?" I asked.

"I asked her if you two were lovers."

I laughed out loud, looking down at my lifeless leg. "I've been a bit occupied. And a gentleman would never say."

"They're bringing the breakfast, Private Coulter," she said. "And then I want you to get some more rest."

"Please call me Mathew," I reminded her.

She smiled and then moved on to the next bed.

Jess leaned in close as we watched her walk away. "She's magnificent, Matty."

"Yes, she certainly is."

"Are you feeling any better?" Jess asked.

"With the drugs there's just a dull ache," I said. "I feel like I'm in a deep fog most times."

"We need to get you home. Get some of Velma's good cooking in you."

Velma was the black cook who had worked for our family back in Atlanta for many years, and my mother's family before that. She had practically raised us Coulter children; Jess, my middle sister Margaret and I. My parents were often too busy with social and business obligations.

Jess saw the medal lying on the table beside my bed. "I'm proud of you, Mathew," he said, reaching for the ribbon and inspecting it more closely. "Just glad those damn Krauts didn't get a bigger piece of you."

I couldn't answer him, knowing what had truly happened that night during the battle. The memories were a harsh reminder that we all must carry some burdens in life. Shame and guilt can be a heavy load.

When he left me that day he said that his unit may be shipped home soon. We hugged as he left and I tried my best to smile, wondering if I would ever be able to face my brother again without a shameful heart.

When a woman feeds you and changes your clothes and your bedpan several times a day, there is a strange intimacy that grows. Celeste was also the first to take me outside when I was finally able to be moved into a wheelchair. It was spring in Paris by then and in spite of the remnants of war, the city was in full bloom in the gardens and the trees, moving on in its own relentless pace. The American Hospital of Paris was a beautiful old school converted to care for the wounded during the War. It was located in Neuily-sur-Seine along the northern stretch of the city.

Over the weeks I learned that Celeste had come to Paris and been trained as a nurse. She hoped to continue in the profession now that the fighting was over. On that first day outside she pushed me along the walks through the hospital property. Ford Motor ambulances lined the drive with young attendants milling about. I asked her how to pronounce something in French. She leaned close and whispered the answer, and then laughed at my awkward pronunciation before we continued on.

When I was well enough, Celeste got permission to take me in the wheelchair for a tour of more of the city. As she pushed me along another bustling street, she leaned over and whispered in my ear, "How do you like our city of Paris?"

When I turned, I saw the delight in her marvelous green eyes. "It's magnificent," I said.

"My parents used to bring me and my sisters to the city on special occasions, to see a museum, or visit friends," she said. "It was always our favorite times together."

"I'd like to meet your family," I said. I watched her face for a response, but she hesitated a moment.

"We will have to see," she finally said.

We continued on and came by a small park. A photographer was set up taking portraits. I convinced Celeste to have him take our picture. I was able to stand and lean against the gate to the park, and Celeste stood beside me.

In broken English, the photographer said, "You are a beautiful couple, no?"

"Yes," I said, and Celeste laughed.

We were gone almost the entire day. I returned exhausted and with pain throbbing in my leg. When she left me at the hospital that night to leave to catch her train home, I almost couldn't bring myself to let her go. I knew the hours before she returned for her next shift would be endless.

I wrote my sister Maggie that night about it. In previous letters I had mentioned Celeste, but in this letter I shared how my feelings for the woman who was helping me recover were growing more strongly every day. At the end I wrote, *Sister, Celeste is so special. I hope that you will be able to meet her one day.*

There had been some discussion among the doctors about my ability to tolerate the cruise back home across the Atlantic. I had experienced some setbacks with my leg healing, infections and other issues. My time with Celeste had also begun to create some doubt in my mind on whether I really wanted to leave Europe.

I was reading a book one morning when she came in. As always, I was delighted to see her, but I sensed a much different mood. She went about her business in the ward with only a quick nod before she moved away. Later I stopped her as she passed and asked her what was wrong.

"It's nothing, Mathew," she said.

"Please tell me," I asked.

She looked around the room at the other men. Most were still sleeping. Some were unconscious and would likely never recover. It was a terribly sad place at times and I was always surprised at Celeste's bright attitude each day in the face of such misery, until that morning.

"My mother is quite unhappy with me," she finally said. "One of our villagers who works at the hospital told her that we have been spending time together."

I just looked at her for a moment. I had not seen such sadness in her eyes since she first told me about her father and the young French soldier. "Can you tell me about Jules?" I asked.

She didn't seem surprised by the question and sat down on my bed, looking out through a window to the courtyard below. "We have been friends since we were small children," she began. "As we grew older it was just assumed that we would be together. We were only eighteen when he left for the War. He asked me to marry him, but I said that we should wait, that I would be here when he returned."

"And you're still waiting?"

"Yes, of course," she said. "But he's been gone so long and there has been no word. Men from his unit have told us that he was missing after the very first battle with the Germans. His body was never found, so they think that he was taken prisoner."

"How long has this been?" I asked.

"Over three years." She looked down and tried to straighten the white apron on her lap. I reached for her hand, but she pulled away. "My mother is right, Mathew," she said.

"Right about what?" I asked.

"Mathew, I so enjoy the time we spend together, I mean beyond here at the hospital," she said. "But my family and the people of my village, they all know about Jules and me."

Later that afternoon, I finally convinced Celeste to take some time to come and read to me as she often did. I listened to her words in the beautiful language of the French. I was caught up in the comforting sound of the words and the closeness of her sitting on my bedside. I watched the lines of her face as she concentrated on the story. I tried not to think about the lost French soldier and what might happen if he were ever to return.

When I was well enough, I invited Celeste to join me for dinner at a nearby restaurant that a doctor had recommended. I had to ask her several times, but finally and reluctantly she agreed. She wheeled me there that night and we sat in the quiet little place, a few candles on the tables providing most of the light. She picked a red wine that was made near her village. I can remember the shine of the candlelight on the glass and in the deep red of the wine. I told her more about my life that night than anyone I had ever been with. She was quite curious about my family back in Georgia.

"And your father sells whiskey?" she said.

"His company is a distributor for beer and spirits, even wine from your country," I said.

"And do you work in this business?"

"I suppose it will be there when I get back," I said.

"You don't sound very excited about the prospect."

"I plan to go to school first," I answered. "I want to study writing."

"You are a writer?" she said and then took another sip from her wine.

"Maybe someday."

When we returned to the entrance of the hospital she kissed me for the first time, slowly on the lips. She pulled away and looked at me for a moment with a confused expression. As she turned to leave, I grabbed her hand and pulled her close again for another kiss. I had kissed a few girls in my life, but this was different. The feeling and the taste of it were soft and wet and staggering. Then she smiled and squeezed my hand. I watched her walk away into the night, the lights of Paris around her.

After so much time in the broken earth of the French countryside and villages where everything around us was brown and burned, and the air lay heavy and rank, I felt that I would never see a green tree again or be able to take a breath of fresh air. Then there were those mornings sitting in the gardens of the American Hospital in Paris with life blooming green and glorious all around us. It was easy to forget, at least for a short while with Celeste sitting there with me, that the War had not been far away.

A wounded man was brought in to the bed next to me one morning. I was told that he was an American soldier, transferred from a distant field hospital for more surgery. He was gravely wounded months ago and had never regained consciousness. That evening a doctor called Celeste over to sit with the man and hold his hand while he changed the heavy bandages around his head. When the doctor left I heard her speaking softly to the soldier, still holding his hand. The doctor came by again later and checked on the man. He asked Celeste to stand back and he pulled the sheet up over the soldier's head. Then he left to find an orderly to have the body taken away. Celeste stood there for some time just staring at the lifeless form of the fallen soldier.

Eventually I was moved to the Army camp infirmary outside Paris. The day that I left the hospital I spent the morning with Celeste out in the gardens. She wrapped her arm in mine and we talked of the future as best we could.

"When will I see you?" I asked.

"There will be time, I hope, before you are sent back to America."

I could sense the hesitation in her voice as memories of her lost soldier seemed never far from her thoughts. There were no promises, only shared assurances that we would see each other again. As I left that day, just before I was placed on the gurney to be loaded onto the military ambulance, she hugged me tightly and whispered on in French with only a few words that I could actually understand.

"I have to see you again," I said.

She nodded and smiled, then leaned over and kissed my cheek. "I would like to see you, too, Private Mathew Coulter."

She stood back as the orderlies lifted me into the ambulance. I saw her smile again just before the doors closed as we drove off.

Several days after arriving at the Army infirmary I had a friend who secured a vehicle. "Coulter, 'bout time we got you out of here," he said one morning. "Let's see if we can find that French nurse of yours."

He was able to load me in the passenger side, and then drove us off the camp. When we reached the small village of Les Mureaux, we asked directions and soon came upon the old brick house where Celeste's family lived near the outskirts of the town. It was a small house with a stable that backed up to a stand of trees. An older woman came out, drying her hands on a towel. I could see Celeste's features in her face, and was certain it was her mother. My friend's French was far better than mine, and he asked of Celeste. Her mother shook her head and spoke quickly. My friend turned to me and translated. "She left a message in case Private Coulter came by," he said. "She is away visiting the family of her boyfriend."

I nodded at the woman and said, "Thank you." To my friend, I asked that he tell her that it was nice to meet her, and to tell Celeste that we were sorry that we missed her.

As we drove away, I was concerned to see that her mother had a much too satisfied look across her face. I had to wonder if Celeste was indeed away visiting the soldier named Jules' family. I also thought it strange that Celeste's father had not spent time teaching his wife to speak English, as he had with his daughters.

The next day I was napping in the infirmary, still not released to make arrangements to return home. An orderly came in and shook me awake.

"Private Coulter, you have a visitor," he said. "And a damned fine looking one."

Moments later Celeste walked into the tent. I had never seen her without her nurse's uniform. She wore a simple blue dress over a white blouse. Her long auburn hair was down and pulled back behind her ears. She came up to my bed and sat beside me. She looked glorious, and there was a smell of fresh country flowers about her. She took my hand, and then leaned in close and kissed me.

"Comment allez-vous, Mathew?" she asked.

"I'm much better now."

"I'm sorry that I missed you yesterday. Can we go for a walk?" she asked.

I grabbed my crutches and we walked slowly out into the heat of the day on the dusty road of the Army base. We found a bench to sit on away from the rushing chaos of the camp. I wanted to put my arm around her and hold her close but felt wrong about doing so.

"My mother told you that I was with Jules' family?" she asked.

"Yes, she did."

"I have become very close to his mother since he's been away," she said.

"I can understand," I replied, meaning it. "I'm still not sure when they're going to send me home."

She didn't answer and just looked down at her hands in her lap.

"Celeste…," I started.

"I'd like you to come to my home for dinner," she said, looking up at me. "I would like you to meet the rest of my family."

The next Sunday I arrived at Celeste's home. Her mother was not pleased with my place at her table that day, but the two younger sisters giggled and gossiped, and seemed to enjoy the visit immensely.

"Mam, thank you for having me here today," I said as we all sat down. She just nodded, seeming to understand. Celeste's youngest sister, Ann Marie, passed a plate of food to me. Celeste poured the wine.

Ann Marie said, "Thank you for fighting in our war, Private Coulter. Thank you for fighting the Germans."

"Of course," I answered, a bit surprised.

"Our father fought the Germans, and he died a hero," she said.

"Yes, I know," I said. "He must have been very brave."

Celeste's mother spoke quickly to Ann Marie in French, and gestured for her to continue passing the plates of food.

The middle sister, Angela, asked, "Will you return to America soon?"

"Yes, I believe so," I said. "I'm waiting for my orders to come through."

"Celeste will be very sad," she said.

"Angela!" Celeste scolded.

Again her mother went on in French, apparently admonishing the girls to get on with their dinner. Angela just smiled at me across the table.

Later, Celeste and I sat out in the back courtyard of their house. Chickens and a pig lingered nearby going about their business.

"My family has lived here for many generations," she told me.

"It's a beautiful village," I said.

"It is so different now," she answered. "So many are gone because of the War."

I just stared at her face as she looked away into the woods behind the house. When she glanced back she stared at me for a moment. "I'm sorry," she said.

"It's all right."

We attended church later that day with her mother and sisters. We sat together along the hard wooden pew, listening to a young boy's choir, the lyrics and the notes from the organ echoing through the high lofted arches. Celeste reached over and placed her hand on mine, out of sight from her mother. Others in the church looked severely at Celeste for bringing an American when they all knew of her boyfriend away and still missing from the War. It was a terrible risk for her, and I felt badly about putting her in that situation. She had insisted that I come, and as we walked out of the church and back to her house, she held her head high in defiance at the whispered comments and disparaging glances.

Later, she and I took a walk together as best I could with my crutches and a leg that hung heavy and stiff. As the sun was going down we walked along a path by the river just outside the village. We sat together on a grassy bluff above the water and watched the sun set through the trees. A few fish rose out in the flow of the stream. I leaned over to try to kiss her, and she hesitated at first, but then moved into my arms. Our passion was clumsy and tentative, but we kissed and held each other close.

Then she backed away and looked down at the river, her hand wiping across her mouth as if she wanted to take the kiss away. "Mathew, I'm so sorry about all of this," she said.

"Sorry?"

"I should never have let any of this..."

"Please don't say that," I interrupted.

"I can't sleep at night thinking about this, thinking about Jules out there somewhere, whether he's dead or alive… thinking about you," she said, looking back at me like I should have the answer.

Later that night I was saying goodnight to her at the door of her house. She kissed me on both cheeks as the French do. Her mother opened the door and pulled her inside. I stood looking at the weathered paint and hardware of the door before turning to find my friend down in the village for a ride home.

I had been moved back into a barracks with a new unit at the base, only to stay on until arrangements could be made for my return home to the States. I met Celeste for lunch in Paris about a week after we had been together by the stream near her village. It was clear that she had been crying. She took my hand and then leaned in close and kissed me across the small table at the cafe.

"Mathew, I spoke with my mother this morning before catching the train to come to the city," she said.

I sat listening, but was captured by the splendid look of her face.

"I told her that I couldn't wait any longer," she said.

"Wait?" I asked.

"I can't wait for… for Jules," she said.

I leaned across and kissed her cheek.

She came around the table and sat down on my lap and hugged me. She was laughing and crying at the same time. "What shall we ever do now?" she finally asked.

"I think I should speak with your mother," I said.

I made arrangements to get leave to go to Les Mureaux the next night. A friend secured a truck and drove me through the countryside toward the little village. My heart was pounding with the excitement of seeing Celeste, and telling her mother that I loved her daughter and wanted to marry her. I had dropped a letter in the mail earlier that day to my family back home, telling them that I might soon be bringing home a special guest.

I was let off at Celeste's house and made my way up the walk as quickly as I could on the crutches and a leg that was still stiff and heavily bandaged. When I managed to get up the three steps to the porch, I pounded the old tarnished knocker on the door. There was a long pause and no one answered. I couldn't hear anyone inside, so I knocked again. This time I heard the scuffling of feet coming to the door. The latch was slid back and the door opened slowly.

Celeste's mother peaked around the edge of the door. Her face was flushed and drawn, her eyes red from tears. She said something slowly in French that I didn't understand.

I shook my head and said, "Where is Celeste?"

Again she went on with a long answer in French, and I had no idea what she was saying. I held up my hand to stop her. "Tell me where Celeste is," I insisted. "What's happened?"

One of Celeste's younger sisters, Ann Marie, came up behind her mother. She said something in French to her mother, and then came out on the porch. She took my hand and started to pull me away from the door. I looked back at Celeste's mother, and she nodded her head in agreement. I thought they were trying to get me away from the house. When I looked back again the woman had her head down as she slowly closed the door.

Ann Marie led me out of the gate and down the road. I asked her where we were going.

"Please come, Private Coulter," she said.

"Where are we going?"

She didn't answer and kept pulling me along, clearly impatient with my slow pace. We walked deeper into the village, and then turned down a narrow street with small row houses down each side. It was near dark and lights were coming on. We stopped at one of the houses and Ann Marie helped me up the steps. She knocked on the door and a boy about her age answered. When he saw me and looked at the uniform his face grew very stern, and he tried to close the door. Ann Marie pushed past and held him away to allow me to come in.

I walked into the dark little house, heavy smells of food and dampness in the air. I called out, "Celeste!" I heard her voice in the back down a long hall and started in that direction. She came out of a room on the left. Her face was drawn and tired, and when she saw me there was a look of panic.

"Oh, Mathew," she said quietly. She stood at the open door and held up her hands for me to stop. Then she looked back in the room when a man yelled out in French. When she turned back to me, we stood staring at each other for a moment, and then she came down the hall. "Mathew, you must go."

"I'm not leaving until..." I said before she broke in.

"It's Jules," she said. "He was brought home yesterday. He was found in an abandoned hospital at one of the German prisoner camps."

I was so stunned I couldn't respond at first, and then finally said, "He's home? This is his home?"

A weak shout came from the back room, "Celeste!"

"He's terribly sick, Mathew," she said. "He was near death when they found him. He was wounded so badly, and he's lost an eye and one of his arms."

"Celeste..." I started to say.

"I'm so sorry, but..." she said, but the man yelled out weakly again. "It's best that you go," she said.

She turned and tried to pull away, tears now flowing down her cheeks. Her hands slipped out of mine. I looked down and saw a gold band on her finger that I was sure had never been there before. She walked hesitantly back to the doorway and then turned to look at me. For just a moment our eyes met, and then she walked into the room and closed the door.

I stood there letting all of the emotions rush through me. Ann Marie came up from behind and pushed me toward the door. I looked down at the little girl, and she forced a smile and nodded again in the direction of the bedroom. She took my hand and led me down the narrow hall. When I reached for the knob on the door I saw that my hand was shaking. Ann Marie pushed the door open for me and in the dim light I could see Celeste sitting on a narrow bed, holding a cloth to the forehead of the lost soldier named Jules. His body was bare to the waist and frightfully gaunt and pale, his right arm missing below the shoulder with a heavy wrap of bandages.

Celeste turned and saw me in the doorway. When she pulled the cloth away from the man's face, I could see the far side of his head was wrapped heavily, covering his eye. I watched her stand and saw the look of sadness and confusion on her face. Then Jules noticed me standing there, and an angry rage flushed his expression. I wondered about what he had been told about Celeste and me. He tried to sit up, but didn't have the strength. He started yelling at me in French, and then even louder at Celeste. She turned and tried to comfort him, but he pushed her away with his good arm and kept screaming at her.

An older woman came in and pressed by me, sitting on the bed and trying to comfort the man. Celeste looked at me and then rushed past out of the room. I looked one more time at Jules. In a low hiss of a voice he spoke directly at me. Although the words were unclear, his meaning was not. I backed away, the image of the broken man etched in my mind forever.

Back in the main room of the house I saw Celeste standing with her sister. Her mother came through the front door and went over to hold her daughters in her arms. Then she turned to me and in a clear voice said, "Private Coulter, I know that you think this is unfair."

Her English was not surprising to me. I had sensed that she had chosen from the beginning not to speak to me in my own language.

"I know how much you care for my daughter," she went on. She walked over to me and put her arms around me. "We all remembered Jules as the young man who left us to join the Army. He was a good boy."

Celeste came up and pulled her mother away, "Mother, please…"

"He will need much care to bring him back," her mother said. "Not just his body, his spirit has been so damaged."

Celeste took my hand and led me out the door to the street. I looked back and her mother and sister were holding each other, the little girl's face pressed into her mother's stomach. Celeste wiped at the tears in her eyes. I looked for some little change of heart in her expression, but I found no encouragement.

"Please don't ask me to explain," she said. "I don't think I can."

"He has family to care for him," I said, and then felt overwhelming guilt at my selfishness.

She just stared back at me, her eyes moist and searching, and for just a moment I saw a flush of hopeful expectation.

I pulled her close and wrapped her in my arms. I felt hers around the small of my back and the full weight of her falling into me.

"Celeste, I love you. I want you to come home with me. I want you to spend the rest of your life with me."

She took a deep breath and then looked away at the house behind us. When she looked back I tried to see some measure of acceptance in her expression, but there was none.

Finally she said, "I told him that I would wait."

For several days after I returned to the Army camp I often sat on the steps of my barracks, staring off into the distance, not able to focus on what was going on around me. Friends tried to get me to go into the city and drink away the problem, but I had no interest in getting drunk. Several times I was on the verge of going back to Les Mureaux to see her again and try to convince her that she belonged with me.

My orders finally came and I was to leave Paris by train in a week to catch a ship out of Calais back home to America. I watched the French coast slip away on the far horizon that day, not thinking about what lie ahead, but only what had been lost.

Chapter Two

Atlanta, Georgia 1926

  I knew from an early age that my family was in the whiskey business, and that my father was a successful and powerful man. His business had supplied clubs and restaurants all across Atlanta with beer and liquor for many years. We lived in a house on West Paces Ferry that rivaled the Governor's mansion, and my older brother and sister and I had attended the finest private schools in Georgia. On Sundays after church we would all go to dinner at the Piedmont Driving Club, and my mother and father would be greeted by the help there like they were local royalty. It was the pretense of it all, I suppose, that troubled me most. I was amazed at the great effort put forth by my parents to honor traditions of family and expectations of Atlanta society, in spite of my father's more recent line of work. Doing what was right and proper was of utmost concern, which I found quite confusing considering that the bread on our table was suddenly borne of illegal smuggling and distribution of spirits.

  I had been back from the War for two years in 1920 when the Volstead Act was passed. The 18th Amendment to the Constitution of the United States banned the *manufacture, sale or transportation of intoxicating liquors*, as I recall the specific language. Prohibition spread across the land like a dark and menacing cloud.

My father, Samuel Coulter, was a good businessman, and he moved quickly to protect his enterprise. It wasn't long before he had a whole network of bootleggers and moonshiners lined up to keep the supply coming. There was a lot of "shine" coming out of Georgia, Tennessee and Alabama. The bootleggers were bringing in good liquor from the Caribbean and Mexico, and by truck down from Canada. The family's business moved quickly and almost seamlessly to its new configuration. As he was most adept in doing, my father was able to preserve honor and position in the midst of all of this new lawlessness. If anything, the Coulters somehow managed to elevate their social position during this transition, owing much to my parents' efforts in maintaining a self-assuredness in their legacy, and certainly even more so in their abundant generosity in community affairs, political campaigns, ongoing bribes and payoffs, and of course, a relentless social schedule to maintain proper appearances.

There was a warm Saturday night in that spring of 1926, when my family was throwing one of their typical extravagant parties. The substantial yard in the back of our house was illuminated with lines of tiny white lights strung through the branches of the trees. The dogwoods were in full blossom with their white flowers floating on the branches like soft cotton, the gardenias sending their sweet aroma out through the air on a light wind. A band was playing dance music on a small stage out beyond the pool. Tables covered with pressed linens were spread with food and attended by servers in white uniforms. The four bars set up on the porch and the far corners of the lawn were surrounded by guests. People had been arriving for hours in their fine cars, coming up the long drive and stopping in the circle in front of the house for the parking valets. Everyone was dressed quite formally, the men in dinner jackets with white starched shirts and black ties; the women in colorful flowing dresses adorned with layers of shining jewelry and feathered hats of every known design and color.

One of my father's business partners and friends was Charles Watermann, a very high ranking officer of the law in Atlanta, who also had an interest in a few clubs in town. They were standing by one of the bars being served some fine Canadian whiskey. Nearby were two other men dressed in dinner jackets, but conspicuous in their lack of gaiety or conversation with the other guests. They were *associates* of my father and his friend, actually their bodyguards. Heavily armed and constantly on alert, they followed their employers most everywhere they went. The liquor business had become not only illegal, but much more competitive and dangerous, and any number of young thugs were trying to break into the business by eliminating the competition.

My older brother, Jess, was standing there with the bodyguards. He was taller and stood above the others, his face a younger version of my father. He was laughing and looking out over the growing crowd, sizing up the gathering of young women. I had walked in Jess's considerable shadow for my entire life, and yet I felt no conscious resentment or ill will. As the youngest of the Coulter children, I had always assumed my position in the genealogical pecking order with a matter-of-fact acceptance and tolerance.

I had just turned twenty-six at the time and had finished school the year before, a few years later than was expected due to a long convalescence following my return from France. Much to my father's disappointment, I had studied journalism at the University of Georgia in Athens and hoped to secure a position working for a newspaper in the near future. I had also begun work on my first book and had been taking time since graduation in that pursuit. My father had been trying to keep me involved in the family business working in the office; *getting my hands dirty*, as he would say. My brother was four years older, and following a wildly precarious and barely successful college career at Georgia Tech right there in Atlanta, was taking on increasing responsibility in my father's operations. He clearly had more of an aptitude for running liquor, and certainly enjoyed it far more than I.

Coulter Imports had moved with the times to distribute soda drinks, coffee and tea as a front for the real and lucrative business of liquor. I knew it was illegal, hell everyone did, and except for a few greedy politicians and cops that had to be convinced with a little cash now and then, most of the town chose to turn its back on the situation. Surely everybody we knew thought that Prohibition was not only the most damned stupid thing the government had ever come up with, but also a short-term nuisance that would soon be a distant memory.

At my side that night was a most remarkable young woman. I was convinced that I had fallen in love again, the first time since leaving young Celeste in France after the War.

Her name was Hanna Wesley and we stood looking out across the lawn from the back steps of the broad veranda, her hand in mine. The white sequined dress that she wore, fashioned just below the knees, sparkled like a thousand stars. Her hair was trimmed short and shining black, even in the low evening light. I turned to look at her, and she smiled back and gripped my hand with confidence and reassurance. I was to introduce her to my parents that night, and I was far more nervous than she about the encounter ahead. I had never been really serious about any of the girls that I had dated or brought home to the Coulter house, but none of them had been Hanna Wesley.

With every intent to ask for Hanna's hand in marriage later that night, I felt that it was only right to have made all of the proper introductions to family and friends. What better timing than a night with everyone in town that mattered, as far as my parents were concerned, assembled for easy and hopefully relaxed encounters with the future Mrs. Mathew Coulter? My parents were always caught up in excessive protocol, as was the custom in their circle of friends in Atlanta. I had no particular interest in formalities, other than an obligation, beyond mere courtesy, to make sure Hanna knew what she was getting into.

I had met her only four short weeks earlier at the library in downtown Atlanta. I was there doing some research for my book. I had told her a lot about my family; everything except the more recent nature of my father's business, which she would surely come to understand fully on this given evening. If she accepted my proposal, which I had every reason to believe would certainly be the case, I was planning to offer to accompany her back to Chicago as soon as possible to ask for her father's blessing.

We started down the steps together, Hanna holding my arm and keeping me steady as I willed my stiff leg to follow along; the old war injury that would prove to be a lifelong nuisance. I scanned the crowd looking for my mother. Someone grabbed my arm and I turned to see my sister, Margaret, with her new husband trailing along beside. She and Desmond Raye had been married the previous year. He was an attorney who had, until recently, been working at a small firm in the city. The Rayes had been friends of our family for many years. Maggie looked spectacular as always, her blonde hair pulled back tight and piled on top of her head, dressed in the latest fashion from New York. All our family were taller than most and Maggie had inherited the same trait, standing nearly as tall as her husband. She had a drink in her free hand, spilling frequently on her white glove as she bounced nervously. My friends had always lusted after Margaret Coulter, and she had been enough of a flirt to allow them to imagine that she was actually interested in boys two years younger, even when we were in high school.

    Desmond Raye was a different sort and we had yet to form much of a bond, although my father had asked him to join the business a few months earlier. I suspected that he felt we would need in-house counsel for anticipated legal entanglements ahead. Unlike the gregarious and ever adventurous Maggie, Desmond was dry and humorless, reminding me of someone more suited to the undertaker's profession than of a dynamic litigator. His dark black hair was greased back flat against his head and parted from the side to cover early signs of baldness. His ever-present scowl further reinforced my opinion of him.

    "Maggie," I said with as much enthusiasm as I could manage and trying my best to hide my nervousness, "I want you to meet Hanna… Hanna Wesley, my new friend." Of all the family, I wanted most for Maggie to approve. She had always been my closest confidant and we had often found ourselves in a self-protective alliance against our older brother or some other unwelcome intrusion in our lives. "Hanna, this is my sister, Margaret, and her husband, Desmond." I turned to look at Hanna. She was smiling graciously and reached out her hand.

    "It is very nice to meet you, Margaret," Hanna said. "Mathew has spoken so often of you."

    "You must call me Maggie, and I trust that you don't believe any of his scandalous lies!" my sister said.

    "On the contrary, he talks like you've hung the moon. It really is so nice to meet you… and Mr. Raye," Hanna said, reaching then for his hand.

    Desmond nodded along with something resembling a grunt, and then looked away across the crowd of people dancing, oblivious to all of us, apparently thinking that we were unworthy of his time and attention. I noticed Maggie giving her husband a frustrated glare, but then she turned back to us and her face lit up again. "Have you met Momma and Daddy yet, Hanna?" she asked, taking a longer sip from her glass of whiskey.

"No, I'm so looking forward to it tonight."

"And where are you from Hanna?" Maggie asked. "Did you go to school in Atlanta?"

"No, I'm from Chicago, actually. I finished up at Northwestern a little over a year ago, and I've been down here working ever since. My friend's father owns a line of clothing stores, and they offered me a position."

Maggie reached out and took her arm and pulled Hanna close to her side so that she could talk *girl-to-girl*, I gathered. "So you're a college girl?"

Hanna laughed. "Yes, my father insisted I get an education."

"Mathew, how have you ever attracted such a beautiful and brilliant girl? Clearly you've fooled her to this point," my sister said in her normal teasing way with me and in a grossly exaggerated, nose-in-the air, old Atlanta southern accent for effect.

"Yes, I'm surprised she ever agreed to even have coffee with me," I said, "but I just wouldn't let up until she said *yes*."

Hanna moved back over and put her arm around my waist. "Actually, I've found your brother to be quite charming," she said, and then turned and kissed me on the cheek. "Not at all what his Southern hayseed accent might indicate."

I watched as Maggie's eyes opened wide at Hanna's display of affection.

"Well, I do believe my little brother has fallen in love and somehow convinced this lovely woman of his merits and abilities," Maggie said

"Please sister," I responded, but she cut me off.

"I'm kidding of course, Hanna. My brother Mathew is the catch of Atlanta… a rich southern gentleman and war hero with looks that can chase your breath away. Just ask half the girls here tonight." She reached over and tried to smooth a stray bit of brown hair back from my eyes.

"Really, Maggie," I started to say, and then Hanna came to my defense again.

"Well then, I have captured the prize tonight," she said. I was so taken with her at that moment and we both lingered far too long in each other's gaze.

Maggie finally interrupted. "Hanna Wesley, it's really been so nice to see you, and welcome to our home. Do enjoy yourself and please sample some of Daddy's best whiskey while you're here." She held up her glass and the amber liquid reflected in the lights from the trees. "You'll have to have Mathew take you down in the cellar where the really good stock is kept." And with that she backed away with a quick and feigned curtsey and a tug on her sullen husband's arm. Desmond managed a slight nod as he was pulled away.

"I hope I warned you sufficiently about dear sister Maggie."

"She is delightful."

"Certainly a bright light in the universe beside her newly betrothed," I said. "I've yet to understand her attraction to *Mr. Raye*. Most clearly a case of opposites attracting, I suppose."

Hanna looked at me then with the most endearing smile and with an expression that always seemed to have me completely at her mercy, she kissed me on the cheek. "I can only imagine how charming your parents must be to have raised such a marvelous daughter, in spite of their efforts with this wayward son."

I pulled her close and felt the smooth softness of her cheek on mine. "You will have to reserve judgment until you meet the older son, my brother Jess." When I looked away I saw my mother through the crowd talking with a group of women who I recognized as her close ring of friends for cards and tennis at the club, and relentless gossip on the latest Atlanta scandals.

"That must be your mother," Hanna said, following my line of sight.

"And how would you know?"

"The resemblance is remarkable. Anyone could see it."

I turned and looked at Hanna Wesley and those wonderful brown eyes. I squeezed her hand more tightly. My heart began beating faster in nervous anticipation of the introductions to the matriarch of our family and all of her friends. My mother, the former Victoria Lancaster, was from an old Atlanta family that dated back well before the War. That would, of course, be the Civil War. The Lancaster's had made their money in land speculation and shipping mostly, and there were now members of the family spread all across the South in prominent families and businesses. One of her brothers was on track to be the next governor of Georgia.

"Are you ready?" I asked.

"Of course I'm ready. She's so beautiful, Mathew."

I nodded and listened to the music from the band play in the back of my mind as I tried to quickly gather my composure.

"Shouldn't we go over?" she asked, wondering about my hesitation.

Chapter Three

    Hanna's smile gave me new courage, and we made our way through the crowd at the party. As we approached, my mother saw me coming and held up a hand to break the flow of conversation with her friends. She could best be described as regal, always dressed elegantly, and on this night holding court again among the elite of Atlanta society.

    "Oh Mathew, I'm so glad that you've finally arrived," she said. "I've been looking everywhere for you." Her friends parted to make room for us. My mother then noticed Hanna on my arm and her expression changed ever so slightly. Only if you knew her well would you be able to detect the subtle change in mood and expression. She stood up slightly more erect, even though her posture and bearing were always impeccable. "Well Mathew, you have a new friend," she said, and I could tell from the frosty tone that this would be the difficult exchange that I had anticipated.

    I knew her friends were assessing Hanna and her dress and shoes. The first impressions seemed to be somewhat positive from the looks on all of their faces. "Mother, ladies," I said, acknowledging all of her friends around us, "this is Hanna Wesley from Chicago."

My mother held out a white-gloved hand and the two women greeted each other politely, but tentatively. I knew that my mother would try to behave in front of all of her closest acquaintances, but I could tell from the look in her eyes that she was less than pleased.

"Hanna... Wesley is it?" she asked.

"Yes, Mrs. Coulter."

"Miss Wesley, welcome to our home. It is really so nice of you to join us, and I hope you're keeping an eye on my son. There are so many eligible young women here tonight who would just love to sweep him away."

The other ladies giggled, and exchanged knowing looks and whispered comments. My mother's tone and intent were very clear, but Hanna continued to smile. She pulled me closer and said, "I'm keeping a very short leash on him."

"I can see that, dear," my mother said, the corners of her mouth pursing the way they always did when she was trying to remain calm.

"Mother, I sense that you're right in the middle of something," I said, and then nodded to the other women. "When you get a moment, I would like to have you spend some time with us tonight."

"Of course, dear. I'll find you a bit later." She took a surprisingly long drink from a glass of champagne. "Miss Wesley, really it was so nice," and she reached for Hanna's hand again. "Make yourself at home and enjoy the wonderful food that Chef Robert has prepared. I'll catch up with the two of you, I promise."

I pulled Hanna away and tried my best to smile at my mother and her whispering group of friends. I could see in her eyes that we would have one of our typical *disapproving mother* and *barely tolerant son* discussions in the very near future. I thought that it would be even more interesting when she learned of my intentions for Miss Hanna Wesley. A waiter came by with a tray of glasses filled with white and red wine, and we both took a glass of cabernet that had been acquired by my father through his connections in Europe. When we were far enough away from my mother, I stopped and held up my glass to Hanna's. "Thank you for enduring that. I'm sorry, my mother can be quite a handful, particularly when she's with the *girls*."

"It's fine really, Mathew. Clearly she loves her son and wants only the best... one of these Atlanta debutantes, I'm sure," she said and smiled, looking around at the other young women throughout the crowd.

The pace of the music from the band slowed. I took the glass from Hanna and placed it with mine on a table next to us. "Would you like to dance?"

At first, I assumed because of my bad leg, she seemed surprised at my invitation, but then she nodded and we moved across the grass to the tile patio around the long pool where a cluster of people were moving with the rhythm of the music. She came close in my arms, and I felt the brush of her hair against my face. All of the stress and worry about the evening seemed to float away on the warm April breeze. As we turned slowly together, I tried to keep some sense of rhythm and grace, in spite of a leg that I had almost left behind in a smoldering muddy shell hole in Europe. I could see my mother standing across the lawn, looking past her friends directly at us. Her expression was strained at best.

"Mathew, this is a lovely evening," Hanna said. "Thank you for bringing me. Your home is just magnificent."

Her soft voice in my ear was soothing and seemed almost a whisper under the sounds from the band. I pulled back and looked at her face. "You're being awfully brave in front of all these people you've never met," I said.

In our short time together we had not become *intimate*, as my sister Maggie would describe it. My big brother, Jess, would be more likely to say that *I hadn't gotten laid yet*. There had been a couple of times when emotion and lust between the two of us had risen to a precipitous level, but a little voice in the back of my head always reminded me that Hanna Wesley was not just any girl, and that our first time together should be special, not some heated thrashing about on the seat of my car. I could tell over recent days that Hanna was beginning to get impatient with my reluctance to *seal the deal* as my old college friends would drunkenly suggest. Her gaze seemed distracted. I turned to look and saw that my brother was coming through the dancing couples toward us.

"And that would be brother Jess," I said.

My brother came up and stood next to us. "May I please have the honor," he said in his most affected southern gentleman flourish.

"Hanna Wesley, please meet my much older and rarely wiser brother, Jess."

They shook hands and Jess pulled her away. "Just one dance," he said as they moved away into the crowd. Hanna looked back at me with a helpless expression. I was standing there watching Jess take her in his arms when I felt a tap on the shoulder. I turned to see my father behind me.

Samuel Coulter was a commanding figure in any gathering, standing as tall as I, but 50 pounds heavier from his years of plentiful food and drink. His flowing hair had grayed and his face was deeply tanned from his many hours on the fairways of the East Lake Country Club, and atop one of his horses riding up in the hills in the country north of Atlanta. The Coulter family was "Old South" and "military" which was the ideal lineage among those who mattered in Atlanta. My grandfather had been a colonel under Jackson in the Confederate Army, and my father had risen to the rank of captain in the Army before turning to a career in business.

"Good evening, son," he said in his imposing voice. He took my arm and led me across the lawn toward one of the bars. I looked back over my shoulder to see if I could spot Hanna and

Jess, but they were lost in the crowd. My father asked for two glasses of Scotch whiskey on ice and handed one to me. He held his glass up to mine and we both took a drink. I noticed Charlie Watermann and the two bodyguards standing a few feet from us, looking the other way.

"So tell me about this new girl?" he asked. "She's quite striking, Mathew."

"She's a new friend, actually more than a friend," I said, my confidence rising for some reason at that moment. "Her name is Hanna Wesley."

"I've wondered where you've been off to so much lately," he said.

"She's a special girl."

His face hardened some and he looked at me with piercing eyes. "Now son, let's not get too caught up here. How long have you known this Miss Wesley?"

"For just a few weeks, but it seems so much longer," I said. "She is just incredible…"

He interrupted by leading me off across the lawn away from the bar. He smiled at people as we walked through the crowd, occasionally acknowledging someone with a quick nod or comment. We reached a cluster of azaleas along the side of the yard, lit up in their spring colors of brilliant white and red.

"Mathew, please tell me you're not getting too serious about this girl."

His words cut through me like razor wire. "You haven't even met her yet!" I said.

"Oh, I'm sure she's lovely, Mathew, but please, let's take things slowly here. Your mother and I have great plans for your future and I…"

I backed away from him and tried as best I could to contain my anger, but then decided to jump right in. "I'm going to ask Hanna to marry me tonight," I said.

My father surprised me by just smiling back, and then he said, "I had a feeling that you were that far down the road with this girl. Mathew. You need to slow down some."

"Her name is Hanna Wesley," I said and I could feel a burning sensation sweeping through my body.

"Are you aware of the consequences of all this?" His question caught me totally off guard, and I couldn't even answer. "Do you know anything about this woman and her family?" he asked, and then he took a sip from his glass of whiskey.

"Of course I do!"

"So you know of the Wesley family from North Chicago?" he went on. "The father is a clothing merchant of some success, I understand."

"And how would you know that?"

He sensed the anger in my tone and said, "Mathew, please listen to me. I've had some people do a little checking on your new friend." I started to interrupt, but he held a hand up and continued on. "We know you've been spending a lot of time with this girl and I just thought it would be prudent to help you learn a little more about what you're getting in to."

"Help me!" I said.

"Please, son." His voice became even deeper, and he looked across the lawn filled with Atlanta society as he continued. "It's very important that we look out for each other and for this family. We have a place in this town that has taken years to establish, and we have to be smart about the choices we make and the implications of those choices."

I couldn't contain my frustration any longer. "What in hell are you talking about?"

My outburst seemed to surprise him, and he looked back at me. He turned and faced me head on, looking directly into my eyes. "Mathew, I'm sure that Hanna Wesley is a wonderful young girl, but you have to know how difficult this will be for everyone."

"What's difficult?"

"You must know that her family will be just as concerned. Hell, her father probably won't even allow you to see her again when he finds out the two of you have been together."

The realization of what he was saying swept through me and I tried to calm myself. "I can't believe you've had her family investigated."

"Mathew, I told you we have to be careful for the family. You'll learn this as you…"

"You have no right to do this."

"Of course I have the *right*!" he said in anger, his voice booming out through the night air. Two couples nearby turned to look at us in surprise. "Mathew, listen to me carefully. I'll not have you making this mistake. A Jewish girl…"

"This is not a mistake," I said, trying to remain calm. "I should have realized it was about this. I know about her religion. I've known about it from the beginning."

"Well, you must know how impossible it will be for everyone," he said.

"Only if you make it so."

"No son, I'm afraid it goes much deeper than that. Even if people in this town…"

"I don't give a damn about people in this town!"

He reached out and took the lapel of my jacket in his hand to stop me. "That's enough, and I don't want to hear you say that again." He paused, seeming to try to catch his breath and calm himself. "Even if people in this town accepted her, and these are our friends and business associates, Mathew," he said looking again out over the people assembled across our back lawn. "These are the people that we share our lives with. Even if there was some chance that they would understand and welcome this girl into our ways here, which I can tell you will never happen; even if that were so, there is no way that her Jewish family in Chicago would ever allow such a marriage. Do you understand this, son?" He let go of my jacket and tried to smooth it down.

"I'm not stupid. I've known from the beginning that this would be a problem with the family, and all of these people and this damned town."

"Have you talked to her about this? Does she know your intentions?" I just stared at him for a moment. "Does she know you were planning to propose to her tonight?"

As his words began to sink in, I thought about the fact that we had not discussed marriage and that, perhaps in my naivety, I just assumed this could all be worked out between the two of us. *To hell with parents and everyone else in this damn town and in Chicago*, I thought.

The first seeds of doubt began to creep into my mind about Hanna and me being together. All I could feel was anger and frustration at the prospects and inevitabilities that our families, and the little worlds that we lived in, were imposing on us. The sudden realization that my future might not include Hanna Wesley was overwhelming, and I just stood there staring back at my father.

"Mathew, I asked if this Miss Wesley has any idea about your intentions?"

I tried to compose myself and was finally able to answer. "No, I don't believe that she does," I said with a dullness in my voice that didn't even sound like myself talking. He put his arm around me and started leading me back toward the party. My mind was racing with the events and discussions with Hanna over the past few weeks, and I searched for any of the signs that would reassure me that she felt as strongly as I about our future.

My father spoke, but his voice seemed a distant echo and I don't even recall what he was telling me. I was just thinking that I needed to find Hanna. We had to talk, and she would have to tell me how she felt about us and about our future. I looked through the growing crowd and couldn't see Hanna or Jess. I pulled myself away from my father and threw the drink in my hand to the ground as I started off across the lawn. They weren't out dancing anymore, and I walked up onto the back veranda, looking at all the groupings of people. Maggie came up to me and stopped me. "Mathew, what's wrong?"

I looked up and just stared at her for a moment, and then said, "I have to find Hanna."

Chapter Four

My sister, Maggie, looked at me with a puzzled and blurry expression from the drink as I left her standing there and walked into the house. I wandered from room to room, looking for Hanna. Then I realized what must have surely happened. Jess had not only interrupted to have the next dance, but also to escort her home; to get her off the property. A quiet rage continued to grow inside me. My family's complicit betrayal was overwhelming. Even my own brother was in on it.

I staggered down the steps across the back of the house. I turned and looked over the crowd of Atlanta's most notable families gathered on this evening to be entertained by my parents; to be served with the illegal alcohol that my father's company now provided to this town; to gorge from the extravagant feast that had been prepared. The whole lot of them, and all of their excesses, suddenly seemed so pathetic; all of their customs and protocols and prejudices.

Our housekeeper, Velma, came up beside me with a tray of drinks. I grabbed a glass of wine and drank half of it in the first gulp. She was a big woman, with an even bigger heart. She stood there in her black and white uniform looking at me with those eyes that always seemed to understand what I was thinking. "Mathew, I want you to take it easy on this drinkin' tonight, you hear me son?" she said. "I been hearin' what your daddy's been up to with this new *little miss* of yours. Best not to get all worked up. Some things just ain't meant to be."

I sensed someone behind me and turned to see my father. Standing at my back, he placed his hand on my shoulder and said, "Son, I'm truly sorry about all this, but it's only what's right for everyone, including this girl."

"She's gone isn't she?" I asked, turning to face him as Velma hurried away into the crowd. "Jess has taken her home?"

He nodded. "Mathew, this world can be ugly at times. How we all feel about each other and our faith is one of those damned things that has been a curse since the dawn of man. I can't say that I like it, but it's the way this world is, and you're going to have to understand that and live with it like we all do. I know you think right now this is the only woman in the world, but you'll meet so many more girls."

"I need to go find Hanna."

"No, you're not going to see her again," he said with a firm grip on my shoulders.

My first reaction was to laugh at him, and then the anger returned. "You can't stop me from seeing her."

His next words caught me totally unprepared, "I rather doubt this Miss Wesley will have much interest in seeing any of us again, Mathew."

I reached out for him, grabbing his arms and trying to keep myself from hitting him. "What have you done? You haven't hurt her?"

"No, of course not," he said. "I've only asked your brother to escort her home, and on the way to explain to her the facts of the situation." He calmly reached to loosen my grip on his arms.

"The facts?" I had to ask, my mind swirling with the sequence of events, and wondering how Hannah could possibly be reacting to all of this. How would I ever be able to explain what had happened, and how my family had treated her?

At that moment, one of my father's men came up and whispered something in his ear. He nodded, and then turned back to me. "I want you to come with me for a moment," he said, and then he was walking away through the crowd, assuming I was following him. Instead, I turned and went quickly through the house and out the front door. I had to go to Hanna and try to salvage the wreckage that my family had created. The driveway was packed with cars parked at all angles, and my car was out closer to the road since we had arrived so late. I began walking down the drive toward West Paces Ferry Road, and closer to the street I found the black sedan parked on the lawn. I started it and was beginning to put the car in gear when my side window was suddenly blocked. My father's bodyguard, William, was standing there. He opened the door and reached in to stop me. I tried again to shift the car, but he grabbed my arm and pushed me back against the seat.

"Mr. Coulter, there's no need to get all excited here," William said. "Your father asked me to find you. He has some business that the two of you need to deal with."

I knew that trying to get away was useless. This goon would never allow me to ignore my father's orders. I looked up at his scowling face and heavy brow, and thought how ridiculous he looked in a dinner jacket, the muscles in his neck bulging at the restraint of the white collar of his shirt. I felt desperate to get away and to find Hanna, but knew that I would have to wait.

I got out of the car and followed William back up the drive toward the house. He was carrying a small lantern, and he turned onto a path that led around the house and down a hill to a creek that ran through the back of the property. We had walked for several minutes before I saw the gas light that illuminated a small clearing along the creek where a gazebo had been built to sit and enjoy the quiet tranquility of the running water and surrounding woods. I could see two men standing in the screened structure, and as we got closer I saw that my father was there with another man that I didn't recognize. William stopped at the screened door to hold it open for me, and I limped up the steps. I felt a numb helplessness as I went over to stand next to my father.

The man that was with him was also dressed for the evening, and must have been one of the guests. He was a smaller man than the imposing Samuel Coulter and he had a desperate, fearful expression on his face. Another of my father's men that I hadn't noticed at first stood off in a corner. My father didn't look up to acknowledge me, but instead continued to stare at the man standing in front of him, and then finally he said, "Mathew, this is Walter. He works for Lenny over on the West Side." Lenny Morgan was one of my father's top associates in the business. Neither of us made any effort to greet the other. My father continued on in a slow cadence. "Walter has been trying to branch out a bit on his own lately…"

"Mr. Coulter," the man named Walter said with panic in his voice, but my father cut him off.

"Walter thinks that there is enough business out there for him to start setting up some of our customers with his own product and cutting our prices."

I watched as the hulking William walked around me and moved over to stand behind Walter. The man was visibly shaking, and even in the dim light from the clearing, I could see the sweat beading on his face and running into his eyes. He used the sleeve of his black dinner jacket to try to wipe it away.

"Really, Mr. Coulter, you don't understand."

"Oh, I understand completely, Walter. I've had to deal with punks like you for years. I give you an opportunity and you get greedy and think you're smarter than me." I could sense the anger building in my father's voice. He moved over so that he stood only inches away from the man's face. "If I let you get away with this, how could I run my business? Every asshole in Atlanta would think they could screw with me and steal from me."

Walter tried to speak again, but only stuttered something unintelligible. I looked down and saw a small puddle of urine starting to leak out from his right pant leg onto the wood floor of the gazebo. You could smell the sickening scent of fear and piss on the man.

My father noticed it, too. "My god, man! You disgust me!" He backed away and nodded to get his man's attention. William moved up close behind Walter, and I watched as his arms came up, one with a hand across the man's mouth to silence him, the other with a long knife that shined in the low light of the gas flame. He held the knife up near the man's face and let it drag down over his cheek, and then up near his right eye. Then my father moved closer and suddenly threw his entire weight into a punch that caught the man flush in the gut. Unprepared for the blow, and desperately preoccupied by the knife at his face, he doubled over in pain. I could hear his breath blow out in a rush of air. William put the knife away, and then turned the man around and held the back of his head as he brought his knee up viciously into his face. I heard the bones in his nose shatter as he wailed out in pain and fell to the floor. Holding his face, blood gushed out between his fingers and dripped on the floor. Everything happened quickly. I was so surprised and sickened that I wasn't even able to respond. I started to back away toward the door, and watched as my father's man moved in and began kicking him unmercifully in the stomach.

My father reached out to stop me. "You need to know what the world is like out there, son. We have to look out for ourselves because there are assholes like this around every corner that want what we have, and will do anything to take it."

There was a vicious hate in his voice, and the distorted look on his face was terrifying. The violence of the moment was so sudden that I was stunned in disbelief. The man's blood flowing out and across the wood floor took me suddenly back to times in the War when such a sight had become so commonplace that men rarely stopped to notice or even care. We lived with blood smeared on our faces and hardened beneath our nails. Violence and brutality became a part of our daily journey from one horror to the next.

    My father's voice became muted and distant in my brain, and I managed to pull away and stumbled through the screen door and down the steps, my head pounding and nausea rising in my gut. I tripped on a root in the path and fell face forward. Trying to catch myself, I felt a searing pain as my hands and face scraped along the stones in the path. I got up and started off again through the darkness. With no light I was soon off the path and into the heavy woods, branches slapping at my body and face. Then I heard the sound of the band suddenly coming through the heavy underbrush. I saw a few lights from the back of the house and the party. I veered to the right to avoid the crowds and continued to stumble along, trying to make my way around to the front of the house to find a car and get as far away as possible.

    I made it back to the front drive. In the lights from the porch, I looked down and saw that my hands were cut and bleeding from my fall, and blood had splattered down the front of my white shirt from the wounds that I could feel throbbing on my chin and cheek. I staggered through the parked cars and eventually found my own. This time no one stopped me and I was soon out on the road and drove away.

    At first I didn't even think about where I was going. I just wanted to get the image of the attack I had just witnessed out of my head. The sickening horror of it exploded again in my mind and I pulled the car over onto the shoulder. The car skidded to a stop in the loose gravel. I opened the door so that I could puke out the bile churning in my gut. It came in waves and seemed to go on and on. Finally I was able to sit back in the seat to try to get my breath. When I opened my eyes, I could see myself in the dim light in the rearview mirror. My face was swollen and bleeding. My eyes were flushed with tears from the puking, and dark circles spread out beneath them. I leaned my head back and closed my eyes. I felt my heart pounding in my chest and my lungs aching to get air.

I'm not sure if I passed out or fell asleep, or how long I was out. I was startled back to consciousness by a passing car that honked because I had left the car door open. They had to swerve around me. I put my hands on the steering wheel and all the images of the night came back to me. Then I thought of Hanna and I knew that I had to go see her. I pulled the door closed and drove out into the night.

Hanna lived in a small apartment above a garage behind one of the big houses down in Ansley Park, closer in to downtown Atlanta. Somehow I managed to drive there without crashing, even though I was barely aware of the road or the traffic around me. I parked out on the street in front of the house and walked back up the drive. A small light was on next to the door to her apartment at the top of a set of stairs that led up the side of the garage. I knew I needed to see Hanna, to hold her and tell her that I loved her and wanted to marry her. The fact that I was bleeding and looking like I had been run over by a truck was the furthest thing from my mind.

As I reached the bottom of the stairs the door opened above me and I looked up with a feeling of relieved expectation. I started to speak, but then a man came out of the door. In the light I could see that it was my brother Jess. He was putting his jacket on, and he had his back to me when Hanna came out. I stumbled back into the shadows and watched as she came into his arms and kissed him. She was dressed in a white silk robe and stood there in bare feet kissing my brother. He pulled her robe open and I could see her nakedness as he put his arms around her waist. Then they were talking in whispers and laughing. I couldn't hear what they were saying. I backed further into the shadows hidden by a large bush at the side of the garage, and I felt myself sinking again into that abyss of darkness and betrayal.

    Later as I drove through the night, headlights blinding as cars passed, I saw the images of my brother holding and kissing Hanna Wesley continuing to repeat in my mind. All I could feel was numb and empty inside. Their betrayal had been absolute and crushing, and I had been unable to move or speak. I had stood there in the darkness of the bushes as my brother came down the stairs and walked away down the drive. I heard the engine of a car start and drive away, and then the door above me closed and the light was turned off. As I stood there in the darkness, I was overwhelmed by the shame of not confronting them. I should have run up the stairs and lashed out at my brother, and told Hanna what a whore she was. I should have gotten all of the bitterness and emotion out, but instead I had hidden helplessly in the darkness like a schoolboy who couldn't stand up for himself.
    It was the shame in all of that, I suppose, that bothered me most that night as I drove out of Atlanta.

Chapter Five

The car seemed to drive itself. I suppose that I knew where I was headed before I had any conscious sense of my destination. My mind was locked on the scenes from earlier that night, the murderous rage in my father's eyes, and the lustful and betraying look of the woman I thought had cared for me. I drove through the town of Columbus, Georgia, and then on into Alabama and down through Eufaula and Dothan, when the sun began to show the faintest glow of light from the coming morning over my left shoulder. It was then that I first realized what my destination had been from the beginning.

By the time I reached the Florida border the sun was up behind me, and in a little town called DeFuniak Springs, I stopped for gasoline and some food. My hands and face still ached from my fall the previous night. The blood had dried and was a dull brown on my skin and clothes. The people in the restaurant that I limped in to were more than a little taken aback by my soiled tuxedo shirt and bruised and bloody face, but they brought out the food without a word. After getting directions from my befuddled hosts, I kept on heading south on the narrow road through heavy wooded swampland. Only a few farms and logging camps along the way broke the relentless isolation of the wilderness, and the further I traveled, the road continued to deteriorate beneath me. By the time I got south of Freeport, the way was not much better than a wide sandy trail. I followed it along the eastern edge of the Choctawhatchee Bay to the ferry at Jolly Bay. As I waited for the ferry to return, I got out of the car and looked out across the water to the south. It was a deep blue from the reflection of the clear skies above, and the west wind kicked up a light chop on the surface. A large flock of ducks flew in low and landed along the tall marsh grasses near the shore. An old man sat in a wooden fishing boat a few hundred feet offshore, and he caught two fish in the short time that I stood there watching him.

When the ferry pulled up, I drove onboard for the ride across the shallow bay to Point Washington, a little town that had grown up around the lumber business. There was a small store there so I stopped in to buy something cool to drink and some food for the rest of the trip. A large woman stood behind a counter and helped me. Her complexion was dark-skinned, almost native. Her face was impassive, and she gave nothing more than a nod in response to my requests. When it was time to total my purchases, I sensed her staring at the state of my clothes and the visible wounds on my body. They had iced cola drinks in a cooler and some pickles and sausages on the counter that I gathered to purchase. There was a phone, and with permission and some money placed on the counter, I called a friend in Atlanta to say that I was going down to the beach and would appreciate being able to stay for a while out at his family's cottage. He immediately acknowledged that I could stay as long as I liked. The family wouldn't even be down this year because they would all be off to Europe for the summer. He told me where the key was hidden out in the outhouse behind the cottage. I asked him not to let anyone know that he had heard from me.

Out behind the store there was a sawmill, unpainted and weathered, with stripped tree trunks stacked high all around and pallets of rough lumber over in another part of the clearing in the trees. A painted sign over the main door read *Bidwell Mill.*

It was midday by the time I was back in my car, and the ruts in the road were growing in size. The car bounced and jostled in the loose sand, and I couldn't make much more than five or ten miles per hour. I sensed that I was getting closer to the shore by the smell of salt and fish in the air. My wheels began to lose grip, and the car swayed and lurched as I accelerated to keep from getting stuck. The engine whined as I tried to keep going, but I knew it was hopeless as the wheels continued to dig deeper into the soft sand.

Then I was stopped and the engine stalled. Suddenly it was very quiet. Only the sound of a few birds up in the heavy live oak trees broke the silence. Sitting there looking out ahead, I kept both hands on the wheel, breathing deeply, trying to get a sense of where I was and how I was going to keep on. Finally I got out of the car and walked around it, looking at the rear wheels stuck up to their axles in loose sand. The sun was beating down hard now and motion above caught my eye. I looked up to see a gray hawk sweep in lower for a better look, and then flare away at the sight of me. The bird lifted up easily on the air currents and continued on its flight, looking ever vigilantly towards the Earth for its next meal.

Sitting down on the front fender of the disabled Ford, I wiped the sweat away from my eyes and tried to consider my situation. I wasn't entirely sure how much farther it was to the little village of Grayton Beach. The directions I'd been given by the reluctantly quiet woman back in Point Washington had been fairly simple, and I felt that I was getting close. Some time ago my friend had described Grayton Beach as not much more than a few random and rustic cottages built into the white sand dunes and sea oats along the Gulf of Mexico. It was the solitude that he had described, I suppose, that had stuck in my mind.

I started off walking down the road. Tall pines and live oak trees grew thick on each side, and I hadn't gone more than a few hundred yards when I was startled by what sounded like some large animal coming through the brush off to my left. Backing up a few steps, I contemplated my options. If it was a wild boar I could run and climb a tree before its lethal tusks made short work of me. Or perhaps it was just a deer that would spook away when it came into the clearing of the road and saw me.

I was certainly not prepared to see a large brown horse burst out through the underbrush from a narrow trail and onto the road with a young woman seated up on top. I noticed her hair first. It was long and black, and floated out behind her in the soft trace of breeze that was blowing. Her skin was dark like a polished mahogany wood. She wore denim pants tucked into high black boots that had a dusty coat of sand, and a loose white shirt with the sleeves rolled up. The horse noticed me before she did and bolted sideways, causing her to rein in the big animal. Then she saw me, and as our eyes met, there was no sense of fear or alarm in her face, just a calm expression of confusion as I imagine my appearance was a bit strange and unexpected for the remote northern shores of Florida. She settled her horse and walked it over closer to me. Then she started to laugh, which surprised me even more. Trying to stifle her snickers, her voice was soft and calm, "You appear to be a bit lost."

I stood there speechless, looking at this girl, too tired to find a response. She slowly climbed down from her mount and held the reins in her left hand as she walked up to me. The dried blood on my face and hands, and all over my clothes, must have been somewhat concerning to her because she stayed just far enough away to be able to jump back up on top of that horse if she had to.

"Are you all right, mister?"

Am I all right? I asked myself. Considering I had just had my entire life pulled out from under me the night before, *no I was not any way near all right*. For a moment, the futility of this trip to the Gulf Coast seemed overwhelming, and I tried to convince myself that it was best that I get away for at least long enough to clear my head and sort out all that had happened back in Atlanta.

I watched as she turned to grab a canteen that was hanging from the horn of her saddle. She uncorked the cap and handed it to me. As I took the canteen, I tried to estimate her age, and came to the conclusion that she was in her late teens or early twenties. I took a long drink, my hands shaking from exhaustion. Water dribbled down my chin and onto my stained shirt. The black bow tie was still around my neck from the night before, though untied. I finished drinking and handed the canteen back to her.

"Thank you," I said as I gulped in air and tried to gather myself.

"My name's Rebecca... Rebecca Bidwell," she said, reaching out for my hand. I took hers and it was warm, and the grip firm. Then she smiled at me.

"Mathew Coulter," I said, continuing to hold her hand.

"You look like you've had a nasty trip," she said.

I looked down at myself for a moment, and then was able to barely manage a smile. Looking back up at Rebecca Bidwell, I said, "If you only knew."

"How'd you get here?"

I glanced back and my car was out of sight around a bend in the road, if you could call it a road. I turned back to the girl and said, "I'm down from Atlanta, trying to get to a friend's place in Grayton Beach."

"You walked the whole way?" she said and then laughed.

"No, my car's stuck up around the bend back there."

"Happens all the time. Guess I'm not surprised. These roads around here are a nightmare."

"How much further to Grayton Beach?" I asked.

"Oh, we're just a ways to the beach there," she said, looking down the road away from me. "Who are you coming to visit? Not many folks around here this time of year."

"You know the Headley family from Atlanta?" I asked. "They've had a place down in here in Grayton Beach for some time now I guess."

Her expression brightened some and she answered, "Yes, I know Jimmy Headley. I've seen him and his family down here in the summers. They have a nice old cottage near the beach, just down from the hotel."

"That's right, the Headley's place," I said, and then hesitated, not sure exactly how to explain why I was headed that way. "So what are you doing out here in the middle of nowhere, Rebecca?"

"Just giving Barley here a little run," she said, turning to rub the soft muzzle of her horse's nose. "Our family lives up at Point Washington. My daddy runs a sawmill and a little store up there on the bay."

I nodded and said, "I just stopped through there."

"That was Momma behind the counter. She was cordial, I expect?"

"Sure," I said, thinking back about the stout woman shopkeeper that had helped me earlier. There certainly was a resemblance with this young girl, definitely in the eyes, although her mother had put on a generous number of pounds over the years.

"Can't always be sure how she'll treat visitors from the North. She's plenty kind to the locals though," Rebecca said.

"She was fine, really," I said, not wishing to get into how the encounter had really gone. I took another drink from the canteen.

"Your bags back in the car?" she asked.

I thought for a moment and realized I had left town with nothing but the clothes I had on and about fifty dollars and change in my pocket. "No, didn't bring much," I answered.

"You want a ride into town?" she asked. "Me and Barley can take you down. Won't be any trouble at all." She turned and pulled herself up into the saddle, and then reached for my hand. I couldn't think of any reason why I shouldn't take her offer. I was frankly about out of strength to continue on alone anyway. I put my right foot into the stirrup and she helped to pull me up behind her on the rump of old Barley, my stiff left leg pushing out at an unnatural angle to the side. I got myself situated and put an arm around her waist to hold on as she kicked the horse and made a little clicking sound in her mouth to get it moving.

We started off at a slow walk, the horse making its way easily in the loose sand. The girl's hair blew in my face and I had to keep brushing it away. There were scents of soap and pine boughs. From this high perch I could see through the trees. Off ahead, the barrier dunes along the beach began to come into view. The sand hills were nearly as white as snow, shadowed across the ridges by the dark entanglements of the low scrub brush and grasses, and shaped over the years by the winds off the Gulf of Mexico. Then I could see the waters of a large lake leading up to the far dunes, laying calm, sheltered by the hills and trees. A line of tall pines rose up along the far east shore of the lake, the trunks bare of any limbs nearly three quarters of the way up. Rebecca just looked ahead like this panoramic view was nothing out of the ordinary.

We traveled on in silence as we came into the settlement of Grayton Beach. The first small house sat on the left, tucked into the trees. It was not much more than a one-room cabin built up on low stilts with a shallow pitched roof over a porch that ran all across the front. Two old wood chairs rested there with a small table with empty bottles scattered about. A large black dog ran out from the back of the house, and Barley didn't even seem to notice as it ran up and barked at us.

Rebecca looked down and scolded the dog. "You stay back now, Pepper. Don't want you gettin' stomped." The dog stopped barking and followed alongside, wagging its tail. A woman came to the door of the cabin. She pushed open the screen and walked out onto the porch.

"Hey Becky," she called, and then waved. She was dressed in a sleeveless white dress open at the neck, and her feet were bare. A small boy came out wearing only short white pants, and wrapped his arms around his mother's leg to watch the horse go by.

"Morning, Mrs. Elliott," Rebecca said.

"Who've you got there?" the woman asked about my place on the back of the horse.

"This is Mr. Coulter. Down from Atlanta to stay at the Headley's cottage," she answered.

The woman waved back. "Welcome, sir," she said. "Hope you enjoy your stay. I'm sure we'll see you around town. We're from Birmingham, but know a lot of folks up in Atlanta. We'll have to have you over for a drink."

I nodded and said, "Thank you." The little boy kept looking at me as we rode away.

Closer to the main street in the little village I began to hear the low rumble of the waves breaking onshore past the sand hills ahead. The sky was still a clear blue with only a few feathered white clouds high off to the south. We came to a stop where the road turned in both directions. A larger building sat off to our left, two stories in height and painted a bright white as many of the other structures in town were. There was a small sign across the roofline that read, *The Beach Hotel*. Just down the road there was an old water tower and a windmill that was turning with a slight rattle in the afternoon breeze. A few other cottages were scattered along the road and through the dunes toward the beach.

The porch on the hotel was lined with wooden rocking chairs, weathered by the salt air and wind. A little girl was sitting in one of the chairs. Her sunburned legs and bare feet were too short to reach the floor and stuck out from a green print dress. Her curly brown hair moved some in the soft breeze, and I guessed that she was near ten or twelve years of age.

Rebecca turned the horse to the left, and as we walked past the hotel she turned to the girl who was staring off across the street as if she didn't even see us. "Hello, Melanee," she said, and the girl looked up and smiled, although her gaze was still off to the side.

"Hi Rebecca," she said. "I thought that was Barley coming around the corner."

"How are you today, Melanee?"

"Oh, I'm just wonderful, thanks Rebecca. Grandma just finished up with my piano lesson, and we're going down to the beach in a bit."

"Well, I'll see you down there, honey?"

Then Melanee asked, "Who's that with you?"

Rebecca introduced us and let the little girl know where I was staying as we passed. She said that she would stop by later down at the beach.

"Yes, please come down," the little girl said with an excited lift in her voice. "The water's been so nice and warm since the spring rains let up."

"You say *hi* to Miss Lila for us now, dear," Rebecca said as we continued on. It was then that I first realized that the girl couldn't see us at all, that she was blind, and I whispered my observation to Rebecca in front of me. She nodded and said, "Little Melanee's been blind since birth. Her momma left her here a few years back with her grandma, Lila Dalton, who runs the hotel there. The woman's never come back for her, and I've heard folks say that she's over in New Orleans, up to no good."

I looked back at the little girl who still sat patiently on the porch, waiting for her grandmother to take her down to the beach. "How did she know I was riding with you?" I asked.

Rebecca turned over her shoulder and smiled at me. "Melanee Dalton is a special one. You'll see."

We turned on another narrow sand road and Rebecca Bidwell pulled the horse up in front of the Headley's cottage, similar in size and construction to the others we had seen along the way. An unpainted and weathered gray picket fence ran across the front along the road with a small gate in the middle. The house had been painted white years ago, but the seasons had taken their toll, and much of the wood siding was covered in cracked and peeling paint. Heavy wood shutters, painted black, covered the windows for protection against storms while the Headleys were away. It seemed that a paint scraper and a few cans of paint would keep me busy for a few weeks, and help to keep my mind off Atlanta. Live oak trees framed the house on both sides and in back, and low branches hung over the rusting metal roof.

"Here we are, Mr. Coulter," she said as she turned to make room for me to slide off. Before I could, there was a shout from the path up from the beach and we both turned to see two young men coming our way. Rebecca waved and said, "That's my brother Jonas there on the left, and that's Seth, Seth Howard…"

She couldn't finish her explanation before the one named Seth yelled out, "Becky, who you got there?" They walked up closer and stopped a few feet away. I slid carefully down off the horse and walked in my stiff and angled way around to be introduced, my hand tracing the back haunches of old Barley. I watched as the two men sized-up my appearance with a not so surprising disapproval on their faces. I started to reach out to say hello when Seth said in a heavy north Florida accent, just short of a snarl, "Who the hell are you, and what in hell'd you run into?"

Before I could answer he looked up at Rebecca Bidwell. "Where'd you find this piece a road kill, darlin'?"

"This is Mr. Mathew Coulter, boys," she said. "He's down from Atlanta to stay for a while here at the Headley's place. His car got stuck up the road there, so I gave him a ride in."

"How are you doing, fellas?" I said, reaching out my hand. Jonas Bidwell took it in a sweaty weak grip and just nodded back. Both were as tall as I and of sizable proportions. They were dressed in denim coveralls worn over short-sleeved shirts that were rolled up nearly to their shoulders. When I turned to Seth, he looked past me to Rebecca. His hair was brown, but bleached from the sun and long over his ears and down his forehead, wet apparently from a recent swim.

"You need to stop picking up strangers on the trail, girl," Seth said. "I been telling you that for some time now, haven't I?" Then he looked back at me and just stared for a moment. His eyes were pinched at the sides and his mouth was a hard line across his weathered face.

I heard Rebecca's voice behind me. "This is Seth. His family owns the hog farm over across Western Lake there. They've got a few hundred acres, but you'll see their pigs wandering through town from time to time. Not much need for fences around here."

"She tell you we're engaged to be married, Mr.… what was your name?"

I turned and looked at Rebecca, still up on her horse. "No, she didn't tell me." I looked back to Seth Howard. "Congratulations, and the name's Mathew." I was quickly growing very tired of all this. He didn't answer and just continued to stare at me. A few awkward moments passed, and I finally decided there was not much more need for introductions and small talk. "Well, I should probably get this place opened up," I said. "Rebecca, thanks again for the ride in."

She smiled back and said to her brother and fiancé, "Boys, maybe the two of you can get out on the road there and help get Mathew's car into town later today."

"Yeah, we can run out there with a couple of horses," Jonas said.

I thanked them both and told them the key was still in the car. Seth Howard started past me without speaking, and with clear intent, bumped my shoulder as he passed. He walked over to the horse and put his hand on Rebecca's thigh. "You best get on over to the house. Momma's been expecting you to help out in the kitchen for the party tonight."

"The Howard's are throwing an engagement party for us tonight down at the beach," Rebecca said. "Everybody in town will be there. You'll have to come down, Mathew."

"Thank you," I answered, ignoring the strained look on Seth's face. "I'll try my best to come down," I said, but thinking that the last thing I wanted was being around a lot of people at a party, trying to explain who I was and why I was in town.

"We'll be there about an hour before sundown," she said. "You just have to be there to see the sunset."

"I'll do my best, and boys, are you going to need some help with that car?"

Jonas said, "No, not a problem. We'll bring her in for ya."

Seth came around and took Barley's bridle and began to pull the horse away. I watched as the three of them headed back in the direction of the hotel. Rebecca looked over her shoulder once and waved.

Chapter Six

I scanned across the panorama of the little village of Grayton Beach, a few rustic cottages tucked into the white sand bluffs and rugged vegetation of wild scrub and live oak, wind-tossed magnolia trees and slash pines; the town's water tower and windmill rising up into the sky. Through a gap in the sand hills to the south I could see the deep blue and green shades of the Gulf of Mexico shimmering in the afternoon sun. Low swells of waves swept up onto the beach in a cadence of muted rumbling. Further offshore a large ketch-rigged sailboat pushed along under full sail toward the east. A flock of a dozen pelicans flew in just above the waves along the shoreline in a V-formation, their wings spread wide to float on the wind currents. The faint smell of salt and stale fish hung in the air.

Rebecca Bidwell, and her brother and boyfriend, had disappeared around a corner. My heart grew heavy again as I thought about the two young lovers, an engagement party being held for them tonight, and how quickly my own plans for the love of a young woman had been dashed on the rocks of my family's intolerance and betrayal. I tried to put the images of Jess and Hanna out of my mind, but I knew of course that they would be forever imprinted there, a grating reminder of misplaced trust.

Again I had to force down the rising anger with Hanna and my family, and the frustration with my own response to all that had occurred the past evening. *Would I ever be able to live with the humiliation of just running away, of letting them have their way with my life?* The indignity of it all left a sour knot in my gut.

    I turned and looked at the Headley cottage, boarded up and lifeless in the warm spring sunshine. Two old fishing poles had been left leaning against the wall on the broad covered porch. There was some welcome relief in the knowledge that I did have friends like James Headley in this world that would be there for me, even as troubles loomed large all around.

    As I walked around the cottage to the back, my feet sunk deeply into the soft white sand, the heat from the sun causing beads of sweat to form across all exposed patches of skin. The old wooden outhouse stood at the back of the clearing behind the house against a cluster of tall oleander bushes, flush with bright red flowers. Hummingbirds darted around in quick bursts of flight, jostling for position among the blooms. The privy needed a coat of paint far more than the main house, and beneath the peeling white flakes, the grain of worn gray pine lumber stood, battered for years by the harsh elements of weather and wind-blown sand.

    Inside the little structure, I found two keys hung on a nail as my friend had instructed. I removed one quickly to extricate myself from the heavy stench of the place. I walked around behind into the bushes to relieve myself, knowing that eventually I would have to endure a more prolonged visit inside the tiny wooden outdoor commode. When I came back around, I was startled by the presence of three small black pigs that had wandered onto the property. As they rooted around in the sand for any morsel of nourishment, I listened to the soft grunts and snorts that they made. They seemed to have no fear or problem with my presence as they slowly moved past and on into the heavy woods; some of Seth Howard's herd, no doubt.

There was a small porch and door on the back of the cottage, and I walked up the two steps and tried the key in the padlock. Like most metallic surfaces exposed to the beach elements, it was corroded some, but with a little shaking and pounding against the wood door it soon popped open.

I hung the lock on the latch and opened the door into the cottage. The close and musty smell of stagnant air and old leather furniture greeted me as I walked into the shadowy room. All of the windows were shuttered and closed tight. As my eyes adjusted, the dim light from the open door revealed a large single room open to the exposed rafters above. Wood siding from the outside was nailed to the vertical studs, all painted white, but in somewhat better condition than the exterior. To the left, a small cluster of cupboards and shelves covered one wall. A round table was surrounded by four brown-stained wood chairs with woven wicker seats. The last visitor had left a covered glass jar on the table, which I suspected to be moonshine liquor, about half full. *Later*, I thought to myself.

To the right, a tight gathering of two brown leather chairs, one with an ottoman and a small couch of the same leather covering, rested in the corner around a low square table that held an ash tray, two large white candles and some old books. Across the wall were two more shelves crowded with books and other ornamental items including some sand dollars and shells that must have been gathered from the beach. A corner table held a small kerosene lamp for reading. Two doors on this far wall opened into a bunkroom and the main bedroom; and that was the extent of the Headley's beach house.

The family had a far more elegant winter home down on the beach at Siesta Key, south of Sarasota. James Headley had told me this place had been used over the years mostly by the Headley brothers and male friends to sneak away from Atlanta to drink and gamble, and chase girls over in Panama City.

GRAYTON WINDS

I walked into the bedroom and pulled a curtain on the wall aside revealing a small closet. There was an assortment of casual shirts and trousers hanging there, and two pair of more comfortable shoes and sandals on the wooden-planked floor. A large-brimmed straw hat hung from a hook on the wall and I placed it on my head, just to check the fit. It was a bit large, but certainly serviceable. A dresser held several drawers full of other necessities including short pants and a bathing suit. I pulled a pair of worn khaki shorts out and took one of the soft cotton shirts from the closet. I threw them on the bed and then stripped off my clothes and walked back into the main room and over to the kitchen area.

I pumped water from the well handle into the small cast iron sink and did my best to wash up with a bar of soap that was lying on the wooden counter. I found myself scrubbing harder to try to wash away the filth and blood that I felt all over me from the past night, as if a layer or two of skin would sluice away the lingering pain and regret. Several large towels had been hung on the wall by the back door. I dried myself and put on my new selection of clothing. It felt somewhat therapeutic, both physically and emotionally, to lose the formal suit of clothes from the previous night in exchange for the more comfortable beach apparel, although it was all a bit large as the hat had been. The Headley boys were somewhat bigger around the middle than I, but the loose fit was actually welcoming. My bare feet also felt pleasant against the cool wooden floor, freed from the confines of socks and heavy leather shoes.

I went back outside and walked around the cottage, releasing the shutters and securing them to the side behind wooden latches to let in some light. The pigs were gone and the streets were empty. I assumed that whatever few residents and visitors in town this time of year were either down at the beach or napping in the afternoon heat. Back inside, I opened all the windows to let some fresher air in through the screens, and then checked the cupboards for any food left behind, finding a sparse collection of stale crackers, two cans of beans, a jar of pickled herring that looked very far beyond fresh, and two more jars of contraband hooch. A small icebox stood in the corner next to the heavy wood stove. Inside were three bottles of Mexican beer, probably secured by James from one of the local smugglers. Without ice for many months from the store over in Point Washington, the beverages didn't look very refreshing.

I walked across the room and sat down in one of the old chairs, checking the selection of books on the table. It was an odd assortment; Flaubert's *Madame Bovary*, Marcel Proust's *Within a Budding Grove*, and Defoe's *Robinson Crusoe*, which I picked up and took with me along with the jar of local whiskey out the front door to the porch where I settled in to one of the old wooden rockers. Placing the book on my lap, I twisted the top off the glass jar and held it up to the light. The contents were the color of a weak tea, and sediment from the bottom floated up from the jostling. I brought it to my nose and took a sniff. The fumes exploded up into my brain. My recoil was so sudden that I almost dropped the whole jar onto the deck of the porch. *What the hell*, I thought to myself. Trying my best not to inhale, I took a quick drink and again, the first sensation was the rush of the whiskey up into my sinuses and brain. As I swallowed, a deep burning sensation flared that I could feel all the way down into my gut. I coughed and gagged, and then let the sensations settle. I had tried some of the moonshine whiskey that my family distributed up in Atlanta, but none of it had the jolt of this concoction. As I contemplated a second swallow, I couldn't help but wonder where this batch had been made, and just how *poisonous* the brew might be.

I rubbed a thin layer of dust from the book cover, and then glanced up across the barren white dunes down to the beach. I smiled for the first time, thinking of the irony of my similar abandonment and isolation with the character from Defoe's novel. I began to read, but within a few pages the events of the past evening and the long trip south finally caught up with me. I dozed off into a deep sleep full of dreams and scattered fragments of memories of lost women and murderous relations.

Chapter Seven

    As I opened my eyes to the blinding glare of the late afternoon sun now down below the roofline, I felt a cramp in my leg and stiff back muscles from sleeping too long on the porch chair. I stretched to get more comfortable, and watched as a fat little bird flew up and perched on the railing in front of me. Its head and breast were a light gray with darker gray wings, and a long feathered tail trimmed in white. Our eyes met, and the bird cocked its head to the side to get a better look. It scratched around for a few moments on the wood rail, then turned back to me and let out a loud cackle that caught me by surprise. It seemed that it was asking to be fed, and yet I found that unlikely for a wild bird with so few people around.

    I got up slowly and walked into the house. I came back a moment later with the box of old crackers. My bird friend was still there waiting. It watched as I pulled a single cracker out and held it over close to its mouth. Without hesitation it stretched out its neck and took the cracker from me, and then placed it down on the railing where it could begin pecking away smaller bites. I watched with great curiosity and amusement, and soon added more crackers for this little character's afternoon snack. When it was finished, it turned to me again and squawked some new bird message that I was supposed to understand; perhaps *thank you*, but more likely, *I want more*. Then a friend flew up and lighted next to the bird. The first made a huge fuss in trying to convince the new arrival that this was his dining room and that there was only room for one at this seating. The new bird finally gave up and reluctantly flew away. I laughed at the proud strut of my friend along the rail.

"Well, we must find a name for you," I said out loud, feeling a bit silly that I was talking to a bird. "How about *Champ*, young friend?" I asked. "You seem to have won that last fight."

The bird bobbed its head and jumped around in a little dance, its tail working rapidly to maintain balance on the narrow rail. And then it was gone in a flurry of wings and bird talk, away up into a tree over to the side of the house and out of sight. When I looked back from the tree, I noticed that I had other company coming through the picket fence gate and up to the porch.

It was a woman, holding the hand of the young girl I had seen earlier on the porch of the hotel. The woman was of a middle age, perhaps near fifty, and her face beamed a bright smile of even white teeth. Her light brown hair was gathered up in random disarray on top of her head. She wore a green colored print dress that fell down well below her knees, with a white apron drawn around her waist. Her bare feet were dressed in open leather sandals. In spite of her somewhat plain attire, there was a commanding presence about the woman that was quite striking. The little girl stared straight ahead as she had before, but her face was a picture of joy and contentment. She too had the light hair of her grandmother, but curly and hanging loose down past her shoulders.

"I see you've met one of our pesky mockingbird friends," the woman said as they stopped at the foot of the stairs. I stood and walked down the steps to greet them. The little girl spoke first.

"You mustn't feed them," she said with a surprising tone of assurance. "They'll be a terrible bother to you."

The woman laughed and bent down beside the little girl. "You should follow your own advice, young lady. We wouldn't have so many birds all over the hotel." She stood again and held out her hand. "My name is Lila Dalton. I own the little hotel over there."

"How do you do, Miss Dalton," I said and took her hand. "I'm Mathew Coulter. I'm from Atlanta, down for a little getaway at my friend's place here."

"Yes, I heard from Rebecca that you had some trouble along the way, but welcome to Grayton Beach, Mr. Coulter."

"Please, call me Mathew."

"Likewise, I'm called Lila by the folks around here, who I'm sure you'll meet soon. There aren't many of us, particularly at this time of year. What on earth happened to your face," she asked, staring at the open wounds along my chin and cheek.

"Just managed not to duck in time," I answered, not wanting to get into the details of the past night. "And who do we have here?" I asked, looking down at the little girl.

"This is my marvelous granddaughter, Melanee. You will find that she is quite something."

Melanee reached out her hand, staring blankly past me. I bent down to shake her hand. "It's nice to meet you, Melanee," I said. "I saw you over on the porch when I came into town earlier."

"Yes I know, and Rebecca came back to tell us all about you. You've come all this way with no clothes or food," she said, not with surprise or as a question, but as a simple statement of fact.

She caught me a little off guard, and then I managed to say, "Yes, I left town a bit unexpectedly. I just needed to get away…"

She was still holding my hand. "Yes, it must have been quite troubling."

"Excuse me?" I had to ask.

Lila interrupted by picking the girl up in her arms. "You must understand, Mathew, little Melanee is quite perceptive." She kissed her on the cheek and the girl turned and kissed her grandmother back on the lips. "We thought you might be a little hungry and thirsty after your long trip, so we brought over a few things for you." Melanee held up a small basket that I hadn't noticed before, and I reached out for it.

"Thank you," I said, pulling back the white linen napkin to see an assortment of bread and meats and fruit, as well as a cold bottle of cola. "This is awfully nice of you." I reached into my pocket for money but realized that my wallet was in my other pants inside on the bed.

"No, really, this is our welcome gift for you, Mathew," Lila said.

"But you must come for dinner tonight, Mr. Coulter," little Melanee said. "My grandma is the best cook in the county, and then Rebecca's party is tonight."

"We serve dinner at six o'clock, Mathew, if you can join us. Another family has made reservations, and I have two guests in for the season."

"That sounds very nice," I said, though I had very little interest in any social interaction. "But I don't think that I'll be able to get ready so soon this evening." I looked down at my wrist and remembered that I had left my watch inside as well. "What time is it?"

"Just a little past four, Mr. Coulter," Melanee said, and again I was surprised by her response.

"We do need to get back now to finish with the dinner preparations," Lila Dalton said.

"Grandma cooks and I set out the dishes," Melanee said with great pride.

"I will try my best," I said. "I've still got a lot of work to do to get this place opened up." I was trying to find some logical excuse to let me hide away in the old cottage for the night, and be alone with my thoughts and recriminations. Lila just nodded.

Holding up the basket, I said, "I'll bring this back as soon as I can."

"Whenever you're through with it," Lila said and smiled. "We'll see you tonight then, Mathew Coulter?"

"I'll certainly try."

They turned and walked back out through the gate and on down the sandy road back to the hotel. The aroma of the food in the basket made my mouth water, and I started up the stairs into the house, turning for a moment to look again at the woman and her remarkable young granddaughter before I went inside.

To clear my head from the nap and the effects of the local whiskey, I decided to take a walk on the beach before considering whether there was any chance that I would ever go over to the hotel for dinner. As I walked in bare feet through the break in the sand dunes, the full view of the Gulf of Mexico stretched out before me. The sight was breathtaking; the long expanse of white sand beach in both directions as far as you could see and the aquamarine blue of the clear water shimmering in the late afternoon sun, which was beginning it's descent into the southwestern sky. A flock of sea birds just offshore had found a school of baitfish and were creating quite a frenzy as they dove repeatedly into the water from great heights to gorge on the little fish.

A boardwalk had been constructed to walk down to the beach, and just past the dunes a long deck with a covered pavilion had been built looking out over the sand and water. There was a flurry of activity as people were setting up tables and chairs, and a band was getting ready to rehearse in the far corner. Several people were standing against the rail with drinks in their hands, taking in the view of the Gulf. I saw that Seth Howard and Rebecca's brother Jonas were among the men getting all of this organized, and it occurred to me that this must be the preparations for the engagement party. I thought back on the extravagant preparations that my parents always stressed over for their parties back in Atlanta. Then I quickly tried to chase away any memories of the city, and of a girl named Hanna.

Seth Howard looked up and noticed me as I walked by. His expression turned sour and menacing. He walked away across the deck to help with something else. I tried not to let his lack of hospitality bother me, but it was clear that he was unhappy with my earlier encounter with his bride-to-be, Miss Rebecca Bidwell. He certainly had nothing to worry about, as another woman in my life was the last thing I wanted to deal with at the moment. Her brother also noticed me and he was at least gracious enough to manage a brief wave and nod as I walked past on down to the beach.

The sand was even softer and more difficult to walk in than up in town. With each step it was like the ground was reaching up to swallow you clear past your ankles. Down closer to the shore break, the sand became firmer as the relentless tides washed against the beach, and walking became less of a chore. I decided to head east away from the sun, and I hadn't gone far before I came to a small inlet with water rushing into the Gulf through a narrow channel that snaked its way back through the dunes and away out of sight. It was only a foot or so deep and maybe twenty feet across. The water was a darker tea color with the ripples of the light sand evident along the bottom. A few small fish darted about as I came up. I followed the channel back to the north, walking in the water and enjoying the cool freshness of it. Tall pines loomed ahead, and as I came around the edge of a high dune, a large lake spread out before me. Marsh grasses lined much of the shoreline and the water was still, but darker than the Gulf by some measure. As I continued on, the sand bottom became softer and then almost a muck. I stepped up out of the channel onto the grass bank. Along the left shore I could see two white cottages tucked into the pines, with docks coming out into the lake. One had a small rowboat tied up. I looked up to see an osprey floating high on the wind, looking down with a lofty and carnivorous attitude.

I walked on a little farther and stopped suddenly as something moving in the knee-high grass ten feet out caught me by surprise. Standing motionless, feeling the beat of my heart picking up, I waited to see what critter I may have stumbled upon. The thought of big snakes came to mind, and I started backing up slowly. Then with a great explosion of sound and grasses flying about and water splashing, a large alligator ran across in front of me into the lake. I was so unprepared for the sight of it that I stumbled back and fell, my heart now hammering in my chest. I crawled backwards a few more yards before standing. I watched as the big gator swam smoothly across the surface of the water and then turned to look directly at me, its two big round eyes and long snout visible above the water.

"Holy mother of…" I managed to say as I stood staring at the big gator. I took a deep breath and then in somewhat of a panic, looked around me in the grass for signs that he might have a friend nearby. I walked warily backward through the grass, which had sharp edges that scratched at my bare legs. If you had just come up and not seen it in full view before you on dry land, the gator now looked like a big lifeless black log floating on the lake.

In short time I was back to the beach and gratefully away from the marshes and snakes and gators, and who knew what other forms of menacing flora and fauna. The wide open expanse of beach and water was certainly more tranquil and welcoming.

Chapter Eight

Back at the Headley cottage, I questioned the decision to even consider the invitation to dinner at the little hotel with Lila Dalton and her granddaughter Melanee. I was in no mood for social interaction, and having to explain my arrival to a room full of strangers was more than I cared to consider. A few nights alone in this old cottage with the left-behind jars of moonshine liquor seemed more appealing to drown the memories of the past hours in Atlanta. I took a glass from one of the cupboards and sat down at the table in the kitchen and poured it half full. The first swallow was again devastating, but I managed the second and third more easily. I could feel the connections in brain function quickly beginning to unravel.

I began to contemplate the actions of my brother the night before with Hanna Wesley. In our years growing up together we had always been as close as two brothers could be, even with a few years between us, although it occurred to me that I was much closer to my sister Maggie in those years. When we were younger, Jess was always running faster, playing harder, always accomplishing more than Maggie and me, and we accepted this, I suppose, as the natural order of things, he being the oldest. It was only when we got into our later years in school, and both Maggie and I began to advance more in our studies, that it became apparent that Jess was not necessarily superior in all things.

As I sat there in the quiet cottage drinking alone, I remembered a day several years ago with Jess that had always troubled me, but suddenly with the help of the whiskey, it seemed much more clear. He had just come back home for the Christmas holiday from college, and he was driving me across Buckhead to a party at a friend's house. On the way he pulled a small silver flask from his jacket and took a drink, and then handed it to me. His offer caught me by surprise, but I took a small drink and handed it back. He went to it several more times before we arrived and he never said a word to me. Finally I asked him if there was something wrong and he told me to *shut up*. I pressed him again when he took another drink. He threw the flask across the seat at me and yelled that he was sick of my pestering and to leave him alone. Later I found out that he had failed three of his classes from the fall term at Georgia Tech, and that my father was furious with him. His resentment with the success that Maggie and I had enjoyed in college was often evident.

Certainly that couldn't have been the sole reason for my brother's treachery with Hanna, but in my rapidly progressing state of intoxication it seemed logical enough. Then I heard a knock on the door of the cottage. I stood up a bit unsteadily and walked over to see who it was. Standing on the porch were Rebecca Bidwell with little Melanee Dalton holding on to her hand. I pushed open the screen door and walked outside to join them.

"Mathew, I asked Rebecca to bring me over to remind you about dinner," Melanee said. "You're late and everyone's waiting for you."

I tried to consider my response before Rebecca replied, "I was walking past the hotel when Melanee yelled out to ask if I had seen you. I was on my way down to the beach to help with everything for the party."

I took a deep breath to mull over my options, and then before I could speak, Melanee again reminded me, "Mathew Coulter, you're being awfully rude by keeping everyone waiting!"

I had to laugh. Finally I said, "Melanee, I am really sorry. The time just slipped away and I can't apologize enough for my inconsiderate behavior. Would you please tell your grandmother how sorry I am, and that I will be over as soon as I can get dressed."

"Well please hurry," she scolded.

"And by the way, what is appropriate dress for dinner at the Beach Hotel?" I had to ask.

Rebecca answered first. "You are dressed just fine, Mathew. Hurry up now and we'll head on over there together."

I looked down at myself to appraise my ability to attend a dinner at the hotel. While a little foggy in the brain, and certainly not dressed to the standards set in Atlanta society, I decided that I had felt sorry for myself long enough, at least for one night.

Rebecca Bidwell left Melanee and me on the front steps of the hotel and said that she hoped to see us later down at her party at the beach pavilion. Melanee took my hand and led me through the front door of what was one of the largest structures in Grayton Beach, but far from what anyone might consider a hotel back in the city of Atlanta. It was two stories in height, and as you walked in the open glass front door, it was only two rooms wide with a small lobby or gathering room with a few comfortable chairs to the left and the dining room immediately on your right. Seated at a long table there was the woman, the Mrs. Elliot that I had seen earlier on her porch with her little boy as I first came into town on the back of old Barley. She was with a man who must have been her husband.

There was another couple who I had not seen yet, but who immediately caught my attention by their extreme and unexpected appearance. The man was exceedingly large in girth, if not height, which I couldn't tell from his seated position. I guessed his age to be somewhere in his forties and the jowls and roundness of his face nearly jiggled as he turned to acknowledge my arrival. His hair was coal black and greased straight back from his face. In spite of Rebecca's approval of my casual attire, this man was dressed impeccably in a starched white shirt with a blue and red striped tie, and a blue dinner jacket, immaculately pressed. Beside him was a woman at least a generation younger who was astonishingly attractive, her brilliant red hair flowing long and carefully groomed, the milky white tone of her skin flushed with thousands of tiny brown freckles. Like her companion, who I assumed to be her father, she was immaculately dressed. Her fine white dress was well tailored and provocatively cut.

Lila Dalton walked into the room from a swinging door across the back wall with a tray of food, followed by a colored man carrying even more. She saw me standing there with her granddaughter.

"Well, Mr. Coulter, so glad that you could finally join us. Fortunately, we have enough for all. Take a seat at the end of the table there," she said, nodding to the place next to the man of ample proportions on one side and Mrs. Elliot on the other. I realized that most of them were a bit shocked at the wounds still fresh across my face. I tried to clear my head from the earlier effects of the whiskey and nodded in acceptance. As I sat down, Melanee ran through the door to the back as Lila came over to stand next to me at the head of the table. It surprised me to see Melanee move about so easily within the place without sight.

"My cherished friends and guests," Lila said, "this is our newest arrival to Grayton Beach, Mr. Mathew Coulter, just down from Atlanta to spend some time over at the Headley's place down the road. Mr. Coulter, I would like you to meet an old Grayton family, the Elliots, Julianne and Thomas. Their family from

Birmingham has been coming down here from the early days. Their little son, Billy, is back in the kitchen keeping an eye on all of the dessert."

I turned and acknowledged the Elliots, and then listened as the hotel proprietor introduced the guests to my right. "And Mathew, please meet our visitors from far to the north up in New Jersey. This is William and Louise Palumbo."

The big man reached out his beefy hand in greeting. I looked into his eyes and could see from his penetrating gaze that he was assessing my worth and the story of my introduction.

"This is my wife, Louise," he said without looking away. His accent was thick from his Jersey origins. When he said *wife,* I had to pause a moment to gather my surprise.

"Mr. Palumbo, nice to meet you... and Mrs. Palumbo," I said with what I hoped was not too much astonishment in my voice.

"Mathew, my boy," Palumbo said. "What a pleasure. Please call me Willie. Did I hear your name is *Coulter* from Atlanta?"

"Yes, that's right," I answered, already on the defensive within my moonshine clouded brain.

"You wouldn't happen to know Samuel Coulter now, boy?" he asked.

I hesitated for a moment and then drunkenly, and perhaps wisely, decided not to reveal my family's true identity. If this man did know my father, I wasn't ready for anyone to reveal my location. "There are a lot of Coulter's in Atlanta, sir, but I don't think so."

He eyed me with suspicion, and then said, "I've known of the Coulter's who are in the liquor business for years. Not even a distant relation?" he asked.

"No, but it's nice to meet you sir, and Mrs. Palumbo," I answered.

"Louise, please," his wife said with a Jersey accent even more pronounced than her husband's. She also reached down the table to shake my hand, and I noticed the freckles on the skin of her long delicate fingers with nails painted a bright red. She held my hand longer than seemed appropriate. I finally pulled it away and looked back at Lila Dalton beside me for some reprieve from the discomforting introductions.

"Mathew, we're so glad you could join us tonight, and welcome," Lila said. "We're having baked flounder from the docks down in Destin. I hope you enjoy."

I thanked her and looked around the table at the guests assembled, and then around the room, appointed sparingly in the practical style of the local beach dwellings. Windows on the front and side walls looked out at the sand dunes and the few other cottages nearby. In the corner was a brightly polished black upright piano with music sheets spread on the rack above the keyboard, and a long bench pushed under. Across the back wall toward the kitchen was a large painting of what looked to be the lake scene I had experienced earlier, prior to my encounter with the large reptile that I thought was going to eat me. It was beautifully done in soft pastel colors, and exhibited a far more welcoming environment than I had experienced earlier.

Willie Palumbo reached for his glass that was filled with a white wine. I then noticed the bottle sitting in the center of the table. He lifted his glass up in a toast to those around him. "To our friends here tonight, old and new. May the world always grant you the best in life and if not," and he paused looking around the table and at Lila Dalton, "take whatever the hell you need anyway."

Everyone laughed and lifted their glasses, and I saw one at the place in front of me and did the same. It struck me, even in my diminished state, that this was a man like my father who took life by the throat and squeezed out all that it had to offer.

Dinner was served and seemed to fly by in a blur with everyone talking at the same time, and the wine's effects raising the noise level even higher. I could hear myself responding to questions, yet my mind seemed far away, detached. As plates were being cleared by Lila and Melanee and their server, Mr. Palumbo leaned over close and asked if I wanted to join him for a cigar on the porch. I had been rude enough through dinner in my drunken state and decided it would be best to accept his invitation. Mr. Elliott did, however, decline politely and stayed inside to continue the discussion with the women over coffee. I had noticed that he was also particularly taken by the lovely Mrs. Palumbo. Outside, my new *friend* pulled two long cigars from the inner pocket of his jacket and handed one to me. We sat down together on chairs, looking out across the sand hills to the beach. The sun was now hanging low to the southwest, casting a brilliant orange and red canvas across the late evening sky. I heard a match struck and turned as Palumbo held it out for me to light my smoke. The taste was smooth and pleasing, and I told him so.

"Cuban," was all he said in response before lighting his own with a great flourish. We sat in silence for a while enjoying the smoke and the view, sounds of laughter and plates being stacked coming from inside. I noticed the smell of rosemary coming from low bushes planted to the side of the porch.

Palumbo finally spoke. "Tell me, Coulter, what really brings you down to this nowhere place all by yourself without a stitch of extra clothes or supplies?" His tone was harsh and accusative.

I turned and just stared at him for a few moments, taking another long draw on the cigar and then letting the smoke out slowly. He looked to be a man accustomed to straight answers, although I was not prepared to comply. "Perhaps I should ask you the same," I responded, and then beneath his coat I saw a brown leather holster on his belt holding a pistol.

His facial expression didn't change, and he continued to look straight ahead. "Oh, I brought plenty of clothes, young man," he said with little note of humor in his tone.

I kept staring at the gun, and then I realized he was watching me. I felt my heart racing in my chest. We just looked at each other silently for a few moments, his eyes seeming to gaze clear through any pretense that I might try to continue. Suddenly it seemed that honesty would be the best course of action. "Mr. Palumbo," I started, a bit unsteadily.

"Willie, please."

"Right, Willie. I'm afraid I haven't been completely honest with you tonight."

He nodded back and said, "So I gathered."

A loud crash of breaking glass from inside startled me, and I looked back through the window to see Lila bending down to pick up the broken pieces. Willie Palumbo never stopped staring at me, and I noticed that his right hand rested even closer to the gun at his waist.

"You need to understand, I've come down here to get away from some nasty business back home in Atlanta," I said.

He just nodded again.

I hesitated a moment and then continued on. "And yes, my father is Samuel Coulter. I'm sorry that I lied earlier, but I was hoping to keep my family connections to myself for a while."

"So you don't want them to know you're here?"

"Exactly, it would be best if I had some time alone."

I could see his body noticeably relax, and his hand moved away from the gun and rested on the arm of his chair. "Well, Mathew, I see that we have some common ground here in quiet little Grayton Beach."

"And how is that, sir?"

He took a long pull on his cigar and let the smoke out slowly, watching it drift away on the light breeze coming across from the west. Then he said, "Louise and I have come down to get away, too. There are some people back home who would prefer to see me looking out at the world through bars, or better yet, from six feet under the dirt." He turned and looked back over at me, but before I could process what he had just told me, or manage a response, I heard notes from the piano inside ring out clearly through the open windows. The tune was hauntingly moving, and while I wasn't familiar with the melody, it was most certainly a classical piece. When I turned to look inside, expecting to see one of the women playing, I was shocked to see young Melanee Dalton sitting on the piano bench, her feet too short to reach the pedals, but her hands moving effortlessly across the keyboard.

"It's Chopin," I heard Palumbo say, but I was too absorbed in the little girl's music to respond. "She's quite a prodigy," he said.

I forgot all about Mr. Willie Palumbo sitting beside me. I stood and walked back into the hotel and over to stand beside the piano. Melanee continued to play, and the others in the room had also stopped what they were doing to listen to the girl. There was sheet music on the piano, but of course she was playing without seeing, the notes coming through her fingers with pure confidence and a proud look of accomplishment on her face.

"Do you like this song, Mr. Coulter?" she asked as she continued to play, and I had to wonder how she even knew that I was standing there.

"It's beautiful, Melanee," I answered. "Where did you learn to play?"

"My grandma helps me. We listen to music on the Victrola, and then I try to play what I hear." Her grandmother, Lila, walked by and just smiled at me.

I was simply amazed at the ability of this little girl, and when she finished everyone applauded and cheered loudly. She slid off the seat and turned to face her admiring audience with a quick curtsey. Then she jumped back up onto the bench and arranged herself to play again. I knew the tune right away, *Let Me Call You Sweetheart*, a song that the band had played the night before at my parent's house when I was dancing with Hanna. I listened to the sweet melody echo through the small room, and then Melanee began to sing. Again, I was dumbfounded. Her voice was angelic, with the most pure pitch I had ever heard.

I noticed the Elliotts stand behind me to start dancing, and Palumbo came in from outside and invited his wife to dance as well. Lila came over and stood beside me and reached to take my hand. I nodded at her invitation, still mesmerized by the little girl's performance, and began moving as best as I could to the sounds of the music with Lila Dalton in my arms. I looked at the face of the innkeeper who had so kindly invited me to join them all on this evening. She smiled at me and said, "I told you she was quite remarkable."

"She is amazing," I answered, looking back at Melanee Dalton. "I understand her mother has been away," I said, and then immediately regretted bringing up the subject.

Lila didn't hesitate, "Yes, her mother Sara is a wandering soul." She paused for a moment, looking over at her granddaughter. "Sara's been gone for almost two years now. She didn't even get back for Christmas this past year. It's so heartbreaking to watch Melanee. She loves her mother so much,, and in her heart knows that she'll be back for her one day."

"I'm sorry, but how could she leave her like this?" I asked.

"Sara has many demons," was all she said, and then the song was over and everyone applauded loudly again.

Chapter Nine

There was music again later that night down at the beach for the party to celebrate the engagement of Rebecca Bidwell and Seth Howard. The small band was set up in the corner of the wooden pavilion. It was nestled into the sand dunes, and kerosene lamps hung from the rafters of the peaked roof that had been built over half the deck as cover from the sun during the day. A railing ran around the side, and torches had been placed in the sand along the rail for more light. Overhead, the sliver of a waning moon hung behind high wispy clouds.

I had tried to go straight back to the Headley place after dinner at the hotel, but Palumbo had been insistent that I come down to the beach with him and his wife. The brief time of social contact and the effects of more alcohol had only served to darken my already dire mood, but Palumbo had a way of being particularly persuasive.

The band was playing one of the new Jazz songs popular back in Atlanta. I stood alone watching the crowd, a glass of local whiskey in my hand. The honored couple, Seth and Rebecca, was leading a group of dancers out on the floor, and I thought about the previous night with Hanna Wesley in my arms on the dance floor back in Buckhead. The whiskey was lending itself to my overall sense of gloom, when a man walked up that I had not previously met. In the dim light I could see that he was an older man with deep wrinkles across a face covered with a thick gray beard and crowned with long flowing gray hair. He wore a black suit, buttoned high in the front with a white shirt and narrow string tie.

"You must be Coulter," he said, his voice a low rumble like the sounds of the waves coming onshore.

"Yes sir, Mathew," I answered.

"I'm Becky's father, Eli Bidwell."

"Nice to meet you, sir," I said.

"Missed you at the store earlier today, but heard you had come through. Looks like you've cleaned up some since then. You gave my wife quite a stir, what with your face all tore up and blood all over."

"I've had better nights," I said.

"Hear you met my daughter, Becky."

I nodded and took another sip from my drink.

He turned to look over at the dancers. "She and the Howard boy are gonna be married in June. Suppose you heard that already?"

"Told me this morning," I answered. "She gave me a ride into town when my car got stuck out on the road from Point Washington." The man kept staring at the dancers and didn't answer me. He had his own drink in his hand, and then seemed to remember he had it and looked down to take a swallow.

"Makes me wonder about young folks these days," he finally said. "Becky there's just 18 and ready to start livin' with a man and running her own house. Don't know how she'll be with kids of her own runnin' around. Sure thing Seth won't be much help," he said, a thinly veiled note of disgust in his voice. He lingered on, gazing at his daughter in silence for a bit, and then turned back to me. "What are your plans down here, Coulter?"

"Just needed to get away from the city for a while. The Headleys are old friends and they're letting me stay at their place," I said, looking back towards town.

"Yeah, I've seen the Headleys when they're down this way."

"Thought I might do a little work on a book I've been writing."

"You're a writer?"

"Working on it," I answered. "Headley place needs a new coat of paint, too."

"Come by the store. Got everything you need. Even got lumber over at the mill if you have to replace any boards."

I thanked him, and he turned and moved off into the crowd. I thought for a moment about his low regard for his future son-in-law and wondered why he had given his blessing. It occurred to me that there probably weren't a lot of options for young women down in this remote place. Then I noticed a woman coming across the floor toward me, and as she got closer, I saw that it was Louise Palumbo, the wife of my new acquaintance, Willie. She also had a glass in her hand, and her walk was a little unsteady. Even as she stopped in front of me, she staggered some. She still had on the same revealing dress from earlier at dinner.

In a slurred and high pitched voice she said, "What are you doing over here all alone, honey?"

I nodded in greeting and held my glass up to hers and said, "*Mrs.* Palumbo," hoping to remind her that I wasn't her *honey*. Her husband wasn't far behind, and he came up and put his arm around her.

"You two havin' a good time," Willie said in his heavy Jersey accent.

"I was just going to ask Mathew to dance, honey," she said, and then I realized that everyone must be *honey* to Louise Palumbo.

"I was just thinking it was about time we get back to the hotel, sweetheart," he said. "It's been a long day." He took the glass from her and placed it on the rail.

She looked at him and I could see that in her inebriated state she was trying to focus on his face. "Sure honey, let me just go say goodbye to our hosts." She walked away, and both Willie Palumbo and I watched her stagger back across the wood decking, the sway of her hips hard to ignore.

"Beautiful, isn't she?" Palumbo said without looking at me.

I wasn't quite sure how best to answer and then thought, *what the hell*. "You're a lucky man, Mr. Palumbo."

He turned back and looked at me with an appraising eye and didn't say anything. When we both looked back his wife was in the arms of Seth Howard out in the crowd of dancers. Palumbo didn't seem to react at first, but just stood there watching for some time. Then he said in a quiet voice almost to himself, as if he didn't really care if I heard or not, "Always a blessing and a curse to love a beautiful woman."

His words made me laugh as I thought about Hanna Wesley. He turned and looked at me with a questioning stare. "And that's funny?"

I took another drink and swallowed, staring back at the big man from New Jersey. "Sorry Mr. Palumbo..." I started to say.

"Willie," he reminded me.

"I'm sorry, but that's part of the reason I'm down here in the middle of nowhere."

"A young pup like you got lady problems?"

I nodded slowly, the face of Hanna clear in my mind, her smile a taunting and mocking vision. "And not the first time," I said.

"Louise, she and I been married now almost ten years, my second wife. Met her in a club up in Brooklyn. She took my heart and I ain't found it since. Better get her home," he said slowly, and then walked away toward his wife.

I watched as he moved into the group of dancers and stood beside his wife and Seth Howard, who didn't notice him at first. He finally reached out and took her arm to pull her away. The Howard boy got an irritated look on his face and pushed Palumbo away. The big man fell back a couple steps, and then stood there for a moment watching as his wife continued to dance with the boy. Then Palumbo started back toward the two of them, his chest all puffed out, obviously ready to do what he needed to do to get his wife away. Another man stepped in between. He was a big man, nearly a head taller than Palumbo and probably older by a few years. He stood and placed two hands on Palumbo's chest, who immediately pushed them away. Angry words were traded that I couldn't hear, and then Seth Howard left Louise Palumbo to come over and join in the exchange.

Palumbo pushed the older man out of the way to get at Seth. He took a powerful swing at the boy that caught him flush on the side of the face, knocking him to the floor. I heard Louise scream, and all the dancers backed away in surprise as Palumbo jumped on the boy and continued to throw punches at this face. Seth tried to get up to defend himself, but Palumbo was all over him and relentless in his attack. The big man, who I would later learn was Seth Howard's father, was trying to pull him off. Then I saw Jonas Bidwell joining in.

Soon Rebecca appeared and was yelling at everyone to stop, tears flowing down her face. The music died down as the band members stopped playing to watch the brawl. I put my drink down and started over to try to help, wondering to myself which side I was supposed to be on. I pushed my way into the crowd and helped pull Palumbo off the young Howard boy, who was now lying with his arms around his face trying to protect himself from the fury of his attacker.

We finally managed to get Willie Palumbo back on his feet as others held his arms. He turned to me and his face was a brilliant red. There was a dangerous rage in his eyes, saliva dripping down the side of his mouth. He kept struggling against his restraint, and he was yelling at the boy that he would kill him if he ever went near his wife again. Rebecca was wailing now, kneeling beside her fiancé, Seth Howard, who was trying to get back to his feet, his face covered in blood and welts from the many blows that Palumbo had inflicted. Louise Palumbo had backed away into a corner as she watched in horror, one of her fists stuck in her mouth and tears flowing freely down her face.

I took hold of the lapels of Willie's jacket and shook him, trying to get him to calm down. He just stared back at me like he could kill me just as easily as Seth Howard. Finally he shook free of the others holding him and pushed away from the crowd, breathing heavily with sweat shining and dripping from his face. The only sound was Rebecca Bidwell, sobbing as she knelt next to Seth. Palumbo continued to back away and held out his hand for his wife to join him. She slowly came over, and then the two of them walked away into the darkness of the night toward town.

Chapter Ten

My first conscious thought the next morning was the sudden awareness that my head was on fire with pain. The left side of my brain felt like a railroad spike had been driven deep inside. I moaned and rolled over in the bed, trying to get my eyes to focus in the light coming in through the window in the bedroom. On the nightstand next to the bed I saw a glass still half full of the amber poison from the night before. I pulled a pillow over my head to try to hide from the morning, and the effects of my overindulgence from the past night. The memory of the fight between Seth Howard and Palumbo came back to me. I could still see the venomous look in the man's eyes as we pulled him off the boy. I tried to piece the rest of the evening together, and could only remember leaving soon after the fight and coming back to the Headley's cottage. I reached over and found my pocket watch. It was a little past eleven o'clock in the morning. I managed to bring myself up into a sitting position. I held my head in my hands, hoping to find some relief from the pain. I noticed that I was still dressed in the clothes from the night before.

I stood and walked unsteadily into the main room of the cottage and over to the sink against the far wall. After pumping the well handle a few times, a steady flow of cold water began streaming from the spout. I cupped my hands to take several long drinks and then put my head under the stream, the cool wetness providing some relief. I took a towel from the wall and dried myself, and then walked out the front door onto the porch. The sun was up high in the late morning and the heat of the day was building. Within moments my friend, Champ the mockingbird, landed on the rail and began jumping around, performing for what he hoped to be his next meal.

"Not now, pal," I said weakly. In bare feet I walked down the steps and across the hot sand of the front yard, and then out through the gate. My first thought was that Lila Dalton might have some hot coffee over at the hotel to help with the hangover, but then decided I didn't want to present myself in this condition. I looked down to the beach, and then settled on heading in that direction. Large billowing white clouds floated slowly overhead on a strong breeze from the south. The wind's direction pushed the surf up higher and large waves were booming onshore down ahead of me. I walked on, each step causing the pain in my head to explode all over again. The beach was empty, and over at the beach pavilion there was only leftover debris from the party.

As I got down to the shoreline, the breaking waves washed up over my feet. The water was still bracingly cold for early spring. I stood there for a few minutes looking out over the vast expanse of the Gulf of Mexico; large green waves rolling into white frothing curls as they came across the shallow sand flats near shore. The cold water helped me momentarily to forget about the pounding in my head, so I decided to venture further out. The first big wave that caught me square in the chest nearly knocked me over. I staggered back a few feet and yelled out at the shock to my body. I determined that there was no turning back, so I started running out as fast as I could on one good leg in the waist deep water. As the next wave approached, I dove into the face of it and felt my entire body react to the chill. I came up on the other side of the wave and screamed again, diving back under as quickly as possible, hoping to adjust to the water's temperature.

Soon I was out past the first sandbar, and as the water grew deeper, the waves subsided into slow rolling swells. I was able to swim then, which helped to warm me even more. The water was a clear translucent green, and I could see the rippled sandy bottom below with every stroke. I rolled over on my back to catch my breath, and as I looked up at the sky, I could feel that the pain in my head was slowly subsiding as my brain was absorbed with other assaults to my senses. I rested there for a while, floating on the surface, being lifted up on the swells coming in. I closed my eyes to just feel the sensation of floating and breathing.

A bigger wave washed entirely over me and when I came back up to the surface, I began treading water, now several feet in depth over my head. I looked back at the deserted shore and marveled at the beauty of the place, the striking white shoreline and dunes set off against the brilliant colors of the water.

Off to my left, something caught my attention, and the serenity of the place was quickly replaced with the paralyzing terror of a large dark gray fin in the water not fifty feet away. I stayed as motionless as I could without going under, watching the fin come toward me and then dip below the surface. I knew it was too far to try to swim in, and I felt my heart pounding in my chest. Now only twenty feet away, I could see the large mass of the fish coming toward me. It apparently noticed me and veered away slightly toward deeper water. Then it rose up out of the water again in a slow and graceful movement. I could see that it was a dolphin, not the toothy shark that I had first imagined. The animal rose up again as it passed by me, and then turned to circle back. I looked on in a mixture of both admiration and uneasiness as it made its way in a full circle around me before continuing on its route eastward down the shoreline.

As I watched the beautiful creature move on, my breath began coming more easily, and my heart settled back to a near normal rate. Then I realized that I was still much too far out to defend myself from other predators much higher on the food chain than myself, and I started back in toward shore. After making it through the high waves of the shore break, I managed to make my way up onto the beach and I turned to sit, looking back out at the sea and the waves. I sat there shivering for a while, water dripping onto the sand, and enjoying the feel of the sun as it slowly warmed my skin.

Later, I heard the sound of splashing and I turned to see Rebecca Bidwell galloping along the shore toward me up on top of Barley, the big brown horse, sending sprays of water out in all directions as they made their way. She pulled up beside me, and both she and the horse were breathing hard. Barley pranced around, anxious to be back on their run. Rebecca climbed down and calmed the horse. She walked over to me with the reins in her hand. The happy glow that I had seen in her face the previous day was gone, replaced by a dull sadness.

"Good morning," I said as she approached. She sat down next to me, still holding the horse, but didn't speak for a moment, just staring out at the water. "I'm sorry about your party last night, Rebecca." I let the thought linger there between us.

Finally she spoke. "I'm so mad at Seth, I could just…" She didn't finish the thought, but instead looked down at her boots, where she was pushing up big piles of sand.

"I'm not sure what happened exactly, Rebecca," I said. "I think Mr. Palumbo is a fairly dangerous man. Seth had better keep his distance."

She turned to look at me. "Knowing Seth, that's probably the last thing he'll do."

"Was he hurt badly?"

"Only his damn stubborn pride," she answered.

We sat there for some time in silence and the horse wandered away a few steps, nuzzling the sand. I was thinking about the gun on Willie Palumbo's belt, and I knew that Seth Howard may have more than he could handle with this man. "When is the wedding?" I asked.

"First Saturday in June, over at the church in Point Washington. About everybody in the county's going to be there," she said.

"Sounds like quite an affair."

She looked up at me again. "You ever been in love, Mathew?"

Her question caught me off guard, and I just stared back at her. I thought about the stunning irony of the question and my recent experience with Hanna Wesley, and years earlier with a young woman in France. The familiar empty pain now returned in my chest. I noticed that she was still staring at me. I nodded slowly and said, "I thought so."

"Who was she?" The girl's questions seemed to cut straight to the bone.

"Her name was Hanna."

"That's a pretty name. You only thought you loved her?"

I chuckled, looking out at the waves, and then answered, "No, I guess I did love her."

"What happened?"

"You've got a lot of questions," I said, starting to get a little impatient with the conversation.

"Did she break your heart?"

I looked back over at Rebecca Bidwell and had to smile in sympathy at her innocent and probing questions. It occurred to me that she was considering her own feelings for a man that had been carrying on with another woman the night before, and almost had his brains beat in as a result. Finally I answered, "Yes, I think she did break my heart."

"You're not over her yet, are you?" she asked.

"No... no it's going to take a little more time," I said, and then managed to smile again. "Have you and Seth been together for a long time?"

"Since we were kids. Our folks are friends, and our families used to get together all the time for dinner or some occasion. As we got older it just seemed to be considered a fact that Seth and I would be married, although lately my papa's been pretty quiet about it. Marrying into the Howard family means a lot down here. Their family's been around a long time, and they have a lot of land and livestock, and Seth can provide well for a family."

She was looking out at the water again. I called her name to get her attention. "Rebecca, since we're being honest, tell me about your feelings for Seth."

She scratched her head and looked away, seeming to contemplate the question. "It's just right that we should be married," she finally said.

"That's not what I asked you."

"Seth is a good man. He works hard and his family is... well it's just that Seth has a hard side too, and I've seen a temper on him that could light up a brush fire."

"Has he ever been mean with you?"

"Oh, we've had our spats, but I can hold my own," she said.

"Yes, I imagine you can," I answered. "Rebecca, one thing I've learned is that you have to be really sure about something like this."

She nodded back, but didn't answer. Barley had wandered further away. She stood up and brushed the sand off her pants and her hands. "I better get going." She walked over and picked up the reins, and then climbed up on her horse. We looked at each other for a moment, and then she kicked Barley in the sides. He jumped forward into a fast trot off down the beach.

I watched them move away down the shore and thought about the life ahead for this young girl. It was sad to think that she may be on a path that would lead to far less than she deserved.

As I walked back up to the house, I noticed that my car was parked out in front on the street along the old picket fence. It surprised me after the revelry and chaotic events of the previous night that someone had been able to get up so early to retrieve it. I looked inside and saw that the floorboards were covered with cans of paint and brushes, and other painting necessities. There was a note on the front seat. I reached in for it. In a rough hand it read…

Mr. Coulter,
Thought you might like to get started on the paint project for the Headleys. You can pay me when you get the chance.
Eli Bidwell

By late morning I was well into the work. I had found an old ladder in the storage shed behind the house and I started in the front, working with a scraper and rough sandpaper to remove old layers of peeling paint. The sun was up overhead now and the heat had returned. Sweat was pouring out of me, and paint chips and sawdust clung all over, but the work felt good and helped to flush the liquor out of my system from the previous night. A voice from behind interrupted my labor.

"Need some help there?"

I turned and saw Willie Palumbo standing in the street next to my car. He was dressed more casually than last night in a loose tan colored shirt open at the neck, revealing tufts of curly black hair. His abundant middle made the buttons strain to keep it all in. His white cotton pants were rolled up at the bottom revealing bare ankles and feet. On top he wore a large brimmed straw hat for relief from the sun. I wondered if his gun was still on his belt under his shirt. His face seemed friendly and passive, much different than the ferocity that I had seen the night before down at the beach pavilion. I backed down off the ladder and tried to brush myself off, but the effort was fruitless. There was a jug of water on the ground, and I reached down and took a long drink. Then I walked out to the fence and gun or not, my anger continued to build. I knew that I had to speak my mind.

He just stared back at me with a blank expression, and then he looked away out to the beach. Finally he spoke in a quiet voice, "Louise is so mad, she won't even talk to me."

"She has every right," I said, my confidence growing in his seemingly remorseful manner.

"I'll be going over to the Howard's later to apologize. I wanted to ask if you would come with me," he said.

"And why would you want me to come?" I asked, thinking that this man had truly lost any last bit of good sense.

He hesitated and I could tell that all of this pained him greatly. I assumed it was mostly because his wife was so upset with him, not because of the damage he had inflicted on Seth Howard. Then I noticed an extremely large man standing away down the street toward the hotel. It was odd that he was wearing a full suit of clothes in the heat of the day, particularly out of place in this out-of-the-way beach town. Palumbo saw the direction of my gaze and turned to look back.

"That's Anthony," he said. "He's my assistant."

"Assistant?" I asked.

"He takes care of odds and ends, and makes sure that I stay out of trouble."

I laughed and then caught myself, remembering that Willie Palumbo was certainly not a man who you could take too many liberties with, though finally I had to say, "He doesn't seem to be doing much of a job."

The look on his face changed, and I saw traces of that dark rage begin to show itself again in the narrowing of his eyes and the red flush in his cheeks, but then he settled himself and forced a smile. "Oh, you mean last night? Well Anthony was away for a few days. I sent him over to Gulf Shores to do a little business for me," he said.

I looked again and Anthony was still standing there staring at us, holding his hands behind his back, occasionally looking around to gauge the prospect of any approaching threats to his employer. "Why don't you just take Anthony with you?" I asked.

"Anthony will be driving. I'd like you to come along, too. You seem to know the Howard's some and I thought it might help to make the discussion go a little easier."

I thought about his odd request for a few moments, the lurking presence of Anthony off behind him. The last thing I really needed was to get more involved in any of this local drama, but there was something about the whole situation that intrigued me, like a moth attracted to a hot flame.

"I'm not sure that I'm Seth Howard's favorite person, either."

"This would be a great personal favor to me," he almost pleaded.

I think my decision to accompany Palumbo on his peace mission to the Howard's ranch, and my odd fascination with this man, had something to do with the strange contrast of danger and vulnerability that I sensed in him. Unlike my father who never let his inner feelings or weaknesses show, Palumbo was almost an open book of emotions, the direction of his sentiments seeming to change like sea grasses blowing in blustery winds.

"Let me clean up some," I finally said.

"What happened to your leg?" he asked, looking down at the scars beneath my short pants.

"A bad night in France, back during the War," I answered.

"Looks like it was a *very* bad night," he said. "We'll be back in fifteen minutes," he continued, a sound of relief in his voice. Then he turned somewhat awkwardly, as if all of this was terribly embarrassing, and walked back toward the hotel.

Chapter Eleven

The road, or rather the trail, out to the Howard's place was not much better than what I had experienced in my crossing from Point Washington. A wide sandy break in the dense brush and trees, our way was pocked with large ruts and loose sand. Palumbo and I sat in the back of his long black sedan, holding on as best we could as we bounced along. The convertible top was down, and Anthony sat in front trying to navigate the difficult terrain. He had added a large black fedora to his wardrobe. Beneath it his face was an impassive mass of hard muscle and heavy black stubble. His right ear was misshapen, as if a portion of it had been bitten off in a fight. When Palumbo had introduced me to him earlier, he never uttered a word, just nodding his head slightly, and then opening the door for me to get in. He hadn't said a word since.

Along the way we skirted several lakes rimmed with swamp grasses and lily pads. The dunes along the beach blocked some of the wind, but there was still a ripple across the surface of the water that reflected rough images of the white clouds drifting above.

Up ahead a gate came into view fashioned from stripped pine logs, two sections of fence coming off at each side; more as an attempt at decoration and pretense than any useful function.

Across the top of the gate hung a sign that had been crudely painted in black on a weathered plank with the name of the landowner, *Howard*. Our car startled a herd of large black pigs with a dozen smaller babies that had been feeding along the road. They all scurried off into the underbrush. The road continued on curving among tall pines. More pigs were wandering about, no doubt the source of a layering stench that was overpowering.

Coming around another bend in the way, a compound of buildings came into view. Most notable was a wide house painted dark brown with a rusted metal roof that came down over a long porch that ran across the front. Off to the side there were many outbuildings including a large single story barn, also painted brown. There was a maze of rough fencing going in all directions, surrounding muddy paddocks filled with pigs, and one with a few head of cattle.

Our arrival was not unnoticed. The sound of the car had brought several people out onto the front porch of the house. The tall man I had seen the night before during the skirmish with Seth Howard, stood in front of a much smaller woman dressed in a plain gray dress. The man was wearing work clothes splotched with mud and other colors of stains and grease. A large straw hat covered much of his face. Behind them, Seth Howard walked out of the house and stood with his hands on his hips, a look of defiance evident on his face. When they realized who had come to visit, the big man, who I assumed to be Mr. Howard, reached to his side and grabbed a long double-barreled shotgun that had been leaning against a chair by the front door. He held it up in front of him, pointed off to the side.

Anthony stopped the car suddenly when he saw the gun. I watched his big shoulders tense up as he reached for something under his jacket. Palumbo leaned forward, put a hand on his shoulder and whispered for him to calm down. He opened his door, and with some difficulty, moved his abundant frame out of the vehicle. I watched as the elder Howard came down the steps from the porch. His son followed close behind. They both stopped at the bottom of the stairs. Palumbo walked out in front of the car. I remembered that I had been invited along to assist in the apology, so I got out and walked around to join him. Seth Howard gave me a look of something just short of loathing, and I again questioned the wisdom of my presence. The boy's face was swollen and bruised, one eye nearly shut.

The father spoke first, "I don't know what in hell you all think you're doin' out here, but I suggest you get your asses back in that big car there and get on outta here," he said with a deep rumble in his voice.

Palumbo put up a hand in what seemed to be an offer of peace and conciliation. "Mr. Howard," he started, "my name is William Palumbo, and I've come to offer my deepest apologies for the events of last night." I was surprised by the formal elegance of his little speech, with only the slightest hint of his rough accent.

Seth Howard pushed forward and shouted, "You can stop right there, you sonofabitch!"

His father took one hand off the gun to hold his son back. "You just stay put," he said. "Don't know why you think an apology would do any damn good after you near killed my son last night. You better leave now or I'll feel compelled to place a few loads of this buckshot here in your fat ass!"

I looked over at Palumbo, who was staying surprisingly calm, and then I heard a car door open and Anthony was getting out to join in the exchange. Palumbo put a hand out to stop him, and the big man stood a few paces behind his employer.

"You're right, there is nothing I can say to make it right over what happened," Palumbo said, "but you need to know that I'm sorry and just feel awful bad about ruining your engagement party."

He turned to Anthony and nodded, and the big *assistant* walked back behind the car and opened the trunk lid. He came back with a large wooden crate with the stamping of a Canadian whiskey on the side. He walked up in front of the Howards and placed it on the sand in front of them, and then returned to stand beside us.

"We don't want nothin' from any of you all, now git on outta here!" Howard said.

Seth had also had enough of all of the formalities and broke away from his father and rushed toward Palumbo, I suppose hoping to salvage some sense of honor from his earlier humiliation. Anthony moved with surprising quickness to cut off the boy, and the two collided in a flurry of flailing arms and kicked-up dust. I sensed another scuffle was about to ensue, and with little thought of what I was getting into, rushed forward to intervene.

A thunderous explosion caused us all to jump back as Howard fired the shotgun into the air. Everyone stopped and Seth backed tentatively away. Howard brought the gun down and aimed it directly at Anthony's head. The smell of gunpowder took me back to memories of France. I stood frozen, standing there beside Palumbo.

"I got one more load in this other barrel. I suggest you get back in that car before I decide to let this one go, too," he said.

Palumbo calmly said, "Mr. Howard, I'm sorry that we have not been able to convince you of our sincerity. We will leave, but again, I say that I am sorry and wish your son and his future bride only the best."

With that he turned and got back in the car. I did the same as Anthony started the engine and turned the big car around for us to leave. I noticed Mrs. Howard, still up on the porch. Her expressionless face did little to betray any emotion from the earlier confrontation. It was as if this sort of thing happened all the time around the Howard ranch.

On the way back toward Grayton Beach, Palumbo didn't say a word for the longest time, but when I looked over I could see that he was struggling to keep his anger from rising up and taking over again. His fist was clenched at his side, and his jaw line was tight beneath the loose jowls along his face. He took a deep breath and looked over at me.

"Thanks for coming along," he finally said.

"For all the good it did…"

"No, thank you. I appreciate you standing up for me there."

"The Howards don't seem to be in much of a mood for reconciliation," I said.

He erupted with a big hearty laugh. "That bastard aims a gun at me one more time, it will be the last damn time," he said with sudden seriousness. I could tell that his comment was no idle threat.

"Anthony and me need to run up to Panama City for a little errand. Would you like to come along?" he asked.

Considering that my most recent visit with these two had ended with a shotgun blast over my head, I was at first reluctant, but then acquiesced when I thought about the alternative up on the hot ladder back at the beach cottage.

The trip down the coast to Panama City was an interesting journey through farms and a few cottages, and small shacks spread along the way. The road improved as we approached the town, set along the Gulf coast about twenty miles east of Grayton. We drove along a beach road that allowed us to see the water on occasion through the smattering of small hotels and businesses. Again, the white sands of the beach stood off against the brilliant aquamarine colors of the Gulf of Mexico. There was a little traffic moving about, and a few people walking along the road. Anthony pulled the car into a sandy lot next to a wood-sided structure built up on pilings and painted white with a green shingled roof. A wide set of steps led up to a front entrance with a sign that announced, "*Georgie's*".

I followed Palumbo up the steps. Anthony was instructed to stay by the car. As we reached the door, Palumbo turned to me and said, "Do me a favor here and just pretend like you work for me."

I was puzzled by his request and thought momentarily about my last business meeting with my father, but saw no particular harm in the ruse, so I nodded in agreement. Double doors opened into a dark room with round tables and chairs set about. A bar ran along the wall to the left, but the shelves behind it were noticeably empty. The liquor was hidden from view. A green neon light behind the bar spelled the name of the establishment. It was mid-afternoon and the place was empty except for two men sitting at a table in the back. Several fans set along the ceiling moved the stale air about only a little.

Palumbo stood and assessed the place for a moment, and then walked back toward the men. I followed close behind, not exactly sure what my role as an employee would entail. Neither man rose to greet us, but instead the one on the left pulled a chair out for Palumbo to sit down beside him. He was an older man with a shock of white hair that was even more pronounced over a darkly tanned and wrinkled face. The other man was a much younger version of the first, his face with remarkably similar features, only with fewer wrinkles and dark brown hair. Both were dressed in white dinner jackets with white shirts and black silk bow ties, looking ready to welcome the evening trade. Palumbo sat down and motioned for me to join him in the other chair.

Palumbo spoke first and broke the uneasy silence. "Georgie, I'd like you to meet my associate, Mathew," he said, tilting his head toward me. The old man looked at me with a snarling expression and then back at Palumbo.

"I thought we told you we weren't interested in doing business," Georgie said.

Palumbo seemed unruffled by the rude and abrupt greeting, and smiled back at the man. "I thought you might have reconsidered my offer."

The younger version of Georgie, who I assumed was his son or a much younger brother, leaned forward across the table and said, "We don't care who the hell you are, Palumbo, there's no room for your kind down here."

Georgie reached over and put a hand on the other man's arm without looking away from Palumbo. "There's nothing to reconsider. I told you the last time that we have our supplies set up just fine down here, and don't need no complications from your connections up North."

It finally occurred to me that they were talking about liquor, and I was taken aback by Palumbo's presumptuous attempt to insert himself into their business so far from his home and base of power in New Jersey.

"I told you, Georgie," Palumbo said in a calm, slow delivery, "I can bring you better product at much better prices. Your boys down here are taking you for a fool with what they're charging for import product."

Georgie took obvious offense at the comment. "Nobody takes us for fools, Palumbo. I suggest you get the hell out of here, and you and your *associate* best not show your faces around here again."

I listened with interest and a faint sense of alarm as my second meeting of the day with my new friend from New Jersey was ending in threats and requests that we remove ourselves from the premises at our earliest convenience. I started to push my chair back, but Palumbo reached over to stop me.

"Georgie, you misunderstand my intentions..." he said, before he was interrupted by the older man.

"I don't misunderstand nothing, you big asshole!" Georgie said as he pushed his chair back and stood up. "Now get the hell out of here, and take your goon with you."

So now I was a goon, I thought.

I could see that Palumbo's patience had finally been exhausted, and he stood as well. I got up to join him in some sense of foolish solidarity.

"Georgie, I don't want any trouble from you or your son, here. I mean only to help you improve your business, but I can see that you have no vision for the future."

"The only vision I want is your ass headed out that door," Georgie said.

Palumbo put his hands up in mock defense and resignation. "You gentleman have a good day," he said with remarkable composure. He turned to leave, and I looked again at the club owner and his son. I traded a steely glare that I felt was appropriate for a *goon*, and then followed Palumbo out the door.

The sun was blinding on the porch, and I squinted to let my eyes adjust. Anthony was still standing by the car as instructed, and I wondered why Palumbo had not brought his real goon into the meeting. Perhaps he felt that I was less threatening than the hulky and brooding Anthony.

"Let's go," Palumbo said. "These assholes have no stinkin' idea what they're doing."

On the way back to Grayton, Willie Palumbo tried to explain the business proposition that he had offered the man we had just visited. Apparently Georgie was a major distributor of spirits across the Panhandle of Florida. He had his own connections and collection of suppliers, both bootleggers of booze from offshore, as well as the moonshiners that provided local product. Palumbo was convinced that he could set up his own distribution, and bring a better level of service and pricing to the communities along the Gulf.

"Coulter," Palumbo started, as we drove back along the beach road, "we should talk with your old man about taking over this whole damn area. In six months we could own this business, and small-timers like Georgie back there would be out on their asses."

With the mention of my father, all my senses exploded in a defensive reaction that was apparent to Palumbo.

"You're not part of the business up there in Georgia, are you son?" he asked.

"I've tried to keep my distance," I replied, and then thought about how unwise it had been to spend any more time with this man, let alone tell him that Samuel Coulter was my father.

"Why in hell are you down here in the middle of nowhere?" he asked. "You need to be straight with me, boy."

I thought about his question for a moment, and then realized that what more harm could be done with being honest about my situation. In a way, there was an attractive sense of reprieve in confiding with someone about what had happened over the past few days.

I told him the story of my father, and our meeting with one of his distributors, including the assault that I had witnessed. Then I went through the sequence of events with Hanna and my intended betrothal before my brother's duplicity, stealing her away and sleeping with her.

Palumbo listened with what appeared to be earnest attention. When I finished my story he said, "First of all, about your father. This is a very tough business and it's not for the faint of heart. You have to protect your interests, and if you let one jerk run over you, every other asshole thinks they can get away with something."

"I understand all that," I answered. "I just don't choose to be part of it."

"It's a very lucrative business, Coulter. I'm sure you're aware of that, and I'm sure that your family lives quite well," he said.

"I don't care about the money."

He seemed flustered with my comment. "Now that's the first ignorant thing I've heard you say." He leaned forward and spoke to Anthony. "Did you hear that? He doesn't care about the money."

Anthony did little to respond, only looking back for a moment in the rearview mirror. Palumbo turned back to me. "Let me tell you something. You can get by in this life and take what comes along, or you can go out and take what you're really due, and enjoy all that life has to offer."

My anger was rising steadily with this little lecture and I finally said, "So here you are stuck in a little hotel in the middle of nowhere, hiding from the law and people that want to slit your throat. Some life, Palumbo."

The big man stared back at me for a few moments and then said, "Listen kid, I've led a great life, and the years ahead will be just fine, too. Right now there's a little trouble back home. You have to expect a few problems now and then, but men deal with these things. And speaking of being a man, what the hell were you thinking letting your brother get away with banging your girl?"

I started to protest but he continued on.

"You should have kicked his ass all the way down Peachtree Street, and then back again. You can't let people take advantage of you like that, and I don't care if he's family. And the girl, you're damn better off without her."

Now I was really angry, but then again I knew that he was right. "Palumbo," I finally said in frustration, "you have no idea about my life. I'm sorry I said anything."

He seemed to take that as the end of the discussion and looked away at the passing scenery. He didn't speak again until

GRAYTON WINDS

Anthony pulled the car up in front of the Headley cottage back in Grayton Beach. As I got out he said, "Kid, if I was you, I'd get my ass back to Atlanta fast and deal with all of this. You stay down here and keep running away from these things, it's only gonna eat at you."

    I didn't answer, closing the door of the car and walking through the gate up to the house. I heard the car pull away behind me and Palumbo's words echoed again in my mind.

Chapter Twelve

There was a basket of food on my porch when I returned, a sandwich and some fruit, and a note from Lila Dalton to join them again for dinner that night at the hotel. I realized how hungry I was, and I sat down on the porch and started in on the meal. Grayton Beach in the late afternoon was quiet, everyone apparently taking a break before the evening's meals and activities. The wind had settled some since morning, and the surf had calmed.

My mockingbird friend returned and landed on the porch rail. I took a small piece of bread and held it out for him. "How's your day going, Champ?" I asked. The little bird jumped back and put the bread down on the railing so that he could start pecking away at it. I watched as the bird finished, and then let out a shrieking "thank you" sound before jumping around, obviously waiting for more. I threw the rest of the slice of bread down on the deck, and walked inside to leave my little friend to his meal.

I sat down in one of the big leather chairs in the main room and considered Lila Dalton's invitation. Knowing that Willie Palumbo and Louise would probably be there again, I had little interest in continuing to be lectured by the big thug. I reconsidered his suggestion about going home and dealing with my father, and with my brother Jess. It had only been two days, but Palumbo was right; the whole situation was eating at me, and there was no hope in sight that the feelings would fade. My spinelessness in not confronting Jess that night at Hanna's house was the hardest matter to deal with. It wasn't just eating at me as Palumbo had suggested, it was burning a damn hole in my gut, and the ache was building every minute that I let myself think about it. I wondered then about what my family must be thinking about my disappearance. My sister and mother would have no idea about what had happened that night, and why I had suddenly been compelled to get away. They were probably both genuinely upset about my vanishing overnight. Certainly my father and brother would have some notion about why I had left, but what did they really think about all of this? My father was probably disgusted with my inability to deal with the realities of the family business, and he could go straight to hell with his damn business for all I cared at that point.

Jess was another issue. I'm sure that my father had shared at least some of the details about what had happened with their man down in the woods behind the party, and my sudden departure. But he wouldn't know that I had seen him with Hanna on the porch that night after the party. The image of the two of them together, kissing and laughing in the open door, infuriated me all over again. It would have been so easy to jump out from the bushes and have it out with both of them right then, but I had been frozen in hiding with my own shame and humiliation. I remembered Palumbo's comment about *being a man* about all this, and I knew that he was right.

And what of Hanna, and was she expecting me to call? What was really going on in her mind? Did she have any feelings for me at all? Was she with Jess again right at that moment, making love again, and laughing about the little brother who had just run away? *They can all go straight to hell*, I thought, and got up from the chair and walked into the kitchen. I reached for one of the jars of liquor on the shelf, but thought better of it, remembering the effects I had endured all day from last night's drinking. That surely wasn't the answer, and I thought instead about my mother and sister, and knew then that I had to get word to them that I was all right.

I had noticed a phone in the front room of Lila's hotel and decided that I should try to place a call to Atlanta. I walked out of the house and down the street, thinking about what I would say if I was able to get through to either of them. And what if Jess or my father answered? More likely it would be our servant, Velma Harold, who would pick up the phone.

I walked up the front steps to the porch of the hotel and Melanee Dalton greeted me there, opening the door.

"Hello Mathew," she said. "Are you coming for dinner? You're a little early."

I was astounded again by the little blind girl's prescience. I walked into the front gathering room and she closed the door behind us.

"Melanee, how are you today?" I finally responded.

"I'm wonderful, Mathew," she said, and I was lifted some by her bright spirit. "It really is much too early for dinner."

"Yes I know," I answered. "I thought I might ask if I could use your phone." Lila came into the room from the back.

"Well hello, Mathew," she said in surprise.

I thanked her for the basket of food, and asked again about the phone.

"Of course, it's right over there. Who are you calling?" she asked.

I explained that I needed to call my home in Atlanta.

"Let me connect you with the operator over in Panama City, and see if she can make the connection for you."

After a few minutes of effort, she handed the earpiece to me. I stepped up to the phone and gave the operator the number in

Atlanta. Lila took Melanee into the back room to give me some privacy. Eventually I heard a phone ringing through a scratchy connection, and then our housekeeper, Velma, was on the line stating that I had reached the Coulter residence, and asking who was calling. Her voice was comforting and reassuring, and I realized how much I missed them all. Then I felt ashamed again at letting myself fall prey to such emotions.

"Velma, it's me, Mathew," I said.

"Mathew Coulter! Where are you boy? You've got this family tied up in knots with worry," she scolded.

"I'm okay, Velma. I just needed to get away for a few days."

"It would have been nice if you had let some of us know. You're mother is having a fit over this, and she is worried sick."

"I know, that's why I'm calling. Is she there? Can I speak with her please?"

"You hold on, Mathew. I'll go find her," Velma said, and then I heard the phone receiver being placed on the counter. I was worried that the connection would fail as the signal grew more garbled with clicks and hissing, and then I heard my mother's voice on the other end.

"Mathew, are you really okay? I've been so worried," she said, and her words made my heart ache for upsetting her so.

"I'm fine, really."

"Where are you?"

I hesitated for a moment, having anticipated this question, but not really sure that I was ready to reveal my whereabouts. "I've come down to Florida for a while to take some time to think."

"Florida? Where are you staying?" she asked.

"I'm at a friend's place." I hesitated again. "It's probably best that I don't say exactly where for a bit."

"Why on earth not?"

"Have you spoken to father about any of this?" I asked.

"When you didn't come home the next day after the party I wanted to call the police, but he wouldn't let me. He told me that you would be okay," she said, and the panic and concern was clear in the tenor of her voice. I had to laugh painfully to myself that my father thought that I would be okay over all of this. "Mathew, I've been so worried about you. You need to come home."

"I need a little more time, but I wanted you to know that I was all right and that you shouldn't worry."

"Jess and Maggie have been acting so strangely, and I asked them about your friend, the Wesley girl." Her comment hung there between us like I would be able to somehow finish the incomplete thought. Typical of my mother to refer to her in such a distant and condescending fashion. Certainly brother Jess had not confided in her on his dalliance with my intended future wife.

"Mathew, are you still there?" she finally asked.

"Yes mother. And what have any of you heard from *Hanna* since I've been away?" I had to ask.

"I've not heard a word, and yet your brother and sister have been quite odd about it all."

"Is Maggie home? Can I talk to her?" I asked.

She hesitated a moment. "Mathew, please tell me what's happened. You need to come home."

"I'll be home as soon as I can. Please don't worry."

"Your father is very upset with you," she admonished.

"Oh, I'm quite sure of that," I said, and was tempted to tell her to offer him a quick path straight to hell, but I managed to keep the thought to myself. "Can I please speak with Maggie?"

When my sister picked up the phone I had to hold the receiver back from my ear. Her voice came through the weak connection with loud frustration. "Have you lost your mind, Mathew Coulter?" she scolded. I let her go on for a minute with her rebuke. Eventually she began to calm down and then she said, "Mathew, you can't just disappear like this and think that no one will care or worry about you. I know that the family has been just horrible about your friend Hanna…"

I had to interrupt. "And what do you know of that?"

"I know that they all disapproved and it was wicked of Jess to take her away from the party like that," she said, and I could hear the sincere regret in the tone of her voice.

Wicked. The word was so appropriate, and yet I assumed that my sister had no grasp of just how *wicked* the night had ended. As younger children, both Margaret and Jess often conspired against me in typical fashion for older siblings, and yet I was quite certain that Jess would not have engaged Maggie in any of his deceit that night with Hanna Wesley.

"Mathew, you need to let us know where you are." she pleaded.

I had decided earlier that I needed to enlist the help of at least one member of my family, and Maggie had always been my most trusted ally. There was a time when as a young teen I had left a new bike in a park to go play somewhere else with friends. When I returned the bike was gone. I knew that my father would be furious about my irresponsible behavior, as he was always trying to instill proper values and conduct; quite humorous to consider when years later he would turn to a life far removed from such. Knowing that my brother would immediately run to my parents to reveal my crime, I turned as usual to Maggie for help and redemption. She had told me to keep the loss of the bike between the two of us until she could think through a proper resolution. The next afternoon when I returned home from school, I walked through the garage next to our house to look for something and there was a new replica of the lost bike. Maggie had spent some of her own money down at the bike shop to rescue me. It was a secret that we had always kept between us, and over the years our alliance grew stronger.

I took her into my confidence again, and told her of my journey down to the Panhandle and the Headley's place in Grayton Beach. While not going into the specifics of the events with our father and brother Jess on the night of the party, I explained to her that I needed to stay away for some time, and that I would be working on the book that I had started. I needed her to send money and my typewriter, and a few other supplies and clothing. She dutifully made the list without further protest, and I was certain from past experience that I could trust her to carry out the request with appropriate caution. I left the number and address at the hotel for her to reach me if she had to, and before we said our goodbyes, she reminded me that she loved me and that she would do whatever was necessary to help me come back when the time was right.

When I placed the phone back on the hook, an overwhelming sadness came over me, and I knew that it was a combination of loneliness and homesickness. I also knew that I would have to overcome such immature notions quickly if I was to manage in this remote place. I turned and Melanee was sitting in a chair across the room. I wasn't sure how long she had been there or what she had heard. She was whimpering and trying to hold back full blown tears. I walked over and sat down next to her, and at that moment her grandmother came out from the back.

"Melanee, I know it's very sad," Lila said. She held a letter in her hand and bent down to put her arm around the little girl. Then she turned to me and said softly, "Her mother was supposed to come in from New Orleans for a visit next week, but she's written that she's ill and won't be able to make the trip."

Melanee's tears came freely now and she placed her head down in her hands. The sobs caused her body to shake in tiny convulsions. Her troubles made my own seem slight in comparison and I too knelt down to offer some comfort.

"Melanee, I'm not sure what's happened," I said gently, "but I do know that your mother loves you like all mothers do, and that she'll be out to see you as soon as she can."

The little girl tried bravely to sniff back her tears, and then was finally able to say, "My mother has been very sick, and we're all so worried about her. I was hoping she would be able to come this time."

Lila looked over at me and there were tears in the corners of her eyes as well. She just shook her head slowly, and then turned and walked away into the back.

Just as my sister had been a source of recent comfort and support for me, I felt that I should try to help this little girl cope with her mother's disappointing news. After speaking for a moment with Lila in the kitchen, I took Melanee by the hand and went out the door. We walked together down the street toward the Headley house. Her familiar cheer and enthusiasm began to return as she told me about how beautiful her mother was, and what a wonderful singer she was. It was unbearably sad to think how any mother could possibly abandon a marvelous little child like this.

When we got to the porch I had her sit down on one of the chairs and told her I would be right back. I went inside and grabbed what was left of the bread from my earlier lunch, and went back out to sit beside her. Within minutes my bird friend, Champ, had returned and we spent a wonderful time feeding the little beggar, Melanee sightlessly holding out a small piece and laughing out loud when the bird would whisk it away.

After dinner that night at the hotel, Willie Palumbo left immediately to go upstairs. He had been noticeably quiet and aloof throughout the meal, and his wife Louise had not come down at all. As the only remaining guest, I felt obligated to help clear the table and clean up, although Lila at first protested. When the dining room was clear, she finally convinced me to go out on the porch and have a smoke and another glass of the wine that we had all shared during dinner. I listened again with pleasure as Melanee played the piano, another classical piece that was familiar, but that I could not specifically identify. The clear notes of the music drifted off through the night and mingled with the sounds of the wind rattling the palm fronds beside the hotel and the distant rumble of waves ending their long journey across the Gulf of Mexico as they rolled up onto the beach.

I was thinking about the earlier conversation with my mother and sister, Maggie. At least they knew now that I was safe, and there was some comfort in knowing that I was no longer causing them distress. Then I heard loud muffled voices above, and soon it was evident that the Palumbo's were having a heated conversation about something. Over the music and other ambient sounds of the night it was impossible to hear what they were saying, but the tone was harsh and condemning, interspersed with the occasional muted crashes of objects flying into walls or bouncing off floors. Then the confrontation subsided as quickly as it had begun.

Lila Dalton walked through the door and joined me, sitting down in another chair on the porch. She had a towel in one hand and a glass of wine in the other. She let out a deep breath and took a drink from her glass. There was one more short eruption above from the Palumbo's, and when it was quiet again she looked up and shook her head.

"I'm afraid my guests are having a bad time of it tonight," she said.

I asked her if she had talked to Louise about the incident on the dance floor the previous night. She told me that the woman had not come out of her room all day. She had taken some food up to her, but Louise had opened the door only wide enough to accept the plate, and had whispered a pained *thank you* without showing her face. Quietly I told her about my trip with Palumbo over to the

Howard's place, and his unsuccessful attempt to make peace with them.

"They're a tough lot, Mathew," she replied. "It's such a shame that Rebecca is getting caught up in that family. She really deserves so much more. At first, I believe her family thought it was the right thing for her future. The Howards have means to support her, but I think that her father in particular is coming to see how difficult it's going to be for her with that joyless bunch."

She took another drink of the wine, and we sat for a while looking out into the night. I was thinking about Rebecca Bidwell and how quickly the bright light in her heart would fade when she moved in with the Howards.

As if sensing my thoughts, Lila said, "There are just so few options for a young girl out here. I'm tempted to help her get away. I have friends up in Montgomery that I know would take her in and help her to get started up there."

I didn't answer, but it occurred to me that maybe she was trying to save another young girl when she was having so much trouble with her own daughter. As if trying to shake the troubling thoughts from her mind, she went on to tell me of her time in Grayton Beach.

"It's hard to believe that we've been down here nearly five years now," she began. "We left Nashville when my marriage ran out of steam. After a few weeks staying with my daughter, Sara, and Melanee in a hotel down the beach in Destin, we took a day trip to explore the area and happened on to this little town. During lunch here at the hotel, the owner at that time had complained that he was trying to sell the place to get back home to Kentucky to get on with his life in a *real town*. Two days later I came back and impulsively offered to buy the place." She paused for a moment and took a sip from her wine. "Sara eventually went back to Nashville with Melanee, and it was two years later before they returned. Sara had been singing with a band that was going on the road. She didn't think that Melanee should be exposed to that kind of life. The father was the drummer in the band, although they had never wed, much to my disappointment. His name was Bobby Sanborn. I agreed to take Melanee for the summer while the band toured across the South. Three months had turned into several years, and Sara eventually left Sanborn. She's living now in New Orleans, singing in a club."

The sorrow in the woman's voice, as she told the story of her daughter, was overwhelming, but I could also tell that there was some relief for her in being able to share the more recent and troubling events in her life.

I had to ask about her daughter Sara. "Has she not been back to see Melanee in all this time?"

"A year ago Christmas she came to see us and we had a wonderful visit. Melanee was so happy," she replied with sadness in her voice. "Sara wanted to take Melanee with her back to New Orleans, and at first I was concerned about what kind of place that would be for her, but it was only right that she should be with her mother. I tried so hard to get Sara to stay here with us, but there was no listening to notions of that sort. There was another man back in Louisiana that she had fallen in love with, and she wanted to get back to him. They had talked of marriage and Sara thought that he would be a good father for Melanee. He owned the club she was working in."

"But she didn't take Melanee?" I asked.

"No, in the end she decided to wait until they were married, and then she would come back for her," Sara said. "Melanee was so heartbroken when her mother left again without her. She's still with the man in New Orleans, but I can tell from her letters and the occasional phone call that we get that things are strained, and that she's looking to get out of there."

I glanced over at the woman and saw tears running down her cheeks. She took the towel in her hand and blotted at her face.

"They've never married?" I asked.

She let out a low strained laugh and then said, "No, there will be no wedding, and that's a blessed thing from what I gather about this man. There seems to be a lot of drinking and other women from what I pick up from Sara. I've tried and tried to convince her to get away, but there's some strange attraction there. When she was last here she was in a terrible state. She looked like she had aged ten years. The late nights in the club and the liquor are taking a dreadful toll on her. I almost didn't recognize her when she showed up at the door.

The music inside stopped and Melanee came out on the porch to join us. With her hands out in front to make her way around me, she found her grandmother and climbed up in her lap.

"You play so beautifully, darling," Lila said, trying to hide her sadness.

I looked at the two of them, little Melanee trying to snuggle into her grandmother's arms to get warm. It was quiet inside now with the exception of an occasional plate clattering in the kitchen as the help finished cleaning up. It was dark even in the western sky and the brighter stars were just starting to show. Melanee quickly fell asleep and Lila took her in to put her to bed, silently nodding good night as she went in. As I walked back to the house, I listened to the sounds of the wind and the waves, and tried not to let my thoughts wander to a loud smoky club in New Orleans where a young woman was slowly letting her life be stolen away.

Chapter Thirteen

A month went by quickly at the beach. I found my days filled with work on the house during the cool of the mornings and writing through the afternoons. Several boxes had arrived from Atlanta after I had spoken with my sister. I had set my typewriter up on the small table in the kitchen of the Headley's place. Notes and discarded pages littered the floor, but the stack of finished pages of the manuscript continued to grow. I had abandoned my earlier story that had seen some progress back in Atlanta, when somehow I had found myself off in a new direction that I found quite promising.

I now took a regular weekly trip into Point Washington for food and supplies, and Eli Bidwell and I were coming to be good friends. He was always anxious to talk about life up in Atlanta, and he would share the trials of their lives on the Gulf Coast and the challenges of the lumber business. Occasionally we would talk about his daughter Rebecca, but he was always hesitant to say much about the upcoming wedding to Seth Howard. I could tell it was hard for all of them, but the beauty and tranquility of the place seemed to grab everyone who came, and some obviously never left. The thought occurred to me that I may never leave, but then again, what kind of life could I possibly make for myself here, a recluse writer locked away in a remote house by the sea? At times it seemed a heroic and charmed existence, but it was terribly lonely, in spite of my new friendships with the Bidwell's, and Lila and Melanee Dalton.

There was always Willie Palumbo to keep things interesting. In the past few weeks he had been away much of the time, often leaving in the early morning with Anthony driving him off to some unknown rendezvous. I would have dinner down at the hotel usually one night each week, and when Palumbo and his wife were there he would typically steer the conversation to things back in the north; the cities, the fast cars, but usually little about his business. He hadn't mentioned anything again about our trip to see the Howards, or the meeting with Georgie down in Panama City, though I suspected that his frequent trips had something to do with the liquor business.

It was late in the afternoon on a Saturday in mid-May and the heat was building in the house, even with all of the windows open, to a point that I needed to get away from the blur of the pages in front of me and down to the beach for a swim. As I walked down through the dunes, the hot sand burned at my feet, but the winds off the water from the south were freshening some and offering a little relief.

I saw a small child playing in the surf off ahead and a woman sitting in the sand watching. As I got closer I could see that it was Melanee. She was running through the breaks in the waves, splashing and kicking at the water, and waving her arms around in wild abandonment. I walked up and started to sit down next to who I thought was Lila Dalton, but was surprised to see a much younger woman sitting there watching Melanee. She looked up and I was taken aback to see the pale and gaunt face that was staring at me. It was a face best described as haunted, almost as if the woman suffered a nightmare, even during her waking hours. Her hair was long and brown, wafting loose in the wind, and she kept pulling it away from her face, revealing gray circles under her eyes that glistened wet and distant in the late afternoon sun. With no makeup, she had a plain and withdrawn look, but I could see the recognizable lines of Lila Dalton's face in this woman. She made no effort to get up, and didn't seem surprised at my arrival. I introduced myself and offered my hand, and then sat down next to her facing the water.

"Hello, I'm Sara," she said. "I understand from my mother that you know the rest of our family here."

"Yes, Lila and little Melanee here have adopted this wayward soul."

She managed a weak smile as she looked back at me, and the expression in her eyes was so intense that it was almost uncomfortable, and I had to look away. Melanee heard us talking and came running up.

"Mathew, is that you?" she asked as she ran up, kicking sand on the two us and plopping down in front of us on her knees.

"Hello Melanee. It looks like you're having a wonderful swim. I've come down to join you."

"Have you met my mommy?" she asked with great excitement.

I looked over at the woman again and smiled at her, although her face remained sullen and distant. "Yes, we were just saying hello," I said.

"She came in this afternoon from New Orleans," the little girl said, and there was a look of such happiness and excitement on her face, wet droplets of seawater dripping down from her hair. And with that she turned and ran back into the water, running as far as she could before she stumbled in the deeper water and fell splashing into the surf. When she stood up, she yelled back for us to join her. I waved and yelled to her that I would be out shortly. I turned back to her mother who looked on blankly, no visible pleasure noticeable at all in the reunion with her daughter. I couldn't help feeling irritated at her behavior.

"Do you know how much your daughter has missed you?" I asked with some regret as soon as I finished the question. I half expected her to be quite angry with me. She continued to look at her daughter with no emotion on her face. Then she spoke very softly, and I had to lean over to hear her above the sound of the spilling waves.

"My heart breaks every day I'm away, Mr. Coulter." She paused for a moment and I saw tears welling up in her eyes. "You can't begin to know the hell I face every waking day that I'm not with her."

Her response so astonished me that I couldn't reply.

"I can't expect you to understand," she said, and then she stood up to walk down to the water. She was wearing a long plain white dress that brushed the sand around her pale bare feet. She called for Melanee to come in and took her hand and led her back away from the shore. As they came near again, she reached down and picked up the blanket she had been sitting on and a small canvas bag. "It was nice to meet you, Mr. Coulter. We have to get back to help with the dinner."

I turned and watched as they walked away and Melanee waved, knowing that I was looking. They stopped after a while and Sara Dalton reached down and picked her daughter up. Melanee threw her arms around her mother's neck and laid her face on her shoulder. I could see that it was hard for the woman to carry the little girl in the loose sand, but she made her way just the same.

That night I sat out on the porch of the Headley house with a notepad, jotting thoughts about my book and watching the sun set over the dunes across the road. The sky was turning various shades of red behind the line of dark clouds along the horizon. I found myself distracted from my work, not only from the breathtaking view, but also from the recollections of my earlier encounter with Sara Dalton. My feelings ran between anger and disgust for a woman who could abandon a daughter who needed her so desperately, to a sad sense of compassion for whatever issues she must be dealing with.

Then I saw Willie Palumbo walk out onto the porch of the hotel and sit down to light a cigar. After some time, he turned and noticed me watching him. He waved and then got up and walked down the steps, and started coming over. In the fading light of the day, his cigar glowed brightly on the end with each inhale as he grew nearer.

"Evening Mathew," he said as he walked up and sat beside me.

"Willie, how've you been?" I asked. "Haven't seen you around much."

He scrunched his face up in a self-righteous look and told me that he had been busy working on a couple of new business opportunities, some land that he was interested in developing down along the beach, and a couple of other things. I was amazed at the determination of the man to find prospect in any new situation.

"And how is Louise?" I asked.

"Oh fine, just fine," he answered quickly. "She was a bit tired after dinner and she's turned in." He puffed from his cigar again and let the smoke out slowly. It drifted lightly away on the soft breeze. "Mathew, thought you might like to join me for a night out. I'm heading into town and hate to drink alone."

"A night out?" I asked.

"Yes, are you up for a little merriment?"

I thought about his invitation for a moment, and at first, was reluctant to get caught up again in his strange encounters, but I was admittedly growing bored sitting home each night, trying to write and trying to forget about the treachery of young women and older brothers. I resigned myself to saying yes with full knowledge and expectation that the coming evening would likely offer more than a few surprises.

Anthony pulled the car up in front of the house a half hour later and we drove off into the night, Palumbo and I in the back of the convertible, the cooler evening air blowing over us. The headlights from the car darted up and about along the way, occasionally catching several small deer feeding by the road. We headed east into Panama City. The little town looked much different at night, dark and foreboding, a soft haze drifting in across the few lights on along the streets.

We pulled up in front of a club that I could have sworn was the place called *Georgie's* that we had visited a month earlier, but there was a different sign over the door that read *The Panama Club*. Anthony pulled away to park the car, and as we went up the stairs and through the front door, I was sure then that I was in the same place. The big open room was filled with tables lit by candlelight and dim lamps along the walls, most filled with customers dressed in dinner jackets and the women in nice dresses. A man met us at the door in a white tuxedo jacket and tie.

"Good evening, Mr. Palumbo. I've kept your table for you," he said.

I looked at Palumbo with a puzzled expression, but he didn't respond. Following him to the back of the room, I noticed that he nodded and waved to several people, and stopped at one table to shake a man's hand and exchange greetings. We sat down and drinks were immediately served to our table in coffee mugs. One sip revealed that it was a very good whiskey. A man was playing piano against the far wall and smoke lay heavy in the air like a low fog in the morning.

Finally I had a chance to ask, "What in hell is going on here?"

"How do you like my new club?" he asked.

"Your new club...?" I started to ask before he interrupted and continued.

"Yes it's becoming quite the spot in town, can't you see?"

"And where is Georgie?" I had to ask.

Palumbo smiled an evil grin and leaned close to say, "That old shit just couldn't stand the pace anymore. Decided to move on and take that asshole of a son with him."

"Move on?" I asked.

"Yeah, suddenly he was quite anxious to sell," Palumbo said.

I thought to myself about what form of persuasion Willie Palumbo must have utilized to prompt the previous owner to so suddenly look for a new livelihood. I decided it was probably best that I didn't know, and I was certainly not going to ask. There was a commotion at the door as Anthony entered, his large frame bumping into the reservation stand at the front of the club. He walked over to stand beside the bar, his hands folded in front of him, looking out over the crowd impassively. Then back at the entrance another person walked in, this time a man in the uniform of the county sheriff's department. The man in the tuxedo who had welcomed us walked quickly up to him. I was surprised to see smiles and handshakes received. The ritual of the handshake was extended just long enough for a roll of currency to be exchanged in a not so subtle manner. No one else seemed to notice or care about the presence of the law officer, and the party continued on. The sheriff accepted a mug that one of the waitresses brought over and then made his exit.

I looked over at Palumbo, who had apparently been paying no attention to the dealings at the front door. Following the direction of his gaze I realized why. Standing at the bar was a striking woman, tall and lean, dressed as one of the waitresses for the club with a short and shiny silver dress cut deeply in front. Her hair was a brilliant white that was almost luminescent in the dim light of Palumbo's new establishment. She picked up a tray of drinks and made her way through the crowd, capturing the attention of most every man in the place as she passed. When she came by our table she gave Palumbo an alluring smile and nod, and then our eyes met for just a moment before she moved on past. I'm not sure I had ever seen legs so long. Palumbo noticed my interest.

"Her name's Eleanor," he said. "Isn't she a piece?"

I could only nod in agreement, captured in the sway of her hips and graceful navigation of the crowded club with the tray of drinks held high overhead. I tried not to stare, but I was certainly not alone. I noticed that several women in the club had to pull their male companions' attention back to their own table.

"You wanna meet her?" Palumbo asked loudly over the noise of the club. Before I could answer, he got her attention as she was returning to the bar. She came over to our table and sat down between Palumbo and me. Leaning over she gave him a big hug, and then a kiss on the cheek that left a bright red ring of lipstick. Palumbo's meaty face seemed to flush, and he returned her kiss on a turned cheek. "Eleanor, honey, this is my good friend Mathew from Atlanta," he said.

The woman turned to me, and up close she looked much younger than I would have first imagined, perhaps in her early twenties. Her face was flawless, if not somewhat over made-up. I tried not to look down at the well exposed swell of her breasts as she leaned over to greet me.

She reached out her hand, looking directly into my eyes and said, "Mathew, why haven't we met before?"

I continued to hold her hand, more than a bit flustered, but I tried to compose myself and said, "First time here. I've just come down to the coast recently."

She stood with a great flourish and said, "Well don't be a stranger." She kept looking at me as she walked back to the bar.

I looked over at Palumbo, and he was smiling a big toothy smile. "I think she likes the young man from Atlanta."

"Sure, and every other man with a big tip in his pocket," I said.

The night passed quickly with a steady procession of people stopping by to give their regards to the club's new owner, and occasional visits from the leggy Eleanor. Our mugs were never allowed to get empty, and as the evening progressed I finally gave up on trying to pace myself on the whiskey. Palumbo and I had great conversations through the night that seemed extremely funny, and none of which I will ever remember. My last memories were a blurring kaleidoscope of laughing faces and bad piano music.

In the morning I woke to the sound of birds in the trees outside the window. I tried to open my eyes, but they seemed crusted shut. It had been several weeks since my last hangover. The familiar pain was there in my brain as I tried to sit up. Turning over and pushing the covers back I was startled to see a shock of tousled white hair on the pillow next to me, and the curve of a long exposed backside.

I tried my best to remember the events of the past night, but nothing was coming back to me; even leaving The Panama Club was a fuzzy recollection. So how did Eleanor end up here at the Headley cottage and what had happened? I was finally able to get up and put my feet on the floor, and I looked down to see that all of my clothes were there at my feet. I reached down for my shorts and put them on, trying not to bend over for too long to prevent my head from pounding. Eleanor wasn't stirring, so I walked out to the kitchen and pumped water from the well, and then placed my head under the cold flow. I filled a glass and drank it down in one long swallow to cut the dryness that was gripping at my throat.

My mind was floating back and forth between the obviously male reactions to waking up in bed with a beautiful woman, to the doubts and guilt about being so drunk that I didn't really know what had happened. I filled another glass and walked back into the bedroom. Eleanor was awake and just sitting up with a pillow propped up behind her against the wall, one hand holding a sheet up to cover herself. Her face was a blurred image of what I had remembered from the night before. Her make-up was smeared around her face in places that it wasn't meant to be, and her hair was a tangled mess.

"Good morning," I said as I walked in to sit beside her on the bed. I handed her the glass of water which she drank before speaking. She glanced around the room, a look of confusion on her face.

"So this is your place?" she asked.

"No, actually I'm just staying here for a while. It belongs to a friend."

"Where are we?" she asked

I laughed at her question. She was obviously as far gone the previous night as I had been. Wondering if either of us was even able to stay conscious when we got back and into bed, I said, "We're in Grayton Beach. Willie Palumbo must have brought us both back. He's staying down the street at the hotel."

"Willie...right," she said, trying to put the pieces together.

I was struggling to figure out what to say about our encounter. She put the glass on the small table next to the bed and started looking at the floor for her clothes. I decided that she might appreciate some privacy.

"I'll wait out in the main room. Can I get you anything else?" I asked as I was backing away.

"How about some coffee?"

"Sure, I'll put a pot on."

"Mathew," she started, and then stopped and looked out the window beside the bed. "I don't know what you think about last night… or how we ended up like this." She looked down at the sheet covering her.

"Eleanor, really it's all right," I said. "We had too much to drink"

"I don't know what you must think about me."

"Really, it's all right," I said, and then left her there to get dressed.

The coffee was brewing when she came out of the bedroom, dressed as she was the night before in the tiny silver dress. This time she was barefoot, carrying her shoes, and she had obviously tried to run a brush through her hair. She saw the well pump in the sink and went over and washed her face, and then dried off. I was sitting at the kitchen table and she came over and sat beside me. She leaned over to kiss me softly on the cheek. With the remnants of her make-up washed away she was still a pretty girl, but she looked even younger without it.

"Mr. Palumbo can be a bad influence," she finally said, and then tried to stifle a smile.

I looked at her face, intent on the soft lines at the corner of her eyes.

"How do you know him?" she asked.

"He's staying at the little hotel up the street there," I said. "Have you been working at the club very long?"

"Almost two years. I moved down from my little hometown in Alabama."

The coffee was finished and we both took a cup out onto the front porch. We sat down to watch the sun come up over the dunes and cottages at Grayton Beach. It must have been around mid-morning, and the heat was beginning to build.

Eleanor spoke first. "I really need to get back to town. I'm working the lunch shift today."

In a way I was grateful for an easy conclusion to this unexpected tryst. When we had finished our coffee, I took her out to the car, and as I was opening the door for her to get in, I saw Sara Dalton walking down from the porch at Lila's hotel holding on to her daughter's hand. She looked over and noticed me and my guest in her distinctive outfit. She hesitated only for a moment before continuing on toward the beach with Melanee. She didn't acknowledge that she had even seen us. I suppose that I would have been embarrassed regardless who had observed me on that morning, but I remember being thankful that Lila hadn't come out to see us; probably that strange mother-figure guilt at work.

The trip back to Panama City was enlightening as Eleanor opened up about her past and growing up in Dothan, Alabama, just a few hours north, before moving to the beach two years ago to find work.

"I've been trying to save enough money to go to New York or Los Angeles", she told me. "I was a pretty good actress back in school. Everyone was always telling me I should be in motion pictures."

I revealed as little as possible about my life in Atlanta, only enough to be polite. She seemed interested that I was working on a book and she wondered if I knew anyone in the movies, which I told her that I did not. She lived in a small house a block back from the beach. She told me that she had two roommates and that both were waitresses at the club. I asked if they might be worried about her not coming home last night. She just smiled and shook her head no. When I stopped in front of the house, she slid over on the seat and kissed me slowly and purposefully on the lips, and I found myself caught up in her apparent affection and secretly wishing that I could remember at least some of the past night's activities. She smiled again as she pulled back and slid over toward the door.

"Can I see you again," I asked.

"You know where to find me," she said, and then opened the car door.

"Sure," I said, and then got out to walk her up to her door. She kissed me again on the porch, and then quickly went inside and closed the door behind her. I stood there for a few moments feeling the wet taste of her on my lips, thinking about our unexpected night together. Then the strangest notion came over me as I thought about what my family might think about me bringing home a bleached blonde barmaid from an illegal club in Panama City. I could only delight in the vision of bringing Eleanor out to one of my parent's parties in her little work outfit. My mother and her friends would choke on their martini olives. With that bit of amusement to fill my time, I drove on back to Grayton Beach.

Chapter Fourteen

When I returned to the Headley cottage from Panama City, there was a note tucked in the front door. It was from Lila. My sister from Atlanta had called, and it was very important that I call her back as soon as possible. I walked over to the hotel and into the front lobby. Melanee was practicing piano and heard me come in.

"Hello?" she said, "Mathew?"

"Hi Melanee…"

"Oh Mathew, thank goodness you've come," the little girl said. "You must call your sister right away. I feel that something terrible's happened."

"What did she say?" I asked.

"I'm not sure. My grandma spoke with her, but I can tell that something's happened."

Sara and Lila walked in from the kitchen. "Melanee told you that your sister called?" Lila asked. "She seemed really upset, Mathew."

Sara went over to sit next to her daughter and avoided any involvement in the conversation. Within a few minutes the operator had connected me with the house in Atlanta. My sister, Maggie, answered the phone and I could tell immediately that something was horribly wrong. She was crying and trying to compose herself to speak.

"Mathew... you must come home right away," she said.

When I asked her what had happened, she started sobbing again, and then there was a pause before my father was on the line. I was startled to hear his voice.

"Mathew, is that you?" he asked.

"What's happened?"

I heard him take a deep breath, and then he spoke in a weak voice. "Mathew... your brother is..." and he hesitated again. "Jess is dead, Mathew."

The shock of his words stunned me, and I felt that I was going to be sick standing right there in the lobby of the hotel. I reached out for the wall to steady myself. When I was able to ask what had happened he simply said that he wanted to wait until I returned home to discuss it.

I was trying to make sense of what I was hearing. I looked over and Lila and Sara were watching, obviously aware that something terrible had happened. Even little Melanee was looking over toward me with a concerned and frightened expression on her face. My father asked me to come home right away. The funeral would be in a couple of days, but the family needed to be together as soon as possible. I was too bewildered to even comment or question anything that he had said. I simply told him that I would be there as quickly as I could, and then I hung up the phone.

I left the hotel without speaking, too stunned to even think about explaining what had happened. Back at the house, I threw a few things into the car and was soon on the road back to Atlanta. Early on as I made my way along the rough country roads, my mind was rambling on about what could have possibly happened to Jess. My anger at his recent betrayal was replaced with overwhelming grief at losing my only brother, someone I had, until recently, always loved and looked up to.

GRAYTON WINDS

I remembered better days when we were younger, when we had been as close as two brothers can be; to a day when we were both caught shoplifting some candy at a drugstore in town. Our father came down to pick us up when the owner had called. He was furious with us and Jess took the entire blame, telling him that it was his idea, and that I only went along with it because he had forced me to. I always felt that I owed Jess an enormous debt for standing up for me that day. We never discussed it again, and he never asked for anything in return.

The long drive back to Atlanta was nearly unbearable. My mind eventually became numb with the grief. The road stretched on through seemingly endless miles of desolate country. I stopped occasionally for gas or food, but pressed on straight through the night and arrived the next day in the late afternoon, pulling up to the long drive in front of our house. A police car was parked at the street with an officer standing outside leaning against the front bumper. After showing him my identification, I was allowed to continue on. Our housekeeper, Velma, must have seen me pull in because she came out right away and met me on the porch. She put her arms around me and squeezed me tight against her stout body. I could feel the wetness from her tears against my cheek.

"I'm so sorry, Matty," she said.

"What in hell happened?"

She just shook her head. "Your father is in his den."

I found him there with the lights off and the shades closed, sitting at his desk with his head in his hands. He heard me come in and motioned for me to sit down across from him. He rubbed his eyes, and even in the dim light I could see that he had probably been up all night as well.

"I'm glad you're here, son," he said, and then took a slow measured breath. "We need to talk about you running off, but that can wait."

"Just tell me what's happened."

I could see that he was irritated by my tone. He sighed and then began speaking very slowly. "Your brother Jess has been murdered. I'm certain it was the O'Leary family. They've been trying to move in on our business." He paused for a moment, trying to calm his emotions. I was listening to him speak, but his words were like a distant echo. I was finding it nearly impossible to comprehend what had occurred and what I was hearing.

"Jess had a run-in with one of the O'Leary boys a day earlier. The kid was at a club that Jess stopped in at and they scuffled before someone stepped in. We found Jess's body dumped on the road out in front of the house the next day. He had been badly beaten and there was a single gunshot wound in the back of his head."

He stopped again and used the sleeve of his shirt to wipe the traces of tears from his eyes. "I have no solid proof that they're behind this, but the old man O'Leary called me the next day to offer his *regrets*. I hardly know the man. They're involved in prostitution and some illegal clubs around town, and who knows what else. He asked if I felt it was time to find a different line of work; that under the circumstances, the dangers of this business were simply too great to risk the safety of any more of our family. I told the sonofabitch that he was a dead man if he had anything to do with Jess. He laughed and hung up on me."

I could barely breathe and felt an uncontrollable rage welling up inside of me. There are no words to describe the anguish that overcomes you in a moment when you realize that someone that you have loved and spent all of your life with is gone in an instant, and the fact he was brutally murdered makes it nearly intolerable. My first conscious reaction was to lash out at my father for getting all of us into this contemptible business, but then I realized that he was as devastated as I by all of this and I managed to throttle my response. He rose and walked over to the window and pulled the shades open, looking out over the long expanse of lawn and trees behind our house. His shoulders seemed bent and defeated, and I realized that I had never seen my father in a weak moment. He rose up within himself and turned to look at me, and then said, "Son, I need you here with me now. We have issues to deal with and we have to come together."

I looked at this man, who only weeks ago I had lost all respect for and seen as a monster as he and one of his men had brutally beaten a man in the interest of business. I had often wondered over the past weeks if the man had survived that night; and now I was faced with the death of my own brother. How could I possibly align myself with his interests? In my father's mind the family *was* his business. The two entities were entwined as one and we both differed considerably on that assumption. My overriding thought was about Jess and how the family would deal with his loss. "When have you planned the funeral?" I asked, trying to bring him back to the essential concern.

"Tomorrow actually," he answered.

"Can we please just get beyond the service for Jess before we talk about any of this?" I asked.

He walked over to the far wall where there was a small bar and poured a splash of whiskey into a glass. He turned and gestured to see if I wanted to join him and I declined. Then he returned and sat behind his desk and said, "Mathew, you are now my only son, and in spite of whatever differences we may have, I need to know that I can rely on you to be here for me and the family."

I had to try with all my abilities to control my first response, which was outrage and condemnation, and finally I said, "There is only one issue right now and that is Jess and the funeral tomorrow." I couldn't help it, but I started to well up in tears, and it so infuriated me to show weakness in front of my father in light of recent events, but I couldn't help myself. Wiping my eyes I said,

"I left this family because of your betrayal and what I witnessed with you that night down at the creek, and because of a woman who I thought I would spend the rest of my life with. I have no interest in any affiliation with you or that business, and I will never forgive you or Jess, frankly, for how you treated Hanna that night."

I watched as the familiar hard edge returned to his face. "She was nothing but a tramp," he said.

I wanted to jump over the desk and throw him to the floor, but somehow I managed to restrain myself. "I know that Jess and Hanna were together that night, and her betrayal was as bad as all that you have schemed, but you need to know that in the end I blame only you." It felt so good to get all of that out, and to confront him with my disgust and true feelings, in spite of the ordeal that our family was facing.

He paused a moment before responding, and then looked at me with a familiar glare of parental dominance. "Mathew, you have a very important decision to make in your life. We will bury your brother tomorrow, and we will all mourn his terrible loss to this family. But then we will move on, and I will need to know that you will be with us going forward... that you will come back and work to deal with these terrible days that lie ahead."

There was no other response than total honesty, and frankly disrespect for all that he stood for. Very calmly I said, "When the service is over tomorrow, I will be leaving, and you can count on the fact that I want nothing to do with this mess that you've created."

He didn't flinch, and I saw the old steely demeanor that had intimidated all of us over the years, and so many others in his life. "You will be lost to me and this family, as well as any financial support if you don't get over this childish anger and come to your senses."

I didn't hesitate for a moment when I said, "Your money is the last thing on my mind."

"I'm serious, Mathew. There is no middle ground here."

I stood up and pushed the chair away and said, "After the funeral tomorrow I will be leaving again, and I don't give a damn about your money or your business and frankly, I hope you rot in Hell for all you've done to this family!" I stood and walked out of the room, and heard no further protest.

I left the house without speaking to anyone else. I got in my car and drove out past the police guard at the end of the drive and down West Paces Ferry Road toward town. There was one other stop now that I was back in Atlanta. A few minutes later I pulled up in front of the house in Ansley Park. I parked the car and walked down the drive behind the main house. It was early evening and the sun was low, shining in scattered patterns of light through the tall trees. I saw the bushes up ahead by the garage apartment where I had hidden in shame that night just a few weeks earlier as I watched my now deceased older brother share moments of intimacy with a woman that I had thought was my own. I climbed the stairs with no thought as to what I might say, only that I needed some closure on all that had happened between us. When I knocked on the door I tried to control the anger and the nervousness that I felt all at the same time. I could hear her coming to the door. When it opened I saw her standing there in her work clothes, looking as beautiful as she had always been to me. There were red circles under her eyes and I knew at once that she had been informed of Jess's death.

I had expected her to show some remorse or regret, but she came into my arms as if nothing had happened between us, and then started sobbing with her face on my shoulder. "Oh Mathew, I'm so glad you've come back."

I was momentarily surprised by her greeting, but then reminded myself of her treacherous behavior at our last encounter. "You've heard about Jess?" I asked.

"Yes, your sister called me yesterday," she answered. "Mathew, I'm so sorry about all of this."

"About all of what?" I had to ask.

"About Jess," she said, and there was an innocent look in her eyes that revealed that she perhaps had no idea about my knowledge of their little affair. I walked past her into the small apartment and looked into the bedroom where she and my brother had surely been together on that night I had planned to ask her to marry me. As I turned to look at her, she stood there with a sad and curious look on her face. I tried so desperately to push any remaining feelings for the woman from my mind.

"Jess is gone," I was finally able to say. "He will never be back. I saw you here with him that night." Her face turned pale and I could tell that she was struggling to respond with an appropriate answer. "I'm not here for answers or excuses," I said. "You just need to know that anything we had together is over."

I walked past her toward the door. She reached out to me and held my arm. "Mathew, I'm truly sorry."

I stopped and looked into her eyes that at one time had captured me so completely. Now all I could see was deceit and betrayal. I turned and started to leave, but she wouldn't let go of my arm. She was crying again and trying to gather herself to speak. I was in no mood for excuses.

Finally she said, "I never meant for any of this to happen…"

"It's far too late for that."

"No, you need to understand," she said, and then led me over to sit on a sofa against the wall.

"What are you talking about?" I asked.

"Mathew, I'm sorry, but you were starting to get so serious, and I just wasn't ready for that," she said slowly. "I never told you, but I was engaged for a year back in Chicago, and in the end it didn't work out. I realized how fortunate I was to have another chance at living my own life for a while."

"Why didn't you tell me this?"

"I just wanted to have some fun. Your brother was very charming when he drove me home that night…" I started to get up to leave, but she grabbed my arm again. "He told me that you were really getting serious about me, and that you might even ask me to marry you soon, for goodness sake. We'd only known each other for a few weeks, and he said your parents would never allow it anyway because I'm Jewish."

"Why did you leave with him?"

"He said you and your father had to attend to some business," she answered, and I thought again about the beating down behind the house.

"So you decided to sleep with him?" I said.

"We had a little bit too much to drink on the way back here, and it just happened," she said. "It was just sex."

"Yes, I noticed." I stood, and this time she didn't try to stop me. I looked down at her and said, "Hanna, you should know that I *was* getting serious. I had planned to ask you to marry me that night at the party. I was in love with you and I thought you felt the same way."

She just looked down at her hands in her lap and shook her head. I left her there and closed the door for the last time.

The funeral was held at the most prominent cemetery in Atlanta, just north of the city. As I watched the coffin that held the remains of my brother being lowered into the ground, I looked around at the faces of family, friends and other business and political acquaintances that were gathered for the ceremony. My sister Margaret and her husband, Desmond Raye, stood next to me, a barrier between my mother and father through the formal service. There was a troubling mixture of emotions rushing through my head as I tried to acknowledge the loss of my brother, and also attempted to deal with the depths of his betrayal and complicity with Hanna Wesley.

I tried to remember better times with Jess; the days in Paris when he came to visit me in the hospital; laughing with Celeste and listening to them carry on in French; all he had done to save what was left of my leg. Then I realized that I had never told him the true events of that last night I was wounded. I pushed those memories away and lowered my head to say a final silent prayer for my lost brother.

After the service I began walking away to my car without speaking to anyone in the family, fully intent on returning to the beach house in Florida and my pursuit of something new in my life. Maggie came running over to stop me.

"Mathew, wait," she said.

I turned and looked at her. I saw that her husband stood behind her, an expression of indifference on his face to all that had occurred. I was so distressed by both anger and sorrow that I knew I needed to get away as quickly as possible.

"Maggie, this is not for me," I finally said. She looked at me with the most pitiable face, and my heart ached for her despair. There was a clear line, however, in my mind between love for family and any sense of loyalty for business or related purpose. "I'll not stay any longer," I said.

Raye stepped forward, and I was surprised by his callous response in light of the day's events. With a maddeningly sour and unsympathetic voice he said, "Your father has asked me to step in and help with the family business in light of the situation and your absence. You need to know that if you leave again, you will be forever cut off from the Coulter family." He paused for a moment for effect, and then finished the message by saying, "…and any right to the family income or estate."

It took only a moment, in spite of my immediate desire to throw a fist clear through his face, to smile, as hard as that was and say, "You can take this whole damn state of affairs and shove it straight up your ass!" I wasn't surprised in the least that he didn't react in any way to my response; however my sister rushed forward and threw her arms around me.

"Please don't leave me now," she said.

All of the old familiar bonds with my sister and brother swept over me, and yet there was an undeniable sense of rage and intolerance with what this family had become that I couldn't deny. I pulled Maggie close and whispered in her ear, "I can't stay and be a part of all this."

The next day I was back in Grayton Beach, and it was a day after that when Maggie called for me at the hotel. When I was able to get back to her she told me among other family news that Hanna Wesley had stopped by to see her, and that she was leaving Atlanta to move back to Chicago; a move that seemed best for all involved, in my opinion.

Chapter Fifteen

Returning to the beach had been somewhat cathartic. Two weeks had passed since my brother's funeral. I had kept busy with work on my book, and I was almost done with the painting project on the Headley place. The news about Hanna Wesley had not been unexpected, and in a strange way I found some sense of relief in the closure that I thought it would bring to the whole situation; although I had no doubt that my father had yet to find closure in any of this.

On a morning that had started like so many others at the beach, I had risen early to write and then to go take a swim in the Gulf. It was early June by then and the temperatures were rising quickly each day. The water was still cool and invigorating, although after my earlier encounter with the dolphin I had stayed much closer to shore. On the way back up the beach to the house, I saw a couple walking together toward me. As they came closer, I saw could see that it was Lila's daughter, Sara Dalton, with a man I hadn't met before. He was dressed quite formally for the beach and it seemed curious; a dark silk vest over a white shirt with cuffs and collar neatly starched. He also wore a jaunty felt hat, a Bowler I believe, and his beard was neatly trimmed. Sara had that same vacant look on her face as she came near. She looked up to acknowledge me, but didn't stop to speak or to introduce the man. I turned and watched them heading down to the shore. The man began to gesture with his arms in a very animated way, obviously trying to emphasize some point that he was making.

Back up on the road in town I saw Lila sitting on the porch at the hotel with Melanee, and I walked over to say hello. I noticed that Willie Palumbo's car was gone. I suspected he was back at his club again for the day. I had not been back with him since my return from Atlanta, thinking it best not to further align myself with the man, but the beautiful waitress, Eleanor, was often on my mind.

"Hello Mathew," Melanee said as I walked up onto the porch. Lila smiled at her granddaughter's uncanny sense of what was happening around her, often even what people were thinking. On the day of my return from the funeral the little girl had come over to the house with Lila to welcome me back and to give me a hug for my loss, before I had spoken to anyone back in Grayton Beach about Jess.

"Did you see my momma down at the beach with Mr. Boudreaux?" she asked. "He's come in from New Orleans to visit. He owns a big nightclub in the French Quarter."

"Yes, I saw them," I answered.

"Melanee, you need to go in and finish your lessons, child," Lila said, and the little girl got up and made her way across the porch and inside. In a few moments we heard the sound of the piano begin to play. I sat down next to Lila. "So you met the famous Miller Boudreaux?" she asked.

"No, not actually," I answered. "They passed without speaking."

"He showed up this morning. Arrived by boat into Port Washington last night and then got a ride out here. He's come back for Sara," she said. "Sara was starting to do so much better. I'm just sick about her going back there."

"Has she already decided?" I asked.

"No, they went off to talk about it," she said, and then stood to walk over to the rail and look out at the beach. "He's a dangerous man, Mathew."

"And how is that?"

"He's a very prominent man in New Orleans, and from all I hear, extremely ruthless in the process," she said, as a tear let loose and made its way down her cheek. "Sara has been together with him for almost two years now. He seems to hold a spell over the poor girl. She sings in the club for him. He apparently provides quite well for her, but she's changed so. I barely even recognize anything about her anymore. Her old spirit is just gone."

I felt so badly for the woman who had become my friend, and I understood the feeling of anguish in dealing with family issues that seemed beyond your control. "Do you want me to help with this?" I asked.

She turned and looked back at me. "I don't want you to get in the middle, but thank you," she answered. "I just feel so helpless and stupid that I ever let her leave home with that band all those years ago. I was so caught up in the ruins of my marriage that..." and then she couldn't finish.

Around the corner from the main road into town we both turned to see Seth Howard riding up on a black horse. He was holding the reins of another horse trailing along behind him. He stopped in front of the hotel and nodded to Lila Dalton, giving me a threatening glare instead. The door opened behind us and Louise Palumbo came out dressed in black pants and boots, putting a large straw sunhat on her head covering her bright red hair.

"Seth has been so nice to offer to teach me to ride," she said as she passed and went down the steps. Seth got down from his mount and helped her up into the saddle.

As the two of them rode away toward the beach without another word, Lila said, "This has been going on for over a week now. Every time Willie goes off on one of his trips to town the Howard boy shows up to take her riding. This is going to end badly."

"Does Rebecca know about this?"

"I don't think so," Lila replied. "They're supposed to be married in two weeks and this kid is running around with a married woman, in broad daylight, no less. If her husband finds out about this, I can't begin to imagine what he'll do."

I had a fairly good idea what Willie Palumbo would do and it didn't bode well for the young Howard boy.

Sara Dalton was coming back up the road from the beach with Mr. Miller Boudreaux. This time she introduced him to me as I came down the porch to return home. I shook his hand and scrutinized his face, trying to get some sense of the man. He stared back impassively.

"And what keeps you here in dis lovely place, Mr. Coulter?" he said in a strong Cajun accent.

I told him that I was a writer finishing a book and staying at a friend's place for the season.

"Well good luck to you then, Mr. Coulter," he said. He took Sara by the hand up into the hotel. "We're famished, Lila," he said. "How about we scare up some food in dat beautiful kitchen of yours?" Lila followed them in, giving me a final hopeless look of desperation.

I was napping that afternoon on the big leather sofa in the Headley's front room, trying to find some respite from the hot sun, when I heard a loud commotion out on the road that woke me. I shook off the haziness of sleep and looked out the window. An old dusty black truck was parked in front of the hotel. Miller Boudreaux was standing by an open door, holding Sara Dalton's arms and talking loudly to her. I couldn't hear the conversation, but it was clear that Sara was struggling to get away from the man.

With no hesitation or second thought, I ran as best as I could out of the house and through the front gate toward the hotel. Lila was up on the porch yelling, and as I got closer, I saw that Melanee was standing behind her, holding her skirt and crying.

"Please just leave us alone!" Lila screamed.

My only consideration at the moment was for young Melanee. To have her mother caught in the middle of such terrible circumstances was unconscionable to me, and I felt an angry and immediate need to intercede. I was hobbling along as fast as I could when I reached the car. I grabbed Sara around the waist and pulled her away from Boudreaux. I almost knocked him over, and he came around with a furious, lethal look on his face.

"Coulter, dis is not your affair," he hissed.

I moved between him and Sara Dalton, pressing close to his face. My heart was beating at a furious pace and I could hardly breathe, but I felt no hesitation. "Get the hell out of here and leave her alone."

Seemingly from nowhere he pulled a long knife that was instantly in front of my face. As our eyes locked, he said, "You back away and don' think I won't cut your balls off."

The familiar feeling of uncertain fear from the front in France returned at that moment. All the weeks of agonizing over my tentative reaction to Jess and Hanna that night in Atlanta, and not confronting my father more forcefully for his dreadful behavior, swept over me in a moment. I felt the same emptiness returning in my gut, but I stood there face to face with the man.

Lila came running down the steps and tried to push between us, screaming, "Both of you stop!"

Boudreaux seemed bewildered by the reaction from all of us. He put the knife back in his belt and looked over at Sara who had backed away up onto the porch with her daughter, Melanee. "I will be back for you, sister," he said to Sara, and then he fell back into the seat of the truck and the hired driver took him away.

As they drove off leaving a cloud of sandy dust in the air behind them, all of us gathered at the bottom of the stairs. Sara now had her daughter in her arms, and Melanee was hiding her face in her mother's hair. There was a sense of dazed tension among us.

I was trying to catch my breath and calm down when Sara said in the saddest voice, "Mathew, this is none of your affair. Best that you not interfere again." Her eyes looked straight through me. I was more than a little surprised by her reaction, and this strange association with a man who had just acted so terribly.

Lila stepped forward and put her arms around me and held me close. Then she whispered in my ear, "Thank you."

I pulled back and acknowledged her with a nod. The three of them walked back up into the hotel. I stood there for a moment thinking about the encounter with Boudreaux. The knife had sent a chill of fear through my body that I had tried to suppress for so many years. Clearly he would be back and it was frustrating to think that there may be nothing any of us could do if, in the end, Sara decided to leave with the man. It was unimaginable to think that she would expose her daughter to such a situation, or even consider leaving her again. What would lead a woman to behave in such a selfish and cruel manner?

As I was turning to go back to the house, Anthony drove Palumbo's big car around the corner and pulled up in front of the hotel in a choking cloud of dust. Palumbo struggled some as he climbed out of the back seat, and it appeared that he had consumed a few drinks during his day at the club.

"Mathew, nice to see you, son," he said as he came over and gave me a big bear hug. I could smell the liquor on his breath.

"Willie," I said simply in greeting, pushing myself away.

"Just saw Eleanor down at the club. She just couldn't stop asking about you. Wonders why you haven't been into town to see her."

I considered that to be a very good question at the moment. The tedium of my existence these past weeks was beginning to wear thin. Perhaps a ride into town was not such a bad idea, I thought. "You give her my best, Willie."

"Mathew, come up on the porch here with me. I want to ask you about something." I followed the big man up the steps and we sat down together. "Been thinkin' about your brother some. It's just a damn shame how this has come down. I have a few connections up in Atlanta if you'd like me to look into this a bit more, son. Who's this family, the O'Leary's? Somebody needs to string their asses out on a line."

While his offer was at first attractive, I was quite certain that his involvement would only lead to more trouble for everyone. "Willie, I'm sure my father and his men are… well, let's just say that they will be dealing with the O'Leary's, I have no doubt."

He looked at me with blurry eyes and nodded back, seeming to take my response with a measure of acceptance, and then he said, "Okay then, enough of that." He turned to look out at the beach. I saw that his wife, Louise, was walking back up through the dunes, her big straw hat in her hands, no sign of Seth Howard and the horses. We both watched her come up the stairs. She got a big smile on her face as she came over, sat on her husband's lap and gave him a kiss. I couldn't help but notice the sand on the rear of her skirt and a twig of beach grass stuck in the back of her hair. I had hoped that she and the Howard boy had sense enough not to be engaging in what her tousled appearance seemed to clearly indicate. Palumbo didn't appear to notice, and I suppose would have no reason to be suspicious. He patted her on the backside and told her to go in and get ready for dinner. As she walked away, I thought to myself that I was definitely not going to be the one to bring this affair to light. Hopefully it would pass and Howard would marry the Bidwell girl, and all of this would be long forgotten. Then again, I was coming to find that events rarely take such a tidy course.

The temptation of those long glorious legs finally were too difficult to ignore, and I found myself that night sitting at the bar at Palumbo's *Panama Club*, a mug filled with whiskey in my hand. As my luck would have it, Eleanor was not scheduled to work that night. I sat and stared at myself in the mirror behind the bar, brooding about my unfortunate sense of timing, oblivious to the crowd and noise around me. The band was playing over in the corner. A few couples were dancing. Smoke drifted heavy on the air, pushed in billowing swirls by the ceiling fans.

I felt a touch on my shoulder. In the mirror I saw Eleanor, unexpectedly standing there beside me. On her night off she was dressed like many of the other female patrons, although in my eye, far more appealing; a black short dress plunging low in front and a gathering of shiny jewelry around her neck and hanging from each ear. Her face was beautifully made up and framed by the wavy curls of that striking blonde hair. She leaned in and kissed me on the cheek. I made room for her to sit down on the stool beside me.

"What a nice surprise," I said, trying to act as if this was all just a mere coincidence.

She nodded to the bartender, who knew immediately what she wanted. He came over and placed a white mug down in front of her on the bar and she took a quick sip, then she placed her hand over mine on the bar. "I've missed you so, Mathew Coulter. I've been tempted to have Mr. Palumbo bring me home to see you out there in the wilderness," and then she smiled, looked deeply into my eyes and took another drink.

I couldn't help but melt into her every word and the feel of her skin on mine was electric. "You look magnificent," I finally managed to say.

She smiled back at me. "It's such a beautiful night. Let's take a walk on the beach." Again she motioned to the bartender. He came over and refilled both of our mugs. I left some money on the bar, and we walked out together. The fresh breeze was welcoming after the closeness of the air inside. It was still warm, although the sun had been down for quite a while. We walked through the parking lot and crossed the road onto a path that led down to the beach. A near full moon was rising high from the east, brilliant white against a clear, starry sky. Eleanor reached down and took off her shoes. I did the same and we left them there against the dunes in the grass. She took my hand and we walked down through the loose sand. At low tide, what little waves there were broke far out in the darkness, slipping almost silently up onto the shore break. We walked west along the beach for some time. There was no one else about and only a few small houses tucked up in the dunes. She turned to me, and in the low light from the glow of the moon, I could see her beautiful face smiling at me. I pulled her close and kissed her.

She pushed me away and said, "Let's take a swim."

My first reaction was to look out into the darkness of the night and the water with thoughts of very big toothy fish swimming in shallow, looking for an easy meal. But then she stepped back and pulled the straps of her dress from her shoulders and let it fall to the sand at her feet. She stood there in only a small pair of white panties and held her hand out for me to join her. All thoughts of predators and danger seemed suddenly far away. I was quickly down to my own shorts and we were walking hand in hand out through the waves. When we were out waist deep I pulled her close again. Her body and her kiss were warm and welcoming in the chill of the water and the waves. The next wave knocked us over and we fell together under the salty water and held on to each other until it passed. She wrapped her arms around my neck and we drifted there in the surf together, kissing and laughing. Soon we were coupled as one in a rising swell of motion and touch, and seemingly weightless, we drifted off with the tide through the night.

Chapter Sixteen

I woke the next morning in Eleanor Whitlock's bed in the house she shared with the two other girls from the club. The sunlight was pressing hot through the thin fabric of curtains hanging across the one window in the room. The door to the bedroom opened and Eleanor walked in with two cups of coffee in her hands. She was dressed in a long pink silk robe that brushed at her bare feet, and showed all of her marvelous curves as she moved across the wood-planked floor. She sat down next to me on the bed and handed me one of the cups.

"Good morning Mr. Coulter," she said with a delightful grin across her face that still showed the signs of sleep and early morning drowsiness. I propped a pillow against the wall and sat up to sip the coffee, and then she leaned down and kissed me. "Did you have a nice swim last night?" she asked.

"One of the best I can remember," I said, thinking back on the night's events on the beach, and then back here at the house. "Are you working today?"

"No, not until tomorrow night, actually," she said.

"Why don't you come out to Grayton with me? We can spend the day at the beach. You can help me paint the house. We'll have a wonderful time."

"I'm not sure about the painting, but…" She put her coffee cup on a small night stand beside the bed, and took mine and put it there as well before climbing into bed beside me. She rested her head on my chest and ran her fingers over my stomach. "Do we have to go right away?" she said, and then looked up at me with an inviting smile.

In the end, Eleanor stayed in town, claiming that she had a full day of errands and chores to do around the house. About midday I drove past the hotel in Grayton Beach, and I was not surprised to see the sheriff's car parked in front. Rebecca Bidwell's horse was also tied up to the rail at the porch. Sheriff Lucas Crowe was a regular at Lila's, often stopping by for a cup of coffee or occasionally something stronger; a small contribution to ensure a blind eye toward all things possibly in violation of the Volstead Act. Lila had confessed one evening that she and Sheriff Crowe had, in fact, become quite close over the past year, and from the few times I had met the man, he seemed pleasant enough. I was happy for Lila that she had found someone to share the solitude of this remote place.

I drove on past and pulled up in front of the Headley cottage. As I was getting out of the car I saw Lila coming down the road toward me, a look of ashen shock on her face. When she came up, I grabbed her softly by the arms and helped her to lean back against the car.

"Mathew, the Howard boy, Seth, was found dead this morning."

As I listened, I felt my heart sink in my chest as I quickly thought through the implications of what she was telling me. Lila was rubbing her eyes with her hands. "What's happened?" I asked.

"Rebecca was out riding and found Seth along the road in from Point Washington. It was just horrible, Mathew. She came riding in early this morning in a panic because she couldn't get him up on the horse by herself. I went out there with her in the car. He was lying by the side of the road. There was blood everywhere. He had been stabbed so many times. We managed to get him in the car to bring him back to town, and I called Lucas who just got here a while ago."

"Lila, I'm so sorry. How is Rebecca?"

"Oh, she's just a damn wreck. Sara is sitting with her."

"Where's Palumbo?" I asked and she looked at me, clearly aware of why I was asking.

"He's been gone since last night. He and Louise had a terrible fight, and he and that dreadful man Anthony left in a huff. I didn't think much about it. Those two have been fighting so much lately."

"So you haven't seen him? He hasn't come back?

She shook her head *no*, and I could see that her hands were trembling.

"Did you say anything to the sheriff about Seth and Louise Palumbo?" I asked.

She looked at me with a frightened stare and started to cry. "Mathew, I'm so afraid of what Palumbo might do if I say anything."

I thought about what she had said for a moment, and then realized that she had been right to keep the affair to herself. Why should she get in the middle of this and risk the murderous wrath of this crazy gangster. And yet how could either of us keep this secret, knowing what this man had probably done. "And how is Louise?" I asked.

"She hasn't come down from her room since I told her about Seth."

"We don't know for sure what's really happened here," I said. "I think it's best that you not say anything about Louise and the boy."

"Lucas will never forgive me if this all comes out," she said.

"Let's just wait a bit until we're sure what's going on," I cautioned her.

We both heard the engine noise at the same time. We turned to see Palumbo's car pull up and stop in front of the hotel. Willie Palumbo climbed slowly out of the back seat, and Anthony drove the car around to park it in back. Palumbo's clothes were rumpled and in disarray, with part of his white shirttail hanging out of his pants and suspenders, his jacket and hat in his hand. He saw us watching him and waved, and then walked over to us. His gait was slow and deliberate, almost a shuffle as if he had barely enough energy to move the mass of his body. Lila looked away as he came up, trying her best to hide her tears.

"Morning folks," he said with a surprising calmness in his voice.

I tried to read the look on his face, but found no sense of guilt or awareness of what had happened. Though my first inclination was to just walk away and not get involved, I suddenly felt compelled to ask, "Have you heard about the Howard boy?"

He looked at me with a quizzical expression, and after a moment said, "Seth Howard?"

I nodded, waiting to see any gleam of recognition or responsibility in his eyes or his reaction.

"No," he said, "what about the little punk?"

Lila spoke first, and I could hear the anger rising in her voice. "He's lying dead over in the parlor."

Palumbo looked at her with a dazed expression, and then back at me. "What the hell happened?"

I just stared at him, again trying to read his expression. Finally I said, "He's been murdered, Willie."

The man scrunched up his face, rubbing the overnight stubble of his beard and said, "Oh shit. That why the sheriff's over there?" I nodded slowly. "That boy had no sense… not surprised at all that he got crossed with somebody," he said.

"Where've you been Willie?" I asked, suddenly not concerned about the obvious accusation.

He stared back at me, and then turned and looked out toward the beach. "Me and Louise had a little go of it last night, and Anthony and I stayed in town at the club."

"Didn't see you. I was in town last night," I said.

"Yeah, heard you left early with Eleanor. Hope you two had a nice time of it," he said and a lecherous smile spread across his face. "That girl is some piece of cake, boy," he said, and then turned and apologized to Lila for his remark. "You two seem to be hittin' it off real good."

I didn't answer and Lila was obviously growing frustrated with our topic of discussion. As she walked away, she said, "I need to get back."

"This is a damn shame, Mathew," he said, as we both watched her start back to the hotel, "that boy getting married and all."

"So you stayed in town all night?"

He looked at me again, and I watched the red flush of anger fill his round cheeks. "You best be careful about who you're accusing of something like this, son. I was at the club all damn night, and I got twenty witnesses can vouch for me."

"You know that Sheriff Crowe had to have heard about the fight the two of you had a few weeks back, and that we went over to the Howard place to apologize."

"People have disagreements all the time. Doesn't mean they're gonna kill somebody," he said.

We both turned and watched as an old truck pulled up next to the sheriff's car. Seth Howard's parents got out, and the elder Howard looked over at us with a malevolent glare. He helped his wife walk up the steps and into the hotel. "Just a damn shame," I heard Palumbo say again.

A few moments later I saw Sara Dalton coming out with her daughter Melanee holding her hand. They walked past the cars and started down toward the beach. I left Palumbo standing there, and that was the end of our exchange. I joined Sara and Melanee on the boardwalk through the dunes. "You two all right?" I asked.

"Hi Mathew," the little girl said. "Did you hear about Seth?" she asked sadly.

"Yes I did. I'm sorry." Sara just kept walking without responding. She had her long hair pulled back in a braid and her pale face was scrubbed clean of makeup, gaunt and sallow. She was wearing a long plain yellow dress, and Melanee had on a bathing suit. We reached the end of the boardwalk and started out across the white sand, and then she looked over to me and said, "Thank you for what you did. Trying to help with my *friend* from New Orleans, I mean."

I smiled back at her, and then reached down and took Melanee's other hand to help her through the loose sand. "Has he been back?"

I heard her take a deep breath and then say, "Yes, he came by again last night, and fortunately Sheriff Crowe was over for dinner. He finally convinced Miller to leave, but it got a little ugly."

We got down to the shoreline and we let Melanee walk out into the shallow surf. We sat down together to watch her. Sara sat with her arms wrapped around her knees. After a while I said, "You can't go back with him." She didn't seem to react, but just kept looking out at her daughter splashing in the waves. "I don't pretend to know anything about…"

She interrupted me and said, "That's right, you don't know a damn thing!"

"Sara, I'm sorry and I know I have no place in any of this, but Melanee needs you."

Tears started to form in the corners of her eyes. "Don't you think I know that?" she said, and sniffed and wiped at her eyes. "Don't you know that it breaks my heart every minute I'm away from her?"

I sat in confused silence for a moment. "I'm sorry," I finally said. "I really don't understand."

She looked at me with the saddest expression. "It's just not right for her to be with me for now."

"What are you talking about?" I asked. "Your daughter needs you to be with her. What's in New Orleans that could possibly keep you away from her?"

"It's probably plain to see that I'm not much of a mother," she said, looking back at her daughter. "It's better if I'm away."

"How could it possibly be better?"

"Like I said, you can't begin to understand," she replied with irritation rising in her voice.

"So you're going to run away with Boudreaux again?" I asked.

She shook her head slowly and then put her face down in her arms.

The Howard boy's body had been taken away to town by the sheriff, and as the late evening sun began to fall near the horizon, I left the house and walked over to the hotel to check on Lila and Sara. I found them sitting together on the porch, each wrapped up in sweaters against the wind coming in off the Gulf. Melanee was inside playing a delightful tune on the piano, a low almost hypnotic ballad that filled the night air with a soft comforting sound. I pulled another chair over close to the two women and sat down. Both acknowledged my arrival with forced smiles after a very long and troubling day. We all sat together for a while without speaking, looking out across the dunes to the water beyond, listening to the waves rumble up onto the shoreline. The sky was melting into darkening shades of purple and orange, and the palms rustled in the breeze.

Sara stood up and pushed her chair back against the wall. "I need to get Melanee off to bed now. You will all please excuse me?"

"Good night, honey," Lila said, taking her hand briefly as she walked by.

We listened as Sara took her daughter up the stairs to her room. Echoes from the little girl's music seemed to linger. I looked over at Lila and asked if there had been any new developments with Seth Howard's murder.

"No, Lucas talked to everyone," she said.

"Yes, I know. He stopped over to the house and asked me a few questions as well," I said.

"Mr. Palumbo went back into town tonight, and Louise hasn't come out of her room," she replied softly. "I just don't know what to think or do about all this, Mathew. I really don't want to get in the middle of it, but I also don't think I could live with myself knowing what's been going on with his wife and that boy."

"I think that we should both let things work themselves out for a day or two, and see what the sheriff comes up with on his own." She seemed agreeable to that approach. Then I had to ask her about Sara, and I told her about our discussion earlier down on the beach.

Lila shook her head, not able to hide the sad expression that came over her face. "Mathew, Sara has a terrible problem that's got hold of her, and I'm afraid it's damn near killing her. It makes me so mad, and I keep trying to help her. When she first left Nashville, she was so young and it breaks my heart everyday to think that I let her go. I thought they were all decent people, the band she was singing with I mean." She paused for a moment to calm herself. She pulled a handkerchief out of a pocket and wiped at her eyes. "I don't know if it's drugs or alcohol, or both, Mathew," she said weakly, her voice cracking as she tried to hold back tears. "That damn Boudreaux's only made it worse since she's been over in New Orleans. He keeps her supplied with what she needs and she just keeps falling deeper into this downward spiral."

I was frankly shocked by all this, and just sat there looking at her for a few moments. "Has she tried to get help?" I finally asked.

"I haven't been able to get her near a doctor."

I thought about Miller Boudreaux and my anger rose trying to imagine how a man could treat a young woman like this, and come between Sara and her family. "We can't let her go back, Lila."

"Don't you think I've tried?"

"Can we get her some help around here?" I asked.

"There's a good hospital over in Tallahassee, but I can't get her to even talk about any of this. I know it's breaking her heart about Melanee."

"And yet she'll leave again." I said.

Lila nodded. "It's a terrible sickness, Mathew, and once it gets its grip into you, well it's just a nightmare. She rarely sleeps, and after we're all in bed I know that she's drinking or doing whatever."

"We're not going to let her go back this time, Lila," I said, and she looked at me with the saddest expression I think I've ever seen.

Chapter Seventeen

There is a graceful cadence to the rhythms of a new day along the Gulf of Mexico. As the first glint of soft light from the coming morning sun shows in the dark sky to the east, the night's predators begin to find their way back to their daytime sanctuary, and the hunted peer out cautiously at the prospects of the coming day. Those with a less nocturnal nature venture out. Seabirds flying high over the water looking for schools of baitfish chased near the surface by bluefish or sharks, slash down into the water and the abundance of morning food. Sand crabs peer out from their holes and scuttle about in their tireless fashion. Sandpipers scurry along the shore break, darting away from the incoming waves and pecking along the sand for any edible morsel.

Cruising formations of pelicans float along the shoreline, rising and falling together on the currents, and just above the rising swells of the surf. Fishing boats and other trade ships make their way out beyond the far sandbar, and a few early rising fishermen stand out in the surf, casting long rods and heavy baits. Depending on the direction of the wind, the water can lay flat and clear with an offshore breeze, or churn dark and foreboding in a relentless series of white-capped swells when it blows from the west or the south. The tall sea oats along the dunes sway on the push of the breeze and after a night of strong winds, wavy patterns of blown sand curve along the beach.

It can also be a time of peaceful contemplation and reflection, a few moments alone before the heat of the day and complications of life's realities become all encompassing. Usually among the first out along the shore as the sun would rise each morning, I came to welcome the steady patterns of life, and more and more began to feel part of all that was happening around me. On this particular day there was a ridge of low clouds rushing off to the south, deep purple and threatening rain. The wind was blowing with a slight chill from over the dunes to the north, providing a welcome relief from the summer heat.

As I walked back up through the dunes, squishing through the soft white sand and enjoying the feel of its coolness oozing up through my toes, my mind was drifting back to recent events, dwelling particularly on the dilemma that Lila Dalton faced with her daughter Sara and little Melanee. Then I saw a car parked in front of the house that I recognized immediately. There was a large man sitting in the driver's seat dressed in a dark suit with a big hat on. My sister Maggie was sitting on one of the porch chairs and my friend Champ, the mockingbird, was bouncing about on the railing, imploring her with various shrill comments that he wanted to be fed. Of course Maggie had no idea as to the interpretation of mockingbird talk, and she kept trying to shoo Champ away, most unsuccessfully. In spite of all that had been happening lately, I had to laugh at the whole situation.

"I see you've met my friend, Champ," I said as I walked through the front gate of the worn picket fence. Champ obviously heard me coming because he jumped back down along the rail and turned his attention to me, the easy mark that had become his meal ticket as of late.

"What is the problem with this crazy bird?" Maggie asked, rising cautiously and coming down the steps to greet me with a long embrace. "How are you, little brother?"

"It's great to see you," I said, holding her close. "Frankly, I've been better." I took her inside and poured coffee for us that I had made earlier. We sat down in the living room and I told her about Seth Howard and the Palumbo's, and then about Lila Dalton and her daughter and granddaughter. I was about to share recent events with the glorious Eleanor, but decided that could wait.

"My, there certainly is some drama in this nowhere little place," she said. "Almost as exciting as back in Atlanta."

"Why have you come all the way down to the coast?" I asked.

"It's just dreadful up there right now. Daddy and his men are almost bunkered down in this fight with the O'Leary's, since Jess, you know?" she said with pain welling up in her voice. "I swear they're all going to kill each other, and my dear husband, Desmond, has got himself right in the middle of it all."

I asked her how bad it was really getting, and she went on to tell me that all of my father's men were carrying guns now and that she and our mother were not allowed to travel around town without armed escorts, including the big bodyguard that was out in the car. She had read in the paper that one of the O'Leary's men had been killed in a shootout on the south side of the city. When she had asked our father about it he had refused to discuss it.

I was still struggling everyday with the nightmare of the loss of our brother Jess, and the empty space that ached inside. His betrayal with Hanna was still a fresh and vivid stain on my memory, but far overshadowed by the tragedy of his death. When she had finished I said, "Please don't ask me to go back up there."

She reached across and placed her hand on my arm. "Daddy asked me to come. He really wants the family all back together in Atlanta where he can make sure that we're safe, and honestly with Jess gone, he needs you to help with this war he's found himself in."

"And he thinks you can persuade me?"

She nodded, and then looked out the window across the barren dunes and scattered cottages. "Mathew, you can't stay down here forever."

"Don't be so sure," I responded quickly.

"What can you possibly do?"

I told her that I was coming to feel at home here, and that I was making friends. I went into some detail then about Eleanor, and that we were getting along quite nicely. I talked about the progress that I was making on my book, but mostly I tried to emphasize that there were people down here now that I cared about and that needed my help, too.

"We're family, Mathew," she said.

"I told him, in no uncertain terms, that I wanted nothing to do with his business, and my conscience is still quite clear on all of that."

She looked at me for a few moments, seeming to contemplate my mood and comments. "Father wanted me to tell you that he won't ask again. He'll cut you off brother, and I mean completely."

I smiled back at her with an easy peace within myself.
"You all will just need to understand that I don't care about that, and I sure as hell don't care about his money."

I could see the sad expression appear across my sister's face. She looked down at the floor and shook her head slowly. Then she quietly said, "I guess I knew that's how you'd feel." She reached in her purse and pulled out an envelope and handed it to me. I looked inside and there was a thick stack of $100 bills. "I figured you were going to need a little more cash to see yourself through down here, for a bit longer anyway. Don't tell Daddy."

I thanked her and tried to give it back, but she insisted. "You're not going to just turn around and head back, are you?" I asked. "You need to stay for a day or two, or as long as you like. This is a glorious place."

"What could possibly be glorious about snakes and sand storms and crazy birds flying around my head?" she asked, and we both laughed. I moved over next to her on the couch and hugged her.

"Thank you for coming down and please stay a while." She nodded reluctantly. "Did you bring any other clothes?" I asked, looking at her finely tailored dress and fitted hat, clearly out of place in this little beach settlement.

"You know me, always prepared." She walked over to the door and yelled for her driver, Sidney, to bring *one* of her bags in. When she had changed into something more casual and appropriate, a pair of slacks and a light blouse, I took her over to the hotel and introduced her to Lila Dalton. Sara and Melanee had gone down to the beach for an early morning swim. We made arrangements for two rooms at the hotel for Maggie and her assigned escort, Sidney. Lila and Maggie seemed to hit it off immediately, and the innkeeper took my sister off on a tour of the little hotel, and then out to show her around Grayton Beach. Sidney went upstairs to put their bags away. He passed Palumbo coming down, who I noticed got very concerned by the arrival of the big stranger, his hand hovering close to the gun under his jacket.

"Who's the goon?" he asked when he came up to me in the lobby.

"He's here to keep an eye on my sister. She'll be staying for a couple of days. Nothing to worry about," I said, trying to reassure him.

"I have nothing better to do than worry," he answered, looking up the stairs again. "It's part of the business." We walked into the dining room and he poured a cup of coffee from the credenza in the corner. We sat down together at the long dining table. "The old sheriff worked me over pretty good about Seth Howard. Told the asshole that I had twenty witnesses in Panama City that could vouch for me. He finally agreed to check them out."

I resisted the urge to tell Palumbo about his wife and the now dead and gone, young Seth Howard. What possible good could come from it, only the real likelihood that he would be furious and take it out on his wife? I watched the man sipping his coffee, trying to read his implacable face. How many other men had he murdered or had killed in his long career of crime and violence? I thought about the strange selection of friends that I had happened across in this little town.

"What's your sister down for?" he asked. I explained everything that she had told me, and about the escalation of the feud with the rival bootleggers. "It's a damn dirty business, a tough business... a real tough business," he said, going up to get a couple of muffins that were on a tray. When he sat back down, he leaned over close to me and said, "Told you I had a few friends up there in the city." I nodded. "Asked one of them to do a little checking on the situation."

"I told you not to get involved," I said, irritated that he had initiated such a course of action.

"I know what you told me. Since when has what you think ever stopped me from doing whatever the hell I care to do?"

"Palumbo..." I started, but he interrupted me and continued.

"One of my friends called me back down here last night. You and your family have a real problem up there."

"That's hardly news," I said.

"Who's this asshole, Desmond Raye?" he asked, and I looked up with sudden alarm. Before I could answer, he said, "Your sister's damn husband, right?"

I nodded, looking him straight in the eye. He took a big bite out of one of the muffins and I waited for him to finish, watching crumbs fall down over his big belly and onto the floor.

"The sonofabitch's rattin' out your family, Mathew."

"What the hell are you talking about?"

"Seems he's playing both sides of this thing," Palumbo said.

"He's working for O'Leary?" I asked, pushing my chair back and standing up in disbelief. He shook his head *yes*, as he took another bite. "Are you sure?"

"Sure as shit, young man," he said. "I got excellent sources up there in Atlanta. This Raye fellow's been settin' your old man up. Wants a bigger cut of the business."

I was completely stunned by all of this, and immediately thought of my sister, out walking around with Lila. I could feel the anger burning up from deep in my gut. I went out the door and found Lila and Maggie a few minutes later down at the covered pavilion at the beach. Sara and Melanee were off in the distance splashing down in the shallow break of the surf. I told Maggie that I needed to speak with her privately, and Lila excused herself to go back up to the hotel. When I told her about Palumbo's story implicating her husband in a terrible plot against the family, she looked away toward the green and blue waters of the Gulf, and stood there silently for a few moments before speaking.

"Obviously, I'm not surprised," she said. I asked her if she had any notion of what he was up to, and she reassured me that she hadn't really imagined it was anything as sinister as this, but that he had been acting so differently since I had left Atlanta, and our father had asked him to get more involved in the business. "Are you completely sure about this?" she asked.

"Palumbo is not one to speculate, or act on rumor," I said.

Suddenly the implications of all of this seemed to catch up with her, and I could see her proud bearing and posture deflate before my eyes. I had always questioned her attraction to the strange and aloof Desmond Raye. Seeming to read my thoughts, she said, "Desmond and I have had such an odd time together. Believe it or not, he was so charming when we first met. I know I had never met another man more caring and attentive."

"I don't recall seeing that side of the man," I answered.

"No, you were away at school back then. Our courtship was the talk of Atlanta, two old families with a son and a daughter making the perfect new couple. It wasn't but a few weeks after the wedding that he began to slip away into these dark moods, and we wouldn't talk for days at a time. I kept hoping that it was just a phase or some difficulty he may be having down at his law office, but it never got much better."

"How have you put up with this for so long?" I asked.

"I guess I'm just too stubborn to admit that I made a mistake."

"And now the bastard's working against the family," I said, my blood reaching a near boil. "If he had anything to do with Jess…"

"Oh Mathew, I just can't imagine."

When we walked back up to the hotel, Maggie called my father from the phone in the lobby. I listened as she tearfully shared Palumbo's story of betrayal by her husband and my father's new lieutenant, Desmond Raye. He asked to speak with me, but I refused and walked out onto the porch. Palumbo was sitting there with the cup of coffee in his hand. "I sure as hell hope you've got your story straight here," I said.

At mid-day, Palumbo pulled up in front of the house with Anthony at the wheel of his big car, and his wife Louise sitting beside him in the back. He yelled for Maggie and me to join them. They were going into town for lunch and some fun, he promised. We debated for a moment, and then decided that we needed to think about something other than what was going on back up in Atlanta. All the introductions were made and we found ourselves bumping our way along on the rough road out of Grayton Beach, Palumbo exuberantly talking away about all sorts of new opportunities the day held in store, his wife quiet and somber beside him.

When we arrived in town and pulled into the lot in front of his club, there were cars parked everywhere and people waiting to get in the front door. Even a sheriff's patrol car was parked over in the sand to the side of the club, but Palumbo seemed to show no concern. I had noticed in past visits that the authorities were as welcome as anyone to come in for a drink and some good food, and of course, a small contribution to their future retirement fund before they left.

A prime table was suddenly available and we sat down as Eleanor came up to take our orders. She leaned over and kissed me, and Palumbo whistled. "Man you work fast, Coulter," he said, and then laughed, holding his big belly. I introduced Eleanor to my sister and they shook hands politely.

"Hi honey," Eleanor said, "nice to meet you."

As she walked away to get our drinks, Maggie said, "She's lovely, Mathew."

"Your brother's quite the lady's man," Palumbo said. "Eleanor can't keep her hands off him."

His wife Louise finally showed some sign of life and slapped him on the arm for his rude comment. "Willie, would you please behave yourself with our new guest here," she said, looking over at Maggie and smiling apologetically.

Eleanor returned quickly with four mugs filled with the house's best whiskey. She leaned over and whispered in my ear that she would be off work in two hours and had the night off. I nodded to her, and immediately began the debate in my mind about abandoning my sister on her first night in Florida for further adventures with my new girlfriend.

Palumbo held up his mug in a toast. "Maggie, welcome to our club. I'm sorry that I didn't have better news for you today. When I heard about your husband, I just couldn't sit tight and let that scumsucker keep on with this scheme of his."

We all drank to his toast, and I could see the sadness in Maggie's eyes as she sipped the whiskey. I reached over and touched her arm, trying to reassure her that all of this would eventually be okay. She looked over at Willie and said, "Mr. Palumbo, thank you for what you've done. I just can't imagine how I could have let this happen right under my nose."

"Sometimes roaches can hide under our own damn shoes," he said. "Don't beat yourself up, honey. I'm sure your old man can take care of this now."

I could tell that Maggie was thinking the same as I that we may have both seen Desmond Raye alive for the last time.

The drinks and food came steadily through the afternoon, and Eleanor was very attentive to our every need. Maggie seemed to find some solace in the whiskey, and soon we were all drunk and laughing at Palumbo's crude jokes. Even Louise finally loosened up and joined in the merriment. When Eleanor got off duty at around 4:00, she came over and joined our table at Palumbo's invitation. She slid in close beside me and tried her best to start catching up with our current state of inebriation. After a while, I sat there looking at beautiful Eleanor, talking with my sister like they were the oldest of friends. Soon one of the bartenders that had just come off duty had joined us as well, and he and Maggie seemed to quickly become very interested in each other. Palumbo was a most gracious host, and cigars and whiskey and platters of seafood kept coming in a steady supply.

The rest of the evening was just a blur of random recollections of drinking and dancing, and walking in the surf with the Palumbos and Maggie, and her new friend Randall. Eleanor and I were pawing at each other like we might never see the other again.

When I woke up the next morning, I was in a room that I didn't recognize, a hotel room nicely appointed with a window looking out over the Gulf. Eleanor was still asleep, her bare back and bottom cuddled up beside me. I tried to shake off the dull ache in my head, and there was a glass of water on the table beside the bed that I drained to try to quench the dryness in my mouth. I got up and walked naked over to the window. The curtains were open. We were on the second floor of the hotel, a beautiful view of the beach and the calm emerald water before me beyond the small deck outside the door. A few people were out on the beach and in the surf, and it looked to be mid-morning by the height of the sun in the sky to the southeast.

I felt Eleanor's hands gently caress my shoulders, and the bareness of her against my back before I even heard her get out of bed. Then she traced her fingers down slowly over my chest and stomach. I turned and she came into my arms and placed her head on my chest, her hair hiding her face. We stood there holding each other, swaying gently together for some time as we both awoke to the possibilities of another day.

I found my sister later down by the pool. Palumbo had brought us all out to this beach hotel late the night before. She had chased the amorous bartender, Randall, away in the end, and had actually managed to get some sleep. There was still no sign of the Palumbo's, and Eleanor was upstairs taking a bath.

The realities of our family's situation had obviously caught up with my sister again as she sat pensively looking out at the water, a cup of coffee steaming in her hands. "I'm afraid to call Daddy," she finally said. "I'm afraid to hear what's happened, to Desmond I mean." She took a sip of the coffee. "That asshole deserves all that the old man chooses to bring down on him, dammit, but as much as I try to hate the bastard," she said, "I just can't get over that we actually loved each other, at least for a while."

"This isn't your fault," I said. "It's best that we found out when we did, while something can still be done."

She came over and sat down on my lap and put her arms around me like a small child looking for comfort from a parent. Her cheek, wet with tears, slid against mine, and we sat there together quietly, listening to the morning sounds of the waves breaking against the beach, and birds squawking overhead.

Chapter Eighteen

Desmond Raye was nowhere to be found.

When we returned to Grayton Beach later that day from Panama City, Maggie had called home to Atlanta and spoken with our father. Apparently her husband had been warned that his treachery had been uncovered. No one had been able to find him through the night, and he hadn't come in to the office that morning.

To get her mind away from all of that, I convinced Maggie to come with me over to Point Washington to pick up some more paint supplies for the Headley house. I was almost done with the project, but had underestimated that last amount of paint needed to finish. The old picket fence across the front of the house also needed a fresh coat, and I was finding the work excellent therapy and diversion.

We took my car and made our way slowly over the rough sandy road up through the tall pines and scrub toward the back bay and the small logging town. We dodged herds of pigs from the Howard's ranch rooting along the road, and left the windows down to keep air flowing through against the heat of the day. It was mid-afternoon before we pulled in under the cover of the huge live oaks that twisted up into the sky in a massive canopy around the Bidwell's little store. A long pier was built out into the channel that led to the Choctawhatchee Bay, allowing the boats from Destin and the Gulf of Mexico to come in with supplies and passengers, and to load the milled lumber and other commodities like turpentine and contraband moonshine for transportation to markets across the South. Rebecca Bidwell sat alone at the end of the pier. We walked out on the old worn planking, the wind blowing down the channel from the west. Pelicans sat precariously atop some of the tall pilings, trying to hold their position against the breeze, and looking down for a fishy meal to swim by.

Rebecca didn't look around until we had come up behind her. I introduced my sister and we sat down on each side of her. On the way over from Grayton I had told Maggie about the death of her fiancé, Seth Howard, and the illicit affair he had been having with Louise Palumbo. Now that Maggie had spent some time with Palumbo, she was as suspicious as I about his involvement in Seth's murder, alibi or not.

I reached over and took Rebecca's hand and asked how she was doing; which I had come to think of as such a stupid question myself when I had been asked the same thing after my brother had died. I was surprised at the gaunt and pale appearance of her face. Her long beautiful hair was tied up raggedly in back. Her feet were bare, dangling out beneath an old pair of torn jeans, but not able to reach the water below. She looked at me in response, and tried to smile, gripping my hand more firmly.

"Did you know about Seth and Mrs. Palumbo?" she asked. The question caught me by surprise, and I looked beyond her to Maggie. Her reaction was the same. In an instant I knew that there was no reason to try to hide our knowledge of the whole situation, and I nodded. "My brother Jonas told me at the funeral," she said, with a tone in her voice that was almost matter of fact.

"I'm so sorry, Rebecca," I said.

"I knew that Seth would be a handful," she replied. "He was such a wild one."

I was thinking, without remorse, that it was surely best that Rebecca Bidwell had been spared the life that had been ahead of her with Seth Howard and his hostile family, and then I thought of all the pigs and I almost smiled.

Off to our left a large steamer was coming in through the channel, a long trail of smoke following it in from the bay. We all stood to make room for it to come alongside. Rebecca's father was coming out to greet the boat. We all helped with the lines in securing the big ship, which reached nearly the entire length of the pier. Maggie and I walked with Rebecca back up to the store.

"Would you like to go for a ride with me?" she asked. "I've got Barley saddled up back in the barn, and I just couldn't bear to go alone today, so I just left him there."

Maggie seemed up for it, and we were certainly in no hurry to get back to the beach. There was very little adherence to rigid timeframes in this remote place. We helped her saddle two other horses in the barn. The stench from manure and stale hay was overpowering in the heat, and the breath of fresh air that we were able to inhale when we came out was a great relief. We mounted up and Rebecca led us back along the narrow road through Point Washington. There was a small clapboard-sided church and a cemetery alongside. I wondered if Seth Howard had been buried there, but I didn't ask. A few houses had been built in the little settlement, and the old lumber mill could be seen back through the trees. It wasn't long before we were out in the wilderness again, and Rebecca led the way as the horses walked in single file in the loose sand. It felt wonderful to be out in the fresh air with a cooler breeze blowing through the trees off the bay. We rode in silence for what must have been at least an hour, all lost in our own thoughts and issues with the unexpected turns, and not so private calamities in our lives.

The trail ahead opened up and we came along a big lake that spread out to the south toward the Gulf of Mexico. Rebecca told us that it was Western Lake, and I realized that it was the same body of water where I had wandered upon the big gator. The water was an odd blend of brackish brown, almost tea colored, tinted in a muted shade of blue reflecting off the clear sky. Across on the far side, perhaps not quite a mile, the striking white sand dunes along the beach rose up, and farther to the east a row of tall pines stood sentry, swaying slightly in the breeze. We continued on along the sandy road by the lake, and when we passed the gate to the Howard ranch, Rebecca didn't seem to slow or hesitate. The trail kept on skirting the edge of the lake, and then it curved down closer to the Gulf shore as we got beyond the water. We could hear the waves crashing up onto the beach on the other side of the dunes. There were a few beach cottages built into the high bluff above the Gulf, and Rebecca led us out past one of them that seemed uninhabited at the moment. We all sat there together atop the high dune, looking out over the most beautiful scene of sparkling water and endless sky. Two parallel sandbars ran as far as you could see down the beach in both directions, a lighter color green against the blue of the deeper water. A few ships were far out on the horizon.

I looked over at Maggie and Rebecca, and they both sat there motionless on their horses, enjoying the spectacular scene. Old Barley dropped his head to feed on some beach grass and Rebecca let him have his way.

"This is magnificent, Mathew," Maggie said. "I can see why you've come to love this place."

"It gets under your skin, sister."

Rebecca looked over at us and smiled. "I've lived here my entire life. I can tell you that this view always catches me by surprise and takes my breath away every time." She pointed down the beach to the east to a larger building that sat high up on the sand bluff. "That's the old Seagrove Hotel down the way there. We all used to go down there to the dances on Saturday night on the pavilion that looks out over the beach."

Down below there was a long trail, a couple of feet wide, that had been left in the sand leading from the dunes below us all the way down to the wet sand of the shore break. I asked Rebecca about it.

"It's the loggerheads… the turtles," she said. "This time of year they come up on the beach and lay their eggs in nests along the dunes. When the babies hatch they dig out and head for the water."

"That must be amazing to watch," Maggie said.

"They come out mostly at night," Rebecca said. "Unfortunately the birds and other predators usually have their way, but a few make it to the water."

"That is so sad," said Maggie. "Can't someone be there to help them all get to the water?"

"It's nature's way."

The sun had started it's progression toward the western horizon, and Rebecca thought that we should start home to make sure we got back by dark.

The ride back was cooler in the long shadows of early evening, and Rebecca pushed the horses at a faster pace. I looked over at my sister's face as we rode along, and she smiled back in the sheer joy of the moment and the wonderful trip down to the beach. Thoughts of husbands and other troubles seemed far away.

When we got back to Point Washington we helped Rebecca put the horses up, and then she led us back over to the store. Her mother had already locked up since it was close to dark by the time we got back, but she came over from the house to let us in to get the paint and supplies that we needed. As we were gathering up to head home to Grayton Beach, Rebecca came over and first gave Maggie a long hug, and then over to me with the same. She thanked us for spending the day with her and then when her mother had gone back into the store to close up, she said, "Mathew, you know Mr. Palumbo pretty well now don't you?"

"Pretty well, I guess."

She hesitated and then went on in almost a whisper, "Jonas thinks it was Mr. Palumbo who killed my Seth." I let the comment hang there for a moment without responding, and then she continued. "Do you think so, Mathew?"

I really didn't know myself, but I said, "The sheriff has talked to him, and he's got a real good alibi for that night. I guess he was over in Panama City the whole night."

"What about that awful man that's always with him?"

"You mean Anthony, the bodyguard?" She nodded. "I think the sheriff has talked to them both. Did Seth have any enemies, anybody that would have reason to hurt him?"

"He was always getting in a scrape with somebody," she said. "He had a pretty fair temper on him."

I noticed that tears were starting to form in her eyes, and realized again that she had loved this boy, in spite of all his faults. "Rebecca, I'm sure they'll find who did this. It's just a matter of time. Thanks again for the ride today."

"Yes, thank you," Maggie said. "I had a wonderful time."

We got in the car and started back to Grayton Beach. Maggie looked out the window and let the air through the open car blow her hair back. I wondered if she was thinking of her husband after all the talk with Rebecca about her loss. It made me think how strange and unpredictable it is, the people we find ourselves attracted to.

It was well after dark when we pulled into Grayton Beach. Lights were on in some of the cottages, and the hotel was lit up brightly. A few guests were sitting out on the porch. As we drove by, I could hear Melanee playing the piano. I pulled over and parked, and took Maggie inside. The little girl was playing with great concentration and a look of proud accomplishment on her face. Her mother, Sara, was sitting over in a corner watching, and she nodded as we came in. As we walked up near the piano, Melanee said, "Oh Mathew, I'm so glad you're here. I have a new piece I want to play for you." Maggie looked at me with a puzzled expression, I'm sure taken aback by the little girl being able to identify me before I had even spoken. I had told Maggie that Melanee had been born blind, but that she had an incredible sixth sense that was always surprising people.

"And is this your sister?" she asked.

"Yes," I responded. "Melanee, I would like to introduce you to my sister, Maggie."

She stopped playing and turned towards us, holding out one of her hands. "Hi Maggie," she said, and my sister shook her hand. "I just love your brother. He doesn't know it yet, but I might just marry him when I get a little older."

We all laughed. Sara came over and I introduced her to Maggie. She was even more sullen and distant than usual, and I had to wonder if her issues were pushing her back close to the breaking point. She told her daughter that it was time for her to get to bed. They both told us goodnight and went up the stairs. We were about to leave when Lila came out of the back.

"Have you eaten?" she asked.

I looked at Maggie. We had been offered a small snack back at the store by Mrs. Bidwell, but it had been a long day and I had worked up a fair appetite. I could see that she felt the same way. "Now don't go to a lot of trouble, Lila, but if you've got something you can warm up quick…"

"You all just help yourself to a drink over there and I'll be back shortly," she said, and then she was off to the kitchen. In no time she was back with two plates of hot food, and she sat down with us at the long dining table. We told her about our trip to Point Washington and the horseback ride down near Seagrove Beach.

She seemed to be hearing what we were saying, but not really listening. I stopped talking and she kept nodding her head as if I was still talking about our day.

"Lila, are you okay?"

She startled some and her eyes seemed to finally gain focus. "Boudreaux came by again this morning," she said at last. "He's given Sara until tomorrow to make up her mind, and then he's going back to New Orleans."

"She told him *no* didn't she?" I asked.

"If I hadn't been standing there with her, she may have run off with him right then. He's got the most frightening hold over her, and when we talk about it she refuses to tell me why."

My anger was rising quickly and Maggie must have sensed my feelings when she said, "Can't you just reason with this fellow?"

"I wish it was that easy," Lila said.

"I'll be here all day tomorrow, Lila," I said. I thought for a moment about the knife that Miller Boudreaux had held to my face, but it only intensified my anger and resolve to help this family stay together. I shook my head and said again, "I'll be here," but I was thinking with a guilty heart that another encounter with Boudreaux was the last thing that I cared to consider.

Chapter Nineteen

I slept fitfully through the night, thoughts of Palumbo and Miller Boudreaux and Desmond Raye chasing in and out of my mind. Sometime in the morning I felt someone pushing on my shoulder, and heard soft whispers from a familiar voice. I opened my eyes, squinting against the glare of the morning sun coming in through the window. My sister was sitting next to me on the bed. I sat up slowly with my back against the wall and felt the heavy burden of sleeplessness weigh down on my whole body. Maggie's face came into focus as my eyes adjusted to the light.

"She's gone, Mathew," she said. "Sara left in the night. Lila is just beside herself, and she hasn't been able to tell Melanee what's happened."

"Did Boudreaux take her?" I asked.

"I don't know... Lila didn't know for sure, but all of her bags are gone."

I got up out of bed, trying to gather myself and think clearly about what could be done at this point. If she had really left with Boudreaux in the night, they would probably be back in Destin by now, and mostly likely on a boat back to New Orleans. Any hope of finding her before they left was remote. I tried to contain my anger and walked around the house muttering about that sonofabitch Boudreaux, and at the same time, chastising myself for not doing more to protect and help Sara. I finally got around to getting dressed and walked back to the hotel with Maggie. When we walked into the lobby, I could tell that Lila had talked to her granddaughter about the departure of her mother. The little girl was sitting in a chair in the corner with her legs drawn up under her, holding a doll tightly in her arms. Tracks of tears shone on her cheeks, and right at that moment I thought that my heart would shatter beyond repair. She sensed that we were in the room and turned her face into the cushion of the chair. I watched as Maggie went over and sat down beside her, taking her in her arms and whispering words of comfort to her that I couldn't hear.

I walked back into the kitchen and found Lila sitting on a stool beside a food counter, staring blankly out the back window. I walked over and held out my arms, not knowing what else to do or say. Lila stood up and came into my embrace, and we stood there together in silence, knowing that nothing could really be said that would help at that point.

Later, Maggie had taken Melanee down to the beach to try to offer some distraction. Palumbo came downstairs and I sat and listened as Lila told him about the departure of her daughter. I could see that he was as upset by all of this as the rest of us. His jaw clenched and the blood flushed to his face like other times I had seen him angry. He turned and looked at me, and then in a surprisingly even and measured tone, said, "Go pack your bags."

The trip to New Orleans was long and miserable. Anthony accompanied Palumbo and me. We found a boat out of Point Washington to get us over to Destin, and then it took a day to find another ship we could get aboard to head down the coast to New Orleans. Before we left, Maggie had offered to stay in Grayton Beach to help Lila with little Melanee. We left Destin late in the evening. The trip across the Gulf coast was windy and stormy. The water kicked up in an unrelenting pounding that sent the small steamer crashing up and through the endless onslaught of tumbling, frothy waves. The skipper of the ship pulled into Mobile Bay early the next morning to find refuge from the tempest we had endured throughout the night. We waited another day, tied up at the docks in Mobile, watching the skies for some break in the storm.

The next day started with just a light breeze from the south and clearing skies as the sun came up across the bay. We started out again, thankful for calmer seas and the continuation of our journey. Several hours out, I stood at the rail on the deck with Palumbo looking at the coastline far to our north. Anthony was still seasick from the previous day and was asleep down below. We both sipped on hot coffee and let the rising sun warm our faces. Palumbo finally broke the silence.

"I've been thinkin' about this dirt bag, Boudreaux," he said. "He's gonna have some muscle and this ain't gonna be no picnic." His reflection concerned me because I had been assuming that Palumbo and the bodyguard Anthony would know how to handle something like this. "And we got the girl to worry about, too," he went on. "She's not gonna just give us a big hug and kiss, and then walk out the door with us. This asshole has got a noose around her neck, and for some reason she can't seem to slip free of it."

Our boat made two more stops along the coast at Pascagoula and Gulfport to exchange cargo before we finally cruised through the Mississippi Sound, and on into Lake Ponchartrain. It was near dark when we were finally tied up at one of the many wharfs along the south shore of the lake in New Orleans. Anthony was finally beginning to recover, and he left us to go find a car to take us into the city. Palumbo and I had made arrangements with the ship's captain to be back onboard by noon the next day if we wanted to make the trip back to Destin with him. Anthony pulled up a few minutes later in the backseat of a taxi, and Palumbo and I joined him. Willie started an immediate banter with the old colored driver, and when he began asking about Boudreaux's club, I grabbed his arm. The last thing we needed was Boudreaux getting tipped off that there were three men just in town, and asking a lot of questions, but Palumbo waved me off.

We learned from the old man, as he looked back and smiled through crooked yellow teeth, that the club was named, not surprisingly, just *Boudreaux's*. It was one of the more popular spots in the French Quarter; booze, women and just about any other vice that you might desire. Palumbo had him take us to a hotel a few blocks away from the club, and paid the driver generously to agree that he had never met us.

While Anthony went over to register, Palumbo and I sat in two overstuffed wingback chairs in the lobby. He pulled out a cigar and offered me one, which I declined. After he had the smoke lit to his liking, he said that he needed to make a few phone calls; friends of friends that might be able to help us. There was a phone on the wall in the corner. He went over and sat down on a stool and rang up the operator. I kept watching the front door of the hotel, expecting Boudreaux and his men to come storming in after being tipped off by the taxi driver, but the only person through the door was a young woman who had all the mannerisms and wardrobe of a prostitute. She walked right by the desk clerk with a quick nod and a smile, and then up the stairs.

Palumbo was on the phone for nearly twenty minutes, and he walked over and threw some bills at the night clerk to pay for the calls. "Come on," he said, "we need to get some sleep." Anthony had rented a large suite, and I had a room of my own. Palumbo had ordered some food sent up, and after we ate, I went in and lay down on the bed. It must have been only minutes before I was asleep, still numb and exhausted from the long crossing over from Florida.

The next thing I could remember was Anthony hovering over me and shaking me to wake up. I looked over at a clock on the nightstand next to the bed and it was just past midnight. I sat up and watched as Palumbo came in and threw a travel bag down next to me. He reached in and pulled out a small shiny black revolver.

"You ever use one of these?" he asked, as he pulled out two boxes of ammunition. My father had taught both Jess and me to hunt up in the Georgia mountains when we were younger, and we had learned to handle weapons at an early age. Then, of course, there had been the Army. I took the gun and opened the cartridge. I saw that it was already loaded. I took a box of the bullets and put them in my pocket. I sensed a slow pounding rhythm in my brain, and yet I felt surprising calm at the circumstances and prospects of possibly shooting up a club in the French Quarter of New Orleans to rescue a girl. I watched as Palumbo and Anthony both loaded two guns each and stuck them in holsters under their jackets.

Palumbo sat down next to me and outlined a plan that seemed both simple and brazen. He had learned that Sara played piano and sang most nights in the club until at least two in the morning. Boudreaux had a table elevated in a corner overlooking all of the guests, and with a vantage point to allow him to watch his lady, Sara Dalton, very closely. Boudreaux would have at least four armed men working the club, and they would be evident by their size and crisply pressed tuxedoes. Getting in the club would require the assistance of one of the men that Palumbo had reached earlier. Unlike Palumbo's *Panama Club*, where patrons and lawmen came and went pretty much as they chose, New Orleans like most major cities had a system of security and passwords to gain access to the private clubs that served liquor and other illegal services.

As soon as we were inside, a planned diversion arranged earlier by Palumbo would allow us to quickly grab Sara Dalton, and if everything went according to the plan, with very little if any need for the guns we were carrying. The pounding in my head had now started up in my chest, and as I took a deep breath to calm myself, Palumbo stared hard at me and said, "You gonna be ready, son?"

I paused for a moment and thought about little Melanee Dalton, and the heartbroken look I had seen on her face the morning we had left to get her mother. I thought about Sara Dalton and the haunted expression that she carried wherever she went, and then I knew that this was the right thing, and that it was worth whatever risk we would soon be facing. "I'll be all right," I answered. "You're damn sure you've got this all worked out?"

Palumbo laughed that crazy laugh he gets usually when he's giddy or drunk, and I was less than reassured when he said, "A plan's just that, son. We'll do what we have to do."

Two cars were waiting out in front of the hotel for us when we walked onto the street. Anthony got in the front car, and Palumbo and I climbed in the back seat of the second. There was a driver and another man in front, and he and Palumbo ran through the sequence of events again as we drove off. Boudreaux's club was a few blocks away on Toulouse Street, just off Bourbon. It was close to 1 a.m. when we pulled up and parked across the dimly lit street.

There were no signs or gaudy entrances for the club. It looked like all of the other two story buildings along the street, most with balconies overhanging from the second floor. We got out of the car and the hot wet air clung to my face and beaded up along my brow. There were a few people wandering along the sidewalks on both sides of the street, but most seemed too drunk to even care that we were there. Anthony headed off with two men across the street, one of them carrying a large bag, and then down an alley towards the back of the building. Palumbo and I stood with the other two and waited as planned for the signal. I looked up and saw heavy clouds illuminated just enough from the city lights to see that another storm was rolling in, and a rumble of distant thunder echoed down the street.

I found that my mouth was so dry that I couldn't swallow, and I tried my best to keep my hands from shaking by keeping them in my pockets. The image of Boudreaux's face holding the knife in front of my eyes crossed my mind, and in that instant, a sudden calm came over me and a sense of purpose that was both clear and urgent.

One of the men peaked around the corner of the alley and whistled softly. He disappeared back down the alley and we started across the street, Palumbo and I trailing the driver of our car and the other man who seemed to be in charge. Willie and I stood to the side as the man knocked four times on the door and waited for the small security window to slide open from inside. Palumbo looked over at me and nodded with a confidence that continued to give me assurance in what we were about to do. The window finally opened and our man exchanged a few words, and the door was opened for us all to enter. I took the deepest breath that I could and felt the rough grip of the pistol in my hand in my pocket as we started in.

My first thought was that there was no music, and that Sara wouldn't be at the piano. As soon as I entered I scanned the large room quickly and saw through the heavy smoke that there were tables filled with people laughing and drinking, girls working through the crowd with trays of drinks. A large green neon sign spelling out *Boudreaux's*, hung over a bar on the wall to our right, and it flickered every few seconds. Then I saw Sara, and she *was* sitting at the piano, but not playing, and my heart sank for a moment when I saw that she was talking to Boudreaux who stood there next to her.

Then the whole scene seemed to freeze for a moment as the thunder of a deafening explosion sounded from behind a wall in the back of the club. The door blew open with a heavy cloud of dark smoke billowing out into the room. There was chaos everywhere as women screamed and people fell to the floor crawling for cover and protection. The concussion from the explosion was so strong that I fell back for a moment myself, and when I looked up I could see that Boudreaux was running to the back. Two big men dressed in tuxedoes followed closely behind. The big man at the door that had let us in started back as well, and I watched as Palumbo grabbed him by the arm to turn him, and then sent the butt of his pistol crashing into the man's temple. His knees immediately buckled and he fell in a heap in front of us.

I looked up and Sara was still sitting at the piano, a look of horror and confusion on her face as she scanned the room. Then our eyes met and I knew that we had to move quickly. The driver and the other man were already rushing up onto the small stage. Palumbo and I took a position to each side to watch for any more of Boudreaux's men. The driver pulled a large burlap sack out from under his jacket and threw it over Sara's head, and pulled it down over her body before he picked her up and threw her over his shoulder. I could hear her muffled screams even above the pandemonium of the bar crowd, people rushing in all directions, most toward the front door.

The driver rushed by Palumbo, moving with the crowd and as we backed away toward the door, I saw Boudreaux come back through the door from the back. He saw me immediately, and the look of recognition on his face turned quickly from surprise to fury. He started pushing through the crowd toward us. I pulled my gun without even thinking about what would happen if I was forced to use it, and I saw that Palumbo was aware of Boudreaux's approach as well. Then Anthony seemed to come from nowhere, and was quickly behind him. He grabbed Boudreaux by the hair and yanked him back off his feet, throwing him to the ground. As we reached the front door, I could see that Anthony was on top of him, hitting him again and again in the face with his gun. When the big bodyguard got up and ran toward us, there was blood down the front of his white shirt and spattered across his face.

We all ran across the street among the crowd of scattering patrons. In moments we were in the cars and away as Palumbo and I held onto Sara, who had been thrown in between us, still covered by the heavy sack. She struggled and screamed, and I started to lift the bag off from her, but Palumbo stopped me.

"Sara, it's Mathew," I said, trying to calm her. "We're not going to hurt you." I looked over and Palumbo's sweat-stained face had a wild and excited expression. He was breathing hard and holding Sara tightly to keep from getting hit by flying elbows under the bag. Ahead, two cop cars with lights flashing were coming toward us. Then I could hear the sirens and Palumbo pushed Sara's head down behind the front seat until they had passed. I looked out the back window and no one seemed to be following us.

As we drove through the night, Sara seemed to calm some and she stopped struggling, but I could feel her heavy breathing under the sack. "Sara, you need to come home. We're going to help you." She didn't respond.

The cars dropped us at the docks, and Palumbo spoke with the lead man in our car as I stood holding Sara beside me. I could see the wisdom now in keeping her covered because it would be impossible for her to try to break free and run. When we reached the top of the gangway to the deck of the boat, the Captain came out to meet us. Palumbo intercepted him and put some bills in his hand when he started to protest. Soon we were below and Palumbo and I led Sara into the bunk room we had used coming over from Destin. I lifted off the sack and Sara squinted in the light, and then she flew at me like a rabid animal, a look of madness and hatred on her face. Her hand slashed across my face and a deep searing pain ripped across my cheek. Then Palumbo had her pinned with his arms around her, and he pulled her back away from me.

"You stupid bastards!" she yelled. "Why can't you leave us alone?" And then she was sobbing as Palumbo laid her down on one of the bunks. He pulled a set of hand-cuffs from a pocket and locked her wrist to the iron rail of the bed. She didn't seem to even notice as she lay there on the bed crying with her other arm over her face. I touched my cheek and felt the warm sticky blood running from the deep scratches, and the pain was sharp and throbbing. Palumbo went over to a sink in the corner and soaked a towel. He threw it over for me to hold against my face.

    I sat down and tried to collect myself, and then finally realized what we had just done. I wondered for the first time how many of Boudreaux's men may have died in the explosion in the kitchen, or any of his men who had tried to stop us. Murder was not exactly something I had hoped to find myself in the middle of. It was much later, after I had returned to Grayton Beach, that I learned from Palumbo that the kitchen had been cleared before the explosion, and the cooks and other help had been chased away down the alley at gunpoint. No one had died in the abduction of Sara Dalton, but Miller Boudreaux and three of his men had been seriously injured. Boudreaux, in fact, had sustained severe head wounds at the hands of Palumbo's unleashed bodyguard, Anthony, and lingered near death for two weeks in the hospital before he regained consciousness and began to recover.

Chapter Twenty

The return trip to Florida was blessed with better weather and seas, but our new passenger was less than pleased with being *rescued*. Later that first night on the boat when Sara seemed to have calmed some, I tried to talk to her about coming home to where she belonged with her daughter, but she refused to even acknowledge that I was there. By morning when I checked in on her again, I noticed that she was sleeping fitfully, and her face was flushed and drenched in sweat. At first I thought it may have been sea sickness, but she was still locked to the bed and didn't appear to have vomited. I asked the Captain if there was anyone on the ship with medical training and there was not, but he offered to look in on her again with me.

The sun was now a few hours up over the eastern horizon, and the light filtered in through the small porthole in the cabin. There was a staleness and lingering stench of diesel fuel and mildew, and I wasn't surprised to see that Sara was having difficulty breathing when we walked in. She was drenched in sweat, and shaking as if she was cold now. She had a desperate and pained look on her face. The captain sat down beside her on the bunk and felt her forehead, and then checked for her pulse on her wrist. As he held her arm out, the sleeve of her dress slipped back and a line of small bruises showed an ugly blue trace against the pale skin of her forearm. I kneeled down and looked more closely. I could see the small pinprick wounds along the veins of her arm, and I felt a sick bile rise in my throat as I realized now the appalling addiction that had kept her tied to Miller Boudreaux.

The captain noticed the tracks of the heroin needle at the same time as I, and he looked at me with a worried scowl. "I don't suppose she had time to bring along her next dose?" he asked.

I knew that she had no purse with her when we rushed her out of the club. I shook my head *no* and thought about the danger we had now placed her in. While I didn't know much about this drug, I did realize that withdrawal could be extremely difficult and dangerous without medical care. "You don't have anything onboard to help her?" I asked.

"We don't carry drugs like that," he replied. "We need to get her to a hospital. We'll be back to Gulfport in a couple of hours, and you can find some help there."

Sara seemed to drift back into consciousness for a moment and tried to speak, but her words were slurred and unintelligible. I went to the sink and filled a glass, and helped her to take a few sips. She gripped my arm tightly, and her frightened eyes held mine as her body began to shake even more. She motioned for me to lean close. She whispered weakly, "I know that you're trying to help, but please take me back." Then her eyes got a glassy and distant look, and rolled back up into her head as she passed out again.

Palumbo walked in and I explained what we had found. He shook his head and went over to look at her arms. Both were lined with the horrible bruises from the injections. "This lady's in real trouble, Mathew," he said. "I've seen this too many times back home in the city. She's gonna get a lot worse before she has any hope of getting better."

"They're going to drop us in Gulfport," I said. "I can get her to a hospital there."

"You can't just leave her there after all we've just been through to get her home," Palumbo scolded.

"No, I'll stay. I can stay with her," I said.

By the time we were able to tie up in the little town of Gulfport, Sara was nearly in convulsions. It was all we could do to hold her down. Anthony and I managed to carry her off the ship. Palumbo had found a car to get us into town to the hospital. They stayed to get back on the ship to return to Destin. Palumbo said that he had business that couldn't wait. My emotions were running at a high pitch, and I felt so beholden to this big hood that I couldn't help myself. I went over to him and gave him a hug around the shoulders, as Anthony sat with Sara in the back of the car.

"You just take care of this little girl now, Coulter," he said, pushing me away. "You get her well and bring her back home."

I took Anthony's place in the back of the car with Sara. She was wrapped in a blanket and seemed to be sleeping, although she was still shaking terribly and her face was a ghostly white. As the car pulled away, I looked back and saw Palumbo and his man walking back toward the ship. They were such an odd pair, the short and squat little Willie Palumbo walking with his waddling gait, and his giant of a bodyguard, Anthony, a step behind. I wondered if Lila would ever truly realize how much these two had done to help save her daughter.

The next two days were a blur of sleeplessness, bad coffee and even worse food. I slept in a chair in the waiting room of the hospital when I wasn't with Sara. One of the doctors had told me that she had been near death by the time I had brought her in. They had her on a treatment program of measured withdrawal that he said could take some time, and that she would have to be institutionalized beyond that and monitored closely.

On the third night, Palumbo got word to me through the hospital office that Sara's mother, Lila, was taking a train out of Destin, and would be arriving in Gulfport the next day. His message also said that my sister would be staying to take care of little Melanee, and that together they would all keep the hotel operating until she could return.

I realized that I hadn't showered or changed clothes in days, and I left that night to find a hotel and something clean to wear. I happened upon a hotel first. I slept that night like I had been knocked unconscious, and it was nearly noon before I woke the next morning. Gulfport was a hot and sticky little town, clustered with small boatyards and warehouses along the waterfront. I found a clothing store and a restaurant to get some lunch, and then went back to the hotel to clean up and change. When I returned to the hospital that afternoon, I found Lila sitting in the waiting room. She ran to me and hugged me, and thanked me over and over.

I felt happy that we had been able to help bring her daughter back, but I was also haunted by the fact that we had almost killed her in the process. "She's awfully sick," I said. "I just feel so bad that we didn't know about the drugs."

Lila touched the scratches on my cheek and hugged me again. I could feel her tears seeping through my shirt and onto my shoulder. "Mathew Coulter, how could you have known," she said. "All the help I've tried to get for this girl and I didn't even know. This is only the latest addiction. I'm just so damn scared that she'll never get over this."

We both went back to Sara's room and she was sleeping. We sat together beside the bed, and I watched silently as Lila held her daughter's hand. The window was up and a slight breeze was managing to find its way through the room, rattling the old blinds that hung at a slight angle. It was an hour before Sara woke and as her eyes focused on the room and the visitors at the side of the bed, I saw her face brighten for the first time that I could remember. Lila leaned over and hugged her.

"Oh honey, I love you so much," she said. "We're going to get through this. I promise you we're going to get through this."

Sara looked over at me, and I think she finally knew who I was. Her eyes welled up with tears, and in a weak and raspy voice she said, "Thank you."

I left the two of them there in Gulfport the next day. Lila went down to the train station with me, and on the way told me that Palumbo had arranged for a full-time nurse to accompany them back to Grayton Beach, and stay with Sara as long as needed to help her get back to her life without the drugs. She hoped that they would all be home soon.

As I was boarding the train, she pulled me close and hugged me, and whispered in my ear, "You've given me the greatest gift, Mathew." We both started crying and I didn't care. The train was starting to move before I could pull myself away. I watched her standing there waving to me until she was out of sight.

Chapter Twenty-one

It was three weeks before Lila Dalton returned to Grayton Beach with her daughter, Sara. We had all been alerted a few days earlier when Lila called the phone at the hotel and my sister Maggie had answered. She told Maggie that Sara was coming along well, and that they would be leaving to come back sometime the next day, accompanied by the nurse Willie Palumbo had arranged for her.

When I had finally made my way back to Grayton Beach by ship and train and borrowed rides, Palumbo had come over to see how I was doing. We sat together out on the porch of the Headley's place. He told me the details of what had happened in the rescue, or abduction of Sara Dalton. Everything had happened so quickly that it all seemed a blur to me. Not only had Boudreaux and his men been subdued in our assault on the club, but half the building had burned and been destroyed from the explosion. Palumbo had just received a message the day before from his contact in New Orleans that Boudreaux had suffered terrible physical injury during the attack, and with the closing of the club there were several of his backers that were fed up with him. In fact, he owed more money than he could ever hope to repay even with the club open, let alone closed for repairs. Miller Boudreaux had been found dead two days earlier, sitting at his desk in the office at the club, his head rolled back in the chair with an ugly self-inflicted bullet wound in the side of his skull.

As I listened to Palumbo's account of the demise of the asshole that had tormented Sara Dalton's life for so long, I found myself somewhat troubled by my delight in his exceptionally fortunate departure from this world. While I rejoiced in the liberation of Sara Dalton from an unimaginable torment, I also cringed at the reality that my collaboration with Willie Palumbo in her escape had put me on much the same level as my father; violence and extreme action as a means to justify an end.

On the day that Lila and Sara returned home, Maggie and I were sitting on the porch of the hotel. It was late evening and the sun was painting a brilliant canvas against the far clouds on the horizon. Maggie was reading a book to Melanee Dalton, who could hardly sit still, knowing that her mother would be there soon. My sister had been tending to affairs around the hotel, working with the small staff to keep things running in Lila's absence. She and Melanee had become almost inseparable during that time, and the little girl had kept a remarkable spirit during the past days, in spite of the absence of her mother and grandmother. When I was around her I couldn't help but feel my heart lifted up by her bright attitude and courage in the face of so much challenge in her life. I continued to be surprised by her remarkable ability to *see* and anticipate events, and to read our thoughts.

Long before either Maggie or I could hear the car's engine coming into town, Melanee jumped up out of my sister's lap and ran over to the rail of the porch, looking off down the road in anticipation. Maggie and I looked at each other in amazement, and then the little girl said, "It's them, Maggie. My momma is feeling so much better."

It was several minutes, but then Lila's car pulled around the corner and stopped in front of the hotel. Maggie took Melanee's hand and helped her down the steps. I watched as Lila got out of the car, and then the passenger door opened and Sara Dalton quickly got out and ran to her daughter. She picked her up and hugged her, and then turned slowly in the sand holding her face close to her own. It wasn't long before all of us were crying. Maggie and I went over to welcome Lila back home, exchanging long embraces and knowing looks of relief that Sara was back and that she was safe, at least for now.

Sara walked over to us with her daughter in her arms. There was a noticeable change in the look on her face, no longer distant and pale, but with a new and fresh glow, flushed now by the tears and excitement. There was a bright glimmer in her eyes that had, for so long, been extinguished. She held out a free arm to me. I put my arms around both Sara and her daughter, and held them close. Sara kissed me softly on the cheek and then almost in a whisper, simply said, "Thank you."

Maggie and the cook had prepared a big meal in anticipation of the homecoming. Louise Palumbo came down to join us as well. Willie had been off in Panama City more often now, and kept a hotel room there. His wife stayed in Grayton Beach and kept mostly to herself, walking alone on the beach or reading on the porch of the hotel. None of us was really sure if Willie Palumbo had ever found out about her dalliance with the young Howard boy. No one had been charged yet in his murder. Louise had drawn into herself since the day that Seth Howard had been found out on the road to Point Washington. Perhaps she knew more about what had happened than any of us might have thought, or maybe she was just caught in that strange place between secretly mourning the loss of a man that she had feelings for and guilt at her possible role in his end.

When dinner was over and the places cleared, Sara led Melanee over to the piano. They sat together on the narrow bench. Sara whispered something in Melanee's ear and the little girl began to play, and then her mother joined in playing an accompanying melody in the higher range of the keyboard. It was a beautiful piece, and we were all sitting there mesmerized by the song. When Sara began to sing I felt a rush of pinpricks across my skin, and I realized that I had never heard her sing in the previous days that she had been here with us. Her voice was soft and full at the same time, and the tone and pitch were so pure that I found it hard to even breathe as I listened. Lila reached across the table and took my hand. She had the happiest look on her face.

As I listened, the song's lyrics of redemption and hope were so moving, and then at the chorus, Melanee joined in with her mother and the harmony was stunning. The music and their voices filled the room with an almost spiritual feeling. When they finished, the notes echoed in the silence as we all sat in wonder, no one wanting to break the spell of the song. Melanee turned and put her arms around her mother, and buried her face in her embrace. Then, finally, we were all clapping and shouting out our praise.

Much later I sat out on the porch of my borrowed home at the Headley's. I had lit one of Palumbo's big cigars and had a glass of some of the better local moonshine resting in my hand. I had been thinking about nothing but the homecoming, and the bright glow of satisfaction in reuniting mother and child washed over me, mellowed by the whiskey. The lights had all gone out over at the hotel, and a bright moon ducked in and out of high clouds passing on the soft winds of the night.

I heard the rusty creak of the gate hinges to the fence across the front of the property, and looked down to see a woman walking up to the house in the dark. I could see the long flowing white robe before I could make out who it was. She walked up onto the porch and I then could see that it was Sara Dalton. I stood unsteadily, a bit off guard. She reached out her hand for mine and said, "Would you go for a walk with me?"

We walked down the boardwalk toward the beach. When the moon came out from behind the clouds the white sand around us glowed in soft focus. We were both walking with bare feet, and when we stepped off the end of the wooden walk the sand was cool and bracing. Sara held my hand and we walked on in silence toward the shore. The wind was blowing almost in a whisper from the north now and pushing offshore, leaving the water nearly mirror calm, the moon reflecting back across the surface toward us.

When we reached the water's edge the sand was firmer from the receding tide, and then Sara turned and came into my arms. We held each other there without speaking, the moon occasionally illuminating us from above as the clouds passed. There was a fresh smell in her hair, a smell of renewal and promise.

I'm not sure how long we stood there together in the sand, but it was one of the most comforting times that I can ever recall. I took so much joy in the knowledge that this woman now had another chance in a life that had been so cruelly taken from her in the past. I felt her squeeze me more tightly for just a moment, and then she looked up and kissed me on the cheek. Then she turned and we walked together back up toward the dunes. When we reached the hotel we stopped and I could just make out the lines of her face in the darkness. I felt her press my hand more tightly one more time before she turned and walked up the steps and closed the door behind her. As I walked home I realized that we hadn't spoken a word to each other the entire time. I turned and looked back at the hotel again, its shadowy edges just barely visible. I felt satisfaction in knowing there was some sense of comfort and peace among those now asleep beneath that roof.

GRAYTON WINDS

In the morning after a quick swim in the Gulf to clear my mind, I returned to work on my book, sitting at the typewriter on the dining table in the Headley's cottage. A cup of steaming coffee rested next to a stack of typed pages, sunlight from the kitchen window brightening the room. The story had taken some unexpected turns, as I suppose is so often the case when the work of writing a novel plays out over time. On this particular morning I found myself writing almost effortlessly, words flowing onto the page, the story unveiling itself before me on the successive blank white pages. There was an underlying excitement in the knowledge that the story was progressing, and the uncertainties of where it might lead were becoming more clear. This would be my first novel, and I took some encouragement in its future potential from the placement of several short stories in literary journals over the past couple of years. A publisher in New York had actually contacted me after reading one of my stories. While he had given me no certain guarantee of publishing the book, he had been very encouraging through the process when I had sent a few chapters for review. I had no grand illusion of publishing fame or success, only a desire to simply tell a good story.

I heard some commotion outside and then there was a soft, almost hesitant knock on the front door, as if someone thought that I might still be sleeping. As I walked over, I could see through the screened door that it was Sara and Melanee. They were both dressed in short pants and their feet were bare. Sara wore a long-sleeved shirt in spite of the growing heat and I, of course, understood that she was trying to hide the traces of her past life, tracked along the veins of her forearms. I opened the door and went out to join them on the porch.

"Good morning, ladies," I said. "You're out calling early today."

"I hope we didn't wake you," little Melanee said, "but we wanted to help you finish painting that fence."

I looked at Sara and we both smiled. My first thought was getting back to the story, but I didn't have the heart to say *no*. "I just happen to have a couple of extra brushes, little lady."

I brought the paint and supplies out from the shed in the back and together, Sara and I helped Melanee put paint to fence. Even in her sightless world, she was obviously taking such pleasure in making the old Headley place look new and shining. Our mockingbird friend, Champ, swooped down and lit on the fence just down from us. He chirped and Melanee jumped up and greeted the little beggar. "Oh Champ, we don't have time to feed you right now. We have to get this work done." The bird seemed to somehow understand and bounded away down the tops of the pickets, and then turned to watch us, remarkably without further protest or screeching requests for a handout.

By mid-day we had finished the work, and the Headley place stood completely renewed before us with a fresh coat of paint and weeds and shrubs pruned over the past weeks. All of us seemed to have more paint on our hands and faces and clothes than had made it onto the picket fence. Lila and Maggie came over toward the end of the project, and they both just shook their heads at the mess we had made.

Lila took her two girls back to the hotel to get them cleaned up. As they were leaving, I thanked them both for their hard work and promised them that I would take them shopping in Panama City to pay them back. Maggie stood with me as we watched them walk away. She put her arm around my waist and pulled me closer.

"Brother, you've done a good thing here," she said.

"What, this old fence?" I said.

She elbowed me in the ribs. "You know what I mean."

"How about some lunch?" I offered. She nodded, and we went inside. After I had cleaned up, I put a spread of sandwiches and fruit on the table, pushing the typewriter and random pages to the side. I noticed Maggie looking out the kitchen window, not paying attention to her food. I asked if she was all right.

"I need to go home, Mathew," she said, and the sadness in her voice was clear. "I spoke to Daddy yesterday and there is still no sign of Desmond."

"If he's smart, he's left the damn country," I said, thinking about the fate that awaited him if my father and his men ever did find my sister's husband.

"I need to find him and put this all behind us. We'll never be together again, but I need to understand what could have led him to do this to the family. He certainly didn't need the money," she said.

"I understand what you're feeling, but I think it's best if you just let it go. Get the family's law firm to do up the paperwork and get the bastard out of your life forever," I said.

She nodded as if accepting my advice, but I knew that Maggie was not one to just walk away from something like this. She had a quiet, inspired tenacity in most everything that she did, from school to the volunteer work that she kept busy with after college, to her fierce competitiveness on a tennis court.

The next morning I said goodbye to my sister as she left Grayton Beach for the long drive back to Atlanta. Again she asked me to come home soon to be with the family. I gave her little encouragement.

Chapter Twenty-two

The days and nights seemed to run endlessly together, a rhythm established in the routines of a life now edged in soft focus between new possibilities, and the old realities of home and family back in Atlanta. It was mid-June in Grayton Beach and the days grew hotter in succession; the only relief a bath in the cold well water or a swim in the Gulf during early morning before the sun brought the temperature back up. In the back of my mind was an ongoing reminder that soon I would have to take some new direction in the affairs of my life. Certainly I would not be able to stay in the Headley's place forever, nor was that ever my intent.

The writing life could perhaps take me off to New York, or some far city, but any possible hope of subsistence from such a course was still only a slim prospect. Returning to Atlanta seemed the last of all options, though my sister had managed to finally plant just the smallest seed of guilt in my mind regarding my hesitance to come back to help the family through difficult times. I had enough money from a family trust fund established when I was quite young, and set to begin paying a steady allowance when I had turned twenty-one. My sister had helped to arrange for checks to be sent to my account at a small bank in Panama City. It was certainly enough to be comfortable, regardless of the direction I took with my life, but I had never planned to be satisfied with such an easy existence, and I cared little if my father chose to cut it off.

My sister Maggie had been gone for a couple of days. I had been able to keep the momentum of my writing going, rarely venturing out since she had left. It was late in the evening when the sun had fallen below the western horizon, and darkness filled the small rooms of the Headley's cottage. I sat at the little table reading over the work that I had completed in the past hours by the light of a kerosene lamp, dressed only in a pair of paint-stained khaki shorts, trying to find some relief from the heat. I heard some low voices out on the street and walked to the door. Light from the moon cast a soft glow over the town, and I could see people coming down the road from the hotel. When I went out on the porch I could see that it was Lila coming up with Sara and Melanee. Lila walked through the gate, and I met her out in the front yard.

I was surprised that she spoke in almost a whisper. "You need to come down to the beach with us. Melanee is certain that the turtles are hatching."

"The turtles?" I asked, with some confusion.

"Yes, the loggerheads. There were tracks to a nest up in the dunes a while back, and now Melanee is sure that they're hatching, and the little turtles are trying to find their way down to the water."

I walked with her out to the street. Sara was standing there holding her daughter's hand.

"Mathew?" I heard Melanee ask.

"I'm right here, kid."

Melanee was whispering too, like the turtles might be able to hear us all the way up in town. "Mathew, we have to go down to the beach. The little turtles are trying to get back to the sea."

I could see her mother Sara's face in soft outline, and she smiled at me with a knowing look.

"What are we waiting for?" I said, and we all started off down to the beach. We walked in the sand, avoiding the boardwalk to be as quiet as possible. Lila told me as we walked that the tracks up into the dunes had been down the beach a few hundred yards to the west. When we got to the waterline we stopped, and looked in both directions. The big moon was rising over Panama City to the east, and sending a bright reflection across the water.

"We have to be very quiet," Melanee said, again in nearly a whisper. "We can't frighten them away from the water."

We started down the beach slowly, looking ahead for any sign of little turtles scurrying about. Lila told me that they would be smaller than my hand, and many might never make it to the water with shore birds often having their way.

Lila walked out ahead of us and back up toward the dunes. We walked on in silence, and then I saw her hold up a hand to get us to slow down. She kneeled down as we walked over carefully, Sara and I both holding Melanee's hands. We all got down next to her, and then she pointed into the soft darkness, the white sand showing starkly against the night. I felt Melanee squeeze my hand more tightly, and then she quietly said, "They're coming, aren't they?"

Lila pointed out ahead, and then I could see this slow mass of tiny dark bodies moving slowly across the light contrast of the sand. We inched a few feet closer, being careful not to interfere with their course, and then we could see them more clearly, dozens of little scurrying critters using their tiny flippers to push through the sand toward the water. I looked around and was pleased to see that none of the pesky seagulls that were constantly hovering above during the day were anywhere to be seen. It would have been pure carnage, but the little things kept on in their instinctual path to the sea, and we were all blessed to be there to see the magical migration.

Sara was speaking quietly to Melanee, describing the scene of the loggerheads to her blind daughter. I watched as the little girl sat there sightlessly, a beaming smile on her face. I seemed to be the only one who was utterly amazed that Melanee had this intuitive notion that the hatch was underway. She reached down every few seconds and picked up a handful of sand, and then let it all run slowly through her open fingers, as if she was sharing the feel of the texture of the beach with the turtles. "Momma, can't we keep just one?" she pleaded.

Sara hugged her close and explained that we needed to let all of them make their way to the water, allowing as many as possible to survive at least this first step of their journey. The water was calm enough that as they began reaching the shore, their little fins flapped harder and they splashed out into the gentle surf, and away into the darkness of the Gulf of Mexico. When the last little turtle was at the shore break, we walked over closer. A small wave came in and swept over it, knocking it onto its back. We waited for a few moments for it to right itself, but it continued to struggle. Sara walked over with Melanee, and they both kneeled by the foundering turtle. She took her daughter's hand and helped her gently pick up the little loggerhead and hold it for a moment near her face, and then she kissed it on the top of its shell before placing it down into the water. And then it was away. We all stood and looked out at the moon-sparkled surface of the water as the turtles made their way out into the current.

Back at the hotel, Melanee had finally been put to bed after what seemed like hours of excited conversation about the turtles. I sat on the porch with Lila, and we sipped a cup of tea together, feeling the slightest breath of wind on our faces as the late evening cooled. The scent of gardenias from the bushes beside the porch was lingering in the air, and even this late, there were bees buzzing around the blossoms. Sara had gone up with her daughter, and now I asked Lila how her recovery was continuing.

"Helen, our nurse, has been wonderful, and she helps Sara through each day," Lila said. "There are some difficult times, and I'm still frightened to death that she could run away again looking for the drugs."

"She seems so much better," I said, trying to be comforting, but also honestly expressing the improvement I had seen in Sara since she had been back in Florida.

"Mr. Palumbo has arranged for Helen to stay with us through the summer, and he told me longer, if necessary. I still can't believe what a saint that old bastard is at times," she said, and shook her head, smiling.

"He's an interesting sort, isn't he?" I replied.

"Helen confided in me the other night and told me that Sara will always be haunted by this terrible addiction, and her mind and body will never be totally free of the craving. It just makes me so sad to think that her life may never be truly free from this poison."

I sat there thinking about the times ahead for Sara Dalton, and hoping that her love for her daughter would overcome the sickness that pulled her in other directions. There would be many more difficult challenges ahead for her trying to raise a daughter who would never be able to see, and totally able to take care of herself. What a burden for a young woman who would have to struggle so hard to keep her own life on track.

We both heard a car off to the left, and I looked over as the headlights illuminated the Headley cottage. It was Palumbo's car, and one of the back doors opened. In the light I could see a woman get out and walk through the gate up to the house. From the striking white hair I could tell that it was Eleanor. I said goodnight to Lila, and walked down the steps and back toward home. She seemed somewhat disturbed about my sudden departure.

Palumbo's car pulled up in front of the hotel, Anthony at the wheel and Willie in the back. He leaned out of the open window. "Brought you a little surprise. Eleanor's been wondering where you've been."

I could smell the whiskey on his breath. I looked inside and Anthony peered calmly ahead, a man of very few words. I thanked Willie for his thoughtful gesture, and continued on down the road. Eleanor was up on the porch sitting in one of the chairs. When I walked up the steps, she came over to me slowly and reached out her arms. We held each other for a while without speaking. I hadn't seen her since returning from New Orleans, but she was often on my mind, and a distraction from my work on the book. I had purposefully stayed away from Panama City to keep my mind focused on the story, and my energy up for the work. She was dressed in a simple sleeveless light dress buttoned up the front. As always, she was a comforting reassurance that there was someone in the world that cared for me simply for the person she knew me to be in Grayton Beach, not my family or their position, or anything else.

Then she spoke quietly in my ear, "Mathew darlin', I thought I was never going to see you again. Did I do something to chase you away?"

We moved over to the chairs and she sat down on my lap, her arms around me and her hair hanging in my face. I told her about the trip to New Orleans, and the work that I had been doing on the book since returning. Then I told her about the turtles earlier that night. She wanted to see for herself, so we walked down to the beach together and along the shore until we came to the tracks in the sand. We followed them back up to the dune line and found the big hole that all those little turtles had crawled from. Looking around in the moonlight there were pieces of egg shells littered about. Eleanor was kneeling beside me, and she reached down into the hole and felt around for a bit, and then she pulled another egg from the sandy nest and held it up for us to examine. It was cracked a bit, and then it moved in her hand and she yelped in surprise. I placed it down in the sand, and we moved back and watched as it continued to twitch and then crack open a little at a time. Eventually the tiny turtle freed itself and lay in the sand, almost seeming to rest and catch its breath as it considered the next leg of its journey; then it was off down the gentle slope of the dune toward the water.

Eleanor took my hand. We sat there quietly watching the turtle move off into the darkness. When it was out of sight she turned and kissed me, and I was caught up in the scent and closeness of her. All thoughts of turtles and books and family dilemmas seemed to drift away on the night air.

In the morning I made breakfast for us and then we made love again, this time on the sofa in the front room, the heat of the day soaking us in a dripping sweat when we lay together at the end. Eleanor had grown accustomed to the unsightly scars and disfigurement of my bad leg. When she asked me about the time away at the War, I had shared very little.

She had brought a small bag with her with a swimsuit. We got dressed and went down to the beach. The wind had come up in a steady blow from the southwest, and the waves had grown to several feet overnight. I thought to myself how fortunate that the turtles had made their way last night during the period of calm seas. We walked arm in arm out into the surf, and the cool chill of it was wonderful as we fell together into the waves. We both came up from under the clear surface of the water. Eleanor's hair was smoothed back away from her face, and tiny droplets of salt water hung on her eyelashes. I kissed both of her eyes. She laughed and pushed me away, and dove out into the next coming wave. I followed her and we swam out to the first sand bar. The water was then only up to our waists, so we walked into the coming waves, holding on to each other so we wouldn't be knocked over with each rising swell.

The beach was deserted in both directions as far as we could see, and the sun was now up an hour or so over the horizon. We made our way back to shore and sat together just beyond the water's break in the wet sand from the high tide. Eleanor rested her head on my shoulder and shivered some from the chill of the wind. I had my arm around her waist. No words were needed at that point. There was just a moment and a morning to be shared.

Chapter Twenty-three

Sheriff Lucas Crowe came into town later that day. I saw him walking with Lila Dalton down to the beach as Eleanor and I were heading back to the house. When they came up to us in the sand, I said hello and introduced Eleanor Whitlock to both of them as my friend from Panama City. I noticed that she squeezed my arm a bit more tightly, and looked at me with an annoyed expression that she clearly would have liked to be introduced as more than a *friend*. Crowe was friendly and cordial in the presence of this beautiful woman, but Lila was again cool and distant. It was clear that she disapproved of my relationship with Eleanor. Lila had become a good friend, and we had been through a lot together in a very short time, but I was getting close to telling her that none of this was any of her damn business. I explained to Crowe that Eleanor worked at Palumbo's club in Panama City, and the sheriff looked at her with an even greater interest.

Sensing that all of this was extremely awkward, I tried to move the conversation in a different direction. "Sheriff, how are you coming with the Howard boy's case?"

The peace officer stood more upright, as if he was now officially on duty, and considered his comments for a few moments before he hesitantly said, "Actually, there are a couple of new developments." He declined to elaborate, but said that some new information had recently presented itself, and he was following up on the leads.

Seeing that this was going nowhere new, I told Eleanor that Lila Dalton was the owner and manager of the Beach Hotel, which she seemed to think was extremely exciting. She went on asking Lila question after question about the operation. Lila reluctantly indulged her, and I pulled Crowe aside and asked, "Lucas, really, what can you tell me about Seth?"

"The kid had more enemies than you can ever imagine," he replied. "That's all I can honestly tell you just now."

Lila and Eleanor had finished their exchange. Lucas Crowe took Lila's hand and they continued on to the beach. As Eleanor and I walked back up to the road to the Headley's place, we saw Sara and Melanee up on my porch. *More awkward introductions*, was all I could think, as Eleanor and I walked up to join them. Again, I introduced Eleanor as my *friend*, and again I received the expected pinch on the arm. Sara Dalton was quite pleasant, and explained that her daughter had wanted to come over to feed my little bird friend, Champ. Not unexpectedly, Champ was ever present on the porch rail and Melanee was excitedly handing him tiny morsels of broken bread crumbs. Then the bird squawked at me like I was interfering with his feeding schedule.

Eleanor broke the uncomfortable moment among us all by saying, "Sara, we just met your mother and her boyfriend, the sheriff, going down to the beach."

Sara nodded. Her face remained impassive and emotionless as she answered, "The sheriff has been a good friend."

I also sensed that Sara was trying too hard to be cordial, and then her daughter made everything even more prickly by asking, "So Mathew, do you really love her?" Her comment caught me off guard. I wasn't ready to answer, certainly not under the present circumstances.

"Do I love Eleanor?" I said, repeating the question to gather more time to either bail myself out, or figure how to change the subject. I noticed that everyone was paying close attention to what my answer might be. My heart and my mind were racing to actually answer the question for myself. Certainly I was attracted to and enjoyed being with Eleanor Whitlock, but was there more to it than that? In my heart I knew that I had been in love before, and I knew the intensity of the emotion. There was something different here, not necessarily better or worse, just different. The feelings for a young nurse in France had faded only a little over the past years; the raw memories of my short time with Hanna Wesley still vivid and painful. Finally, without really knowing the consequences of my words, I said, "Yes, I do love Eleanor, she's a wonderful girl."

Sara looked at me and managed a smile, and I tried to read the expression on little Melanee's face, but she turned away toward Champ to feed him another crumble of bread. Eleanor, on the other hand, responded with a grand show of affection, and a big hug and kiss on my cheek.

Sara reached for her daughter's hand. "We really need to go, sweetie," she said. Melanee protested, but Sara was insistent that they needed to get back over to the hotel to help with the lunch preparations. I watched the two of them walk off, and my thoughts were mixed emotions of delight that they were together and that Melanee had been reunited with her mother, but also a lingering sadness that even together, they were still mostly alone in the world, and both had a difficult road ahead.

Eleanor had to be back at work that night at Palumbo's club, and I offered to drive her into town. Along the way we spoke occasionally about passing sights or things happening at the club, but nothing about my earlier expression of *love*, which I found both troubling and relieving at the same time. I really didn't want to explore the sentiment expressed in any more detail, at least for now. I did find myself looking over at this woman next to me, and in one moment being totally mesmerized by the loveliness of her face and the incredible proportions of her bare legs stretching out from the hem of her dress on the car's seat; while in the next, thinking that I really knew very little about her. We seemed to be plunging too fast into this *relationship*. Again I thought of Hanna and how certain I had been about my emotions and feelings for her, right up until I realized how misguided that had been. *So how did I really feel about Eleanor Whitlock?* Passion and love can prove to be far different fellows, as I had learned in previous affairs of the heart. In the end, before we pulled up in front of her house, I rationalized in my mind that why shouldn't I take comfort in the arms of this woman? If all of the emotions around that weren't terribly clear right at that moment, certainly all such things would sort themselves out eventually.

I walked Eleanor to the door and we kissed goodbye.

"Can you stay in town tonight?" she asked.

"Sure, I'll see you down at the club later," I said, and she kissed me again before going inside.

I drove down the beach road in Panama City, looking out at the few shops and small hotels along the way and people walking along the road. Having been away from Atlanta for so many months, even this little town was beginning to seem crowded and bustling; the flurry of activity certainly a contrast to the tranquil existence I now lived in Grayton Beach.

One of the shops along the strip suddenly caught my attention, and I hit the brakes hard and turned into the parking area. I walked through the door of the storefront, and my senses were assaulted by the sounds and smells of animals of all sorts. The pet shop seemed abandoned, other than the many furry, feathery and finny creatures that all seemed to react wildly to my arrival. Then a little man came out through a curtain in the back. He was quite small actually, barely able to see above the counter that he now came around. His hair was graying, nearly white in fact, and thinly sparsed across the sunburned dome of his head. The features of his face reminded me of a dog breed, a specific name and breed that escaped me. *A boxer perhaps,* I thought later. Heavy jowls on the sides of his face seemed to pull his lower lip down revealing an uneven line of stained teeth. When he spoke, the animals seemed to calm and listen as well. "You look like you need some assistance," he offered.

A short while later I walked out of the store with exactly what I had hoped to find.

When I arrived at Palumbo's later that night, the place was characteristically packed to the seams with people of all walks of life; many I now recognized from my previous visits. Palumbo was holding court as usual at his regular table over in the corner, a position that afforded him a clear view of who was coming and going. His bodyguard, Anthony, was standing near the door again, making sure that all was safe and secure for his notorious boss. I decided to leave Palumbo to his entourage and I sat down at the bar. Eleanor noticed me come in. She came over and greeted me affectionately. All I could think was that she would jeopardize her tips for the evening if she aligned herself too publicly with me in the club. She hurried away to one of her tables. My drink came and I sipped at the whiskey, looking at my face in the mirror behind the bar. Then there was another face there beside me, and I turned to see Sheriff Lucas Crowe standing next to my stool. I held my hands out as if to be cuffed and said, "I confess, I've been drinking some very good hooch. Are you going to take me away?"

Crowe laughed hard, and then looked around at the club and all its patrons. "I don't have near enough handcuffs, son."

"Is it appropriate for me to offer to buy an officer of the law a drink, under the circumstances of the Volstead Act, and your duty vows and such?"

He didn't laugh this time, and simply said, "Just buy me a damn drink, Coulter." When it was delivered and he had taken a thirsty draw from the cup, he looked out across the crowd again, his eyes coming to rest on Palumbo. "Your friend and his ape over there," he said, now glancing toward Anthony, "seem to have extremely solid stories for their whereabouts during the time that Seth Howard was killed."

I was honestly relieved to hear that Willie Palumbo was no longer a suspect, but the sheriff's next comment nearly knocked me off my stool. "I do know that Mr. Palumbo's wife had been having a little action on the side with the Howard boy." I tried not to overreact, and struggled to seem surprised. "Yeah, he was banging Palumbo's wife," the sheriff said. "If the old crook didn't kill Howard, he sure as hell would have if he'd found out. I also heard about the fight they had down at the beach during the engagement party."

I assumed that Lila had finally decided to share all that she knew about the situation. I thought immediately how critical it was that Palumbo never learn of her role in giving this information to the police. I had to trust that Crowe would be discreet. I asked the obvious question, "So you're sure that Palumbo had nothing to do with this?"

Crowe nodded in the affirmative as he took another sip from his drink. "You probably know that Howard and his dad were running moonshine." I shook my head *no*. "Yeah, guess there wasn't enough money just raising those damn pigs. I got several families across the county making shine. None really appreciate the work of the others, if you know what I mean."

"So you think the liquor business got him killed?" I asked.

"Pretty damn good chance." Then Eleanor walked up. I watched as Crowe made room, and then took a long appraising look up and down. "Well, hello Miss Whitlock," he said, taking her hand. I was surprised that he remembered her name. Eleanor smiled back, and then I noticed she was trying to get her hand back from the sheriff. When she managed to free herself, she told us that Palumbo wanted us to come over and join him at his table, and then she was off again.

Crowe finished his drink in one long swallow. "I gotta go." I could see why he wasn't particularly interested in socializing with Palumbo. "Give the old bastard my regards," he said, and then he walked toward the door. I watched as Anthony stepped aside slowly for him to leave the club. Then I looked over at Palumbo. He was watching me, and nodded with his head for me to come over. When I reached the table he pushed out a chair next to him. As I was sitting down, a young couple who had been sitting there had gotten up to leave. They lifted their glasses in a toast to Palumbo as they walked away.

"How you doing, son?" he asked, and didn't wait for an answer before he continued. "Keeping some interesting company these days." He was looking at the door that Sheriff Lucas Crowe had just departed through.

"Crowe tells me that he's convinced you had nothing to do with Seth Howard."

"He better damn well believe it," Palumbo said.

"Did you know that Seth and his old man were running moonshine?" I asked.

"Shit yes," he responded with a snort and a laugh. "Damn amateurs, but yeah, I even brought a little of their supply into the club, but it ain't worth a damn." He wiggled in his seat to get more comfortable, and then he leaned close. "Been looking for you, Mathew. My friends in Atlanta got in touch with me today. They've got a line on your sister's husband up there. Seems he took off to Miami. They know where he's staying down there."

I looked at the old gangster, and just had to marvel at the reach of his contacts and connections. I tried to remain calm as I thought about Desmond Raye on the run in Miami.

"You should let me talk to your old man," Palumbo said. "He and I can work out the details on this. That sonofabitch, Raye, will have his ass back in Atlanta served up on a platter in no time."

As I listened to Palumbo's offer of assistance I had to ask, "Willie, why are you going out of your way like this?"

"What, you don't want my help?" he said with an irritated growl.

"Don't misunderstand. I appreciate what you're doing, but don't you have enough going on to keep you busy?"

Palumbo smiled and looked out across his crowded club. "It's business, kid," he said. "I've always got time for business."

As the evening progressed and the liquor continued to flow, the prospects of spending the night here in town with Eleanor Whitlock seemed even more attractive. While Palumbo continued to chat away about this and that, I couldn't help but watch her work the room, moving gracefully among the crowded tables, laughing with the customers and slapping away hands that tried to get a little too friendly. The tip jar that she carried on her tray was spilling over with bills. Occasionally she would stop to check on us, and usually whisper something in my ear about what she had planned for us later that night back at her place. She was just walking away again when I noticed one of the bartenders coming up to Palumbo and handing him a note. He unfolded it and read the message, and then turned to me with a different expression. Suddenly the jovial look on his face faded, and he leaned over to speak to me above the din of the crowd. "Your sister's on the phone in the back, kid. Sounds like your old man's sick."

A few minutes later I found myself in the backseat of Palumbo's car, Anthony up front driving us out of town. Palumbo had offered to have his man take me to Tallahassee to try to catch a train into Atlanta in the morning.

When I had picked up the phone it was difficult to hear, and Maggie was crying, but eventually she was able to tell me that my father had been found slumped over his desk unconscious earlier that evening. She was down at the hospital with our mother. The doctors seemed to think that he had suffered a severe stroke. They had been able to stabilize him, but he had still not regained consciousness. I didn't hesitate for a moment in telling Maggie that I would be there as soon as I could.

Eleanor had seen me heading toward the door and stopped me. When I explained what had happened, I was surprised to see her eyes well up, and then a tear fall down her cheek. I asked if she would take care of my car and the present I had purchased earlier that day. She hugged me and said that she would miss me, and to please hurry back as soon as I could. The taste of her kiss was still lingering as I looked out at the lights of Panama City fading behind us.

Chapter Twenty-four

    Maggie met me at the train station in downtown Atlanta the next day. It was nearly five in the afternoon, and the long trip had been dreadful from the beginning. The summer heat intensified inside the tight cabin of the train, and even with all of the windows down, it was stifling. As we pulled through one small town after another, and on through endless farms and hilly woodlands across southern Georgia, I kept thinking about my father and how we had left things between the two of us. My emotions reached from deep sadness and fear that he may die and that we would never be able to make it right between us, to a guilty feeling of acceptance that the old bastard had got what was coming to him.

    In the waiting room at the hospital, which was just a mile from our home, we met my mother who had not slept since they had brought my father in. She looked a terrible mess, and the fear in her eyes was unsettling to see. After long embraces and tears, she said, "He's been showing some improvement. He opened his eyes an hour ago, and seems to be aware when people are in the room." She paused. "But he still hasn't been able to speak or even react to anyone."

    Maggie led me down a long corridor, and a nurse who was working on some papers outside my father's room nodded that it was okay for us to go in. The room was dimly lit with the shades pulled down tight. The antiseptic smell of the place was overpowering. My mother and sister stood back as I walked up to the bed. My father was lying there with his eyes closed, a sheet covering only his lower half, as the room was terribly hot. I was startled to see that his face looked as if it had aged ten years overnight and his skin had a gray, ashen cast. I reached out slowly and placed my hand on his arm. It was cool and clammy feeling. I leaned in close and whispered, "Pop, I'm here. It's Mathew."

His body stirred some, and then I watched as his eyes opened slowly like he had barely enough energy to lift his eyelids. At first he looked straight up at the ceiling, but then very slowly his gaze turned toward me. Our eyes met, and he just stared at me with no change of expression for a few moments. I squeezed his hand and said again, "I'm here, Pop."

The deep wrinkles along the outer edges of his eyes seemed to tighten, and then one corner of his mouth started to quiver. He was able to will it to turn up just ever so little to show a weak smile. Then I could feel the weak grip of his hand tighten some. It looked like he was trying to speak, but couldn't find enough energy to form the words. I pulled up a chair and sat down next to the bed, taking his hand again. Maggie and my mother said that they would go find something for us to eat.

I ended up spending the entire night sitting there by the bed, and woke the next morning with my head lying on the sheet next to my father. When I realized where I was, I tried to stand. A pain shot through my neck and back from the odd angle that I had slept. I managed to stretch out the kinks, and looked down at my father who was still asleep. Through the night and fitful periods of dozing, I kept thinking about what this all meant to the family and to the business. My brother Jess was sadly gone, and my father's other lieutenant, his son-in-law Desmond Raye, had turned on us all. Maggie and my mother had never shown any interest in the business, which ultimately led this trail of management succession back to me. I found myself racked with guilt when I thought angrily about where all of this had now put me. The last place I ever wanted to be was moving into the position and responsibilities of my father. I had absolutely no interest, and after the events before I had left Atlanta, I was sure in my conviction that I would never be a part of that world again. It wasn't just my abhorrence of the violence that now seemed to inundate my father's world, but oddly, some vague notion that all of this was just so needless. Yet, how could I abandon my family at a time like this? What kind of man would just walk away and say, *sorry, not interested*?

Later, Maggie convinced both my mother and me to go home for a break. Coming up the long drive through the trees to the big house sent memories running through my mind. I saw Jess dancing with Hanna Wesley that night at the party in our backyard; my father and his bodyguard attacking the man down at the gazebo by the creek; and later when I had watched my brother coming out of Hanna's apartment after they had slept together. I had been gone for over three months, but it seemed like I had been away for years. So much had happened. So much had changed.

After a shower, which helped me to recover some from the long trip and night at my father's bedside, I found a closet full of clothes in my old room. Wandering around, the bedroom felt strange as I looked at the books and things arranged on shelves and dressers that at one time had been so familiar, but now seemed a part of a life so many distant years away.

I found my sister sitting out on the back veranda with a pitcher of cold sweet tea. She told me that Mother had gone up to get some sleep. I sat down beside her and poured a drink, the cold glass sweating in the heat of early evening. The sun was down below the far tree line giving us some relief. All signs of the party from my last time out on this porch were, of course, gone now and the large yard was eerily quiet and deserted. Random chatter from birds up in the trees was all that broke the stillness of the place.

I told Maggie that Palumbo's contacts had found Desmond hiding out down in Miami, and that he had offered his help in bringing him back. I watched as my sister looked blankly out over the big lawn, and didn't seem to react. I reached over and touched her arm and said, "Maggie, did you hear what I said?"

She turned to look at me. There was so much sadness in her eyes, and they were red and moist. When she spoke, it was barely above a whisper. "Mathew, all of this is just incredibly sad, and I feel like everything that we've known is slipping away." She pulled a handkerchief from a pocket and dabbed at her eyes. "As far as I'm concerned, my *former* husband can go straight to hell, and I don't care if he ever comes back." Then the tears overwhelmed her. She covered her face with her hands.

I placed a hand on her shoulder and felt her gentle sobs. "Let's worry about him later," I said. "I'm sorry, but I had to tell you." She nodded back and sniffed loudly, trying to swallow back the tears, and then she wiped her face with the hankie as she gathered herself.

"Mathew, I know it's not fair to ask you to do anything at this point, but I'm terribly afraid of what's going to happen to this family," she said, her voice now more composed. "What if Daddy never gets any better?"

I slept off and on through the night in my old bed, images of my life in Atlanta flashing across my mind; school and old friends, familiar places, better times with my brother and family. Then I would find myself drifting back to even more recent memories of the Florida coast, the people I had become close with and the places that were now becoming as familiar as even my home here in Atlanta. The song that Melanee and her mother, Sara, had sung together that night at the little Beach Hotel became stuck in my half awake brain, and the melody echoed within me as I lay in the quiet room.

In the morning, our cook, Velma Harold, had a big breakfast waiting for all of us. When my mother joined Maggie and I at the dining room table there was a brief moment when all seemed right again. But those reassuring feelings soon faded as we began to talk about my father and the problems we were facing.

Velma came back in to let us know that a visitor had arrived, my father's friend and business confidant, the police captain, Charles Watermann. My mother sent Velma back to show the man in. Watermann was an imposing figure, standing several inches over six feet and built full in the chest so it looked like he had taken a deep breath and never let it out. He came into the room and walked over to my mother, and then expressed his regrets at my father's situation. She offered him a seat, and he nodded to both Maggie and me as he sat down.

"I just stopped over at the hospital," he said in a heavy South Georgia drawl. "Sam is a tough old bastard. Please excuse my language, ladies." Velma put a cup of coffee down in front of him, and he sipped at it. "The doc says that he's showing some improvement," he said, taking my mother's hand. She tried to smile but didn't answer, and just looked across the table and out the windows into the woods beside the house. "I wanted to let you all know that you don't have to worry about the business. Sam and I worked very closely together, and I can certainly help to keep things afloat until he's feeling better," he said. "Of course Mathew, you are welcome to get involved at any level you feel inclined."

I bristled as I sat there and listened to this man position himself in the business of our family. Of course he was here to help when there was so much money on the table at stake. I really didn't know Watermann well, although my father had always placed considerable trust in the man. But, I had to wonder how trustworthy a crooked cop could be. In a way it would be a relief to have someone else take on the burden of my father's affairs. "Captain Watermann," I said slowly, my point of view on all of this still forming slowly in my mind, "it is very thoughtful of you to stop by today, and we really do appreciate your offer of support."

"Son, your father has been my closest friend for twenty years. I owe him an awful lot," Watermann said. "You can rest assured that we will do everything we can to cover for him now."

By the reference to *we*, I had to assume that he was speaking of other members of the Atlanta Police Department who were in his employ, and also my father's payroll. "We need to go over to the hospital now and check in on him," I said. "Do you think we could meet later to discuss all of this?"

"Of course, Mathew. Whenever it's convenient for you." I thanked him and we shook hands before he gave his best to my mother and sister, and then left.

An hour later we were all walking into the hospital, when I froze in total astonishment. Sitting in the lobby with a newspaper and a cigar was Willie Palumbo. Anthony sat beside him reading another section of the newspaper. Palumbo hadn't seen us yet and I walked over, still amazed that the man had found us up here in Atlanta, and then wondering why.

"Willie," I said and he looked up from the paper, and then stood quickly.

"Hello, kid."

"What the hell are you doing here?" I asked.

"Well, I just thought that you would need a friend at a time like this."

"How'd you get here?"

"Caught the train last night out of Tallahassee," he answered. "Just got in a few minutes ago. Got a taxi up from the station. How's your old man?"

I told him the latest we knew on his condition, and then took him over to meet my mother. Maggie of course recognized him from her visit to Grayton Beach, and she smiled as we walked up. "Good morning, Mr. Palumbo. How nice of you to stop by," she said with a smile, and more than an edge of sarcasm.

Palumbo took her hand and bowed slightly, and then turned to my mother. "Mrs. Coulter, it's a pleasure to meet you, and I'm so sorry about your husband. I do hope he's doing better today."

"Mother, this is a friend from Florida, Willie Palumbo," I said.

"Mr. Palumbo," my mother said formally, and then shook his hand. "You will excuse me please. I would like to go up to see my husband."

"Of course, of course," Palumbo said. "I certainly hope they have brighter news for you this morning."

My sister walked away down the hall with my mother, and I told them I would be up in a few minutes. I turned to Palumbo. "Willie, really, what the hell...?"

"Mathew, I got to thinking about all you would be facing with your father's health, and all the other issues he's been dealing with."

"Well, I do appreciate your efforts to get up here. That train ride's a bitch." Palumbo laughed and pulled me over to sit where he had left his newspaper. In spite of an all-night ride on an old train, he looked as refreshed as if he'd been relaxing at the beach for a week. His standard suit of clothes and starched shirt even looked pressed... and where had he managed to shave? I sat down beside him, and the thought occurred to me that a lot of people were suddenly coming to our aid. *Probably had nothing to do with my father running one of the most lucrative liquor networks in the South*, I thought.

"Had another interesting visitor this morning," I told Palumbo, and then went on to describe the visit of the police captain, Charles Watermann, and his similar offers of assistance. Palumbo squirmed in his seat a bit, and looked around the room. We were alone except for a nurse up at the check-in desk.

Palumbo leaned close and said, "I know of this Watermann guy. He's highly placed and very well-connected. He's close to your old man, right?"

I nodded. Palumbo let all of this sink in for a while, and then said, "Why don't you go up and see your father, and then when you get a few minutes, I'd like to go for a walk and discuss some important business."

I decided not to get into any of the discussion at that point. I really needed to get upstairs. I told him I'd be back when I could, and that if he needed a place to stay he could have Anthony run him up West Paces Ferry Road a mile to our house on the left, and that he was welcome to stay with us. He was very appreciative of the offer, but said that he would wait for now in the lobby, and for me to obviously take as much time as I needed with my father. I walked away from Palumbo thinking through all of the possible angles he was working.

In my father's room the blinds were open this time, and the light filtered in and lifted the overall mood of the place. He was sitting up on several pillows against the wall, and the color seemed to be returning to his face, although his arms rested limply at his side, and he was still unable to speak or even turn his head to acknowledge me when I came in. I walked over and took his hand, and again he tried weakly to smile. He managed a low grunting sound. I just nodded and held his hand more tightly with both of mine. I looked over at my mother and Maggie who were standing at the foot of the bed talking to a doctor. I knew very little if anything about the recovery from a stroke of this magnitude, but it seemed clear that it would be a very long time before my father was anything near the man he used to be.

An hour later my father was asleep again. The doctors informed us that he had obviously made a little progress overnight, but that the recovery would be long and difficult; that it was quite likely that he would never walk again, and that his speech would be impaired at best. It was a sobering discussion that left all of us teary-eyed and worried. Maggie wanted to stay with my mother as long as she needed to be at the hospital, but my curiosity with Palumbo got the best of me. I explained that I was going to take him and Anthony back to the house to get settled in. My mother was too tired to even consider protesting the presence of company at this point, and in fact our house had always been open to guests of the family, sometime for prolonged periods, often to the dismay of my father.

I drove Palumbo and Anthony back to our house in Maggie's car, a sporty roadster that was much too small for Anthony to be comfortable in the back, but he managed without protest. It occurred to me that I hadn't heard him speak more than an occasional grunt since I'd first met him. Velma greeted us and arranged for our guest's few bags to be taken upstairs. I led them both through the house and out back to the lawn, and then down a path through the woods. Anthony walked a dozen yards behind us, ever mindful of security for his boss. Finally Palumbo got down to the discussion he had promised.

"Mathew, with all due respect for your father and his present condition, your family is terribly vulnerable at this time. This is a dirty business and assholes from far and wide will see this as an opportunity to move in." He paused for a moment, I suppose to let his words of warning sink in. "As you know, I have many contacts here in Atlanta and I have a very good feel for the nature of the business… not so different from what we're running up in New Jersey."

It occurred to me that somehow he was still managing to keep his power over the enterprise to the north, and I marveled at his ability to keep everything apparently under control. "Will you ever be able to go back home?" I asked.

"It's still a little hot up there. There are more than a few federal and local authorities that would love to put my ass away for a very long time," he said. "Fortunately, I have some good people, including my two sons." It was the first time that he had mentioned his family. It made me realize how little I knew about this man.

We reached the gazebo down by the stream where I had watched my father and his man beat a person nearly to death. As we walked up on the platform I looked to see if the blood was still evident on the planking of the deck, but it seemed to have been cleaned away.

Palumbo came up next to me and stood at a railing, looking off into the dark woods. "Mathew, I am in a position to do your family a considerable favor."

"And what would that be?" I asked, very unsettled about what he could possibly be ready to offer.

"The Coulters are accustomed to living a very fine life," he said, looking out across our vast property in the middle of the north edges of Atlanta. "Your father and all of you have worked very hard to earn what you have, and you deserve to continue to enjoy the fruits of those efforts."

"Willie, what are you talking about?" I finally said, trying to get him to come to the point.

"With a substantial sum of money invested in the accounts of you and your family, now and in perpetuity, I can assure you a life that will be free of worry and labor, and free of this dirty liquor business once and for all."

I had considered several possibilities, but I was shocked at what he was proposing. "You want to buy us out?" I said, totally flabbergasted at what he was proposing.

"Think about it, son. I doubt that your father will ever be in a condition to allow him the strength needed to run this operation, and with your older brother gone now, the bloodsuckers like Watermann are already moving in," he said. "I know how you feel about all of this, and that it's the last thing that you ever want to be involved with."

My mind was spinning with the implications of what he was proposing, but foremost was the disbelief that Palumbo could simply step in and take over. What would Watermann and other powerful members of the system here in Atlanta do in reaction? I looked into Palumbo's eyes and saw the same resolute confidence and assurance. Finally I had to ask, "How do you propose to simply walk into a town like this and take over a business and a network that has taken my father decades to build? Watermann won't just step aside and give you a key to the city."

Palumbo laughed his self-assured and jolly laugh, and I was amazed again at his confident air. "Watermann is only about the money, and that's the easiest damn thing to take care of. He'll be *my* new best friend tomorrow if we move forward with all of this."

I wasn't so sure about Watermann or any of the other power brokers in town that my father had worked with for so many years to establish his current position. "And what if you fail, Willie?" I asked. "Where does that leave my mother and Maggie?"

He looked at me for the longest time, and was just nodding his head slowly up and down. Then he said, "Son, we've known each other for only a short time, but I hope you've come to know that, in spite of the nature of my business, I'm a very loyal man… loyal to my family and to my friends, and I will do whatever it takes to care for them and protect them." I thought back to our raid on Boudreaux's club in New Orleans to pull Sara Dalton out of the hell that she had been trapped in. Before I could speak he went on to say, "What you may not know is that I'm also a very successful businessman, and I have resources beyond your imagination. Even if something didn't happen to work out right here in Atlanta, and trust me, I don't fail; I would still keep my obligations to you and your family."

It was this last comment that got me to thinking that in agreeing to Palumbo's proposition, I would be committing my family to a life beholden to a gangster, regardless of how successful he may be now or in the future. But then it also occurred to me that my father was cut from the same cloth now that Prohibition had sent him to the far side of the law. Was there really any difference in the arrangement? As I quickly thought through the implications, I realized that the only true disparity in all of this would be that my family and I would no longer have to deal with the ugly world of bootleggers and contraband whiskey. It seemed a convenient rationalization at that moment.

"I'm sure you've got a good family lawyer, kid," Palumbo said. "We can make this as ironclad and legal as you want. The first issue, however, will be making sure that we have *power of attorney* for your father."

It was all sinking in and frankly, it seemed too easy, which was always a trigger point for worry as far as I was concerned. Doing business with the devil always leads to the same fiery destination.

"Willie," I said, "I appreciate what you're trying to do here, but you need to understand that this is a huge decision for the family and with my father incapacitated, I just don't know how quickly we can even begin to consider such a thing."

Palumbo didn't hesitate for a moment and said, "I'm telling you kid that the sharks are in the water and they smell blood. You don't have the luxury of time to sit back and ponder. I know this is a big decision and you're caught in the middle here. What I would suggest is that we get your mother and Maggie together for dinner tonight, if and when they get back from the hospital, and allow me some time to explain all of this in more detail for all of you."

I took a deep breath and tried to balance my concern for trading away the family's legacy, as jaded as it had more recently become, with my elation for a possible escape from having to try to run the damn enterprise.

"Fair enough," I finally said.

A week later, my father had been moved to a recovery home where he would receive constant care for his rehabilitation, as limited as it appeared that it would be. The doctors were now even more pessimistic about the ultimate state of his quality of life in the future. It appeared that his mind was slowly recovering, but his body and speech would probably never come back even close to fully functional. He was still unable to talk or move even his fingers, so communication was impossible although he seemed to understand some of what we would discuss with him.

Palumbo had stated his case to Maggie and my mother that night at dinner after we had discussed the arrangement down at the gazebo. Surprisingly, both of them were more than open to the proposition. I suppose all of us were looking for a way out of the dilemma that we faced. I learned later that night from my sister that the family's banker had paid a recent visit following my father's stroke. He had informed our mother that the family's accounts were at dangerously low levels, and that my father was far overextended. Apparently his efforts to carry on the illusion of prosperity had been fueled by excessive optimism in future receipts. Suddenly Palumbo's proposal took on a more immediate sense of urgency.

I spoke to my father one morning when he seemed more lucid, and I explained in great detail about who Willie Palumbo was, and what he was proposing. His face seemed impassive throughout my explanation, and his eyes looked at mine with a blank and expressionless stare.

Chapter Twenty-five

It was several weeks later before I was back in Grayton Beach at the Headley place. Palumbo had stayed on to work through the transition of power and frankly, I truly believed that he would be there for months trying to grease all the right palms to keep the business on track. My father had shown very little improvement, and would likely be in the recovery home for months, if not more.

Both my mother and sister had agreed to the settlement that Palumbo had put on the table, and my mother did indeed have *power of attorney* for my father in the event that, as the lawyers described it, *he may become incapacitated or die*, of which fortunately only the former had actually occurred. The financial offer that Palumbo had made was staggering, and the first installment was deposited as promised on schedule. This initial down payment on the business transition was enough money for all of my family to live out the rest of their lives in easy comfort, although I chose to accept none of the compensation. It was actually a bit troubling to think that my father's nefarious business was worth so much, and I couldn't help but worry that they would all be living on blood money from a gangster for the rest of their lives. Yet how different was this from the standard of living that my father had been providing for all these years.

On the trip back I had also started to think about where my life was headed. Sticking my head in the sand down along the sleepy Gulf Coast was an interesting consideration, and one that held some appeal at that moment. My family was cared for better than could ever have been expected. I certainly had enough money from the family trust fund for me to buy my own place to get settled in more comfortably. I cared about the friends I had made along the beach, the Daltons and the Bidwells. I imagined that Palumbo would be back down as his business and flight from the law required or allowed. And of course, there was Eleanor Whitlock to help keep me warm at night. I had been thinking more about my somewhat forced declaration of love for the woman that day on the Headley's porch with Melanee and Sara. When someone fills your mind and your absent thoughts as much as Eleanor had these past weeks back in Atlanta, surely there must be something there, I thought.

Palumbo had arranged for a car to drive me back to Grayton Beach from Tallahassee, and on that last leg of the journey I also started thinking about the tenuous recovery of Sara Dalton. I hadn't spoken to anyone down there since I had left, and there was a nagging fear in the back of my mind that Sara may have succumbed to the death grip of her demons and the drugs, and perhaps even run away again. The car pulled into Grayton Beach late on a Saturday evening, just before dark, and as we drove by the Beach Hotel, I scanned the front porch and inside looking for Sara. There were a few summer guests sitting out and conversing, but no sign of any of the Dalton family. With dinner cleared it was possible that they were down at the pavilion at the beach with some of the other guests, a ritual I had found that was observed on most weekend nights through the busy season. Grayton Beach and the Gulf Coast were surprisingly more of a summer destination, rather than winter when the migration was to South Florida for the more tropical weather along Palm Beach and down to Miami. In the summer, more and more families from Birmingham and Montgomery and over in Atlanta were coming down to the Gulf beaches to find some escape from the heat, with somewhat cooler breezes and the water, of course.

I had brought a few more things with me on this trip back from Atlanta, some clothes and books mostly. After unloading and tipping the driver for his trouble I made a drink, and then walked down through the dunes to the beach. There was a crowd of a dozen people milling around the pavilion, drinks in hand. The small quartet that Lila occasionally hired out of Point Washington was setting up to play dance music. Lanterns were lit along the corners, and there was a beautiful light cast across the gathering revelers. Then I saw Lila over talking to some guests. When she saw me, she excused herself and came rushing over. I scanned the crowd looking for Sara and her daughter, but they were not around. Lila came up breathlessly and gave me a giant hug. Some of the new guests that didn't know me looked on in surprise.

"Well, isn't this a nice welcome home," I said.

"We've missed you, boy," she answered, and then kissed me on both cheeks. She had a big glowing smile on her face that reassured me some that everything was okay with her family. As usual on a big summer night, she was dressed extravagantly in a beautiful long dress and all of the appropriate accessories.

"Where are the girls?" I asked. She looked down at the beach and pointed, and I could see them now. Sara was walking along the waterline with her little daughter, who had a big long-handled net in her hands, helping her to catch blue crabs in the shore break. "Everyone's all right?" I asked, almost afraid to hear the answer.

"They're fine, Mathew," she said to my great relief, and then she asked me about my father and Maggie, and how everything was going back in Atlanta. I took a few minutes to fill her in on my family and my father's health, although I certainly left out the particulars of our recent deal with Palumbo.

"I'm so sorry to hear about your father," she said. "I hope that he'll be comfortable and continue to improve."

"It's going to be a long road back," I said, and the familiar sadness returned again that came with the images of my father lying lifeless in a bed, unable to move or speak. I excused myself and told Lila that I wanted to go down to see Sara and Melanee. The present that I had bought for Melanee back in Panama City before I had to leave so suddenly for Atlanta was hopefully still under the care of Eleanor, who had agreed to look after it when I left.

As usual, Melanee sensed my approach before she could have possibly heard me coming. She turned from her work scraping along the beach with the net at her mother's direction and yelled out, "Mathew, that's you isn't it, Mathew?"

I called out and said hello, and then hurried down and picked her up. I gave her a big hug. Sara stood there smiling at us, and I was pleased to see that her face still had that new healthy flush of color in her cheeks that had returned with her continued recovery.

"Mathew, look at the crabs we've caught," Melanee said, and she wiggled with excitement for me to put her down so that she could take me over to the pail. Indeed there were a half dozen little blue crabs crawling about inside, each trying to climb on top of the others to attempt to get out of their confinement. I turned to Sara and she came over and welcomed me as well with a warm hug. She smelled of fresh flowers, and I saw that both of the girls had blossoms stuck in their hair.

"Welcome home," she said, and I had to stop and think for just a moment that indeed this was my new home, although my existence still seemed tentative and uncertain. She asked about my father and of Maggie. I told them both about what had transpired back in Atlanta.

Then Melanee said with sudden impatience, "We need more crabs, Mathew. There's barely enough for a snack here." Sara and I both laughed and returned to the work of spotting blue crabs in the wash of the waves, and helping little Melanee to get into position to smash the net down on top of them and scoop them up. It was a grand game and we kept after it until well after dark; a lantern that Sara had brought down helping to illuminate the little buggers.

Back at the hotel, Lila's cook steamed up the crabs and served a tray of lump crab meat on crackers for the guests to munch on. Melanee helped to serve, proud of her catch. The day was winding down and I was exhausted from the long trip back from Georgia. I excused myself, and Lila walked out with me when I had said goodnight to all of the others. She placed her arm in mine as we walked down the stairs. We stopped and looked down toward the beach, a billion stars now shimmering overhead.

"What are your plans now, Mathew Coulter?" she asked.

A dozen thoughts seemed to push through my mind all at once as I contemplated my answer, and all I could manage to say was, "Wherever the tides may chose to take me."

I slept late into the next morning, and woke refreshed and alert for the first time in weeks. With a pot of coffee next to me at my writing table, I started looking through the work I had done before leaving for Atlanta. Before I knew it, half the day was gone and I was lost again in the story and the writing. I planned to clean up later in the afternoon and drive into Panama City to see Eleanor. Something outside broke my concentration and I walked over to the screen door at the front of the house.

Rebecca Bidwell, the shopkeeper's daughter from Point Washington, had just come up and she was tying her horse, Barley, to the fence in front of the Headley's place. Melanee Dalton was sitting up on top of the big brown horse, a look of pure delight on her face.

"Look Mathew, Becky's giving me a ride on old Barley," she said.

"You look like a real cowgirl up there, kid," I yelled back. I walked down and greeted Rebecca as she stood at the fence.

"Welcome back, Mathew," she said. "I just wanted to let you know that Sheriff Crowe stopped by our house earlier today. He still hasn't found out who…" and then she hesitated for a moment, "who killed Seth."

"Yes, I know, I spoke with him before I left for Atlanta, but he seemed to have some positive leads."

"He keeps coming by and asking all of us more and more questions," she said, and I could tell that she was more than a little concerned. "And he won't tell us anything. My pa and brother, Jonas, are getting real upset about it."

"He's just trying to do his job, Rebecca," I said, trying to comfort her, but thinking how strange it was how Crowe was moving forward so tentatively with his investigation.

"I just thought," Rebecca said, "that since you've come to know Sheriff Crowe, that you might be able to speak with him and try to learn more about what's really happening. Maybe you and Lila could speak with him?"

I promised her that I would talk to Lila, and that we would do our best to find out what he was really working on.

"It just keeps me up at night knowing there's someone out there who did this to Seth. It's been so long."

"Let me see what we can find out," I promised again.

She went back and took the reins, and said goodbye before climbing up on the horse behind Melanee. The little girl waved as they rode away back toward the hotel.

Later, I drove into the parking lot at Palumbo's club in Panama City. It was just before dark and the place was filling up. Inside I found out that Eleanor wasn't working that night, so I got back in the car and drove down the beach road toward her house. One of her roommates there told me that she had gone for a walk on the beach. As I walked down through the sand on the narrow path through the dunes, the breeze picked up and pushed the tall sea oats about in a slow rhythm with the currents.

I made my way down through the dry white sand to the water. Looking first to the east, I could see only a couple walking along the shore together, and then back down to the west I saw a solitary figure some distance off, a shadow in the fading light. I took my shoes and socks off and left them in the sand. I rolled up my pant legs and started walking down the beach, the low waves washing up over my feet at times, feeling fresh and cool. The distant figure grew closer, walking slowly toward me. Soon I could see that it was a woman, her flowing skirt blowing in the wind. Then she stopped and was looking out at the water as I approached. I was only a dozen yards away when she turned again, and I could see that it was Eleanor, and when she realized who it was she ran quickly down the remaining space between us, water splashing up as she ran in the falling tide. She threw herself into me, almost knocking us both over into the water, and I lifted her up in my arms and backed up away from the surf. I tried to speak and say hello, but she was kissing me all over my face, and we were both laughing. Then we fell down on the sand. She pushed me over on my back and kissed me again, this time slowly and full on the mouth. Her hair was spilling down around my face, and she pulled it back with her hand.

"I was wondering if I would ever see you again," she said.

"I'm sorry that I didn't call or write," I said. "It's been a little difficult back there." And then I told her about my father and my trip back.

"Your little present is still okay," she said, referring to the gift for Melanee that I had left with her that night at the club. "I'm not sure I'll want to give it back," she said with a big mischievous grin on her face. "I'm getting kind of attached to the little thing."

It was a mockingbird that I had seen that day in the old pet shop along the beach, and I knew that Melanee would love having a new little companion, caged where she could always play with it, and sing to it and feed it. "You wouldn't take a present from a little blind girl?" I teased.

"No, but you may have to buy one for me, too." Then she kissed me again and I felt her shiver. The bottom of her dress was wet from the surf and the wind was getting cooler. We walked up closer to the dunes, and there was wood from a previous fire. We gathered some more drift wood from around the beach and soon had a big warming fire going. Huddled next to each other, we sat looking at the fire and out across the Gulf of Mexico, dark and rolling in the night. Above, a few clouds drifted across the starry landscape and several gulls squawked overhead as they floated their way down the beach to their night's roost.

Later as the light from the fire began to ebb, we made love on the sand and I lost myself in Eleanor and the glorious comfort of her arms and legs and smooth skin, and the graceful rhythm of two people who were coming to know every move the other would make.

Chapter Twenty-six

A steady routine returned to the beach through the summer. My time was full with writing and welcome breaks down at the beach, and occasional dinners with Lila and her family at the hotel. At least once a week I would break away to drive into Panama City to see Eleanor, and on those times when she had a day or two off, she would come back to Grayton Beach with me. Our relationship was becoming more comfortable and indispensable, and my earlier declaration of *love* was proving to be surprisingly prophetic.

My book was progressing as well as I could have expected. Before I knew it, the routine of the beach eased into early September, and while the temperatures stayed hot and humid, subtle changes in the weather and environment began to show. The patterns of fish and birds began to change noticeably, and cloud formations in the mornings and evenings took on new character. The late afternoon thunderstorms that had blown in through the summer began to shift north of the beach, and it was a marvelous time of transition to the coming months of fall and winter.

I hadn't received a word from Palumbo since I had left him back in the summer in Atlanta, and each day a few moments of my conscious thought were on Willie Palumbo and his progress in taking over the Atlanta liquor business. Having always been surprised by his tenacity and capability, I was fairly certain that he would be successful in putting this new operation together. But, I also knew that there were many factions and powerbases in the city that he would have to navigate and overcome. Interestingly, his wife Louise had stayed in Grayton Beach this entire time in her tiny room at the Beach Hotel. She rarely ventured out, and Lila was always fussing about her and how worried she was about her current state of affairs.

I did receive a letter from my old friend and beach housing benefactor, Jimmy Headley, indicating that he wanted to stop down to Grayton Beach to see me before he headed back after a long summer's break to rejoin his father's firm. There was no specific date in the letter, and I assumed that he would arrive on his own schedule. I was frankly looking forward to the company of an old friend from my younger days in Atlanta.

He showed up at the most unexpected time, and true to form, caught us all by surprise. Jimmy was of medium-height, a very round sort with a wild head of reddish brown hair and freckles from head to toe, who through the years has come to be one of the most jovial and interesting people I had ever known. He had also established himself as one of the more accomplished revelers at parties, and certainly proved his mettle upon arrival.

It was late on a Saturday night and I was down at the beach pavilion with Lila and all of her guests from the hotel. The band was playing and people were dancing. Drinks were in plentiful supply, in spite of the mandate from the federal government according to the Volstead Act. I was out on the dance floor that night with Lila Dalton in my arms, and we were twirling in a truly intoxicated attempt at the latest dance steps. While Lila was twenty-five years older than me, we had become close friends and nearly inseparable at times such as these. Her daughter Sara and granddaughter Melanee had continued to progress well together through the summer. Sara was careful not to get too close to the parties and the alcohol for fear of any relapse, and we were all sensitive to that. On this particular night she was back at the hotel with her daughter, working on music and reading stories.

Jimmy Headley must have heard the music when he pulled up to his cottage and found no one home, and then ventured down the beach path to find someone who might know where the "freeloader", Mathew Coulter, may be hiding out. He spotted me out on the dance floor before I had any indication that he was in town. Rather than just walk in and announce himself, which would have been terribly boring in Jimmy's estimation, he instead wandered around the periphery of the dance floor making sure that I didn't notice him. Then he found a nice looking young woman, who happened to be Rebecca Bidwell and asked her to dance. Out on the dance floor I was suddenly pushed from behind and turned to see my friend in the arms of the attractive young Miss Bidwell. It was quite a pleasant surprise to see Jimmy there as if it were the most natural thing, as if he had been there all summer. I quickly explained to Lila who this new visitor was, and she reminded me that she had known Jimmy and the Headley family for some time. I excused myself momentarily from our dance and turned to face my old friend.

"Damn, Coulter," he said. "Didn't even recognize the old beach house with that new coat of paint. Did you have half the county out painting the place all summer?"

I moved a few steps over, leaving Lila for a moment and gave him a big hug. "Where have you been all summer?" I asked. "I've been out there painting my ass off and you're nowhere to be found!"

He just laughed and took a sip from a drink he had grabbed from the bar that had been set up in the corner of the pavilion. "Meet my friend…," he said, turning to look at his dance partner, and it was clear that he had forgotten her name. Rebecca held out her hand in embarrassment and said *hello*. She seemed very intrigued with my friend, James Headley.

"Headley, really, what have you been up to?" I asked in mock accusation, knowing that he had been traveling with his family in Europe.

Jimmy turned to look at his new dance partner, Rebecca, and said, "I don't know why the hell I haven't been here. Damn, they've got pretty women in Grayton Beach. Should have remembered how nice it's been down here these past years."

We both excused ourselves from our dance partners and walked back over to the bar and refilled our drinks. "Coulter, what the hell have you been up to all summer?" Headley asked.

All of the events of the past months swirled through my mind. I really didn't know where to start. It was like a kaleidoscope of people and events, tragedies and surprising delights. "You should have been here, Headley," I finally said. "You can't even imagine."

"All I can imagine," he replied, looking at his new friend and dance partner, "is young Rebecca there laid out bare in the sand with me in about twenty minutes. Boy has she grown up!"

"Take your time, Headley," I said, and then laughed. "You don't want to sully the Headley name in Grayton Beach on your first night back this year."

"Hell, she's a big girl," he said, and then took another long drink from the moonshine he had poured from the bar table. "We could very likely fall in love tonight."

I looked over at Rebecca and saw her talking with her parents near the rail of the pavilion. She was particularly striking on this night, tall and lean, her long black hair flowing and wearing a dress that sparkled in the fire lights from around the dance floor. She also held herself in such a confident manner that she literally stood out and shined like a beacon among the other guests. Clearly she was letting everyone know that she was moving beyond her mourning for Seth Howard, and I had to agree that it was damn well about time. I doubted that Jimmy Headley would have much luck luring her away into some illicit rendezvous on the beach, but then again, as I thought back to our time together at the university in Athens, Georgia, I was never surprised by the audacity of his conquests.

I managed to find my way back to the cottage at a reasonable hour, sometime after midnight, and sipped a short drink and smoked one of Palumbo's cigars out on the porch, waiting for Headley to return. When the music stopped down at the pavilion and the lights went out and people milled up through the dunes back to the hotel, or to their cottages, I finally gave up on Headley and went to bed. In the morning, my first conscious thought was that someone was shaking my shoulders. I managed to open my eyes and then focus in the bright glare through the shades in my room, the ache in my head a quick reminder of last night's excess. Headley was sitting there on my bed. His mop of hair was in disarray, shooting off in random angles. His face was flushed and tired looking, and yet his ever present smile was still radiating out from the carnage of the drink and apparent lack of sleep.

"Morning, Coulter," he said.

"What time is it, and where in hell have you been?" I asked.

He looked at his watch. "Just past seven."

I rolled back over and pulled a pillow over my head. "Find a bed, Headley and get some sleep," I said, but he had to tell me about his night on the beach with young Rebecca Bidwell from Point Washington. Apparently she had arranged to stay over with a friend for the night in Grayton Beach, and then she snuck out after everyone else was asleep and met him back at the beach. The details seemed all a bit fuzzy in my half-conscious state, but I did gather that they had taken a long walk down the beach toward Seagrove, and then a swim in the late night surf. With that comment, I was awake enough to remind him about the nocturnal travels of big sharks along the shoreline after dark. He just laughed and continued to tell me that they had fallen asleep in each other's arms in the sand and woke when the sun started to show off to the east. He had just gotten her back to the house before anyone was up, and then he told me that he was desperately in love with Rebecca Bidwell. She had reminded him that they had met before a couple of summers earlier, but she had certainly *matured* as Headley called it since then.

    I had heard Jimmy express his undying love for a dozen different girls over the years we had been friends, so I didn't take the comment with much credence. He obviously sensed my skepticism and said, "Coulter, I'm serious. This girl is incredible and I didn't even sleep with her. I mean I slept with her, but you know, we kept most of our clothes on."

    I just laughed and threw my pillow at him. "Really, you need to get some sleep," I said. He reluctantly backed out of the room, but was still chattering about the marvelous Rebecca. I heard him go out to the kitchen to pump some water in the sink and soak his head. I fell asleep again, almost immediately, and woke some time later to the smell of bacon. I stumbled out into the main room of the cottage trying to wipe the crusted sleep from my eyes, and scratch in all the places that needed scratching. Headley was there at the wood stove working over a frying pan full of eggs and crackling bacon. The smell was marvelous and mixed with the aroma of fresh coffee. I cleared room on my writing table and Headley served. The food was so good that neither of us spoke until it was quickly consumed.

    "So you kept your pants on last night," I finally said, and smiled at my friend.

    "You know it's not nice to talk about a lady," he teased. "We're talking about my future wife, Coulter."

"Right, until I introduce you to one of my girlfriend's roommates later today."

"She has roommates?"

"Gorgeous roommates," I said.

He jumped up quickly and threw the dishes in the sink. "We need to get cleaned up and on with the business of the day. Come on Coulter, we need to get moving. We're burning daylight."

On our drive over to Panama City later that morning, Headley went on to tell me all about Rebecca. I decided not to get into the details of her recent engagement to the now deceased Seth Howard. His undying love paled some as we drove along, perhaps as the whiskey had worked its way through his system, or the bright lights of reality of a new day and the prospects of beautiful roommates in Panama City loomed just ahead.

It was mid-afternoon when we got into town. I knew that Eleanor didn't have to be at work until later in the evening. We pulled up in front of her house. The shades were down and there were no signs of anyone around. Jimmy and I got out and started walking up the narrow sandy path to the front door.

"She's got two roommates, right Coulter?" he asked for the fifth time.

And then the door opened. I stopped and looked on in complete astonishment as Sheriff Lucas Crowe walked out onto the porch, adjusting his uniform, and then turning to face Eleanor Whitlock who was squinting in the opening of the door in the bright sunlight with an arm in front of her eyes, her robe half open and untied. Crowe hadn't seen us and he turned and pulled Eleanor close and hugged her, and then handed her a wad of bills. When he pushed away, Eleanor looked out and saw me standing there. Both she and the sheriff stood for a moment in stunned surprise. My eyes met hers and her mouth fell open as if she wanted to speak, but had no capacity to form the right words.

Crowe recovered more quickly and walked down the steps toward us, and as he passed, said, "Hell of a piece of ass, Coulter."

A rage that had just begun deep in the pit of my stomach, now instantly boiled over. I lunged at the man and catching him off guard, knocked him to the ground. I fell on top of him, and as he struggled to get me off, I started throwing punches wildly at his face. Headley quickly pulled me off and held me as I struggled to go back after him. I watched as Crowe stood up, a red fury now burning on his face, and he came over next to me. I felt Headley free my arms and I stood staring at Sheriff Lucas Crowe, breathing heavily and knowing in my heart that at that moment I could kill the man.

"She's just a damn whore, Coulter," he said, and then he laughed and started to walk away. I was trying to catch my breath, and Headley had a handful of the back of my shirt in case I decided to go after him again. Then Crowe turned and with a malevolent glare said, "I wouldn't suggest that you ever hit an officer of the law again, Coulter." Then he kept walking down the street. I could see his car was parked about a block down in front of a small restaurant that Eleanor and I had eaten in many times.

Then I turned back and saw her still standing in the doorway, her face showing a mottled expression of panic and shame. She had managed to cover herself and held the collar of her robe tightly up around her chin, tears streaming down her face. She started to walk down the steps and I put a hand up to stop her, my own tears now welling up in my eyes. I tried to wipe them away before I simply said, "No."

She came down anyway, along the narrow path until she was standing right in front of me. Wiping away the tears on her cheeks, she tried to reach out for me, but I pushed her arms away.

"Mathew," I heard Headley say. "We should go."

I looked into her eyes for some sense of explanation, but all I saw was sadness and fear. When she spoke it was in a small and crackling voice that I had never heard before and she had to stop several times to fight back the sobs that shook her body. "Mathew, please this just isn't right…"

"It sure as hell isn't *right*!" I screamed back at her.

"You need to understand, Mathew," she said. "It wasn't supposed to happen."

"What wasn't supposed to happen?" I asked, and with all my will I had to hold myself back from lashing out at her.

"I wasn't supposed to fall in love with you."

I stepped back away from her, letting what she had just said sink in for a moment, and then her next comments sent my emotions into a total frenzy. "It was Palumbo," she said, and then she looked down at the ground as if this was the ultimate shame of what had just transpired.

"Palumbo?" I asked in complete shock and disbelief.

She came up to me again and put her arms around me, and this time I was so off kilter that I let her hold me, my own hands hanging at my side. Then she looked into my eyes and said, "He paid me to get close to you."

Immediately my mind started racing back over the sequence of events of our time together, and I quickly felt the sickening realization that I had been played. Then I started to think through the implications and motives. "Why?" was all I could manage to say.

"I never knew for sure, Mathew," she replied, "but he often spoke about your family's business up in Atlanta, and how he wanted you to help him get close to your father."

A lightening bolt of clarity shot through me, and all of this suddenly became very clear. Palumbo had ultimately worked his way into position, and our family had taken the easy way out in turning over the business. My feelings of rage and frustration welled to the surface again. Then I felt Headley pulling me back toward the car. I let her slip out of my arms for the last time, and as Headley drove us away, I looked back at Eleanor Whitlock standing on the front walk of her house with her face in her hands.

Chapter Twenty-seven

We drove in silence back to Grayton Beach. Jimmy had the good sense as a friend not to make some lame joke about not being able to meet Eleanor's roommates. I kept looking out the side window at the passing landscape and occasional cottage or farm. It all went by in a clouded blur, as my mind was focused on trying to retrace the times I had spent with Eleanor Whitlock these past months. She was certainly no saint, but how could I have missed the indications of her true nature and occupation? I was also struggling with my embarrassment at having been duped for so long, and now in front of one of my best friends who I had spent all morning telling how wonderful this woman was, and that I was in love.

Finally, Headley apparently felt it was time to offer some solace. "Look friend, I don't know what the hell just happened back there, but from what I could see, you're damn well better off knowing now." He let the comment hang there for a moment. "I know you had feelings for this girl, but there are a lot of women in this world."

I looked at my friend and said, "I know you're trying, Headley, but just shut up." He obviously got the message and we went on the rest of the way back to his cottage without speaking.

When we arrived, he announced that he really wanted to head over to Point Washington before going back to Atlanta, I'm sure with thoughts of Rebecca Bidwell fresh in his mind. I helped him load his car, and as he was about to pull out, he leaned his head out of the window and said, "Stay as long as you like, Coulter, but I'd stay away from Panama City for a while if I were you."

I thanked him again for the shelter and sanctuary, and then he was off down the dusty road out of town. I turned toward the beach when I heard thunder off in the distance over the water. A heavy bank of dark clouds was moving in from the south, and in the last light of day, lighting was flashing off behind them, illuminating the sky. I noticed for the first time how strongly the wind had picked up since the morning. The tall pines and live oaks were thrashing about, and gusts of wind sent swirls of white sand rushing by. Out along the beach I could see that the waves were rolling higher than I had ever seen them and crashing hard down along the shore. And then what struck me was that the sound of birds was gone, and I wondered about little Champ, the mockingbird.

Going into the house, I closed the door against the wind. I lit two of the kerosene lamps and found a bottle of good whiskey in the cupboard. I heard a knock on the door and when I opened it, Lila Dalton stood there trying to hold her dress down in the strong winds. "Mathew, I just saw you get home. This looks like a big storm coming. You better get everything outside put away.

I was still staggering from the shock of Eleanor and the Sheriff, and I thought for a moment about telling Lila that her boyfriend was sleeping with prostitutes in Panama City, but decided there would be a better time and place. I had to cope now with the reality of the moment and the coming storm. "Do you need my help with anything?" I asked.

"No, we're fine," she said. "Some of the guests decided to leave earlier when the weather started to turn, but the rest of us are pretty well settled in. If it doesn't get too bad later, please come over and join us for a drink and some company."

I thanked her and closed the door as she walked back out into the approaching storm. Then the rain started to fall and the lightning seemed even closer out over the water. When the lightning flashed, the sky turned an ugly and ominous purple and black. I pushed the door closed again and reached for the bottle I had left on the writing table. Somewhere in the back of my mind a random thought caused me to look at all of the loose pages on the table. I sorted them and stacked them, and took the whole pile into the bedroom and put them in a suitcase, and then shoved it under the bed.

Looking out one of the front windows, rain now slashed against the glass and the old metal roof above creating a deafening clatter. I grabbed the bottle from the writing desk and a glass from the kitchen, and then sat down in the old worn upholstered chair in the corner. I twisted the top off the bottle of whiskey and took a long ragged breath. I knew deep inside that there were no answers or relief to the disturbing events of the day in this bottle, and yet I felt compelled to believe that there was some hope of escape toward the bottom of it, at least for a few hours. I poured the glass half full and held the amber liquid up to the dim light beside me. It glowed golden and warm and welcoming, and I threw my head back and swallowed it all. As the liquor burned down my throat and into my gut, images of Eleanor Whitlock flashed in my mind; better times that we had shared, moments of intimacy and lust, laughter and tears. I couldn't help but wonder how much of our time together had been a pretense, a performance, paid for by the gangster, Willie Palumbo. And then I remembered her telling me that she had fallen in love with me. I poured another half glass full and just took a sip this time. I laughed to myself as I thought about

GRAYTON WINDS

Eleanor Whitlock's love; how she must have been thinking about how much she loved me when she was screwing Lucas Crowe and who knows how many others.

The sounds of the wind and the rain continued to build outside, and the lightning flashed every few minutes, followed soon by the roar of the thunder up in the heavens above the little town of Grayton Beach. I thought for a moment about closing the storm shutters outside, but was distracted again by the whiskey and images of Eleanor Whitlock. After a while, the thunder seemed a continuous growl out in the night sky.

I don't know for sure if it was minutes or hours later, but I had fallen asleep or passed out. An even louder crack of thunder had startled me back to consciousness. I looked over and the whiskey bottle was half empty. The house now seemed to shudder and creak with each gust of wind, and the roar of the thunder and the wind mixed in a frightening wail. The bushes and live oaks beside the house scraped against the clapboard siding. I thought about my new paint job and managed to smile for a moment at the futility of my labor.

I reached for the glass again and filled it this time to the top, and then held it in my lap. I started to think back over my pilgrimage to Grayton Beach all those months ago after fleeing the betrayal of my family and a woman that I thought I had shared a future with; the new people who had come into my life and those that I now considered friends. And people like Willie Palumbo who I thought I had been able to come to trust, only to find that everything with him was an angle, another line on expanding his base of business and power.

I held the glass up in front of me and yelled into the roar of the storm, "You can go straight to hell, Willie Palumbo!" Then I took another long drink and the whiskey hammered my brain again as I threw my head back into the cushion of the chair. Rational thoughts and concerns faded with the effects of the liquor, and I started laughing out loud, laughing maniacally at the storm and my life and the people that now haunted that life.

Through the haze of the liquor, the effects of the storm seemed now only a roaring crescendo of sound and chaos. The window behind my head was shaking against the fury of the wind, and then there was an explosion that crashed through the house as the window in the kitchen blew out and glass shattered across the floor as the knifing wind found its way into the Headley cottage. There was madness all around and I struggled to stand against the force of the wind blowing through the hole in the wall above the sink. Papers and books and other debris flew through the air, and the roar of the wind grew even louder now that it had penetrated the barrier of the house.

I staggered against the gale, trying to get over to the kitchen to do something to close the howling gap in the wall, but even in my sodden state, I quickly realized that it was a hopeless pursuit. I turned and let the wind almost blow me into the bedroom, and I struggled with whatever energy I had left to close the door behind me. There was a temporary escape from the wind, but not the howl and booming thunder of the storm outside or the shuddering effects it was causing on the house. Then there was another explosion of glass out in the living room that caused me to fall back, and I tripped on some clothes on the floor and landed on my back near the bed. Looking up, the rafters and planks of the roof seemed to be moving, as if they were preparing to fly off into the night. I thought for a moment about Lila Dalton, her daughter Sara and little Melanee down the street at the hotel, and I prayed that they were in a safe place, protected from the bedlam that was howling across the sand and dunes of Grayton Beach.

The bedroom door was shaking violently in the wind, and a near squall was blowing through under the gap at the bottom. I sensed that the old house would crumble and fly apart into the storm at any moment. I looked around frantically for any safe harbor. The tiny closet against the wall seemed the only shelter available, and I crawled in and burrowed against the back corner of it, holding my hands over my head. In my drunken state I was convinced that I heard water and waves crashing against the side of the house. Later I would find that the storm surge had indeed brought the surf well up into the village. My last conscious thought was of Melanee Dalton and her piano, and a furtive hope that all would be safe by morning.

Then there was the sound of birds again, and at first it was off somewhere in the deep recesses of my brain, only a distant echo of song. The chorus continued to build and I opened my eyes, the past night's fury and pandemonium now beginning to return in my mind. I looked around and saw that it was light, probably early morning and I was still sitting in the tiny closet. Peering out into the bedroom there was nothing but clothing and debris and wreckage all about. When I looked up, I was surprised to see that the roof was still attached to the house, although there were several leaks where water was dripping in.

Trying to stand, I pulled myself up along the opening edge of the closet, and my legs and back ached from sleeping on the wooden floor of the small space, and my head was pounding from the effects of the whiskey. The door to the bedroom had blown open during the night. There was sand and water everywhere among the debris. As I walked out into the main room, it looked like a bomb had gone off and tossed everything in random disorder about the house. All of the windows appeared to have been blown out or partially shattered. I walked carefully on broken glass and splintered wood.

Almost afraid to look outside at the destruction the storm must have wreaked upon tiny Grayton Beach, I unlocked and opened the front door slowly. As I walked out onto the porch, my mouth fell open and I blinked several times to make sure that I was focusing. Giant pools of water lay all about across the roads and nearby yards. Many of the structures that I could see seemed to be stripped and battered by the winds and water, several knocked entirely over and lying in shattered wreckage in the wet sand. My car was still parked by the leeward side of the house and though covered with palm fronds and debris, it seemed relatively serviceable.

As I looked down the road toward the hotel, I was stunned to see that it was virtually gone. With a less protected path up from the beach from dunes and other structures, only a portion of the lower floor remained in broken remnants. I started running down the street as best as I could, my mind exploding with images of the most horrifying of outcomes. Surely no one could have survived the night if they had stayed in what was left of the hotel. I started yelling Lila's name as I got closer, but there was no response, only the sound of the pounding surf down at the beach. Down past the hotel I saw two people walking out of their cottage and almost in a daze, staggering around and taking in the destruction. The windmill and water tower were nowhere to be seen. The wind had died to almost a calm breeze, and the dark gray clouds were now distant to the north, the sun shining across the beach and the town from down toward Panama City.

I ran up into the yard in front of the hotel and struggled to climb over debris that blocked my way. I kept yelling for Lila and then Sara Dalton, but there was no response. When I was able to climb up onto what was once the front porch, I saw a woman's legs sticking out, lifeless and bloody from under a collapsed wall. I was frantic, and started pulling at splintered boards and furniture, throwing as much as I could to the side, while at the same time looking around for signs of any of the others. With all my strength I pulled hard on a piece of wooden wreckage that lay across the woman's head. When I was able to move it enough to see, two lifeless eyes stared back at me. The woman's face had been badly injured, but it wasn't anyone that I recognized, perhaps one of the summer guests. I reached down and shaking badly, placed my fingers on the woman's neck. Her skin was cold and wet and there was no sign of a pulse.

I moved on across the battered ruins looking for others, tears running down my face as I feared what I was soon to find. Then I heard a sobbing noise from somewhere out behind the main structure and started in that direction, my hands and arms now bleeding from splintered wood and broken glass. There was a wall still standing at the back of the hotel where the kitchen had been and the door was still in place. When I opened it and walked down into the back alley, a large tree had fallen and blocked the way to where I was now hearing the crying sounds. I ran around to the side and saw the tiny storage shed that Lila used to keep supplies. To my surprise it was mostly intact. The door was open and my heart nearly stopped beating when I saw Sara Dalton walking out of the darkened doorway with her daughter Melanee in her arms. Sara's face was cut badly and bleeding on her left cheek. Melanee was crying, her face buried in her mother's hair.

I ran up to them and held them both in my arms, my tears joining theirs. Then several others started coming out of the shed, some were guests that I recognized, others were unfamiliar to me. Louise Palumbo stumbled out and held her hand in front of her eyes to shield the bright morning light. I turned back to Sara and her face was an awful mix of tears and dried blood, her eyes clouded in a terrified gaze. Melanee looked up at me and her expression of fear and sadness nearly broke my heart.

Then she spoke in a hoarse whisper. "Grandma's gone, Mathew."

"She's gone?" I asked, nearly numb with my own fear.

Sara spoke for the first time, strained and distant, "She's dead, Mathew." My worst fears were realized and I pulled them both closer to me. Sara went on to tell me that Lila had herded everyone out behind the hotel into the old storage house when the storm had peaked and windows and walls began to break in, thinking that there may be more protection from the wind. Most of the guests had managed to get out; although she knew that several were still missing. Everyone was huddled in the shed with blankets over their heads for some protection from flying debris when Lila went back one more time to look for her remaining guests. They all heard the giant live oak tree moan and then crack loudly before it fell, taking out part of the back of the hotel porch.

"When I heard the tree coming down," Sara said, as she tried to control her voice from crying again, "I looked out the window of the shed, and a bolt of lightning illuminated everything as one of the big limbs of the tree fell right on her."

Melanee was sobbing again and wouldn't lift her head from her mother's shoulder, but then she cried out, "I told Grandma not to go."

Sara tried to comfort her, and then I looked over under the tree and a blanket had been laid down among the broken branches. I walked over slowly and knelt down and pulled back the edges of it. Lila Dalton lay with her face to one side in the sand, her hair pushed back away to reveal a peaceful expression, even with her eyes closed. She could be taking a nap on the beach and not look any more serene. The huge limb from the tree that had knocked her down and taken her life, lay across her back, nearly two feet around and impossible to move. I placed the blanket back over her face and turned to Sara and Melanee, who had been watching me. There were no words to express my grief, no offer of sympathy that could have possibly been given. There was only a deep, gnawing and dark hole in the pit of my stomach that made it difficult to even breathe. That morning we all stumbled around in the wreckage, numb to our loss and heartache. Later, even as the winds continued to calm and the sky cleared, I truly felt that there might never be a respite from the memories of that terrible night to help ease our loss.

Chapter Twenty-eight

The service for Lila Dalton was held two days later at the small church in Point Washington. The cemetery was adjacent to the old wooden chapel, and a sizeable crowd had gathered now on this morning to pay their respects. The Bidwells had come over and Rebecca stood with her parents with a bible in her hands, listening with the rest of us to the words of the pastor. Jimmy Headley had made it as far as Point Washington, and then was forced to ride out the storm there with the Bidwell's. He was also there with Rebecca. I stood holding hands with Sara and Melanee Dalton to my sides. They were both looking down at the casket that was about to be lowered into the ground. The sky had been clear since the storm had passed, and the shade from the tall trees all around us was welcome relief against the rising heat of the morning.

The pastor finished a final prayer, and then came over to Sara and shook her hand, expressing last words of sympathy. I thought about how fragile our brief time in this world can be. Only a short while ago I had been back in Atlanta for the service for my brother, Jess. The flame of his life had been so suddenly extinguished, without warning and with no sense of the terrible pain that would be left behind in those who had loved him. Now this beautiful and kind woman had fallen and left us. Family and friends stood in quiet anguish and if like me, they were considering their own mortality, it was certainly a sober awakening to what may lie ahead.

The Bidwell's had offered to host a small reception back at their house, just a block down toward the bay from the church. They had all weathered the storm fairly well. Being several miles back from the beach they had been somewhat sheltered, although several large trees had come down near the house and the tidal surge had raised the Choctawhatchee Bay waters up near their house and the store. We all started off in that direction when I saw a solitary figure standing back among the trees. It was Sheriff Lucas Crowe, and fortunately he had sense enough not to come closer. We exchanged looks, and he turned and walked back over to his car. I watched back over my shoulder as he drove away.

At the Bidwell's house everyone milled about in solemn respect for the passing of Lila Dalton. Louise Palumbo stood alone by the table set with food and cold tea. I walked over and she smiled when she saw me and then gave me a long hug. Her pretty face had seemed to age noticeably over the summer; the death of Seth Howard and the constant tumult of being married to Willie Palumbo, taking its toll.

"Mathew, I feel so badly for Sara and little Melanee," she said. "They were doing so well with Sara back and getting healthy again."

I looked at Sara Dalton, standing with her daughter and talking to the pastor, all with plates of food in their hands, but not eating. Her face had taken on some of the old troubled and withdrawn look from when she had first returned. I was worried that her mother's passing and the responsibilities of life on her own with a young daughter would be too much for her to cope with.

"She and Melanee will need help from all of their friends," I said. "I hope you'll be able to stay a bit longer." Louise had been staying at one of the neighbor's houses up in the woods that had received less damage. I had cleaned up the Headley place enough that it was habitable, and Sara and Melanee had been staying in the spare bunk room, although with most of windows blown out and the screens ripped to tatters, the bug and flies were a constant bother.

"I haven't heard from Willie," she replied. "The phone lines must still be down. I expect he'll be trying to get down here as soon as he can."

I tried to think how I would react the next time I saw the man. Murder was more than a little extreme, but certainly a wistful option that I had laid awake at night contemplating. His man Anthony would protect him from any physical harm I might try to inflict, and my sensible side kept reminding me that attacking gangsters is usually to be avoided.

Headley came over with Rebecca on his arm, and I could tell that they were smitten with each other. They both expressed their sadness again with Lila's passing. Jimmy said he'd be staying another couple of days with the Bidwell's until the roads were better before starting back to Atlanta. I wondered if Rebecca would ever let him leave.

Sara walked up with Melanee and said that she would like to get back home, and that Melanee was tired and needed to take a nap. I looked down at the little girl and placed my hand on her shoulder.

"Mathew, I tried to be very brave today and not cry so that Grandma could go to Heaven and be happy that we were okay," Melanee said.

"You *were* very brave," I reassured her. I looked up at her mother and saw far less strength and composure in her face, and I noticed that her hand was shaking as she held her daughter's.

"We really must go," Sara said again.

We all gave our thanks to the Bidwell family, and Rebecca and Jimmy Headley walked with us out to the car. Rebecca was holding Melanee's hand. "We'll try to bring old Barley out to the beach tomorrow to give you a ride, honey," she said. "Would you like that?"

"I would like that very much," the little girl said, trying not to show too much excitement on the day of her grandmother's funeral. Sara thanked her again and then we drove back to Grayton Beach, bumping around fallen trees and huge puddles of rain water.

They both sat in the front with me. We had been traveling for a few minutes when Sara said, "Did I tell you that Melanee warned us about the storm?"

I look over at her in surprise. "When was this?" I asked.

Sara explained that two days earlier, Melanee was sitting at the kitchen counter when she told both her mother and grandmother that a big storm would be coming soon, and that they should really leave the beach for a while. I looked down at Melanee beside me and she was crying now, her defenses finally down from the burial service.

"I told Grandma that it was going to be a very bad storm," Melanee said sadly. I looked over at Sara and we exchanged knowing glances of how much this would haunt her little daughter in the days ahead.

The process of clean-up and repair continued over the coming days, although there was no hope of salvaging what was left of the hotel. It would need to be torn down and rebuilt. I had taken Sara and Melanee into Panama City to meet with Lila's bankers. Sara was devastated to find out that her mother had invested almost all of her money in buying and fixing up the place, and there was very little left, certainly not enough to rebuild. She had carried no insurance either. I had offered to give Sara the money and she was grateful, but said that she wanted to think more on where she should really be to raise her daughter properly. Her comments gave me comfort that perhaps she was going to take some responsibility for her life, and remain stable enough to carry on and take care of Melanee.

While the Headley place had remained standing, it had sustained severe damage. The front porch roof had been entirely ripped off, and we found pieces of it scattered up in the woods behind the house. Many of the metal roofing panels had been ripped away, and others were bent back and away at twisted angles. Several holes in the roof had been caused by a fallen tree. The wind and sand had scoured the outside of all the homes in Grayton Beach, leaving the paint worn and pitted. I just shook my head when I had first walked around to assess the damage, a full summer's work wasted. Although Jimmy had told me not to bother, I had given Bidwell a list of lumber and other supplies that I would need to start the repairs, and they had been delivered the day before by one of his big horse-drawn trailers. His son Jonas had agreed to hire on to help. While I could handle a paint brush, after a while I knew that I was way over my head when it came to construction and carpentry.

Sara and I had spent much of our time sifting through the wreckage of the hotel looking for the family's possessions and anything that could be salvaged if she were to rebuild. It was too dangerous for Melanee to be in there with us, and after Jimmy Headley had left for Atlanta, Rebecca came over most every day to help take care of her. Louise Palumbo was also being very helpful and looking after Melanee when needed.

The first morning that we had begun the salvage we found the piano under a pile of debris, totally destroyed. I looked at the sad expression on Sara's face, and knew that she was thinking about her daughter and how much she would miss playing.

Sadly, three people had died the night of the storm in the hotel. Beside Lila Dalton, the woman I had found in the lobby was a guest who had been down from Birmingham with her family. A young child was upstairs when a window blew in, and had been wounded severely. The little boy died the next morning before he could be taken into town for medical care.

The remaining residents in the little town had miraculously survived with only minor cuts and scrapes, although all were emotionally scarred and shaken by the storm's fury. We learned later that the Hurricane of 1926 had started days earlier down in the Caribbean and then swept across South Florida, nearly leveling Miami, turning north up across the Gulf of Mexico before reaching landfall again along the beaches of the Panhandle of Florida. It was a devastating storm that had left many dead in its wake.

The beach had been drastically altered by the fury of the wind and waves, swept nearly clean of vegetation, the dunes battered and eroded. Walking along the beach, those homes and cottages that had been built close to shore had been nearly decimated by the wind and storm surge.

Melanee's new pet bird had been saved when everyone took refuge in the shed. The little girl kept the bird on the table in the living room of the Headley place. There had been no sign of Champ since the storm, but many other birds had returned, somehow able to survive the ferocity of the winds of the hurricane.

It was more than a week after the storm when Willie Palumbo's car pulled back into town. I was out working on the front porch of Headley's cottage when I saw him drive up in front of the wreckage of the hotel. Phone service had still not been restored, and I was sure that he had no idea what to expect or what had happened to his wife. He got out with Anthony and they both walked up into the mass of broken beams and walls. I watched as he stood there helplessly looking around. I had little empathy for the man, considering what he had done with Eleanor, but I knew that Louise was anxious for him to arrive.

I walked over, and when he saw me his face lit up, obviously not aware that I had discovered his secret pact with Eleanor Whitlock. "Coulter, thank God you're all right," he said, and walked up to greet me with a big bear hug. I didn't return his embrace and he stood back with a puzzled look. "What's wrong, son?" he asked.

"I'm not your son, Willie," I reminded him. "Louise is okay, by the way. She's staying a couple of blocks back with another family." I could see the relief on his face as I gave him the directions to find the place.

"We had no idea how bad it was down here," he said. "It's taken this long for the roads to get cleared so we could get through. God, what a mess," he said, looking over the ruins of the hotel and the rest of the town. "Must have been a helluva blow?"

"You can't imagine," I said. "Three people died there in the hotel that night." He looked at me with the question that didn't need to be asked. "Lila's gone, Willie. She was killed that night and two of her guests. Sara and Melanee managed to get to safety out back there. They're staying with me over at Headley's."

Palumbo looked down in sadness and shook his head. "What a damn shame," he said. "She was quite a woman." He looked up at me and obviously detected my look of scorn. "Coulter, what's wrong? What the hell is going on?"

I wanted to launch into a full and angry rant on my last encounter with the prostitute he had arranged to seduce me, but I knew that his wife had been waiting for days for his arrival. "It can wait," I said. "Louise will be happy to see you." He nodded and backed away, and they drove off around the corner.

Sara was leading Melanee by the hand up from the beach when I started back to the house. They had gone down for a swim and taken a picnic lunch with them. I had been invited to go, but wanted to keep on with the work on the house. My last minute efforts that night of the storm to put the pages of my manuscript away proved beneficial. The suitcase had survived the night and the pages had remained dry. There had been no time to return to the story and the typewriter had been badly damaged.

"Mathew," Melanee cried out as they came closer. "The waves are down today and we were able to go out in the water."

"That's great," I said. The pounding surf had lingered for days after the storm, and the currents had been too dangerous for the little girl to venture in. I took her other hand and walked with them back up to the house. Looking over at Sara, I saw that her mood seemed to have brightened some from the trip to the beach. She had been terribly quiet and sad these past days, understandably so with the tragic loss of her mother. I knew that it would take time for all of our grief to fade. The sight of the battered hotel every day didn't help to let any of us move on beyond the terror of that night.

Back at the Headley's house I had set up chairs on the front yard for us to sit in the evening until I was able to get the porch rebuilt. We sat Melanee down and Sara went inside to bring out her bird in its cage. I sat down next to the little girl. "Mathew, can grandma see us from up in Heaven?" she asked. "I hope she can so that she can see that we're all right."

"Yes she can, honey," I said, trying to reassure her. "She's up there with God and she knows that we're just fine." Sara came back out with the bird and placed it on a small table in front of her daughter. The bird chirped and jumped around on its perch, and Melanee reached in to feed it a cracker. Then I heard some commotion behind us and I turned to see little Champ, our wild mockingbird, jumping around and squawking on a pile of lumber.

Melanee heard him, too and yelled out, "Champ, is that you, Champ?" I took her hand, and we walked over together and knelt beside the wood pile. Melanee held out another cracker and

Champ hopped right up and took it out of her hand. I was amazed that the little bird had managed to find refuge from the storm. I assumed that it had perished when we hadn't seen him for days after the hurricane.

Melanee had named her new little bird, *Maggie*, after my sister. She looked at me now and asked, "Do you think Maggie would be happier being free with Champ?"

Sara had come over to join us. "She might not come back, sweetie," she said.

"But Champ needs a friend, and I think she'll be happier," the little girl said. "Would it be okay, Mathew?" she asked.

"I think you're right," I said, and then I brought the cage over and opened the door. Melanee reached inside and the little bird jumped on her finger. Slowly pulled it out and held her hand down near the board that Champ was bouncing around on. Sure enough, Maggie jumped down and hopped over to check out her new companion. Champ seemed delighted with her by the sound of his chirping reaction. Melanee fed them both another cracker, and then a gull swept in close and both of the mockingbirds flew away up into a tree behind the house.

"They'll be back," the little girl said.

Chapter Twenty-nine

Palumbo came by later that afternoon and got out of the car to speak with me. "Wanted you to know that the bastard O'Leary, the one who killed your brother Jess…"

"Yes?" I said, my attention piqued.

"Well we took care of the sonofabitch for you. Part of the payout I guess," he said.

"You killed one of the O'Leary's?" I asked in amazement. "The old man?"

"*Kill* is such a strong word, Mathew, and highly illegal, as you know," he said, and then he smiled that wicked smile of his. "We just allowed him to disappear, a very painful disappearance I might add."

"I don't know if *thank you* is appropriate at a time like this," I said, "but I do appreciate what you've done."

"It was nothing, kid. The bastard had it coming." Then he asked if I wanted to come into Panama City with him. Louise was in the car, and he said that they would be staying at a hotel in town. I told him *no*, and again debated on confronting him about Eleanor, this time with his wife there in the car.

"I'll say hello to Eleanor for you, son," he said. "Have you seen her? Is she okay after the storm?"

"No Willie, I just haven't had time."

"I'll give her your best," he said, giving me a strange look before getting back in the car.

"Sure," I responded, trying to keep my temper under control in front of the man's wife. As they drove off it occurred to me that Eleanor would tell him everything about my discovery of their alliance, but I was getting to a point that it seemed far less important than what many others were now dealing with along this battered coast. I was still troubled about the financial arrangement that we had made with Palumbo, but I kept trying hard to remind myself that my mother and sister would continue to be well cared for with no further worries about the illegal liquor business. A letter had just arrived yesterday from my mother, the first mail to get out to Grayton Beach since the storm. I had dropped a note in the mail to her the day that I had gone into Panama City with Sara to visit the banker. In her note she wrote that she continued to be so worried about me since the hurricane, and was waiting each day to hear news of how things were progressing. She also wrote that my father was showing little improvement, and that Maggie had filed for divorce from Desmond Raye.

It dawned on me that I hadn't even asked Palumbo about the business. It seemed the least important thing just now, and actually I cared very little if he was successful or not.

Sara Dalton came out of the house with a sandwich and glass of water for me, and we sat in the chairs on the front lawn. I proceeded to eat my lunch, still stewing on Palumbo. Melanee was off riding with Rebecca Bidwell. They had headed off up the beach about an hour ago.

Sara was looking off in that direction when she said, "I was wondering why you haven't been into Panama City lately?"

Her question caught me unprepared, and I almost choked on my sandwich before I could swallow the last bite. I hadn't told anyone else about Eleanor and her tryst with the sheriff, let alone her scheme with Palumbo. "I've just been a little busy here," I said. Trying to change the subject, I continued, "Have you thought any more about your plans? About the hotel, I mean."

Sara looked over at the rubble that was the life that her mother had tried to build. Birds were pecking around in the debris. She kept looking at the hotel when she said, "I just don't know if this is best for Melanee and me. Is it really fair to keep her out here in the middle of nowhere? She needs special schools and teachers, let alone friends that she can play with."

"You know that she loves it here," I offered.

"Yes, I know, but she really doesn't know much else. She was so little when I brought her here," she said, and I watched as the memory caused her face to flinch in an anguished expression.

"Please don't worry about the money," I said. "I can take care of that for you."

"I know, and that's so sweet of you to offer, but sooner or later Melanee and I need to make our own way and build our own life. I just don't know what, or where that might be."

"You don't need to rush," I said.

"I've been thinking a little about going back to Nashville. I could get a job singing somewhere…" She let the thought trail off on the breeze blowing in from the Gulf. Finally she spoke again. "And what about you, Mathew? You plan to spend the rest of your days out here on the edge of nowhere?"

She knew about my book and had been encouraging me to get back after it. "I have work yet to do here," I said, looking back at the Headley place. I knew that I wasn't obligated to do any of this; that the Headleys could afford to have it all taken care of, yet I felt an obligation after their hospitality, and I was actually enjoying the labor and hard work. And something about this little beach town had gotten under my skin. I was really starting to feel at home, in spite of the series of unfortunate and often tragic events these past months.

"I still can't come to terms with the fact that she's gone, Mathew," Sara said suddenly, catching me by surprise. She had been fairly strong the past few days, but I could tell all of this was weighing heavily upon her.

I took a deep breath and scratched at my unshaven face before I replied. "When I lost my brother a few months back, I felt the same. There was this feeling that it was all just a bad dream. I'm not sure those feelings will ever go away, Sara."

"I know," she replied softly. "It's just that we were finally back together and…" Then she started to cry and couldn't continue for a moment. She tried to compose herself and said, "She was so patient with me and what she's done for Melanee…" Again she couldn't finish.

"Your mother loved caring for Melanee, and she loved even more seeing you back and healthy, and with your daughter again," I said. "You know how pleased she was that you're healing and ready to get on with your life with Melanee?"

She nodded, and then got up and came over and kissed me on the cheek before turning and going back up into the house.

It was just past dinner and the sun was falling low to the west. I was sitting out in the yard. Melanee and Sara had already gone to bed. A car drove up the road past the wrecked hotel, and then stopped in front of me. When the headlights went out I could see that it was the sheriff, Lucas Crowe. He got out and walked up, and then sat down beside me.

"Evening, Coulter."

I didn't respond, but took another pull on my cigar, and looked off at the sunset.

"Wanted to let you know something." When I didn't turn or answer he kept on. "Picked up a piece of shit drifter yesterday down near Seagrove. He was drunk and had broken into a couple of houses, looting after the storm."

"And why should I care," I finally said.

"Got to talking to this asshole down at the jail. Seems he knows your friend Palumbo. I gave him a little more to drink and he kept talking."

I was getting more irritated by the minute, and finally said, "Crowe, what the hell do you want?"

"Seems this fella does some work for your friend now and then."

"All right," I said, "just get to the point."

"Well I let the guy get pretty liquored-up and he just kept talking, and I started putting things together," Crowe said. "Asked him if he knew Seth Howard."

This got my attention and I looked over at the man who I had seen paying my former girlfriend for sex. I tried to put the images out of my head, as I had been for some time now. "Howard?" I asked.

"Yeah, he got real squirrelly when I asked him about Seth Howard, so we kept talking about it."

"Just get on with it, Crowe," I said.

"I could tell that this guy knew something, and I told him if he had anything to do with that boy's murder that I'd personally take him down to Tallahassee to let the State of Florida hang him by the neck. Well then he got real nervous."

"You think he killed Seth?" I asked.

"Hell, he finally confessed. I told him that if he told me who had put him up to it, that I could probably save him from the gallows. Well he was so damn drunk and so relieved at not getting his neck stretched, that he told me everything."

I sat up in my chair. "Palumbo paid him to kill Seth Howard?" I asked.

"Damn right he did, and I got the asshole he paid sitting down at the jail ready to testify against him," the sheriff said. "Just thought you'd like to know."

"Yeah, right," I said.

"Stopped down to check on Louise Palumbo to see if she had heard from her husband. Seems he came through town today I didn't say anything.

"You see him when he came through?" he asked.

"Yeah, said he was going into Panama City," I said. "Took Louise with him."

"Suppose he'll be down at the club tonight?" he asked.

Again I just looked at him.

"Your girl, what's her name, Eleanor?" he said, and the hair on the back of my neck bristled. "Suppose she'll be down there, too. Seen her lately?"

I stood up and reached over and grabbed him by the shirt, and lifted him up to face me. I moved so quickly that I caught him by surprise, but he recovered and pushed me away. "I told you once, Coulter, don't ever pick another fight with the law."

I was seething with anger and about to ignore his warning, and proceed with the ass-kicking that he deserved. Then I heard Sara behind me. I turned and she was standing in the darkened door.

"Everything okay out there, Mathew?" she asked.

"Just fine, just fine," I answered. "You can go back to bed. She hesitated for a moment and then went back inside.

"So you got yourself a new girl, Coulter," he said, and laughed.

"Damn you, Crowe. Get the hell out of here!" I yelled, and I moved at him again.

"Boy, I'd like nothing better right now than to throw your ass in the slammer for a few days for assaulting an officer of the law," he said, "but I got a little appointment with your friend, Palumbo, down the beach there."

He backed away, smiling, and then got in his car and drove away. I sat back and let myself settle down a bit. My heart was racing and my hands were shaking. I thought about Palumbo and his role in the Howard boy's death, and I certainly wasn't surprised. He was a ruthless sonofabitch, and of course he had gotten revenge for his wife's dalliance with Seth Howard. I thought about Louise and the life that was ahead for her. *The bastard wouldn't let her live in peace with that transgression between them.*

I realized that Palumbo would probably be spending the rest of his life in prison, if he wasn't executed for the crime of murder. Louise would be free of the monster, and then I thought about Atlanta and the business. All of that would fall apart without Palumbo's influence and power. But did it really matter? My family had already been paid extravagantly for his access to my father's suppliers and connections. The only thing that stuck in my gut about this was that the O'Leary family would now be free to take it all over. First they had killed my brother, and now they would have everything else that my father had worked for his whole life. Palumbo's gesture of revenge on the man who actually killed Jess did little to lessen my rage at the situation.

I sat there for a while thinking about all the implications of Palumbo's arrest. One minute it seemed the best possible outcome for a dangerous man that deserved what he had coming. The next I was thinking that Seth Howard was a piece of shit, too, and Palumbo had only done himself and Rebecca Bidwell a favor by taking him out of this world.

The thought of O'Leary and his family taking over my father's enterprise kept eating at me as I sat there and finished my smoke.

Five minutes later I was in my car driving toward Panama City. I knew that I couldn't beat Crowe to the club, but I hoped that Palumbo was still at the hotel where he had always stayed. It seemed one of the longest drives into town, as I kept thinking about the repercussions of what I was about to do. I kept thinking that I should let the bastard rot in hell, or stretch from the hangman's noose for all he'd done in this world. His little plot with Eleanor Whitlock seemed the least of his crimes, but I was certainly not ready to forgive and forget. And it wasn't the money from the future payments that Palumbo had promised our family from the business. That was the last thing that I cared about, and I'm sure my mother and sister would agree if they knew all of the details of this sordid affair.

In my mind, I finally rationalized that I was doing this for my father and my lost brother; that both of them would do the same thing if faced with the situation. The fact that I was about to aid and abet a murderer was not lost upon my conscience, however.

It hadn't occurred to me on the trip into town that the hotel along the beach could possibly be closed from the storm, and my heart sank as I pulled up into the parking area and saw the damage the place had taken in the hurricane. There were a few cars parked, but very few lights on. I went into the office and an older lady was sitting behind the desk, her head down asleep in a book. I walked up and nudged her on the shoulder, and she didn't move. There was a little bell on the counter, so I rang it loudly a couple of times, and she sat up and rubbed her eyes. I had thought it best not to ask for Palumbo specifically if anyone ever came around inquiring about me. I asked her if she had taken in any new guests today. She told me no, that they were closed and were referring everyone to the Palmetto Motel, inland a mile or so.

I drove through the night and found the little place tucked in along the back bay of water that ran through Panama City. Palumbo's car was parked in front of one of the rooms. Anthony was nowhere to be seen, and I figured that he had taken an adjacent room. I looked at my watch and it was just past ten. I was surprised that Palumbo hadn't headed down to the club by now. I knocked on the door and heard shuffling inside. Then the door next to this room opened and Anthony peered out. When he saw me, he nodded with little expression and went back inside. The door in front of me opened and Palumbo stood there in a sleeveless undershirt with his suspenders hanging from his pants. I looked into the small room and saw Louise sitting on the bed in a nightgown, holding a towel to her face. She had been crying, and when she saw me she let the towel down for a moment. I could see the welt of the bruise on her cheek. I shook my head in disgust and started to turn and leave.

"Coulter, what the hell is it?" Palumbo said, grabbing my arm.

"You sonofabitch," I said, "just let me go." In that instant seeing his bloodied wife, I decided that he could face his own fate with Sheriff Crowe.

Palumbo looked back at his wife and then at me. "This is between a husband and a wife, kid and you got no right to judge," he said.

I stood there staring at him for a moment, and then I decided on a new course of action. "Willie Palumbo," I said, "I'm about to do you the biggest favor you ever got."

"And what's that, kid?" he said defensively.

"But you need to swear to me that you'll never lay another hand on that woman there," I said, gesturing at Louise Palumbo.

He got a strange and puzzled look on his face. "What the hell are you talking about?"

"Just swear to me, Palumbo," I yelled, "or I'll let you rot in hell."

"All right, kid," he said. "Just settle down."

"Swear to me!"

"I swear, you asshole, now what the hell is this all about?"

I took a deep breath, and then told him about Crowe and the man he had arrested earlier today. He listened carefully to everything that I said, and I watched his face lose its color in the low light of the porch of that seedy motel.

When I finished he said, "You're not shittin' me are you, kid?"

"Could I make this up?" I said. "You hired this guy, right?" He just looked at me, and of course he wasn't going to admit anything. "Crowe's probably waiting down at the club for you right now."

He seemed to think this all through for a moment, and then said, "You done the right thing, and this conversation never happened."

"Palumbo," I answered, "I'm only doing this to protect my family's interests back in Atlanta. You better never let those pieces of shit O'Leary's get another sliver of business in that town."

"You can count on it, Coulter," he said with an evil smile. "You better get the hell out of here."

I looked in at Louise and she tried to manage a smile of gratitude but she winced in pain. I wanted to slug Palumbo right there, but knew I had to get back to Grayton Beach and let him work out the rest of this.

I started to leave, but Palumbo stopped me and said, "By the way, Mathew… about Eleanor. I'm sorry, it was just business."

This time I couldn't stop myself, and I let loose with a right hand that started somewhere down deep inside me, and when it landed on the surprised chin of the big gangster, he fell over like a house of cards and landed on his fat ass in the doorway. He picked himself up, and I prepared myself for the worst from either him or his goon next door, but he just smiled and rubbed his chin.

"You better get out of here now before I lose my sunny disposition," he said.

As I got back in the car I felt good in knowing that I may have just created some safe harbor for Palumbo's wife. On the way

GRAYTON WINDS

back to Grayton Beach I was thinking about nothing but the second deal I had just made with the devil.

Chapter Thirty

It was a week later that I heard from Eli Bidwell when I was over in Point Washington picking up some supplies, that Sheriff Crowe had been found dead, floating in the Choctawhatchee Bay. There was a gunshot wound in the back of his head, what was left of him, at least, from what the crabs and gators hadn't chewed away. I was certainly not surprised that Palumbo had found a way to eliminate this latest threat. I was also sure that the man that he had hired to kill Seth Howard would have met a similar fate by now. Anthony had certainly been busy these past days.

My complicity in these murders was more than a nagging concern. In fact, I was nearly nauseous when Bidwell had told me about the sheriff's demise. As I drove back to Grayton Beach that day, I realized what a steep price I had paid to protect my family back home in Atlanta. For the rest of my life I would live with the guilt of these deaths, and for whatever other trail of carnage that Palumbo would leave behind him in the future.

When I got back to the Headley place, Sara told me that Palumbo had been by earlier. He had left a message that he was going back to Atlanta with Louise, and that *everything would be all right*. He had also left me a sealed envelope. I took it from her and started walking down to the beach. I told Sara that I would be back in a while. I didn't open the envelope until I was down to the shoreline. I had been sitting for some time, looking out at the emerald water and rolling surf, thinking about the events of the past weeks.

Inside was a note written in Palumbo's sketchy hand.

Kid,

You did the right thing. I'll take care of Atlanta for you. I won't be back down this way any time soon, so I thought you might take care of the place for me.

WP

I opened the other piece of folded paper that was with the note and it was the deed to his club in Panama City.

I walked into the Panama Club the next night at about eight. The place was filling up, and already buzzing with music and laughter. Palumbo had obviously alerted the manager, Larry, about new ownership. The man came right up to me and shook my hand. "Welcome, Mr. Coulter."

So I was Mr. Coulter now. He showed me over to what was *my* table now that Palumbo had moved on. A waitress brought my drink before I even had to order, and Larry promised that a big steak would be out in a few minutes. Several people at other tables were looking at me and whispering something back and forth. Obviously word of new ownership was spreading quickly.

Then I saw Eleanor Whitlock come out from the kitchen. She saw me and froze for a moment, a look of sudden embarrassment on her face. I was struck again by her beauty, and the memories of our better times together came back to me. She hesitantly came over and then sat down beside me at the table. I didn't say anything, and we just looked at each other for a few moments.

Finally she reached over and put her hand on my arm and said, "Mathew, I'm so sorry about all of this."

"What are you sorry about?" I said, and she seemed confused by the comment. She shook her head as if she didn't understand the question. "Why are you sorry?" I continued. "You got paid."

My words were like a slap across her face and tears started to well up in her eyes. "Mathew," she was finally able to say, "I really did fall in love with you."

I couldn't help myself and had to say, "Do you fall in love with all your men? You must really love Lucas Crowe. Looks like he pays very well."

She stood up quickly and started to rush away, but I grabbed her arm and motioned for her to sit back down. Her face was blotched and flushed with tears. "I told you that I was sorry, Mathew and no, I don't feel that way about the others," she said. "I just need the money. I need to get out of this town."

"That's a hell of a way to make a living," I said, surprised at myself in how calm I was about all this. "Well, I have a business proposition for you." She looked at me with a confused expression again. "I want you to get into a different line of work," I said.

"And what would that be?" she asked, wiping the tears away from her cheeks.

I took Palumbo's deed to the club out of the pocket of my jacket and slid it across the table in front of her. I let her read it, and then she looked up at me and I said, "You just need to promise me that you'll never turn another trick."

"I don't understand," she said.

"Palumbo's gone. He gave me this club. I'm giving it to you. It's as simple as that." Then I stood up. "This is a new start,

Eleanor. Don't waste it." As I started to walk away, I turned and asked, "What about that promise?" She nodded and managed a thin smile.

I walked over to the manager, Larry, who was standing at the bar, and told him that he had another new boss for the second time today. I gestured over to Eleanor Whitlock who was still sitting at the table watching me, the deed to her new life in her hands. I took one last look at her before I walked out the door, certain that I would never see her again.

The beach house was dark when I returned. I walked in quietly, trying not to wake Sara and her daughter. Then I was startled to hear a movement over in the corner, and I turned to see the glow of a cigarette. As my eyes adjusted to the dim light, I could see that it was Sara and that she was lifting a bottle to her mouth. I went over and sat down beside her. I could smell the sweet, and at the same time, sickening smell of the whiskey. I tried to take it away from her, but she pulled it back. When she spoke her voice was slurred from the liquor.

"I thought you were staying with your lady friend over in Panama City," she managed to say.

All of this was coming at me too quickly. My first reaction was concern that she was drinking and might be falling back into old patterns. "Please let me have that," I said, and she gave me the bottle. I sat it down over away from her on the table. "Let me make you some coffee." I got up and lit one of the kerosene lights, and went into the kitchen. I started a fire in the stove and filled the coffee pot. In a few minutes it started to perk, and I walked back over to Sara. She was sitting there on the couch with her head in her hands.

"I'm sorry, Mathew," she said. "I'm just so scared."

I moved over next to her and pulled her close. She buried her head in my chest, and I let her cry it out as I held her. She had been so much better for the past month that the nurse had gone back to leave her on her own.

When the coffee was done, I poured two cups and we sat together in silence. A little later she asked for more and then said, "Let's go outside so we don't wake Melanee."

I followed her out and held her arm when she staggered a bit. We sat together on the chairs in the front yard. It was cool so I gave her my jacket. The new moon was a thin sliver above, and soft winds were pushing scattered clouds by it every so often.

Finally I said, "It's over with me and Eleanor."

In the darkness I saw her look over at me. "I'm sorry," she said. "I didn't mean anything by what I said earlier. Really, I'm sorry."

I let her comments hang there. I looked up at the sky and wondered about where I would be sitting a month or a year from now, and how that moon and those stars would look from wherever that might possibly be.

Chapter Thirty-one

I had ordered a new typewriter from the Bidwell's store, and it came in on a boat shipment from over in Destin. Jonas brought it over the next morning when he showed up for work. While he got started on the day's work on the roof, I set the typewriter up on my writing table inside, and then went into the closet and pulled out the suitcase that held what was the current state of my unfinished manuscript. I laid the pages out and began to sort back through the story to get caught up on where I had left off. Sara and Melanee both woke while I was working, but I got so lost in getting back into the story that I barely acknowledged them. Before I realized it, the sun was up high in the mid-day sky. The girls had left to go down to the beach. Jonas was pounding away on the roof, but I hardly noticed. The story was back inside me again, and I was enjoying the familiar feeling of it seeping into every part of me. The characters were so familiar, and I realized that I had missed them and was anxious to delve back into their tale.

My back was aching so I got up to take a break and poured some water from the pump, and then walked out to see how Jonas was coming. Up on the roof he had repaired most of the damage to the structure, removing twisted metal and broken boards. I told him that I would be up soon to help, but that I wanted to go down to the beach first to take a swim and check on the *Dalton women*, as I had begun calling them in the past few weeks. I asked him to take a break and join me, but he declined and kept on with the job.

Sara was lying on a blanket down at the water's edge, dressed in shorts and a sleeveless shirt. Melanee was a few feet away building a sandcastle with a small garden shovel. It was a blustery day, although still hot and muggy. The waves were being pushed in hard on the wind from the southeast, churning up the sandy bottom and turning the water a dull brown. The sun darted in and out around big feathery clouds blowing by quickly overhead, their tops a brilliant white and darker blue and purple beneath.

Sara had food laid out for a lunch. I sat down and grabbed a sandwich. She looked over at me and tried to smile. She still had a look of remorse from her behavior the past night. I had poured out all the liquor in the house when I first woke that morning. No need for further temptations for the vulnerable and fragile Sara Dalton.

"Mathew, it's too rough to go in swimming today," Melanee said, and as usual, she surprised me as I didn't think she had even heard me come up in the roar of the surf. She just kept digging and piling sand on her new creation. Sara and I sat there watching her play for a while without speaking, and then out of the blue, Melanee said, "Do you love my momma, Mathew?"

Sara started to choke back her embarrassment, and I just looked at the little girl in amazement, trying to think quickly of an appropriate response. *Did I love Sara Dalton?* I knew the answer without having to think more than a second. My trust issues with women were such lately that I doubted at that moment that I would ever allow myself to fall in love again. Sara was a beautiful and amazing, troubled and flawed person that was still an enigma to me. She had so much love and compassion for her daughter and mother, and yet, harbored demons that drove her down unimaginable paths.

"I love you both, Melanee," I said, hoping that would suffice to move the discussion. "What are you building there, little squirt?" I asked.

"It's our new hotel."

We made a fire that night on the beach, and most of the Grayton Beach residents came down to join us and enjoy the sunset, all trying to put thoughts of the storm and reconstruction out of our minds, at least for a while. Everyone brought food, and it was a grand party and celebration of survival. The boardwalk and pavilion that Lila had built had been swept away in the force of the wind and storm surge, so we all found our place in the soft white sand, looking out over the glorious waters of the Gulf. Most everyone was drinking some form of illegal locally brewed or imported drink, but I sat with Sara and Melanee, and kept sober with a glass of cold tea in my hand. It was really a marvelous night of recovery and jubilation in our mutual survival.

The Bidwell family drove over from Point Washington and joined us, and Rebecca came up to me right away and asked about James Headley. I told her that my friend was truly taken with her, and that she should expect the most outrageous signs of affection and devotion to arrive any day. I also noticed that her older brother, Jonas, had taken a particular interest in Sara Dalton, and had quickly moved over to sit next to her and start up a conversation. He had cleaned up for the evening and looked so much different than the sweaty and grimy carpenter that had been working around the house, his black hair slicked back, and wearing clothes that he probably reserved for the most important church Sundays. I looked at the two of them sitting there on a big wool blanket that Sara had brought down. I didn't know if I should acknowledge the feelings of father and protector, or friend.

Everyone was having a good time sharing stories of weathering the storm and how the reconstruction had been going, although those sitting close to Sara were respectful of her loss. I was standing and talking with Eli and Priscilla Bidwell. They were asking question after question about my friend Jimmy Headley and his intentions regarding their daughter. I noticed another man walking down to the beach from town, someone that I didn't recognize. He walked forward tentatively, obviously not sure of where he was, or whether he was welcome.

The first person to react to his arrival was little Melanee Dalton. I looked over and she stood up on the blanket where she had been sitting next to her mother. She turned back toward town and looked on sightlessly at the approach of the stranger. The man was dressed in light colored suit pants with a vest over a starched white shirt rolled up at the sleeves. He was tall and gangly, and walked with a clumsy stride. He kept looking across the crowd as he approached, obviously with someone in mind.

Then Sara turned from her conversation with Jonas Bidwell when she noticed her daughter's preoccupation. She looked around, and when she spotted the man approaching I was purposely watching her face, trying to gage the reaction. She saw the man coming toward all of us, and she tensed at first, and then her whole body seemed to sink into itself, but she kept staring at him. Finally he saw what he was looking for, and it was Sara Dalton. He altered course and walked straight toward her. Melanee was still looking off in his direction and as he walked by her, she held up a hand to stop him and she brushed his arm. He looked down at her, but didn't stop or acknowledge the little girl.

I watched as Sara stood, and as the man came up to her she reached out and welcomed him with a tentative embrace. I could still see her face, and she was clearly struggling with her emotions. Melanee stood next to them, holding out her hands as if she was waiting to be noticed. Sara and the man knelt down in front of her, and Sara said a few words before Melanee jumped into his arms. He lifted her up and twirled her around.

I walked over to check on this interesting homecoming. Sara reached out and took my hand before she said, "Mathew, I want you to meet Melanee's daddy, Bobby Sanborn."

I had excused myself early from the beach celebration after being introduced to the new arrival, Mr. Bobby Sanborn, taking enough time to slip away without being noticeably rude. Sitting back at the Headley's place on the newly constructed porch, I thought about this Sanborn fellow. Lila Dalton had told me some time ago that he was Melanee's father. He had been a drummer in the band that Sara had traveled with earlier in her singing days. Ultimately, the two of them had not stayed together, and Sara had unfortunately found her way down to New Orleans, and eventually a life clouded by fear and drugs and alcohol with Miller Boudreaux. I knew very little more about Sanborn. Sara had rarely spoken of him. My first limited impression was that he was a reasonable man and had truly missed both Sara and Melanee, and that perhaps it would be best for the two of them to have him back in their lives. But then I found myself wondering about a man who could ever abandon them in the first place.

I watched as people from the beach began making their way back up into town. Through the darkness I saw the shapes of Melanee and Sara, holding hands with Bobby Sanborn. They came up on the porch and noticed me sitting there. Sara said, "I told Bobby how much you've done to help us since the storm."

"Yes, thank you Coulter for taking care of my girls," the man said. I felt like reminding him that he had lost the right of possession by walking out on them. Sara took Melanee inside to go to bed. "Sara had sent me a letter a couple of months ago that she was back down here with Lila," he said. "When I heard about the storm I knew that I had to get down as soon as I could to check on them. Just a damn shame about Lila."

"Nice of you to make the effort," I said, not trying very hard to mask my declining opinion of the man. "I'll grab a blanket for you. The couch isn't too bad."

In the morning Jonas Bidwell was back for work, and I asked him to wait a bit before starting in on the house to allow the girls to get some more sleep. I could tell that Jonas was bothered by something, and I asked him about it.

"It's this Sanborn fellow," he answered. "Who the hell does he think he is just waltzing back in here after all these years?"

I looked back at the house and all was quiet inside. When I had walked out, Sanborn was snoring on the couch. "Well, he is the little girl's daddy, and he has every right to make sure she's safe," I said with little conviction.

"Shoulda thought of that years ago," Jonas said.

I looked at Jonas Bidwell in a different light that morning. In the past I had seen him as a rough kid from a nowhere place and as Seth Howard's best friend, I had always had to question his true character. Getting to know him better recently working on the Headley cottage, I found a sense of maturity and intelligence that had not been evident in our previous encounters. He had much of the same curiosity and wonder about the world around us, beyond the shores of the Gulf of Mexico, as his younger sister Rebecca.

"I noticed that you and Sara were deep in conversation last night before Sanborn arrived," I said.

He looked away toward the beach with an embarrassed expression. "Guess it shouldn't be a secret that I think Ms. Dalton is a fine woman." I was fairly certain this was coming. "I know that she's a little older," he said, "but that doesn't really matter."

"Sara's dealing with a lot right now," I said. "Don't be surprised if she's a little off kilter about things for a while longer."

He looked at me and nodded, and I had to think that now Sara would have to deal with the attentions of two new men in her life, in addition to the loss and chaos of her recent past that she was still trying to sort through.

Chapter Thirty-two

Jonas and I began work up on the roof later that morning. We really needed to get the roofing repaired before any more rain came through the area. The noise and pounding finally woke Sara and Melanee, who came out sleepy-eyed together around ten. Sanborn was apparently still sleeping. They both waved, and then went around back to the outhouse. I noticed that Jonas watched them all the way until they were out of sight.

A half hour later, Sara came back out with a pot of coffee and we came down to take a break. She poured two cups for us, and Jonas and I sat down across from her on the chairs set up out on the front yard. Melanee was up on the porch with crackers in her hand, hoping that her bird friends might finally return. It had been some time since she had released the bird that I had given her, and it had flown off with Champ. There had been no sign of them since, and Melanee was growing quite upset about it.

Sara took a sip from her coffee, and then said, "You all met Bobby last night?" Of course, she knew that we had. When she saw us acknowledge the fact, she went on, "He was back in Nashville, and when he heard about the storm…" She didn't finish the thought, and looked out over the dunes down toward the water. Her eyes were distant and sad, and I felt so bad for the complications in her young life. She was such a talented woman with a beautiful daughter, and yet so many issues to deal with. The sun was just coming up over the house, and it caught her face and her hair in a beautiful light.

"What are his plans?" I heard Jonas ask, and I looked over at him. You could see the pained expression on his face like he didn't really want to hear the answer.

Sara looked over at him, and then shook her head. "I really don't know, Jonas," she said, and then she looked at the boy and smiled. I felt like I was intruding on this time between the two of them.

I excused myself and poured some more coffee, and then went up on the porch with Melanee. She was sitting in one of the chairs, listening for sounds from the birds, crackers spread along the rail. I sat down next to her. "They'll be back, honey," I said. "Who knows where birds travel on their little routes."

"I'm just very worried about them," Melanee said. "Champ's never been away this long."

"Who knows with that little rascal," I said. "He may have ten more houses on his route before he decides to get back to us, and he needs to show Maggie now, so maybe it's taking longer." I hoped this feeble attempt might possibly make her feel a little better.

"Did you meet my daddy?" she asked.

Before I could answer, there was a scuffling noise behind us, and Bobby Sanborn stuck his head out of the door. His eyes were closed against the light of the day, and he was trying to push his hair back from his face.

"Mornin, folks," he said, and then seeing Sara down on the front yard, he walked down the steps without even saying anything to his daughter. I watched as he whispered something to Sara, and she pointed off around the back of the house. He was obviously looking for the privy.

When he came back, he took her hand and they walked off down through the dunes. I looked over next to me at Melanee, and while she couldn't see, it was clear that she knew what was happening because she looked off in the direction of their departure. It occurred to me that the little girl must be wondering about another man coming to see her mother, and usually that meant that she would be leaving without her. I couldn't imagine how a little child could deal with abandonment like this. I asked if she was hungry, and she said she was starved, so I took her inside and pulled together some breakfast. I heard Jonas back up on the roof a few minutes later. It seemed like he was pounding particularly hard.

Sara and Bobby Sanborn must have been gone for over two hours. I had cleaned up the breakfast dishes and was reading to Melanee out on the porch when I saw them walking back through the dunes. Melanee sensed them coming, and stood up and held her hand out for me to help her down the steps. The pounding up on the roof stopped as Jonas had obviously seen their return. We met them out by the road. Sara picked up her daughter and gave her a big hug, turning around in the mid-day sun. I exchanged looks with Bobby Sanborn. He smiled back at me with this assured air that puzzled me under the circumstances. Sara set Melanee down and held her hand as she kneeled in front of her.

"Honey, your daddy's gonna stay here in Grayton Beach with us and help us rebuild Grandma's place," Sara said, and then she looked up at me as her daughter hugged her fiercely around the neck. Sanborn knelt down next to them and put his arms around both of them. Sara kept looking at me. I wasn't sure how to react or what to say. It was marvelous to see Melanee so happy with the fragments of what had been her splintered family starting to come back together, but I also had a hollow and sick feeling deep in my gut that this was only a temporary reunion. The pounding began again up on the roof behind me. I looked back and saw that Jonas had gone over to the other side to keep working.

The Elliot family who had the first place on the way into town, had invited Sara and Melanee to stay in their guest cottage after the storm. It had been fairly protected and received minimal damage, and now that Sanborn had arrived, Sara mentioned that she thought it might be better if they all moved down there. I helped them later that day take what little belongings they had been able to salvage from the wreckage of the hotel down to the Elliot's. As I was walking away, leaving the Dalton girls with Bobby Sanborn, Melanee yelled out, "Do you think Champ and Maggie will be able to find me down here?"

Her sweet little voice nearly broke my heart, and I felt a lump rise in my throat before I was able to say, "I'm sure they're trying to find you." Melanee waved as I walked away.

On the way back to Headley's cottage I was trying to convince myself that this was the right thing, and that Melanee and Sara needed the little girl's father back in their lives. Hopefully he was a good man who would care for them. I had told Sara earlier after her announcement of their plans for the hotel that I would still like to honor my offer of financial help in rebuilding the Beach Hotel. I also told her that I had already ordered a new piano for her and Melanee through Bidwell's store, and that it would be a gift for the new hotel. She had given me a warm and lingering hug, and then walked away with a brief and teary-eyed *thank you.*

When I got back to the cottage, Jonas and his truck were gone. I wondered if I'd see him back on the job after what I was sure was very disappointing news today about Sara's intentions and plans. The old cottage was dark and quiet when I returned, and I forced myself to sit down at the writing table and get myself back into the story.

It was another month before the work on the Headley place was completed. Jonas had indeed come back that next day and had worked hard beside me in putting the cottage back together. His mood had been quiet and brooding, but he worked hard and we never mentioned the Dalton's. I had gone over to the Bidwell's to call Jimmy Headley up in Atlanta to let him know that his family's cottage was almost as good as new. He was extremely grateful, and of course, wanted to speak with Rebecca when we finished with our conversation. He was planning to come down in the next couple of weeks to see her, as soon as he could get away.

I bought a good bottle of whiskey from old man Bidwell's private stock and started back to Grayton Beach. I drove by the Elliot's place and there was no sign of anyone around. The guest cottage was around back and I could see Sanborn's car parked beside it. At the Headley's cottage, I walked up the steps and for some reason, looked over and noticed that the crackers that Melanee had left several weeks ago for the birds that had fallen on the deck in dozens of broken pieces were now gone. I wondered if Champ and Maggie had indeed returned, or maybe some other little scrounger had happened across an easy meal.

I walked down to the beach as the sun headed toward the far horizon. A dull gray reflection lay across the water that was calm in a light offshore hint of breeze. A heavy layer of clouds hung along the distant waterline. I had the bottle in one hand and a few of the recent pages from my book that I had been working on in the other. When I reached the shore, I sat down in the soft white sand and pulled the top off the whiskey. I took a short drink and tried to read through the pages I had brought along, but couldn't seem to stay focused on the words. Out past the far sandbar two dolphins rolled lazily along, coming up and surfacing every few moments for another breath of air.

I started thinking about my own prospects. I had also spoken to my sister and mother by phone when I was over at the

Bidwell's, and they told me that my father was continuing to improve some. They had heard nothing from Willie Palumbo, and I convinced myself that was a good thing. Charles Watermann, my father's old friend and partner had stopped by recently to reassure them that Palumbo had moved quickly to assume control, and that most things were progressing well. Watermann had smartly aligned himself with the old gangster. Self-preservation is a powerfully motivating thing. The O'Leary's had been put in their place. There had been a few skirmishes and hot spots of trouble, but for the most part, the business was falling into much of its old routine.

    I was thinking that it had been a little over six months since I had come down to this place in my flight from Atlanta. As I thought back over the sequence of events and calamities that had transpired, it was nearly inconceivable how much had happened, and how different I had come to feel about the world around me.

    By dark I had loaded my few belongings into my car and shut the old Headley place up for the last time. I hung the key on the nail back in the outhouse and drove out of town. A work crew had begun rebuilding the hotel, and the first floor was fully framed. I had left money with Bidwell and had set up an account to pay for the rest of the repairs. I stopped at the Elliot's to say goodbye to Sara and Melanee, but the car was gone and no one was around. I took some paper from my case and left a note.

Chapter Thirty-three

New York City, September 1927

Just over a year after the big storm in Grayton Beach had almost swept us all away, I was sitting in the lobby of the Plaza Hotel in New York, right there off Central Park South, sipping a cup of coffee and watching the well-dressed crowd drift through the elegant lobby. My editor had set up an appointment for me to interview an actress that was in town from the West Coast for the season. I had secured a job with the *New York Times*, and after months working in obituaries and other even less exciting assignments, I had been assigned to the entertainment beat.

My book was finally finished about six months after I arrived in New York. A few publishing houses had rejected the manuscript, when I had been referred to another by an associate at the newspaper. The editor got excited about the story and I had sold it soon after. I was told that it would be released early the next year.

That summer at the beach along the Gulf Coast of Florida seemed so long ago. I had been terribly busy and moving in so many directions that I had little time to think back on how it all came to pass.

GRAYTON WINDS

I had an hour before my appointment with the actress. The front desk had just handed me a note that she would be late. It appeared to be a beautiful morning in the city and I needed a break to get some fresh air in my system. Walking out through the main entrance doors I was greeted politely by the staff, who must have thought that I was a paying guest. I headed north up into the park. The horse-drawn carriages were already lining up to take tourists on excursions around the city. There was the earliest trace of fall in the air, and in the changing colors of the leaves above me. As usual, people were moving about in careless disregard for other fellow pedestrians and traffic in the streets.

I walked for a few hundred yards down one of the sidewalks into the park and found a large pond with benches set around the perimeter. It was a Saturday and families had gathered to sail small model boats and feed the ducks. I sat down and looked across the scene before me, certainly a far less grand body of water than the Gulf of Mexico. Taking a deep breath, I allowed myself to put the newspaper and book business aside for a moment, and I thought back on other events that had seemed to pass in a disturbing blur these past years.

My father never recovered from the stroke that he suffered during that summer of 1926, and in fact, six months later died from another. He had improved enough to be sent home, but my mother found him collapsed over the desk in his den one morning, and he was gone. The funeral was a grand event in Atlanta that spring, attended by his many business and social connections. My mother was in her element, attending the many related gatherings and services; managing the role of grieving widow with incredible aplomb and dignity. My sister, Maggie, later told me that all of our mother's friends were quite impressed with the entire production, particularly the food and flowers.

Maggie had finalized her divorce from Desmond Raye, who by the way, never returned to Atlanta. Our last report, at the time, had him working for a gem importer in Miami and living with a Cuban woman. Maggie found a new boyfriend and they were engaged a few months later. Much to my mother's disappointment, he was a Catholic from Boston who had come south to work in the railroad business with a family friend. He and his family had considerable wealth, but existed far below the social strata that my mother and her friends would have preferred for the daughter of the Coulters from Atlanta.

Willie Palumbo had attended my father's funeral service, and I spoke with him just briefly afterward. He had stayed in the background throughout the day's events, trying to be discreet. He and Louise had bought a house just north of downtown Atlanta, and he was still spending much of his time in the South. Apparently it was still a little too uncertain with the law in New Jersey. He had asked me about the people back in Grayton Beach, but I had had very little contact since leaving and was unable to provide much of an update. I did tell him that I had given his club away to Eleanor Whitlock on the same day that he had given it to me. He just laughed a big belly-shaking laugh and said that it was certainly a grand gesture considering what had happened. His payments to my mother and sister had continued on the schedule agreed to, and there was very little reason to discuss anything else about the business that was no longer part of our lives.

A few months after leaving Grayton Beach, I received a letter from Sara Dalton that she had sent to my sister to be forwarded to me at my current address. In her note I learned that the hotel had been finished and was open for business again. She said that they had adjusted well to the demands of running the place, and that Melanee was enjoying singing and playing for guests on the new piano that I had given them. When I had left, I also arranged for a special tutor from Birmingham to come down and stay to help Melanee with her schooling. Sara seemed quite grateful in her letter and said that the teacher was working out very well. She provided no news of Melanee's father, Bobby Sanborn.

In the occasional letter and phone call from my friend, Jimmy Headley, I kept up to date on the progress of his love affair with the beautiful young Rebecca Bidwell. Her parents had finally allowed her to travel to Atlanta to visit the Headley family. According to Jimmy, she had handled herself quite well in the social pressure cooker that his parents thrived in. They were still very much in love and he was considering asking for her hand. His last letter had been some time ago, and I had been waiting for the latest.

When I arrived in New York, I secured a small apartment where I could walk to work at the paper. There were many good clubs and restaurants in the area. I had made a few friends, mostly from work, and I had enjoyed the pace of the city again after my brief respite from civilization down in Grayton Beach. I had taken a few women out to dinner or a show, but nothing serious had developed and I, quite honestly, just wasn't finding myself that interested in getting attached. My experience with women the past years had been far from encouraging.

In general, I saw very little to be gained by revisiting paths previously traveled, and I tried not to let myself dwell much on the past. There was enough work and distraction here in New York to keep me focused on the future. There were times however, usually late at night lying awake, when thoughts of past women in my life came back to me in, unfortunately, vivid detail. Even after all this time away I still found myself wondering how I could have been so trusting and naïve. Certainly it had hardened my heart since arriving in New York, and most women that I met were immediately scrutinized in my mind for the slightest traces of insincerity. It was terribly unhealthy and quite off-putting for the unfortunate woman sitting across from me in whatever restaurant or club I had chosen to escort her to.

Sara Dalton also found a way back into my thoughts from time to time. I worried that she and Melanee would face some new challenge in their lives, and that Sara would not have the emotional strength to endure it. Hopefully now that she had to take care of herself and her daughter without her mother to fall back on, she would be able to find some level of confidence and self-reliance.

The interview with the actress was uneventful, except that she was two hours late, not one. She was an up-and-coming star from one of the big studios out in Los Angeles, and her new film would be debuting in New York later in the week. She was distant and ditsy, and I had to wonder how she could ever possibly create a likable image on the screen.

I left the interview and walked down the street to a small restaurant that I frequented on occasion, and went in to get some lunch. When my eyes had adjusted to the dark interior, I asked for a table by the window and a waitress brought a menu over for me. After ordering, I was reading the morning edition of the *Times* that I had brought with me when I noticed someone standing by my table. I looked up thinking it was the waitress and was shocked to see a face that I had never expected to encounter again.

Eleanor Whitlock stood there looking down at me with a beautiful smile filled with even white teeth. Her hair had been trimmed short in the current style, and she was dressed very professionally in a gray tweed suit, smartly tailored. I couldn't even start to come up with anything appropriate to say, and I sat there staring with my mouth hanging open. She sat down across from me, and then reached her hand across the table and took mine. "How are you, Mathew?" she said.

"Eleanor?" was all I could manage to say.

"It's Ellen White now," she said. "My new stage name."

"Ellen?"

"Yes, do you like it?" she asked. "My agent, Rick, feels that it's more of a show business name."

"It's fine," I said. "So you're in show business?"

She smiled again and squirmed with excitement. "I've got a great new part in a show down on Broadway. Can you believe it?"

"That's wonderful, Eleanor... I mean Ellen," I said. "When did you come to New York?"

"Oh, it's been almost six months now. I sold the club, and thank you again for that," she said, and then looked down, a little embarrassed.

"So you're really working in a Broadway play?" I asked.

"Isn't it just grand?" she said. "I've been working steady since I got here and connected with Rick. He's really helped me meet the right people."

Then I looked down at her hand on mine and saw a ring with a big diamond. "And who's the lucky fellow?" I asked.

"Well Rick," she said. "I'm sorry I forgot to mention it. We were married last month."

I congratulated her on her work and new marriage. She asked me why I was in New York, and I brought her up to date on my job at the paper, and told her that my book would soon be published. As I looked at her face and into those incredible eyes, I couldn't help myself from thinking back to the times we had spent together and the intimacies that we had shared. I remembered the feelings I had held for this woman during those months down on the Gulf Coast and how, once again, I had been misled and betrayed. Remarkably, I found that I wasn't angry with her anymore. I was actually pleased that she had changed her life and found a new start, and I took some pleasure in knowing I helped her in that direction. The fact that she was married didn't bother me, and when her husband walked over from across the restaurant, I greeted him cordially and wished them both well as Eleanor, or Ellen, got up to leave. Rick was already out the door when she ran back over and quickly kissed me on the cheek, and then traced her fingers along the side of my face before she left again. Through the window I watched them walk down the street, their arms entwined, and away through the crowd. I couldn't help but feel just a small tinge of regret deep in my gut that things hadn't worked out differently.

Chapter Thirty-four

My novel was indeed published in February of the next year. I had been in New York long enough to have made a few of the right contacts, and my publisher hosted a nice reception to introduce the book at the Waldorf to help broaden that circle. In addition to meeting all the appropriate people to help launch the book, I also met a woman that night that caught me completely by surprise.

I first saw her across the room speaking with a group of other young women, laughing and looking out over the crowd of notable New York literary and entertainment people. She seemed terribly confident in her manner, but stood out as so different from the rest. My first impression was that she was so clearly out of place. There was a certain look that women seemed to migrate to in New York City, and particularly in the publishing business. There was a hard line to the cut of their clothes and the style of their hair, the heavy make-up, affected mannerisms and speech. To the opposite extreme, this woman was all smooth edges and flowing curves. Her light brown hair bounced around her face in soft natural curls, and her clothes were functional, not necessarily fashionable, and yet she cast a compelling presence across the crowded room.

I watched as my editor, Sam Keller, walked up to her and interrupted their conversation. He took the woman's arm and whispered something in her ear. Then in surprise, I watched as he led her over in my direction. As they came up, Sam flashed that big smile that I had become accustomed to over the past months, working closely with him on the final drafts of my book.

"Mathew Coulter," he said, "I want you to meet Annie Martin." Then to my surprise he went on to say, "Annie is a publishing assistant at the firm and I've asked her to work with you on the book introduction."

"Hello Mr. Coulter," she said, and shook my hand.

"Please, it's Mathew," I answered, and up close I could see the shine of her marvelous brown eyes.

"Annie has been with us for a few years now," Keller said. "She has a great future in the business. You're in very good hands."

"I loved your story, Mathew," she said.

"Thank you. And what do publishing assistants do?" I asked, hoping she would say that we would be working endless hours together.

"Annie will be handling all of the details," Keller said. "Anything you need."

"I was so excited when Sam asked me to work on the book," she said. "I think it's going to do quite well." She smiled with an easy confidence and took a sip from the glass of punch in her hand.

"I'll leave you two to get acquainted," Keller said, and then he was off across the room.

"I understand you're from Atlanta," Annie said.

"Yes, originally, though I've been in the city now for long enough that I'm beginning to lose the accent. What do you think?" I asked.

"Oh, I can definitely hear a touch of Old South there," she said, "but I'm used to all of these heavy New York dialects. I'm still trying to sort through Brooklyn and Long Island."

"And where are you from?" I asked.

"From Michigan," she said. "Have you ever heard of a little town called Charlevoix?"

"No, I don't believe I have."

She held her right hand up to illustrate the mitten shape of the state, and pointed with her other hand to a location that would be in the far northwest of the Lower Peninsula.

"Charlevoix," I repeated. "What an interesting name. How did you ever find your way to New York?"

"When I finished school at Michigan State, I wanted to work in the publishing business. I love books and writing," she said. "There's not a lot of that work in Michigan," she said with a smile. "Particularly up in the cold North. I had a friend who had moved here a year earlier after school and she invited me out. I was lucky to be introduced to Sam at a party and got the job."

"You seem very excited about your work," I said.

"It's a tough pace, but I love it."

"So what is your job here tonight," I asked.

"To introduce you to all the right people."

"And who would that be?"

She looked across the room and started to point out some of the more powerful people in the business, and their background, to prepare me for later introductions. She was marvelously engaging and fun. We laughed as she told me inside stories about the business and some of the more prominent people in the room. She had been to many of these kinds of events during her tenure, and helped me through all of the protocols and introductions.

She was someone out of the ordinary; someone who when you first meet you sense that you've happened across something special that you had misplaced years ago and then suddenly found right where you should have looked all along. As the night progressed, there were two voices in my head; the one that was following the conscious conversation with Annie Martin and all of the people she was introducing me to, and the other that was whispering that this was a remarkable person that, seemingly out of nowhere, had so fortunately crossed my path.

Later, I invited her to join me for a celebration drink, and we went to a nearby club. We talked that night about the business, but more about ourselves; how we had found our way to New York, and where we thought our lives were headed.

"So you must tell me about your family," she said after a second round of drinks had been delivered to our table. "Sam tells me that the Coulters are high on the social register in Atlanta."

I shook my head and laughed. "Oh you have no idea," I said. "It's just my mother and sister now, and they are still quite involved in all the society nonsense."

"Nonsense?" she repeated. "So it's not for you? I thought you handled yourself quite well tonight with all these New Yorkers."

"Oh, I'm used to the scene," I said. "I just don't really care for all the pretense and bother."

"I can imagine you'll become a reclusive writer, hidden away on some remote island?" she said and laughed.

"Actually that would be perfect," I said. "I'll have to show you Grayton Beach some day."

We sat there sipping on our drinks, captured by the incredible good fortune that I sensed we both felt in our new relationship. We made quite a late night of it, and I escorted her home, both of us dreading the early start to another day in the office. She shook my hand on the steps of her apartment building. It was all I could do to keep from taking her in my arms and kissing her goodnight, but we both kept up our professional façade.

She went inside after agreeing to meet me for dinner the next night... to discuss the book business, of course.

During that first dinner with Annie Martin the night after the preview party, I felt an almost electric connection, as if we were wired together and completed a circuit. The conversation flowed like we had known each other for years, and I found myself astounded that I had happened to meet this woman. After an hour of talk about the book and what lie ahead with the work she would be doing, ultimately the conversation approached the topic of relationships and why neither of us was married. I was the first to broach the subject.

"And how have you managed to stay single in this town with so many eligible young men?" I asked, and then immediately felt foolish for doing so.

She didn't seem embarrassed or put off. "I have so little time. I don't even remember the last date I've been on," she said.

"Forgive me, but I would think that you'd have offers every night," I said.

"Oh I suppose there have been a few interested suitors," she answered and smiled. She took a bite from the remnants of the dessert in front of her. "And I've heard nothing from you about the girl back home," she said.

I thought for a moment about the women that had crossed my path, even the surprise in seeing Eleanor in New York. "No," I finally said, "there's no one."

After I left her at her apartment that night, I laid awake almost until morning thinking about this person named Annie Martin, and frankly, overwhelmed in the fact that we had chanced to meet in this vast city.

The book editor at the *Times* was a friend and fortunately he felt that my book held some promise. He personally reviewed it for the Sunday section. He also allowed the publicity department at the publisher to send his endorsement and review out to editors that he knew around the country at other major newspapers and magazines, encouraging them to read and review the book. It seemed that the story held some interest for readers. Within several months it had achieved a reasonable measure of success for a first novel from an unknown writer, and continued to gain momentum. My publisher was very excited and paid a fair advance for me to begin work on a second book which I had yet to start, being incredibly busy with the work at the paper.

Annie Martin and I became nearly inseparable in those first weeks, working long hours in the evening after my work at the paper was finished. While we tried our best to keep focused on business, invariably our conversation would stray and we continued to learn more about each other. I found myself struggling not to reach for her hand as we walked down the street after a dinner to discuss the upcoming events and activities for the book release.

I took a few days off from the paper to go to Chicago at Sam Keller's request to meet with reviewers and book industry people. My boss seemed to understand that it would be beneficial to the newspaper to have a writer who had found some success in publishing. Sam had asked Annie to accompany me to help navigate the schedule and make the proper introductions. We took the train out on a rainy night in New York, leaving Grand Central Station in time to have a meal in the dining car as we were leaving the lights of the city behind.

Annie sat across from me, talking on with so much enthusiasm about everyone we would be meeting and how important this trip was to properly introduce the book in the Midwest. I was hearing her talk, but finding it difficult to pay attention to what she was saying. I sat enjoying the sight of her across from me at the little table, the quiet rumble of the train making the dishes rattle.

Finally she said, "Mathew Coulter, have you heard a thing I've said?"

I smiled and said, "Every word."

"How do I ever put up with you? This book is going to be successful in spite of its wayward author."

"I have excellent help," I said.

"You certainly do," she answered, frowning at me and pulling her loose papers and notes together. She placed them in her bag on the floor beside her.

"I'd like you to see Atlanta," I said, surprising even myself at this sudden suggestion.

"Atlanta?"

Trying to recover, I said, "I'd like you to see the town I grew up in. You've never been there?"

"No, I've never been in the South," she said.

"Don't you think you need to see the local roots of your *not yet famous* author client?" I asked. "To round out the story and background you're trying to package."

"Mathew Coulter, you are truly impossible."

"I think you'd like my sister, Maggie," I said.

She stared at me with an amused expression. "And your mother?"

"That's another story."

We stayed at The Drake Hotel in Chicago, an elegant place along the shore of Lake Michigan on the north edge of the city. We arrived late in the afternoon the following day, and after checking in, I asked Annie if she would like to go for a walk down Michigan Avenue. It was early spring in the city and the wind was blowing fiercely through the tall buildings. A strong gust caught me as I was lifting my stiff leg up on a curb and I stumbled forward. Annie caught me by the arm and prevented me from falling on my face.

"You've never told me about your leg," she said as we continued on. "Sam's told me that you were decorated in the War."

I kept walking, trying to think how best to change the subject.

"It was my brother who was the hero," I said. "He had a whole chest full of medals."

"And he's gone now?" she asked.

"He was killed over a year ago."

"Killed?"

"My father was in a very ruthless business," I said. "He ran liquor in the South."

She stopped and looked at me with a surprised expression. "But I thought…"

"You thought we were *high society*? My parents were very good at holding their position in town, even during these years when my father's business changed with the times," I said. I noticed that she was still holding my arm. We kept on along the sidewalk and then across a bridge that spanned the river, the water a deep green below us.

"Jess was killed by a rival family trying to take over my father's business," I finally said.

"My God!" she said.

"My father became quite ill after Jess was gone. He had a stroke and wasn't able to run the business any longer. I had no interest in bootlegging. The family is no longer involved."

"Oh Mathew, I had no idea," she said. "I'm so sorry about your brother."

We walked on in silence for another block.

"I came close to losing my leg after a shell exploded near me during a battle outside Verdun," I suddenly said. She looked at me and held my arm tighter. "I was lucky. I had very good care."

The comment took me back for a moment to a young nurse at the American Hospital in Paris.

Our business in Chicago over the next day was hectic and fruitful. Annie felt that we had made a good impression with all the right people. There had been little time for more personal conversations. We caught the late train out of Chicago and went to the dining car for something to drink before retiring for the long night's ride back to New York. We sat facing each other in the cramped cabin, glasses of soda water with lime in front of us.

"Thank you for putting up with me," I said.

"You've done wonderfully," she said.

"I mean about all the old family stuff."

"I was the one who was so nosey," she said, swirling the ice in the glass and then looking out the window into the night.

"I'm surprised Sam let you come along with me unchaperoned," I said. "Won't your office be scandalized?"

"Should I be worried?" she said.

I shook my head and smiled.

"We work in New York, Mathew. It takes a lot to create a scandal."

"Thank you for all you've done," I said. "I would have been lost in this crowd, and all that's gone on back in New York getting this book out."

"It's my job."

"And you seem to enjoy it," I said.

"Some clients are better than others," she said, and then smiled at me before she took another sip of her water. She put the glass down and stared at me with sudden seriousness. "When *are* you taking me to Atlanta?"

We were both finally able to clear our schedules in June, and Annie joined me on a train trip to Atlanta to visit my mother and sister. They threw quite a party for my homecoming and to impress my new lady friend, although I could tell that my mother and her friends were noticeably disappointed in Annie's lack of social position. My sister, Maggie, thought that Annie was just wonderful and the two of them hit it off splendidly. Our cook, Velma, fawned over her like she was another Coulter sibling under her care.

We spent a day with Maggie touring the city of Atlanta, lunching at the Piedmont Driving Club and shopping downtown, much to my dismay. But Annie was enjoying it all, and she and Maggie were chatting on endlessly about the city, and often about their good-natured frustrations with me.

During lunch, Maggie asked me about Sara and Melanee Dalton. I told her that I hadn't heard anything since Sara's letter. Annie wanted to know more about my time in Grayton Beach. I spent most of our lunch telling her about my time at the Headley cottage, and about Lila Dalton and her family. I decided it was best not to go into my unfortunate affair with Eleanor Whitlock, and only briefly mentioned my friend the gangster, the notorious Willie Palumbo. Annie was very intrigued with Melanee and her talents. I could see that her heart opened to the miseries that the little girl had faced in her short life.

We ended up back at our house on West Paces Ferry, sitting on the back veranda, looking out over the dense woods beyond the pool and spacious lawns. Velma brought out lemonade for us as the dinner was being prepared. I thought of the night I had brought Hanna Wesley here to meet the Coulter family. I could almost hear the music playing, and the crowds of people seemed ghostly images before me; Jess and Hanna dancing close. I turned and looked at Annie Martin's wonderful bright face, and past memories quickly faded.

"So what's to become of the two of you?" Maggie suddenly said with unabashed candor that was so common from her.

Annie looked at me first, as if it was my place to talk of our future. I put my arm around her shoulders as she sat next to me there. "This young publishing assistant has been so successful helping with my book that I'm sure she's going to get a big promotion and never have time to deal with this hick-town writer from the South again," I said.

Annie elbowed me in the ribs and pulled away, clearly irritated with my response.

I reached across for her again and pulled her back close. "I don't think I can let this one get away, sister," I said. I leaned close and kissed Annie Martin.

On the trip back to New York, Annie and I were sitting across from each other finishing dinner on the first night out. As we stood to say goodnight and return to our cabins, Annie held on to my hand and led me back down the aisle and into the next car where her sleeping berth was. I kissed her good night and was turning to leave for my own car, but she wouldn't let go of my arm. I watched as she looked both ways down the corridor, then she opened the door and pulled me in.

Closing the door behind us, I heard her moving across the small cabin in the dark, and then a small reading light over the bed switched on. Annie came back to me and put her arms around my neck. "No chaperones on this trip either, Mr. Coulter," she said in a quiet whisper, and then she kissed me. The warm wetness of her lips moved against mine and I pulled her tight. When she moved her face away and looked up at me, the most beautiful smile greeted me there in the soft light.

"I love you Annie," I said for the first time. "And please call me Mathew."

She laughed quietly, concerned for the noise in adjoining cabins. "I love you too, *Mathew*," she said, and then she reached up and started to loosen my tie. I started kissing her again as she unbuttoned my shirt, and then we were pulling at buttons and belts in a frantic attempt to pull clothes aside. She stepped back and let her dress fall to the floor, kicking off her shoes and standing there in pale silk underwear that I couldn't look away from as I struggled to strip down to my shorts. She smiled at my clumsy attempts, and then came back into my arms.

As we kissed again, I reached behind and tried to unfasten the clasp of her bra, and then she finally helped and let it fall down over the front of her shoulders between us. I felt the soft roundness of her breasts push against my chest. My hands traced the smooth curves of her back as our lips came together again. Then she pulled away and went back over to the bed, pulling down the covers and laying down, leaving room for me to join her.

Sunlight through the window woke me the next morning. I saw Annie sleeping there beside me, her hair covering most of her beautiful face and lying on her bare shoulders. I pulled her closer, and still half asleep, she moved into my arms and rested her head on my shoulder. We lay there together, and I watched the countryside pass by outside the window, savoring the soft warmness of Annie Martin.

The taxi dropped me at my apartment after we had left Annie off. It had been a long trip back from Georgia. We were exhausted and both had to report back to work early in the morning.

Back at the *Times* the next day, I was pleased to see reports on my desk that my book was continuing to do well. I also had several assignments from my editor that would require considerable work in the coming days, and I started right in on it. About mid-morning, I heard a commotion over on the other side of the large newsroom where my desk was set near the perimeter. When I looked up, I saw one of our guards trying to stop a big man from coming on the floor. It was Palumbo's man, Anthony, and then I saw the old gangster himself step forward to argue with the guard. I got up and walked over, very surprised at their arrival. I reassured the guard that everything was okay, and that I knew these men, although when Willie Palumbo entered a room, things would seldom be okay for long. He gave me a big hug, and many of my associates in the newsroom looked over with puzzled expressions.

"Coulter, you look like a million bucks," he said, and of course, Anthony stood off to the side without speaking with the same unemotional expression. "And congratulations on your new book. I really liked the *bad guy*," he said and laughed. "Reminded me of someone we both know, don't you think?"

"Willie, what the hell are you doing in New York?" I asked quietly. "I thought you were a wanted man around these parts."

"Hell," he answered, "I'm a wanted man about any damn place I chose to go," and he was laughing that same old hearty laugh that I had come to know down in Florida. "Man needs to get home now and then." He took me by the arm and led me out into the hall. "You got time for a lunch break?"

I looked at my watch and it was about lunchtime. I had been working steadily all morning. "Sure, I've got a few minutes."

We walked around the corner to a little Italian place that I thought he might like. He asked for a table in the back. When we sat down, he looked at the menu and then proceeded to order just about everything listed. Soon our table was mounded with dishes, and Anthony and Willie didn't hesitate to sample most of it. Finally, he took a break from chewing and wiped his mouth with a napkin before he said, "Was down on the Gulf Coast last month to check on my interests. Went over to Grayton Beach to see how all of our old friends were doing."

I thought to myself that Willie Palumbo didn't have many friends down there.

"Stopped in at the old Beach Hotel," he said. "Sara was pretty busy in the back and just stopped out to say hello for a minute. Little Melanee played us a song on her new piano. That was damn nice of you Coulter, and they've done a hell of a job on the hotel. Looks ten times better than the old place. Headley's joint is still standing in spite of that repair work you did," he said with a smile.

"So they're doing all right?" I asked.

Palumbo took another big bite of pasta that he had swirled on his fork. It took some time for him to almost finish chewing before he continued speaking with remnants of chicken and white wine sauce sloshing about, in and around his mouth. "Little Melanee asked if I had seen you. She asked me to give you a message," he said. "Damn, she's a cute little kid. Grown a foot I swear. You wouldn't recognize her. What is she, twelve now?"

"What did she want you to tell me, Willie," I said, growing impatient with his chewing and rambling.

"She wanted you to know that the loggerheads had been back again last summer," he said. "The turtles, you know?"

"Yes, I know," I replied.

"She also said to tell you that her mom has been sick again," he said, and then he stopped and looked up at me with a serious look for the first time. "Sara's not well, Mathew. She looked a damn mess. Think she's been drinking pretty hard."

"Where was Sanborn?" I asked.

"You mean the kid's old man? He split a few months after you left. I thought you knew."

The news of Bobby Sanborn's abandonment hit me hard in the gut, but not as much as the revelation that Sara's demons had taken hold again. "Didn't you try to help?" I asked in an accusing way that didn't seem to rile the man.

"You know, kid, I did try to help," he said slowly, looking directly into my eyes. "Found a doc over in Panama City that went to see her, and I arranged for a full-time nurse to stay there again, but Sara wouldn't have any of it. She sent them both away in a screaming fit. Told them to stay the hell out of her life."

My spirits were sinking fast as I thought about the child and how this would all affect her again, let alone what Sara was going through.

"Seems she's taken up with some asshole from over in Tallahassee that stopped through one day on his way to somewhere," Palumbo went on to say. "Met him before we left. Bad sort."

My anger was boiling over. "Willie, how the hell could you leave her down there like that?"

Again he remained calm as he replied, "Look Coulter, I've done more than enough to help this woman, particularly because I cared deeply about her mother, Lila, and the little girl. Hell, you know we all nearly got ourselves killed down in New Orleans trying to spring her," he said. "Had a notion to take care of this new scumbag she's hanging out with, too."

"I've seen how you *take care* of people, Willie," I said. "The body count is high enough."

All afternoon I sat at my desk thinking about Sara and Melanee, and their precarious situation. I couldn't stand the thought of Melanee going through more heartache in her life, and I was growing less patient by the minute with Sara Dalton's behavior. Somehow I managed to finish a story that I had been working on and submitted it to my editor. I left a few minutes early, and then walked out of the building and down the sidewalk. The late afternoon shadows covered the streets, and it was noticeably cooler than when we had gone to lunch. I kept thinking about the situation in Grayton Beach, and of a little girl who was faced again with a helpless situation.

After several blocks I turned east, down to my publisher's building and the office of Annie Martin. She was up on the fourth floor and I rode the elevator alone, still stewing about Florida. When the doors opened, I walked down the hall and into the big room where Annie's desk was located. There were a dozen other men and women scurrying about, working on typewriters or talking on the phone. Most looked up when I walked in, as strangers were apparently not very typical on this floor. Annie was the last to see me, her head buried in a stack of manuscripts. When she finally glanced my way, a big smile spread across her face, and then a look of curious confusion. I took her hand and told her that we needed to take a walk. She leaned into Sam Keller's office and told her boss she was going out for a few minutes, and then we went back down the elevator and out into the street.

As soon as we were outside, I turned and took her in my arms. I kissed her right there in front of a hundred people walking by. A few of them clapped and whistled as they passed. Then I leaned back and looked into her confused and shining eyes.

"Will you marry me?" I asked.

"Excuse me?" was her startled reply.

"I love you and I want you to be my wife, Annie Martin," I said, my heart beating at double time. She just stared back at me with that beautiful grin on her face, and the longer she stood there speechless, the more I thought she was going to turn me down for being such a strange and pathetic character. "A proposal is usually followed by an answer," I said.

"Mathew Coulter, you are an original," she replied.

"And is that a good thing?" I asked.

"Yes, that's a very good thing... and *yes*, I will marry you!"

I took a deep breath and sighed with great relief before kissing her again and holding her tightly, not wanting her to ever get away. I took a ring out of my pocket that my mother had given me years ago. It had belonged to her grandmother. I tried to keep my hands from shaking as I took her hand in mine and slid it on. She looked at it and smiled, and then kissed me again. "I love you, Annie," I said.

But, there was another matter that needed to be dealt with, and for some reason I couldn't let the elation of the moment linger. She could see the concern on my face.

"And what's the matter?" she asked. "Was that not the answer you were hoping for?"

"No, of course not," I said. "There are some things back in Florida that I need to take care of."

"In Florida?"

"I'll only be gone for a while, but it's something that has to be done."

"I assume this is about your *second family* down there," she said. "It's Sara Dalton, isn't it?"

"Yes, she's in trouble again, and I'm very concerned about her little daughter," I said. "Something needs to be done."

"So you ask me to marry you, and then tell me you're going to run off to Florida for another woman?"

"You know that's not the case," I replied. "Sara has gone over the edge again and someone needs to deal with her." I continued to explain what Palumbo had told me at lunch.

When I had finished, she said, "I understand, Mathew. I suppose it's why I love you, but I'll be damned if I can truly understand why at times."

Chapter Thirty-five

I made arrangements at the office to take a short leave, much to the consternation of my editor. In the end, he told me that my job may or may not be waiting for me when I returned. The next morning I was on a train to Florida. It took nearly three days to make the trip. I finally got a ride on a boat out of Panama City to run over to Point Washington. I knocked on the Bidwell's door late that night. They were, of course, surprised to see me, but welcomed me in. Rebecca was there, and I was amazed how she had grown up and matured. I could see why Headley was still smitten. I found out that her brother, Jonas, had eventually given up hope of ever catching Sara Dalton's eye, which was obviously for the best. He had married a girl from up in DeFuniak Springs. He had moved there and built a house for them, and he was working for a construction company.

When I asked about Sara and Melanee, Rebecca's face turned grim. "I'm truly afraid for little Melanee, Mathew," she said. "I've offered to have her stay over with us for a while to give Sara a chance to get back on her feet. It's that man she's hooked up with."

"Who is this guy?" I asked.

Eli Bidwell said, "We don't know much about him, other than he's from over in Tallahassee. He was a merchant sailor but he got put off his last boat, and he's nothing but trouble."

Rebecca's mother, Priscilla, spoke for the first time. "Every day he comes over here for supplies, I feel like I need to take a bath after he leaves. How in the world Sara puts up with him, I'll never know."

The Bidwell's made up a spare room for me and offered to drive me into Grayton Beach the next morning. I slept very little, trying to think what I could possibly do to help Sara and Melanee Dalton. I also wondered about what I had left behind back in New York.

When morning finally arrived, I had at last fallen asleep, and Eli had to wake me. I splashed some water on my face and threw my things in the back of his truck. We rode mostly in silence, as I thought about what sequence of events may lie ahead. Eli asked me a few questions about James Headley's feelings for his daughter. I did my best to reassure him that Jimmy was a good man and had nothing but the best intentions. In the back of my mind I was hoping that was indeed the case.

We pulled into town around ten that morning. I asked Eli to drop me at the Headley's place. Dark clouds were blowing in fast from the west, an angry purple and dark blue, the wind swirling about and pushing the trees in all directions. When we drove by the Beach Hotel the doors and windows were closed, and no one was about. I thanked Eli for the ride and told him I would probably be heading out in a day or two. I asked whether it was okay if I called him from the hotel for a ride back. He said *yes*, and then before he drove away went on to say, "You need to be careful Mathew, and you let me know if you need any help."

I unlocked the Headley place and put my bags in the back room. The old place was blistering hot, having been closed up for so long, but comforting and haunting at the same time as the memories of my time there came back to me. I opened all of the windows and doors, and let the cooler wind from off the Gulf blow through the screens. I looked at the old table that I had toiled at for so long in writing my book. It sat there empty and seemingly neglected.

After all of the time coming down from New York to think through the situation, I still didn't know what I was going to do. Finally, I just decided to go and see for myself. As I walked over to the front door to leave, I saw Sara and Melanee coming up the steps onto the porch. I walked out to meet them. Sara held Melanee's hand and helped her up the stairs. I was shocked at how gaunt the woman's face and body looked. She was slight to begin with, and had seemed to lose even more weight. Dark circles hung low beneath her eyes, and her skin had a sickly pallor. I also noticed a large bruise on the side of her neck, and I felt my anger welling up to the surface again.

Melanee was a good head taller than the last time I had seen her, and as she reached out in front for the porch railing, she said, "Mathew, it's you isn't it? When Momma said that someone was over at the Headley's, I knew it was you."

"How are you, kid?" I asked, and she walked carefully over across the space between us with her arms held out. I knelt down and gave her a hug, and she clung to me like she would never let go.

"Mathew, I've missed you so much," the little girl said. I looked up at her mother, who stood there without speaking. She was having a hard time standing steady, and her gaze was distant and indifferent.

"Hello Sara," I said as I stood up, holding on to Melanee's hand. I could see that she was having a difficult time focusing on me.

"Welcome back," she finally said, and her voice was weak and almost a whisper.

"Mathew, you have to come over," Melanee said. "Champ and Maggie are here. They've finally come back, and you just have to see them." When I looked down at her to answer, I could see that she also had an ugly bruise on her forearm.

"Sara, what's happening here?" I said, trying to contain my anger and holding up her daughter's arm for her to see. She tried to understand what I was showing her, but her head wavered back and forth, and I thought she was going to fall. I stepped over and grabbed her arm to steady her. I could smell the drink on her breath. I looked down at Melanee and asked, "How did you hurt your arm, honey?" Her face tilted down and I lifted her chin up. "Tell me what happened, Melanee."

"It was Farley," she said slowly and cautiously. "He got mad at me again."

I turned back to Sara and I finally lost my composure. "How in hell can you let anyone treat your daughter like this?" Again, she looked right through me in a drunken blur. Then over her shoulder I saw a man coming down the street. He was a large man, dressed roughly in old and dirty work clothes, the shirt sleeves rolled up high to reveal big arms. As he came closer, I could see that he was staggering a bit, having trouble walking in a straight line. His face was unshaven, and his hair was oily and uncombed. When he saw me holding Sara's arm, I could see a fury build in his eyes, and his fists clench.

"This must be Farley?" I said. Sara turned and saw him coming and then pushed me away, a fearful look on her face. A flash of lightning on the horizon was followed by a low rumble of thunder a few seconds later. The sky out toward Destin was almost black in the middle of the day. I turned and opened the screen door and helped Melanee inside. "I want you to go in and sit over on the couch for a few minutes, honey," I said, and she touched her way along the furniture and then sat down. I came back out and this

Farley fellow was just coming up the steps, his face bright red in anger.

"Sara, who the hell is this asshole?" he said. She didn't answer and I pushed her over to the side with my arm to stand right in front of the man. He was also clearly drunk, and then it started to rain and the thunder crashed again. I told Sara to go inside, and then I pushed her in that direction when she didn't respond.

"Get your hands off her, you piece a shit!" he spat.

"Sara, just get inside," I said again, and then with all the force that I could muster, I rushed at the man and grabbed him with both hands by the front of his shirt and just kept pushing him backwards until we were both falling through the air and down the steps. I landed on top of him on the planked walkway, and I heard his head smack on the boards and the air blow out of his lungs as he gasped to get his breath back, a stunned expression across his face. Before he could begin to recover, I hit him as hard as I could with a wild punch that came from as far back as I could manage in my frenzy. I felt the bones in my fist break against his nose and cheek, and I screamed out in pain. I hit him again in spite of the white hot jolt of fire that shot up my entire arm. His eyes went blank as blood started pulsing out of his smashed nose. I grabbed the hair on the top of his head with both hands and started pounding the back of his skull against the wood planks as hard as I could. There was a roar in my brain that wasn't the thunder. It was a frightening rage that I hadn't felt since a night many years ago in France. I knew, even in such a crazed state, that I was going to kill this man named Farley with no thought or concern for the consequences.

Then I heard a shrill scream behind me and Sara was pulling at my shirt, yelling for me to stop. I kept on, and then she was slapping me on the back of my head and screaming at me to stop. I suddenly felt exhausted and I was out of breath. I stopped banging the man's head, and he lay there motionless beneath me, his eyes open, but not seeing, blood covering most of his face and all over my hands.

I sat back and tried to catch my breath. I could hear Sara crying behind me. The rain started down harder and splashed in the dry sand and on the boards. The rain caused splotches in the blood on the man's face, and soon it was running down his cheeks and pooling on the walk. Lightning crashed almost directly above us and the thunder clap was deafening, almost an explosion. I looked back down at Farley who was now moving some, and for the first moment of rational thought, was grateful that I apparently hadn't killed the sonofabitch.

I watched in the pouring rain now as the man was able to get to his knees. He held his head down as blood poured from his nose, splashing down into the rain puddles. Sara ran over to him and helped him up. I was so stunned and charged from the attack, and what I had done, that I wasn't able to react or even move. Sara helped him to his feet and held her hand up over his nose to try to slow the bleeding. It ran down her thin wet arms and on to her clothes. She yelled back for Melanee.

I finally reacted and said, "No, she's staying with me." Sara looked at me for a moment. I could see her begin to think clearly for the first time, and she didn't protest. She tried to get Farley moving back toward the hotel, but he almost fell when he tried to walk. He yelled out something vicious and unintelligible in my direction, and then Sara was able to turn him and get him moving away toward the street. I went up and sat on the porch, stunned and breathless.

Then the sights and sounds of the French battlefield were, again, all around me and men were yelling. My friend Billy was at my side running with me, and then he was knocked over by another wounded man. I reached down to help him up and we kept running. Our ranks were growing thinner as men fell, and others slowed in the face of the terrifying barrage of fire from the German line.

Billy and I both dove into a large hole formed from a shell explosion. We fell on a German soldier, wounded and left to die. He was as surprised as we were, but still conscious enough to try to defend himself. He had a pistol in his hand, and he shot my friend dead through the forehead before we had even a moment to realize what was happening. As Billy fell face down, unmoving in the mud, the gun swung in my direction, and I could see the German's face in the distant light from a flare. It was covered in grime and blood, and only his eyes seemed alive in a body that was twisted and broken and near death.

A sudden rage surged through me, and I moved before I could even think or grasp what had happened. I hit the man across the face with the butt of my rifle. His jaw and teeth shattered, and his eyes went blank and distant as he fell back against the dirt wall of the shell hole. I hesitated for a moment as the pistol fell from his hands into a puddle of muddy water near his feet. He lay there motionless, but the roar of rage and anger in my head was so strong that it dulled all other sounds of weapons and men's screams. Without thinking, I took the butt of my rifle and smashed it into his face again and again until it no longer resembled a man. Then I fell back, breathless and crying, and yelling out all at the same time.

Shells exploded all around me, lighting up the sky and leaving my ears ringing. There were sounds of machine guns in the distance and bullets whizzing by my head. I was growing more frantic in the desperation of not knowing where I could go to escape the chaos around me. I looked down one more time at the crumbled body of my friend, Billy Gregory, and then at the dead German. Suddenly all that mattered was getting away from all of the slaughter. I scrambled up over the edge of the shell hole, stumbling in the mud and dropping my rifle. I started back to where I thought our line had been, and then up ahead I saw a soldier, an American soldier, staggering and about to fall over. There was shouting off to my left, and I saw men looking over the edge of an embankment, waving their arms at me and yelling words that I couldn't understand. The man ahead of me fell to his knees, and I felt compelled to go to him. Still running, I reached down and put my arms around his chest and pulled him with me as I stumbled and fell to the ground.

I don't recall the sound of the explosion, only the compression of air and dirt flying in my face as we were both hurled across the ground, and then lay in a heap together. Before I lost consciousness that night, my last memory is of the lifeless face of that man staring back at me.

The pain in my right hand was throbbing and I was still gasping for breath, a rush of adrenaline still coursing through my veins causing a strange rush and light-headedness. I heard Melanee crying behind me again, and I got up to go back inside the cottage. I turned to see that Sara and Farley were managing to stagger their way along the road back toward the hotel. It was at that moment that it occurred to me that this certainly was far from over, and my next encounter with this man named Farley would be much worse.

Chapter Thirty-six

The rain continued to clatter down against the metal roof, and Melanee was sitting beside me on the couch, curled up and whimpering. I reached over to try to comfort her. She slid over and put her arms around me, and buried her face in my chest. We sat there together, listening to the storm crash above us, my mind trying to make sense of what had happened, and what may lie ahead.

Suddenly, I jolted up and realized that I had fallen asleep, not knowing if it had been for a minute, or hours. My first thought was that the storm seemed to be raging even more fiercely outside, and then I realized that Melanee was no longer with me on the couch. I looked around the room and yelled out for her. I went into both bedrooms, but she was gone. A sickening fear churned up in my gut, and I yelled out again for her, but my words were lost in the roar of the storm. I went out onto the porch and, again, there was no sign of her.

I ran down the steps across the yard. The rain was pouring down in sheets that rushed down the street on the wind. The sky was still dark and foreboding, and lightning crashed all around. I kept on down the road, struggling against the wind and rain. A tree had fallen across the road and I stepped over the big trunk, and continued toward the hotel. Up on the porch there was some respite from the rain, but not the relentless wind. I pounded on the door and yelled for Sara with no thoughts of the man that I had tried to kill just a short while ago.

When she opened the door, I could see that even in the dim light she was bleeding from a large gash beneath her right eye. My anger rushed through me again, but then I thought of Melanee and I tried to calm myself as much as I could. I pulled Sara out onto the porch with me. She seemed stunned from either the blow to her face, or more alcohol or both. I shook her to try to get her to look at me. "Sara, Melanee is gone," I said, almost shouting against the din of the storm, my panic rising again. "Did you hear me? Melanee is gone. Did she come back over here?"

Sara finally seemed able to understand what I had said. She started shaking her head *no*, and then I could see the panic growing in her own expression. "No, she hasn't come back." And then she was screaming at me. "No, you were supposed to take care of her!" She started hitting me in the chest. "You were supposed to take care of her!" I grabbed her arms to stop her screaming, and then I held her close to get her to calm down.

"Go inside and make sure she's not hiding somewhere," I yelled. "I'm going to go down to the beach." I left her there standing with a dazed expression on her face. There had been no sign of Farley. I walked back out into the rain and the wind. I thought to myself that there was no way a little blind girl could make her way in this storm, but I also realized that Melanee knew the area instinctively and could have followed the boardwalk down to the newly built pavilion, and even down to the beach to the sound of the waves breaking.

As I walked down through the dunes, the roar of the surf crashing up ahead grew louder and louder. I had a sick and helpless feeling that was almost paralyzing. I had to keep wiping the rain out of my eyes to see, and with each flash of lighting I would duck instinctively, sure that the next bolt would hit me directly and blow me into a thousand charred pieces. When I was able to get far enough down the beach to see in both directions along the waterline, I was furious to realize that the heavy rain and dark clouds allowed me to see only a few hundred yards. I yelled out for Melanee again, an almost hopeless gesture against the fury of the elements. I ran up into the dunes to the west where we had watched the turtles nest, but she wasn't there. I started turning in a slow circle, trying to think where she might have gone, the rain stinging against my face, my clothes drenched and hanging tight, and soaked against my skin. I felt the most helpless fear that I had not been able to protect this little girl, and that something terrible had happened. In a near panic, I began running in my crooked gait back toward the hotel. After a while, I was out of breath and couldn't run anymore. I staggered on as quickly as I could through the wet loose sand back toward town.

When I got to the hotel, Sara came out onto the porch to meet me. "She's not here, Mathew," she said. "I've looked everywhere."

"Where's Farley?" I asked, looking at the cut on her face, and the dried blood on her swollen cheek.

He ran out to find Melanee when I told him she was gone," she said, and her voice sounded as if the fear for her daughter was bringing back some measure of sobriety. "He said he was going down to the lake where she liked to feed the ducks with us."

"Where by the lake?"

"Just past the Headley's cottage and down toward the beach," she said. "We found a little shelter in the heavy scrub when Bobby was still here. We used to take her down there. It was like her little sanctuary."

"Show me," I said, and I took her hand and pulled her down the porch with me into the rain and gusty winds. We were almost pushed down the road toward Headley's place by the force of the wind. The road led on by the little cottage, and then turned to a sand trail through the scrub brush and trees down to the lake. The rain swept across the rough surface of the black lake in relentless gusts. Sara led me on a narrow path edged in tall grass along the shore. Up ahead, I could see a sandy beach area that came up into the grass from the lake and heavy growth of scrub trees up to the right. Sara turned into a small opening in the blowing branches of the scrub growth that I would have never even seen in passing. I ducked down and followed her, and then we were under a small canopy of branches that I could stand up in. There was finally some relief from the rain with the cover. Then I heard Sara yell out, "Oh Melanee, thank God!"

I came around her and saw Melanee cowering back in the corner of the little clearing. Sara ran to her daughter and threw herself down next to her. She put her arms around the little girl and rocked her. I fell down to one knee and hung my head down, trying to catch my breath. I said a silent prayer of thanks, and looked over at mother and daughter reunited. Then I thought about Farley for the first time and looked around for any sign of the man.

"He's gone, Mathew," I heard Melanee say in the most eerie voice. I looked over at her and she was staring sightlessly up into the canopy of the limbs and leaves, water dripping down all around us, and the wind still rushing by overhead in a deafening roar.

"What do you mean *gone*?" I asked, crawling over toward both of them.

Sara looked at me with a bewildered expression. "Where did he go, Melanee?" she asked.

Melanee turned her face toward me, and in a calm voice said, "He's out by the lake." Then she pointed toward the opening we had come through.

I wasn't sure what to think, but I started back out and had to stoop over so I could get through the opening. Outside again, I noticed that the rain had let up some and the sky was beginning to lighten. The wind was still whipping across the surface of the lake, and the tall grass was thrashing about. I walked down the sand bank to the edge of the lake and looked down to my right.

Feelings of shock and horror ripped through me. It was a staggering sight, and I actually fell back a few steps in recoil from what I was seeing. Farley lay half in the water, only his legs up on land, twisted at grotesque angles. In the water two large alligators were ripping at the man's back and arms, throwing their heads high with the torn bloody flesh, only to swallow and go back for more. Instinctively I started forward to try to do something. The closest gator flared up and hissed at me, not ten feet away. I backed away slowly and watched as it went back to feeding on the lifeless form of the man who had been called Farley. I turned and felt a nauseous bile rise up in my throat. I fell retching in the sand, over and over.

When I was able to stop, I crawled slowly back into the shelter where Sara and Melanee were still huddled. Even in the shadows of the heavy brush and darkness of the storm, I could see that Melanee had a look of calm serenity on her face as her mother rocked her slowly back and forth.

I woke on the couch at Headley's place the next morning, my head and hand aching, and a dreadful sour taste in my mouth that almost made me gag again. I had brought Sara and Melanee back here through the calming storm, avoiding the path that went near the gators and the carnage of Farley's body. They had fallen asleep in one of the bedrooms. I got up and went over to the sink and pumped the well handle until the cold water began to flow. I held my head under it and took a long drink, spitting out the bitter taste of the previous night.

I walked out through the screen door onto the porch and sat down on one of the old chairs. Thoughts and images of the terror of the past night caused me to shiver. I looked down at my right hand and saw that it was swollen and bruised, surely broken in several places. The storm had passed and there were patches of blue sky showing through the remnants of the clouds. Debris was spread across the yard and out in the street. I heard the door squeak open and I turned to see Sara come out. She sat beside me in another chair. Her face was ghostly white.

"Farley is gone," I said. "There were gators down by the lake."

"Yes I know," she said. "Melanee told me last night."

I looked at her in disbelief and asked how she could have possibly known. Sara just stared back at me and shook her head. She turned and looked out across the vacant expanse of the little town, deserted at this early hour.

"We need to go back to New Orleans, Mathew," I heard her say, and then she looked back at me. "I have friends there who can care for us, for Melanee and me. I can't be here anymore. It's just too much."

Chapter Thirty-seven

Grayton Beach, December 1928

    I decided to let my wife sleep a little more. I looked over at her lying on the pillow beside me with her pretty brown hair falling all about, and the most peaceful look on her face. I pushed the blankets back carefully and got out of bed as quietly as I could, walking barefoot to the closet to grab a robe. Out in the main room I looked around at what had once been the Headley's cottage. A month ago I had convinced Jimmy that they should sell it to me. Their family was committed to traveling to south Florida now, and the old place sat mostly vacant. I had brought a few new comforts and necessities in, but for the most part it was as I had found it when I first came to Grayton Beach. The small Christmas tree in the corner with presents beneath was the only noticeable change.
    I put coffee on and rinsed out a cup in the sink. When the pot of coffee was done, I walked out on the old porch that had been blown away in the hurricane and rebuilt by me and Jonas Bidwell. There were a couple of creaky boards, but it was serviceable. The few homes in town were mostly vacant. The hotel was also dark and quiet, and no guests had been registered for some time. Jonas and his new wife had recently arranged to purchase the place and

were planning to come in the first of the year to work on getting it ready for the spring season.

The dunes off toward the beach were just getting the first light from the sun coming up over the lake behind our cottage. The sand was almost a blinding white in the early morning hour, and the Gulf water out beyond was calm and shimmering in brilliant tones of green and blue. The coffee was hot and steaming, and kept my hands warm against an early chill in the air.

I heard them before I saw them, the two little mockingbirds that Melanee and I had befriended and kept fat and happy with too many crackers. They both flew in and landed on the rail in front of me, Champ first, followed by the one that Melanee had named *Maggie* after my sister. They jumped around and squawked at me, and I quietly went back inside and brought out the box of crackers that was kept for them. I gave them each their own snack to peck away at. Champ looked up at me between every mouthful and bobbed his head and made little mockingbird sounds that I'm sure had some special meaning.

The screen door pushed open slowly and Sara walked out, her eyes still swollen and sleepy from the night's rest. She pulled her white robe up around her neck and settled herself down into my lap. After burrowing in and shivering a bit in the cold, she turned and kissed me on the cheek.

"Merry Christmas," she said. "I see your little friends have come for their presents."

"Every day is Christmas for these two," I said. "Merry Christmas, Mrs. Coulter." As I said those words, a pain stabbed at my gut as I thought of Annie back in New York.

On my long trip back to New York after leaving Sara and Melanee with the Bidwells, and with the danger of Farley no longer a threat, but the next calamity surely only a short time away, I couldn't stop thinking about the little blind girl and the uncertain life that she faced. When I was finally back in the city, I met Annie for dinner the first night. For days on the train I had been thinking about the women in my life that had abandoned or betrayed me, and here I was staring at a woman that I loved, knowing in my heart that I was about to do the same. I recall only a shattering sense of complete self-loathing as I told Annie about my trip to Florida, and the events that had transpired. She looked on, speechless, as I told her of the death of the drifter, Farley, and then Sara's decline and declaration of returning to the dangers of New Orleans.

We both had tears in our eyes as I continued on. "Annie, I'm so sorry about all this…" I said.

"Mathew, please stop!" she said, and then took the napkin to dry her eyes. "You're going back to them, aren't you?"

I couldn't answer. I couldn't stand to say the words. My heart was bursting in my chest. I was hoping that it would explode and I would be out of this life and away from hurting this woman any more than I already had.

"I couldn't live with myself if anything happened to Melanee," I said.

She took a deep breath, trying to compose herself, looking around the restaurant blankly at the others around us. Then she rose slowly and placed the napkin at her plate. She came around the table and stood beside me. I looked up at her face, the devastation of what I was doing etched in every strained feature. I reached for her, but she pulled back. She took my grandmother's ring off her finger and placed it on the table. Then she reached out and traced her hand along the line of my jaw before she turned and walked out of the restaurant and into the night.

"What time are Jimmy and Rebecca coming over?" I heard Sara ask as she tried to pull her robe down to cover her bare feet.

I tried again to put thoughts of Annie Martin out of my head, as I had found myself doing so many times since that last night in New York. I told Sara that I expected them around eleven. Jimmy had finally come around to ask Rebecca Bidwell to marry him. The wedding was scheduled for the spring up in Atlanta with a big affair that his mother had insisted on. Jimmy was staying with Rebecca over at her parent's house for the holidays, and they were planning to join us later for Christmas dinner."

"Do you really think we should go back to New York?" I heard Sara whisper, her face tucked down inside the warmth of our robes.

"I think it's best," I said. "Let's go make some breakfast." We both slowly got out of our comfortable little nest. I dropped two more crackers on the rail for the birds before following my wife back inside.

We were rustling around the kitchen getting the stove lit and the food out of the icebox when I heard a scuffling of feet behind me. We both turned to see Melanee in the doorway of her bedroom, the long wool nightgown hanging over her bare little feet. She also had a new stuffed bear in her arms, a gift that I had brought down from New York. Sara walked over and leaned down to give the little girl a warm hug.

"Merry Christmas, honey," she said. Melanee put her arms around her neck and hugged her close.

"Did Santa come?" she asked in that playful and innocent tone that children have, trying to keep the spirit of Old Saint Nick alive for one more year.

I walked over and knelt beside the two of them, and swept them both into my arms. "Didn't you hear him last night?" I asked.

There were wrapped boxes lined all around the base of the tree, and we led my new stepdaughter over and sat down next to her, handing her the first present to be opened. The expression of joy and excitement on her face was so marvelous, and as I watched

Sara help her with the gift, I felt the most overwhelming sense of love and connection at that moment that I may have ever experienced.

I heard Melanee squeal, and I looked over as she pulled a beautifully finished violin out of its case. I had been so impressed with her musical ability that I wanted Melanee to get formal training when we returned to New York. I watched and listened as Sara showed her how to place the instrument beneath her chin and how to hold the bow. As Melanee pulled the bow across the strings for the first time, I was caught breathless at the most lovely note that hung in the air.

A final gathering.

Grayton Beach, May 1985

I was married to Sara Dalton in early December of 1928, and soon after filed papers to legally adopt Melanee. We did indeed return to New York that winter, and I continued on with the newspaper for five more years before my second book seemed to catch enough attention that I was convinced that I should turn my efforts full time to writing fiction.

I think often of Annie Martin, and the sad and painful moments we shared when I first came back to New York after running off to help Sara and Melanee. I don't believe that I even slept on that long train ride back north, thinking only about the choices before me.

I had stayed on in Grayton Beach a few more days to help Sara recover some after the terrible night that her daughter was lost and Farley was killed. I finally convinced her to stay on for a while with the Bidwells over in Point Washington, yet I was terribly concerned that she would leave at the least provocation to go back to New Orleans or down some other destructive path.

I'm sure that Annie Martin has never forgiven me for my decision, and I know I broke her heart that night because I'm not sure mine has ever completely healed. I was pleased to hear some *years later that she had returned to Michigan and married, and raised a large family there while teaching in her hometown.*

We are all back in Grayton Beach this spring. We will celebrate my 85th birthday later today with family and friends. The old Headley place that I bought in 1928 is still here, although updated considerably, and is now used as a guest house. After the second War we built a new home on the property next door, and we have been coming down on holiday almost every year since. Sara and I had spent much of our later years down here as well.

This old beach town has fortunately kept much of its familiar charm. Many of the original cottages remain, and the blight of high-rise condominiums and t-shirt shops have been kept far to the west and east down in Destin and Panama City. It's certainly more active now with tourists flocking in each day to visit the few quaint galleries and shops, and of course, the bar and restaurant just down the road that's in the old general store that was built in the 30's. Lila's old hotel was closed years ago, but is still standing and now features the work of local artists. The beach and the water remain as marvelous as ever, and with a permit you can attempt to drive one of those big SUV's out through the loose sugar white sand to the shore to set up for the day. The sunsets are still simply spectacular.

Sara and Melanee both found their way fairly well, living in New York when we moved there in 1929, Melanee in particular. Fortunately we were able to navigate the years of the depression with little discomfort. The Coulter money, for the most part, had been safely invested and diversified.

Melanee was enrolled in a very good school for the blind that helped her to grow into an even more special young woman. She was accepted at Juilliard and studied music, eventually playing violin for the New York Philharmonic for much of her later life. She also married a man she had met in the orchestra and they have lived a fine life, still in the city, their two daughters grown now with families of their own. Her uncanny sixth sense has continued to amaze us all.

Sara struggled throughout her life to control the darker forces that constantly pulled at her, although with love from our family and much professional help, we managed to keep them at bay for most of our life together. In 1935 we had a son, our only child together. His name was Patrick, and he was a terrific fellow. He followed the Coulter tradition of the military life, and eventually chose it as his career. He was lost to us in 1967, one of the casualties of that war in the jungles on the other side of the world. Ten years ago, cancer suddenly took Sara from us.

I've never considered remarrying, and there has been no one romantic in my life since Sara's parting. At this age, it's enough to try to find energy each day to move on with just my own issues to deal with. Our life together was a true blessing, although we certainly got off to a rugged start those first months that I met her and Lila and Melanee down in Grayton Beach those many years ago.

Our daughter, Melanee, was a steadying force that we could always find comfort and direction from. Her love and incredible spirit kept us and everyone around her, centered and whole. She and most of her family are down here for my birthday celebration.

The Headley's have come down from Atlanta. Jimmy and Rebecca have kept their family roots here in the area as well, and they have a place on the beach over in Seaside, a newer development just east of Grayton Beach.

In the late 50's, I received a call from Louise Palumbo. She and Willie had moved to Havana, and lived there for many years before they finally moved back to the States to live in Miami. Willie had managed to keep all of his business interests running well with the help of his sons. Unfortunately, he finally crossed someone who he couldn't handle. He was shot and killed by two men as he was walking out of a restaurant in Coconut Grove in 1959. The big bodyguard, Anthony, was also slain that day, taking several rounds from the assassins in trying to save his employer. Palumbo's funeral was quite a spectacle back in New Jersey, and attended by more federal agents and media than family, it seemed. Sara and I were both there that day and stood with Louise as her husband was lowered into the ground. She told us that she was moving back to New Jersey to be near her grandchildren.

I've struggled my entire adult life with some of the decisions placed upon me during my time with the old gangster, but I did what I felt was best for my family and those close to me. I try not to dwell on some of the less pleasant outcomes.

There was news of Eleanor Whitlock, or Ellen I suppose I should say, sometime after the second war. I don't recall the source, but apparently her acting career had run out of steam, as had her marriage to the agent I had met that day in New York. She had moved to Las Vegas and worked at one of the big hotels. I never knew any more detail, and always hoped that her work allowed her to keep her clothes on.

There was no further correspondence or contact from Celeste, the young nurse that was my first love in France during World War I. Though I traveled extensively in Europe later in life promoting my books and traveling with my family, I always resisted the temptation to contact her or to visit the little village of Les Mureaux. It would have been incredibly unfair to all involved, though I still think of her often.

My mother and sister, Maggie, were able to live out lives that were certainly comfortable financially, thanks to our arrangement with Palumbo, if not occasionally thrown off course by affairs of the heart. My mother married the old cop, Charles Watermann, a year after my father died, and they have both passed on now. When Prohibition was repealed, Watermann retired from the police force and eventually ran for public office, later becoming a prominent state legislator in Georgia. My mother kept on quite passionately with her civic and social pursuits. In their last years, she and the senator lived much of the time in south Florida and were among the early social elite down in Naples.

Sister Maggie remains an indelible force in our lives. Soon after the Depression, she and her third husband moved west and bought a large cattle ranch in Texas, although they knew little of cows and prairies. Her husband did know about oil, and they have prospered quite well as a result. Margaret Coulter Conrad carries on among the Who's Who in Houston society. She and our Melanee remained very close through all these years, and Maggie was often in New York to visit with us and to see Melanee perform with the Philharmonic, and of course to shop some.

Her first husband, Desmond Raye, didn't fare as well after escaping the family's wrath and running away to Florida. He fell in with a bad lot and began doing legal work for drug runners out of the Caribbean, though unsuccessfully. He spent most of the second half of his life in prison and died shortly after his release from complications attributed to a virulent strain of some social disease.

The stories all seem to run together now, and the echoes of the voices of the past only come to me when I lie awake at night and let my old mind wander.

But my young granddaughter's voice is real. Meredith is there at the bottom of the stairs by the door.

"Grandpa, don't be rude," she says. "You have a guest."

I hear the woman's voice again. She walks into the house and pulls a red silk scarf from her hair. The wind rushes through the door, and the scarf blows from her hand across the space between us before it settles on the floor.

"Mathew," she says again.

I can see her face now. The years have taken their relentless toll, but her eyes are as young as the first day I saw her *those many years ago. I manage the last few steps, and my granddaughter hands me the scarf. I open my arms and feel the fragile weight of her as she comes to me.*

"Celeste."

THE END

GRAYTON WINDS

MICHAEL LINDLEY

Book group discussion guide, and questions and answers from the author.

Comments, feedback and questions can be sent to the author at michael.lindley@comcast.net.

A *Sage River Press* Book
© 2011

GRAYTON WINDS

Book Group Discussion Guide

What was your overall impression of the story, and which characters were you most drawn to?

How did the setting of the story in the remote village of Grayton Beach contribute to the overall context of the story?

Mathew Coulter had many interesting women in his life. Who do you feel he would have been best suited to spend his life with?

Sara Dalton was truly a flawed and troubled character. Can you imagine a mental state and addictions that could cause a woman to treat her family so horribly?

How would you describe the relationship that Mathew had with the young French nurse in Paris during the War? Did he make the right decision?

Was Mathew right in trying to distance himself so completely from his family?

Mathew certainly faced several bitter life choices. How did you feel about his ultimate decision with the young publishing assistant, Annie Martin?

The ruthless gangster, Willie Palumbo, seemed to have a good heart at times, but was Mathew another of Palumbo's victims?

Young Melanee Dalton had an eerie sixth sense for events and people's thoughts and feelings. Do you feel she purposely saved her mother by luring the drifter Farley to the lake during the storm that night?

Lila Dalton, the innkeeper, was a stabilizing force in so many people's lives. And yet, do you feel she was equally to blame for the troubles and calamities that her own daughter, Sara, was causing?

Did the book give you a genuine feel for what life might have been like along the South Walton beaches nearly 100 years ago?

Do you believe that Mathew Coulter was a sympathetic character? Did he make the right decisions along the way?

In the prologue, you find that one of the women in Mathew Coulter's life will come back to him at the end of the story. Did you guess the right person before her identity was revealed? Who would you have preferred to return?

MICHAEL LINDLEY

Questions and Answers from the Author

What made you decide to set the story in Grayton Beach?

My previous novels have been set in idyllic and remote resort communities. Our family has been coming down to the South Walton beaches since the early 1990's, and we now have a vacation home along Highway 30A. I've always been so fascinated by Grayton Beach, and how the town has been able to preserve so much of its early heritage, and to keep the blight of overdevelopment at bay.

And why the time period of the 1920's?

In my research into the area, I was particularly drawn to the early years of Grayton Beach, and to the region as a whole. The 1920's in the South I found to be an intriguing period with fascinating potential to create characters and events that could portray the unique cultural upheaval of those times.

You chose to write the story in first person, from Mathew Coulter's perspective. Your previous novels have been written in third person, giving many character's points of view. Why the change for *Grayton Winds*?

This book encompassed the lives of so many different characters, that I felt early on that it would be best to have Mathew narrate the story for us, and allow us to see this remarkable place and the many people who influenced his life there, through his eyes alone.

GRAYTON WINDS

You included a quote at the beginning of the book from Dickens; *there is a wisdom of the head, and a wisdom of the heart.* **What drew you to that quote in the context of the story?**

When I came across this quote one evening, it struck me that it captured the difficult dilemmas and life choices that the lead character, Mathew Coulter, was facing. As his character developed in my mind and on the page, I found Mathew to be an extremely intelligent and practical person, and yet, his decisions were often driven more from the heart than from any practical or logical place.

How do you build your stories? Do you work from an outline?

All of my books have begun with selecting an intriguing place to tell the story. I then try to gain some insight into the history of the place, and any interesting events or cultural issues. Characters then seem to invent themselves and the story begins to come together in my mind. I do typically write a rough outline, but I find the story takes many different routes in its development, and that it's usually best to let the story have its way and not be overly committed to earlier directions.

What themes did you try to capture in *Grayton Winds***?**

I'm always drawn to stories that create challenging life choices for characters, and I think the best stories often have characters that take unexpected paths. In *Grayton Winds*, I saw the opportunity to present the lead character, Mathew Coulter, with several very difficult life choices that would impact not only his own destiny, but those that he loved. Thematically, how will any of us react to decisions that we know will ultimately hurt some of those who we love, in the interest of doing what we think is truly best?

MICHAEL LINDLEY

GRAYTON WINDS

MICHAEL LINDLEY

CPSIA information can be obtained at www.ICGtesting.com
Printed in the USA
LVOW131309101012

302300LV00007B/2/P